PJ Grondin

A Lifetime of

Exposure

PD House Holdings, LLC

PD House Holdings, LLC
4704 Venice Road, Suite 201
Sandusky, Ohio   44870

Library of Congress Control Number: 2009902965

ISBN10: 0-9815333-4-5
ISBN13: 978-0-9815333-4-6
Published by PD House Holdings, LLC
www.pjgrondin.com
pjgron@pjgrondin.com
Sandusky, Ohio

Dedication

This book is dedicated to the victims of sexual predators. The explosion of camera and film technology, coupled with internet access, has opened the door for perversion, privacy invasion, and exploitation of children on a massive scale. Child pornography and voyeurism are crimes that violate people's bodies and souls. Society has yet to find even a starting point to address these crimes. When we figure out how to address these issues, we must never forget the victims. They are the ones who bear the physical and mental scars for life.

Acknowledgements

As with past projects, thanks go to my wife, Debbie, my brother, Patrick, for their critique of the manuscript, both technical and creative. Thanks, also, to Kathy Nesser for a great job reviewing the story and providing editorial feedback.

A big thanks to Jody Owen for allowing the use of her name in the story line. The character that bears her name has no real connection to her likeness or personality traits.

Finally, thanks to the Vermilion, Ohio police department for their efforts in finding and prosecuting predatory adults. Though I had no direct contact with them prior to writing this story, local newspaper articles about their successes inspired me to include the storyline regarding the methods used to identify and apprehend this particularly perverse breed of criminal.

A Lifetime of

Exposure

Prologue
1976

The pit was dug in preparation for the basement of the new house. Located nearly one hundred yards off of a lightly traveled back road in eastern Virginia, south of the Quantico Marine Corps Base, the only path back to the pit was a rough construction road. It was intended for trucks delivering materials for the new home and for construction workers vehicles. The thick stand of pine trees prevented anyone from seeing the site from the road.

Even though it was early in the morning, long before dawn, a young man was hard at work. He was digging a smaller hole inside the pit. It wasn't a perfect hole, a little over two feet deep, two feet wide and four feet long. A slab of Virginia granite kept the hole shallow. The spade wouldn't break through that barrier. It would have to do. The early morning was wearing on. The dark, moonless night worked in his favor. The humidity, though, was taking its toll.

But he was young and fit. Except for the time, a workout like this was not unusual. Working in construction had its advantages for keeping the weight off. Even so, sweat poured from his forehead and soaked his shirt. There was no turning back now. Fear kept him going. It wasn't a fear of the darkness as much as what the darkness might be hiding. Anyone could be watching him, wondering what he was doing, working into the early morning, like a man possessed.

His next fear was the mechanical noise that might attract attention. It was unlikely. The construction site was isolated from any other homes or businesses. But in these parts of Virginia, sound carried a long way, echoing off hillsides and into the valleys. When he started the cement mixer, it sounded to him like a noise that would raise the dead. The motor made the whirring sound that rang in his ears. Ever since working in the engine room of an aircraft carrier during the Vietnam War, his ears never stopped ringing. Every time he was near a running motor, it amplified the ringing. It seemed like the noise in his ears was out of synch with the noise from the motor. It drove him crazy. This early morning it was particularly bad. The motor seemed to pierce the darkness. He was sure that anyone within miles would hear the noise and wonder about its origin. Surely, someone would come to investigate.

But he had no time to worry about that. The deed was done. The evidence was literally at his feet. There was no time to waste fretting over what could have been or how the situation might have been handled differently.

As the cement mixer spun, he poured in two bags of concrete and the right amount of water. He let the mixer spin and do its job to create the first batch. A noise, coming from beyond the walls of the hole, startled him. He froze as he tried to listen more intently. He spun around quickly trying to catch a glimpse of its source. The sweat poured over his forehead and chest even more as his nerves worked overtime. As he looked up at the dirt walls of the pit where he stood, his anxiety jumped another notch. *Get a grip. There's nothing there except the darkness and your nerves. Maybe a raccoon.* He shook his head in an attempt to shake off the tension. He took one more look around the entire perimeter of the hole. The silhouette of the mounds of earth on the edge of the hole looked like distant mountains from his vantage point. In the dark, he could barely make out their shape. He couldn't see a single, living thing. The walls of the pit were only six feet high. The plan was to use backfill to allow the lawn to slope up to the entrance to the three bedroom home that was to be built here.

The first batch was nearly complete. It was time. This was the part he feared most. He scampered up the ladder and made his way to the beat up Ford Econoline Van. The panel doors were locked. He dropped the keys twice, his nerves getting the best of him, as he tried to rush. Finally, he unlocked the doors and flung them open.

There they were. Three trash bags. There was no time to waste. If he was caught standing here with these three bags within his reach, he'd surely pay a price, possibly with his life. He grabbed the first bag and lifted. It wasn't very heavy so he carefully draped it over his shoulder. The contents made metallic, scraping noises as it settled onto his back. Quickly, he made his way down the ladder to the hole where the concrete footer for the new basement would be poured on Monday. He eased the bag in the hole, trying to remain quiet. He hurried up the ladder for the next bag. This one was heavier. There was no metallic sound from this bag. It made more of a squishing, wet sound. When he heaved this bag over his shoulder, something hard hit his back. *Damn, that hurt. Have to be more careful.* He looked down and noticed something dark staining the ground. He set the bag down and noticed a hole where the sharp object protruded through the bag. *Damn.* He adjusted the bag so that the hole was pointing upward. Nothing he could do about the bone sticking out of the bag. Soon it wouldn't matter. He followed the same routine as with the first bag, placing it in the hole. *One more to go.*

The third bag was lighter. It was soft on his back. This trip went quickly. It was a good thing because the mixer was finished with the first batch of concrete. He placed the final bag in the hole. Using a shovel to move the bags around in the hole, he poked too hard. The second bag split open wide. He gasped.

Two horrified eyes stared up at him. They were lifeless eyes, but they showed the terror that the last breath of life must have experienced. He remembered the look. It hadn't changed in death. But they seemed to be staring directly at him.

After the momentary shock wore off, he returned to his task. The bags were in place. He dumped the first load of concrete into the hole. It was obvious that he would need at least four more loads. That meant another thirty minutes with

the mixer. Then he would cover the concrete with a layer of
dirt. He'd be gone by 4:00 AM at the latest. That's okay. It was Saturday morning. It would be
another fifty hours before anyone would be back at the site. By
then, it would look like it had when everyone left on Friday
afternoon. The problem would be gone forever. The crew was
to pour the footer on Monday. The basement walls were
scheduled for later in the week.

It was a fitting grave.

Chapter 1
October 1997

Jillian Rockledge was on cloud nine. She looked around the bedroom while stretched out on her back in the middle of her king-sized bed. She adored everything that she could see. The master bedroom of her new 6500 square-foot home was nothing short of sensational. It was gigantic; 720 square feet, not including the two walk in closets and master bath. The bath opened into the bedroom. No doors separated the combination shower and dressing area from the rest of the bedroom. The walls were painted pastel peach with contrasting dark walnut trim. The trim alone had such exquisite carved patterns that it must have cost a fortune. In the bedroom a bay window looked out over the back yard, which was essentially a forest. There were no neighbors within a quarter of a mile.

She not only loved the sight of her new bedroom, she loved the scent. Everything was new. The aroma of new carpet and the scent of newly cut hardwoods hung in the air throughout the house; her house. The feeling of owning such a beautiful home was like no other.

Jillian and her husband, Nelson helped design the home with the professional designers from Messier Homes. Messier was the builder of choice for young up-and-coming professionals in Virginia, west of Washington, D.C.

Jillian and Nelson fit that profile perfectly. Jillian was an attorney with the law firm of Forest, Harbridge, Weston, and Gross. Nelson was also an attorney working on the staff of Senator William T. Barnhouse, Republican from the State of Ohio. Their combined income was a comfortable $425,000.00 per year; impressive since they were both in only their third year at their respective positions.

Their future was promising indeed, not that it was of

concern to either of them. Jillian came from a prominent, wealthy family near the nation's capital. She had a trust fund in excess of $3,000,000. They planned to leave the trust intact since they had adequate incomes to support their surprisingly conservative lifestyle. Their new home was the most recent departure from the Scrooge-like hold they'd had on their savings and investments outside of the trust. Their other two major expenditures were Nelson's dark green BMW 540i and Jillian's cream colored Volvo 850. The new cars were necessary status symbols for them to fit into their respective positions.

Jillian was one of the newest of the twenty-three associate attorneys in the firm, but she was on the fast track to junior partner. That was no small feat considering the firm's policy to only hire top graduates of the best law schools in the country. In her first year on the payroll, she managed to build a clientele that generated income to the firm that outpaced many of her senior associates. She was noticed with admiration by many of the partners and jealousy by those that couldn't compete with her talent.

Besides being absolutely brilliant, Jillian was drop-dead gorgeous. Her hair was brunette, shoulder length, and perfect. Her smile was radiant and her complexion was flawless. And if none of that caught a man's eyes, her body was a masterpiece. She was tall and slender with curves in all the right places. She had a natural, powerful sex appeal. At work she wore conservative business clothes, never revealing anything that would cause an office scandal or cause her bosses to call her on the carpet for improper dress. She didn't need to draw any undue attention. In fact, she made it a point to present herself in the utmost professional manner. This gained her the respect of the senior partners of the firm. In short, she had the total package for a professional attorney with a brilliant future.

At home she wasn't nearly as cautious as she was at work. When she closed and locked the doors to her beautiful home, her hair came down and she kicked off her shoes. After work weeks that were usually on the long side of sixty hours, she let loose with a little wine or a mixed drink and she wore as little as possible without running around completely naked. This was only if she and Nelson didn't expect company, of course. This evening, she was on her second glass of wine. She'd already showered and was in bed flat on her back, wearing only a pair of light pink, French-cut panties. She was waiting to ambush Nelson for some pre-late-night-dinner sex. She knew he'd be up for the challenge.

As she relaxed on the comfortable pillow-topped mattress, she started to doze off. Her mind wandered to the construction phase of the house when the basement had just been poured, then to when the electricians installed the wiring throughout the house. Finally the drywall was installed. The one and only flaw in the house flashed in her mind. There was a slight, musty smell in one corner of the basement. They couldn't figure out the cause, but as Nelson put it, they were blessed if that was their only complaint. It appeared that the odor wasn't spreading so they decided to live with it unless it got worse. Their Golden Retriever, Fenton, had gone into the basement as soon as the stairway was completed and started to whimper when he got near that corner. He even scratched the concrete block walls as if trying to dig for a bone. Jillian could see herself taking the dog by the collar and guiding him up the steps.

Then her dream shifted back to the tradesmen performing their work. The muscles of the workers rippled as they moved lumber to saw horses. The mental scene was so vivid that she could smell the wood being cut. Her nose tickled from the sawdust as she breathed in the particles. She sneezed and awoke as she did. She was surprised to see her husband holding a feather, lightly brushing the end of her nose. She rubbed her nose then rolled to face her husband. She smiled but with a mock sneer.

"You can be such a troublemaker."

He looked her over from head to toe then lay down beside her. He was fully clothed in his white dress shirt and dark gray dress pants. He'd taken his suit coat, tie and shoes off. They were neatly placed on the chair across the room.

His gaze settled on her breasts. "So, what's for dinner tonight?"

She smiled then said, "I thought we'd start with a little 'Treat a la Jillian' then move on to the main course."

"What would the main course be?"

"That would be the Nelson special." She smiled a seductive, sensuous smile that made Nelson sweat.

He leaned over and kissed her passionately then pulled back. "I'll be right back."

She lay back in bed again, her eyes following him to the bathroom. He stripped out of the rest of his clothes and headed into the walk-in closet. She wondered what he was up to as she heard him moving things around. She heard a zipper noise like he was putting on pants or opening a carrying case or a . . .

When he came around the corner of the doorway to the closet, he was holding their mini-camcorder up to his right eye and he was heading towards the bed. At first, Jillian giggled at the thought.

"Very funny, Nelson but I'm not in that business." She smiled at the camera but her smile was tightening.

"Come on, Babe, it'll be fun. Think how turned on we'll get watching ourselves on video."

"No way! What if somebody finds the tape? What then?"

"Who's gonna find it. We'll lock it up in the safe. We're the only ones who know the combination. What can it hurt? Really, it'll be a blast. I'm getting excited just thinking about it." And she could tell with one look that it was true. But she clearly wasn't comfortable being taped in the nude much less having sex. He really intended to tape their love-making.

Now her smile was gone and she was more forceful. "Nelson, turn the camera off and put it away. I'm not going to end up like some Hollywood slut in the tabloids. Something like that could ruin our careers. I mean it. Just our luck we'll end up on some porn site."

* * *

Her statement drew laughs from nearly three thousand people from all across America who, unbeknownst to Nelson and Jillian, were watching the entire exchange on the Sensual and Exotic Club Network. Those watching didn't have to wait for Nelson's tape. They were enjoying the live feed.

Chapter 2

The entire house smelled of garlic and tomato sauce, the result of a fantastic Italian dish. Pat McKinney's wife, Diane, made stuffed shells with a mixture of Italian sausage, hamburger, ricotta cheese, mozzarella cheese and homemade spaghetti sauce. It was Pat's favorite meal. He always ate more than he should. And he almost always regretted it.

He stood in the spacious living room of their Dunnellon, Florida home, stretching, and rubbing his stomach. He felt a belch coming on. The large, stuffed pasta shells were working on his insides. He and Diane had just finished cleaning the kitchen. They'd planned a nice, quiet evening. Their children, Sean and Anna, were with Pat's mother for the evening. For the first time in months, Pat and Diane were alone together. He'd planned a romantic evening, but his over-indulgence at the dinner table threatened to end his plans. He stretched again, trying to get his food to settle a bit.

"I told you to stop at five, didn't I?" Diane came into the living room and patted Pat's stomach. She smiled and asked, "When are you due?"

"Hey, watch that. Do you want this thing to explode?" He reached out and put an arm around her shoulder and pulled her close. He kissed her on the forehead as he wrapped his other arm around her. "That was a fantastic dinner."

"How would you know? You inhaled those shells so fast your taste buds probably didn't even know what you ate. It's like someone was going to steal them from you." She smiled up at him, her shoulder length, sandy brown hair framing her face. "You're really going to have to start watching what you eat, mister. Have you weighed yourself lately?"

Pat's face turned a slight shade of red. He just did that morning and discovered he'd gained nearly five pounds in the last three weeks. He'd stopped working out and was eating way more than he should. "I've only gained two pounds, but I'm planning to start back at the gym again. I talked to Joe and he said he'd help."

Her look was beyond skeptical. "More like two pounds on each butt cheek and a few more spread around the mid section. The first thing you should do is cut down on your portions. My word, you ate enough shells for three people in there." Diane stayed in his clutches but looked directly into his eyes. "We both need to get back in the habit of eating better and working out. Is it a deal?"

"Deal. We can start tomorrow."

"We're starting right after the news. We're walking around the block tonight. It won't be dark for a while so there's no excuse."

In a voice like a scolded child, Pat said, "Yes, Ma'am."

"That's better. Let's see what great news is on this evening."

"They turned on the *Channel 8 News*. A young woman was in the middle of a story about a convenience store robbery. She was explaining that the store's surveillance video recorded the perpetrators. The film was rolling on the screen, showing the robbery in progress. The clerk was shot, but was expected to live. As she spoke, the video of the robbery shifted into slow motion, showing the two young men with hooded sweatshirts hiding their faces. The film slowed several times to show a brief view of the robbers' faces. Then the screen switched to artist's sketches of the perpetrators. They played the video again and pleaded with viewers who knew anything about the robbery to contact the *Call for Action* line at an 800 number at the bottom of the screen.

The camera went back to the anchor desk. "In another story that *News 8 at Six* is following, several cars at the *Cinema 16* parking lot were broken into last evening. The brazen thieves got away with cash, CDs, and other personal property.

Lisa Alverez reports live from the parking lot at the *Cinema 16* parking lot. What can you tell us, Lisa?"

"Well, Jim, the perpetrators selected cars in the middle of the lot." Pointing to an empty space outlined in police barrier tape, she continued, "They parked in this spot among several late model cars. A surveillance video camera caught the robbers in the act."

A grainy film rolled but there was little detail to the shapes as they went to four different cars, first trying the door with no luck. The car alarm went off in two of the cars but the thieves ignored the noise. After a few seconds, one of the thieves used something to smash several car windows. The thieves reached inside and took several items from each of the cars. Then the two suspects got back in their own vehicle and fled.

After a commercial break, the news returned with a story about a bank robbery, the third in the Dunnellon area in less than a month. Again, a surveillance camera captured the crime. This time the film was very clear. The robber's features were easy to distinguish. The news anchor said that the thief was caught just two miles from the bank with the bag of cash still in the front seat of his car. The bright colored paint canister exploded in the bag and was all over the eighteen year-old perpetrator, and the interior of his car.

"I can't believe all the video cameras. Everywhere you go, you can't escape them. I mean, look at this. Who would think you'd be caught on video in the middle of a parking lot in front of a movie plaza?"

Diane smiled and said, "Well, Dear. I almost forgot. I have a surprise for you." She went into the kitchen and returned with an envelope. Smiling, she handed it to Pat, and sat down next to him.

Pat looked at the envelope. *Marion County Sheriff's Office?* "What's this?"

"Open it and see." Her smile broadened.

Pat reached in the envelope and pulled out the letter. He read the brief salutation then launched into the body.

Dear Mr. McKinney,
Your car was observed running a red
light by our newly installed traffic
cameras at the corner of E.
Pennsylvania Avenue and North Florida
Avenue. Since this is a new installation
for our camera program, we're not
issuing a citation at this time. Consider
this a warning to more closely observe
traffic laws. Safety is our goal, Mr.
McKinney. Slow down. Stop at red
lights. The life you save may be your
own.

At the bottom of the page was a snapshot of his car entering the intersection where the traffic light had clearly turned red. An enlargement of the license plate clearly showed the plate number. The caption under it read, "Florida license plate number HET376, registered to Patrick McKinney, October 4, 1997." A second snapshot was of a wrecked car at the same intersection. The caption under it read, "This driver thought he could make it. August 25, 1997."

Pat wasn't impressed. On the contrary, he was angry. "How can they get away with this in the United States of America? What ever happened to due process under the law?"

Diane was nearly laughing at Pat's outburst. "Wow, aren't you Mr. Self-righteous?"

"Well, this is ridiculous. I didn't run that red light. I was already in the intersection before it turned red." He looked down at the picture to try to prove his point but it was no use. The camera didn't lie. His car wasn't in the intersection, and the light was clearly red. He shook his head, "Regardless, there wasn't anyone there to charge me. What if someone had my car and did this? Why should I get charged with this?"

Diane was shaking her head, a smirk on her face. "You know you were driving that car. You never let anyone borrow your car. Besides, you're not getting a ticket. Didn't you read the rest of the letter? It's a warning, like a reminder to use your head." Diane smiled again.

"But this isn't right. There're cameras everywhere these days. You can't go anywhere without being filmed." Pat's face was getting red now. This was really upsetting him. "What if we decided to get a little frisky in the parking lot at the grocery store? And what if some fruitcake security guard decided to sell it on the internet, or worse, tried to blackmail us with it? It's just not right."

"Pat, most people aren't like that. Most people are honest, especially people in law enforcement and security positions."

Pat stared at his wife for several moments. He couldn't believe that she was naïve enough to believe that security guards, making barely above minimum wage, were above doing some very shady acts. Many security guards had criminal records. Just because they wore a uniform that looked like a police officer's didn't mean they put on a layer of integrity with the threads. But he didn't want to continue arguing with Diane. It would put a real damper on their evening. This was supposed to be a night of bonding, just the two of them. That left no room for quarreling about cameras, tickets, and the integrity of law enforcement. That would have to wait for another night.

"Okay, Mrs. Rose-Colored-Glasses, you're right. Most, and I stress, most people are honest, at least to a large degree. But there is that small minority, those bastards with a scheme, that you have to watch out for. They're out to get you and your money. With all these cameras, you can't let that power fall into the wrong hands. They'll screw you every time."

Diane was looking at Pat with a sideways glance. She knew what Pat was saying, but she still believed in the good in the vast majority of people. But she, too, had more important things on her mind. She loved her children, but tonight was a break from the constant, day-to-day grind. Taking care of children was a labor of love. She was glad to be off-the-clock for an evening.

She had a surprise for Pat. She'd bought a silk teddy for their night alone together. She was going to put it on later and surprise him when he least expected it. Then she looked around the room, thinking, what if there are cameras hidden in our house? She shook her head. *Pat's got me spooked.*

Pat yawned, feeling the effects of overeating. He glanced at the TV as the sports came on. An amateur video of a spectator at one of the professional baseball playoff games came on. He'd climbed out of the stands and started to tackle a player who'd just received a base on balls to force in the go-ahead run. Within seconds there was an all out brawl on the field. The man who'd entered the field was getting pummeled by players from both teams.

"See what I mean? Cameras are everywhere. You can't escape them."

Now Diane's mind was working overtime. Maybe Pat was right. Maybe there were too many cameras. *No. It isn't the cameras that you have to worry about. It's the camera operators.*

Even as she thought this, a satellite camera was taking high resolution pictures of the Florida peninsula. A study of the growth of the Sunshine State was underway. Every week for the next ten years, cameras would be recording changes to the landscape. The proliferation of cities and subdivisions would tell demographers about growth patterns in the state. The pictures were so clear that you could see alligators lying on the beaches of lakes near population centers.

Pat was scared of alligators, but he was more concerned with the two legged animals that roamed the state. He turned and watched Diane as she was deep in thought. He could see the wheels turning as something in her mind held her attention. He couldn't believe how beautiful she was, and how lucky he was to have her to himself. Finally, she turned to look at him with a questioning glance.

He said, "I'm just enjoying the view. Penny for your thoughts?"

"You'll have to pay more than that. They're X-rated. But first, let's go for that walk." She stood and reached down for Pat's hand to help him off the couch. "It's pretty cool out for October. It should be refreshing. When we get back, we can shower. Then I'll give you a back rub." She smiled.

He smiled back. He was already reaching for his tennis shoes.

Chapter 3

The morning sun was angling through the stand of pine trees to the east of the property. The sky above was a bright blue and the early fall temperatures were a cool sixty-eight degrees. Theo Messier stood at the front door of the newly constructed home of Charles and Jody Williams. He was holding the three-ring binder that held the final walkthrough checklist which he insisted be completed prior to turning over the keys to the new owners. Theo developed the checklist over a number of years as he learned about building top quality homes for the wealthiest clients in Northern Virginia west of Washington, DC.

The years had not been without challenges. He'd been sued a number of times early in his career due to poor workmanship or promised features that were required per the contract but not delivered. Those problems proved to be invaluable lessons as he learned to cater to the wealthy, satisfying their taste for the most luxurious amenities to suit their pampered lives. Those lessons, in time, placed his building expertise in very high demand. Over the years, Messier Custom Homes enjoyed a strong reputation for constructing exceptionally high quality homes. He no longer had to advertise for clients; they sought him out. In fact, he had a backlog of clients long enough to keep his company busy for the next two years. He was actually screening his clients and turning those away who could afford his price but who were simply not the type of customer Messier Custom Homes sought.

He looked at his watch; 9:55. He looked up in time to see Charles and Jody Williams' white Mercedes-Benz CLK pull into the long driveway. The drive ended directly in front of the house in a circle around a large fountain with two stone dolphins spitting a stream of water at each other. Charles was proud of the fountain. He was a former United States Navy submariner, having served on the USS *Nevada*. The ship was ported at the Kings Bay Submarine Base near Saint Marys, Georgia. Dolphins were the symbol of qualification in submarines, so Charles designed the fountain to celebrate his time on the ship. Had it not been for his experience on the ship, he'd never have achieved the financial success he was now enjoying.

Since leaving the service, Charles had developed a device that helped reduce the noise emitted from electric motors. Submarines had hundreds of motors performing all kinds of functions. These motors made the submarine 'visible' to enemy sonar which, after years of the United States Government giving away its military secrets, had improved significantly. Charles' invention, the Noise Buffer Module, reduced the emitted noise levels by more than eighty-five percent. In theory, it was a simple matter to reduce noise by emitting an amplified wave that was equal to, but opposite the original emitted noise. In practice, it was much more complex. But after only a year of research and development, the prototype was ready for marketing. The NBM was an instant success and Charles was the beneficiary. He received over $12,000,000 in royalties from the production and sales of the NBM and his new company was on retainer to maintain the devices that were installed on each submarine. His net worth was projected to climb by nearly $6,000,000 annually for at least the next five years; the life of the government contract with Charles' company. He was already working on an invention for headphones and other communications devices to reduce background noise and therefore increase the quality of the delivered sound. Their financial future was rocketing.

Charles was a handsome young man, six feet tall and slender with short, sandy brown hair and brown eyes. He had feet that appeared to be larger than would fit with the rest of his body. They made him look as if he'd be a bit clumsy, which he was, but he learned over the years to slow down. Now his

manner was very smooth. His face was thin and slightly drawn
but he always appeared to be smiling. When he wasn't engaged in conversation he appeared
to be analyzing things. Jody said his mind was working over
the speed limit. He was always commenting to Jody how
different things could be improved if only the manufacturer
would make a slight change to this or that. He would even
make some of the changes himself and most of the time, he
was right. Now he was enjoying the fruits of his tinkering.
    Theo walked down the three steps and opened the car
door for Jody. Extending a hand, he assisted her out of the
luxury car. Jody's cheeks flushed slightly. At just twenty-
three years old, Jody was a short, slender, and beautiful young
woman. Her platinum blond hair was thick and slightly wavy
as it hung down to her shoulders. Her large, green eyes
contrasted with her light complexion. No matter where she
went or what she wore, her stunning looks drew attention.
    She was still getting used to being treated like royalty.
From a humble background, her parents were working class
folks. When Jody first introduced Charles to her parents, they
were suspicious. They wondered why she got involved with a
sailor. After they got to know her new boyfriend, they knew
that he wasn't a typical sailor. He acted more like a computer
nerd. When Charles made the big score on his patented
invention, they were awestruck. Being hardworking
Americans, they were disappointed when Jody and Charles
purchased the Benz. They expected them to at least buy a
Cadillac or a Lincoln, but Charles insisted that they go for the
Benz.
    When Charles told Jody that they were instant
millionaires, she didn't believe him. She became angry with
him when he kept insisting that his invention had made a
bundle of money. 'Stop dreaming, and get back to reality,'
she'd yelled; until he showed her the first check and the
newspaper articles about his invention. At times she still felt
like she was in a fairy tale and the dream would end, taking all
of her new luxuries with it. But the dream kept getting bigger

and better.   She was still learning how to handle life in the spotlight.

When Charles told her that they were going to purchase a home from Messier Homes, she didn't even know who Theo Messier was.   She told her parents that they were going to build a home.   When she said Theo Messier was their contractor, her father nearly fell out of his chair.   He explained to his daughter that only surgeons, high priced lawyers, and corporate CEOs could afford Theo Messier.   Jody Owen Williams finally realized just how wealthy she'd become.

Theo, Charles, and Jody stood in front of the fabulous brick home, looking up at the entry.   Theo stood back a step from the couple and allowed them to take in the elegance of the front of the home.   Theo learned that the home should speak for itself.   If the client was speechless at the first view, the rest of the tour would be easy.

Theo liked Charles and Jody.   He knew that they were both from humble backgrounds and were yet to be spoiled by their newly acquired wealth.   They were impressed with the luxury and lavish amenities that would greet them inside their new home.   This would be an easy final tour.   Many of the young, wealthy couples that toured their homes complained about everything, from variations in shades of paint and wallpaper to the intricate patterns in ceramic tiles.   They were never happy only because they were used to Mommy and Daddy providing a new, expensive toy at the first sign of a whimper.   Theo was only too glad to accommodate their desires because it meant an expensive change order where he made nearly four times the profit for the minor change. *Spoiled rich kids.*   That was one reason he found Charles and Jody to be so refreshing.   They'd come from a background similar to his own and had found a niche to make a fortune. For that reason he had great respect for them.

As Charles and Jody surveyed the grounds, Theo simply watched and smiled.   They were his last clients before he turned the company over to his sons, Jeremy and Aaron. Theo was in his late fifties.   He'd mentioned to Charles and

Jody that he and his young wife Natashia were retiring to a chateau in France. "She's been over there for over two months. She just loves it there."

From now on he would have only minimal involvement in the business, but would still receive income. His sons would split the remainder of the profit. Theo was afraid that his sons fell into the category of spoiled rich kids. He didn't allow them to whine and he didn't give into their complaining like other wealthy parents, but they did have many expensive toys. He'd insisted that they learn the ins and outs of Messier Homes before he would turn over the reins of the business, but he was still worried that they were too young and too inexperienced. But he had other plans.

He came back to reality as Charles and Jody moved into the entry of the home. The high, vaulted ceiling opened up above them and Jody let out a slight gasp. To her, it looked like the entry to a cathedral. She was in on the planning of every detail of the home, but the reality of the finished product had her nearly in tears. She held Charles hand tighter as they continued their walk through.

Part of the deal for Charles and Jody, as with many of the customers of Theo Messier, was that the home came completely furnished. During the planning phase Charles and Jody selected furniture for every room in the house. They sold their old house along with all the furniture except a few prized pieces. Now that they saw the home, they wondered why they bothered to keep anything from the old house. Most of what they brought into their new home was personal items such as family photos, wedding gifts, and other things that only have value to the owner. The family pictures were already in place throughout the house. But many of the other personal items were still in boxes in the garage or on a shelf in the master bedroom closet. They would be opened later when Jody finally came down from the cloud she was riding.

The entire walkthrough took over an hour. Theo explained every detail of the construction and pointed out special features of the house; such as the computer controlled ventilation system which included motorized curtains. The curtains closed when the sun was shining in during the summer to conserve the cool air in the house. In the winter, that same curtain would open to allow the sun to shine through. Charles was already talking about ways that the timing might be changed to improve the efficiency of this system.

The grounds were equally impressive with the landscaping completed just as they had designed. When the tour was finished, Theo completed the checklist and had Charles and Jody sign the last page. Theo counter-signed on the designated line. He gave the couple their copy, shook Charles' hand, hugged Jody and handed Charles the keys to the young couple's new home. He bowed slightly and left, his last deal complete. Theo walked to his own Mercedes and drove away.

Charles and Jody looked at the door as it closed behind Theo. They stood in the entry for a moment, stunned by the elegance and the fact that they now owned the most fabulous home in which they'd ever set foot. It was as if they didn't know what to do first. They turned to each other and embraced.

Charles asked his young bride, "So, what do you think? Did we do alright?"

Jody smiled. She looked up into her husband's eyes. "You are going to be so tired."

He looked back at her, the expression on his face a question mark. *What do you mean?*

"I am going to do things to you that you've only dreamed about. Let's go upstairs. I need a shower. Then I want to tour the master bedroom again." Her smile was broad and sensuous. Like a couple of kids, they ran up the stairs that split at the landing and went in two different directions. Charles nearly tripped on the third step, his large feet getting tangled with each other. He jokingly said, "No running in the house miss, or you're going to get a spanking."

Jody smiled back at him and said, "Umm. I'm counting on it."

Moments later they were in their brand new king sized bed, naked, entangled in each other's arms.

* * *

The small room was crammed tight with electronic equipment that emitted a quiet hum as fans worked to keep the gear cool. LCD lights glowed steady, some red, some green. Nine fifteen inch flat-screen monitors were above the counsel at eye level in a three by three arrangement. To the left of those, a thirty two inch flat-panel monitor was angled towards the control station. A headset was hanging on a hook to the right. Another headset was worn by a man sitting on a stool in front of the control panel. To the right of the nine monitors, a digital recording stack was tapped into the control panel. The receiver had multiple channels and the digital recorder could record the audio and video for all nine small monitors and the large flat panel monitor. If the system were to expand, the recorder was already capable of recording up to 32 channels of audio and video. Behind the stools there was a small box with more blinking lights and a keyboard on a slide out shelf. This was a MircoBranch server that was hooked into the internet. It emitted the hum of a cooling fan as it processed digital data at lightning speed. Cables fed all of the data from the recorder to the server in saved files that were stored and cataloged in folders. The server was password protected to limit access to the files.

Two stools were in front of the control panel. One was occupied as the monitors displayed the images of various rooms. The other stool was empty. The images were sharp and clear since the cameras were top of the line in micro electronics. They were the best equipment currently available on the market.

The man sitting on the stool at the control panel was making adjustments to the cameras making sure they were positioned properly. He thought about making some other changes but the light, color, and contrast were all set perfectly. They had to be ready to capture the action they knew would be happening at any moment. On the center monitor, a green light blinked on the screen indicating that it would be the monitor being displayed on the large monitor to the left. That could be changed with the touch of a finger in the corner of the screen of any of the small monitors.

Twenty minutes later, another man walked into the control room. He looked the monitors over as he always did, then ordered the controller to make various adjustments, like he always did. "This camera needs to be zoomed out slightly."

The man at the controls mumbled, "It looks fine to me." He gave his partner a look of annoyance. The two men barely fit in the room crammed with equipment. It was a blessing that the air conditioning was capable of handling the heat emitted from the electronic gear. The heat in the room would become unbearable if the primary and backup air conditioning units were both to fail.

The man replied with a bit of an edge in his voice, "Why don't you just adjust the focus instead of being hard-headed?"

Mumbling so low that it was almost inaudible he said, "Because I've already adjusted that about ten times. It's fine."

"Well it doesn't look fine to me, so zoom the damn thing out a touch. Look, you don't have the whole bed in the picture."

With an exaggerated eye roll, the young man at the controls clicked a mouse on the zoom button to adjust the camera. The last corner of the bed's headboard came into view.

"Happy?"

"Perfect," he said with a smile. "How many hits are we getting right now?"

'Hits' were the number of members currently watching their internet site. The site was very popular with wealthy folks who wanted to remain anonymous. The company promised that no names would ever be sold on a mailing list and no disclosure of site members would ever be made. For that promise, members paid a hefty sum to view live sex over the internet.

The man at the controls typed a few lines into the keyboard and the screen above the server displayed a report of the system activity. "Six hundred thirty-three. Not bad for a Saturday morning. I guess all these rich kids don't have anything better to do." He looked at the date in the lower corner of the monitor. October 4, 1997.

He heard a noise in his headset and immediately turned to the control panel and flipped a switch. The green light on the monitor turned to red indicating that they were recording the images. Moments later, Charles and Jody Williams appeared on the screen, slowly working their way towards the bed, passionately kissing, their bodies still wet from the midday shower.

"I'll adjust the audio, but it looks just about perfect already."

"Transmit this one live," the older man said, pointing to a camera that provided a fairly wide angle of the couple. "From this angle they should be on screen the whole time while they make it to the bed."

He was right. When Charles and Jody finally landed on the king-sized bed together, the camera was at a perfect angle to capture them both, grinding away, passionately kissing and touching each other.

"This is hot. Zoom in some now and get some close ups."

They watched as the scene on the monitors heated up. As the couple moved around the bed, the controller switched cameras and zoomed in and out to get the best view. The action went from wide angles to close ups.

"Nice," the older man exclaimed as he rubbed his hands together and smiled.

The controller didn't respond, but he agreed. When all the recording was complete, he'd be able to create a full length video of the action that would rival any professionally made film. They'd make this available on their network for viewing on demand by their members.

Across the USA, members of the site saw the signal on their

computer screens that indicated a new, live streaming video was available. Ninety-eight percent of those on their internet site switched from various archived recordings to the live action. Charles and Jody, believing that they were having their own private celebration of their good fortune, unknowingly became instant internet porn stars.

Chapter 4

The round dining room table next to the kitchen was covered with the classifieds from Thursday's edition of the Orlando Sentinel. They were opened to the 'Homes for Sale' section which was seven full pages long. In between the newspapers were two aluminum pans of Chinese food; spicy garlic chicken over fried rice and chicken chow mein over white rice. A small plate with two partially-eaten eggrolls sat between the pans. The aroma from the food filled the two bedroom apartment. Two nearly-empty Bud Light long necks sat next to the half eaten dinners. Two more empty bottles were in the trash near the kitchen. The living room television was muted and angled towards the dining area. The six o'clock news was just starting.

Joe McKinney and his fiancé, Lisa Goddard sat at the table, picking at their Chinese dinners, drinking Bud Light, looking at houses . . . again. They wanted to take their time and find the perfect house but, it was proving difficult. Joe's idea of perfect differed significantly from Lisa's. Lisa wanted a house that they could move into and not change anything. Joe wanted a hobby house that he could tinker with. After all, he had a lot of time on his hands. He'd just been released from active duty in the Marine Corp, for the second time, and had no need to get a job. He wasn't a military retiree and he wasn't filthy rich but he had investments that provided all the income he and his bride-to-be would ever need. She intended to go to school, something that she would never have been able to afford on her own. He wanted to pick up several hobbies, one of which was supposed to be fixing up their new home. They both knew that a compromise was necessary. Joe was afraid that Lisa's idea of compromise was '*You do the compromising, I get what I want.*' Joe knew if it came down to that, she'd win.

Joe was still fit, in Marine Corps shape. He stood five feet, eleven inches tall, two hundred fifteen pounds of lean muscle. He didn't have the muscle bound features of a body builder but, he didn't have an ounce of fat anywhere. He carried himself erect and held his head high when he walked. His chin was slightly square and he had a small dimple in the center. His brown hair was still close cropped but not strictly within military specs. His most striking feature was his light gray-blue eyes. When Lisa looked into those cool eyes, she melted.

Joe was proud to be a Marine. While in boot camp, he'd learned the errors of his youth. He was ashamed at what he'd previously allowed himself to become. But, unlike his brother, Pat, he'd come to terms with his past. It wasn't easy. He still had pangs of guilt when he watched his now-legal investment portfolio grow, but he knew his previous life was already in the books. *What's done is done.*

The apartment they currently shared was originally Joe's. Lisa had lived in the same complex but across the parking lot on the first floor. Joe's apartment was on the second floor which gave him a bird's eye view of the walkway between Lisa's old apartment and the pool. He used to admire her from a distance as she made her way to the pool for her afternoon tan. She drew a lot of attention with her slim, tight, tan body, beautiful face, and flowing sandy blond hair. Joe's life was complicated back then, and he had no time to start a relationship. But fate intervened.

They met in the apartment complex' weight room. As usual, Joe was working out like a mad man, so mentally focused that he didn't hear Lisa walk in. Lisa took one look at Joe and thought he was having a heart attack. He nearly freaked out when she spoke to him. When he saw that it was Lisa, the beautiful woman that he watched from his apartment window, he was momentarily at a loss for words. Finally regaining his composure, he introduced himself and they found that they had a lot in common. He challenged her to a friendly competitive swim, which she won. But she won more than the race, she also won his heart. They fell in love and the rest is history.

Their relationship had a rocky start. It wasn't because of old lovers. It wasn't because they disagreed about politics or religion or any of the usual hot button topics. A number of events appeared to conspire to knock their relationship off track.

Joe had a history that seemed to be chasing him. Like many high school kids, he and his brothers, Pat and Mike, used to smoke pot regularly. When their habit got too expensive to simply buy the weed, they started to sell small quantities to their friends. As word got around, their small business grew and before they knew it, they were dealing in serious weight. Their small business turned into big business and their big business turned into big problems. Their friends and business associates turned against the brothers. Finally, their new enemies stole hundreds of thousands of dollars from the brothers.

But that was nothing compared to the ultimate act of vengeance. Four of the McKinney's new enemies broke into Mike McKinney's home. They raped and killed Mike's wife. They were never brought to trial. A detective who was on the take for a major drug dealer stole the key piece of evidence from the evidence room. The four murderers walked free.

Pat and Joe vowed to get revenge. They both left Florida for the military; Joe to the Marine Corps, Pat to the Navy. After six years, they finished their tours of duty and came home to execute their plan of revenge, but their plan seemed to execute on its own. The brothers were dismayed, but sat back and watched while their enemies were killed, one by one.

All this time, Mike was overwhelmed with grief and despair. He'd moved west, trying to flee his sorrow, but it followed him and ultimately took his life.

It was in the middle of this quest for revenge that Joe and Lisa met. Lisa didn't know of Joe's past or the fact that he'd made a small fortune selling grass. When she found out, she was furious. Her family had been torn apart by her own brother's involvement with drugs. It left her parents near bankruptcy, paying for legal bills which he never repaid. Lisa struggled with reconciling her love for Joe and her hate for his past. Joe convinced Lisa of his true remorse for his past. He knew he couldn't change it but he also knew he could put the financial gains that he'd made to good use now and put Lisa through school.

Just when Joe and Lisa felt that they were ready to start their new life together, fate pulled another fast one. Joe was recalled to active duty to investigate a series of thefts of military personnel and embezzlement of government money. When he reported for duty, he received word that his father was struck with a serious heart attack. Within weeks, Lisa's father also fell ill and had a massive, fatal stroke. The two lovers were miles apart, dealing with their individual grief. They both were concerned that their relationship was doomed.

In the end, their love survived all the challenges and they were finally able to get back together in their apartment in the western suburbs of Orlando, Florida. They planned to buy a home together and get married at the home surrounded by friends and family. The plan was a good one. It was the execution that was proving difficult.

Joe was looking at the ads that Lisa circled while she looked at the last of the classifieds. He was starting to come to terms with the idea that there would be no compromise. He would move into a very nice, complete home that needed little or no tender loving care. He'd talked with Pat about his situation and Pat already warned him that his plans were doomed. Pat said, 'Little brother, you'd be far better off to give in now and be supportive than try to fight it. She's going to win. Besides, you'll be the beneficiary of the joy of a happy bride. Trust me. It will be better in the long run.' While Joe reviewed the listings he looked up at Lisa and saw the intensity in the way she studied the ads. *She really wants this to be her dream home. Maybe Pat's right. Maybe I'd better give in. There are other things that are more important than getting my way. I could always get a guitar and take lessons.* As he reviewed the ads, he made his own marks next to the ones that Lisa circled indicating that he'd be willing to take a closer look at the properties. They were looking at homes to the west of Orlando near Winter Garden, a rapidly growing area and one with which Joe was familiar. He hoped that they'd be able to find a home in a new subdivision that had no relation to his past. That might be difficult, but it was worth a try.

Lisa started looking at homes in the $95,000 to $120,000 range. Joe quickly reset the price range to $275,000 to $325,000. She nearly fell off her chair but he assured her that there would be no issue with making the mortgage. Once they established the price range, they agreed to a number of other features and listed them into categories from 'must have' to 'can't have'. That limited their choices to where they only circled about six homes per edition. They planned to call a realtor and start looking at the homes the next day. They would start with homes that had been listed for several weeks running and not sold followed by any recommendations from the realtor. They figured that they'd look for several weeks then make an offer from the list of those that they liked. Joe wasn't very patient with the process, but he looked to Lisa to help him with self control. She was the calming force in his life.

As they looked through the papers, a story on the six o'clock news caught Joe's eye. The news anchor's lips were moving and a picture behind him was of a naked woman with her breasts blacked out by a censor bar. The caption in bright letters said "Internet Porn Exploding". Joe smiled slightly, grabbed the remote and clicked the mute button. The TV audio came on with the anchorman in mid story.

'. . . *explosion of internet pornography is costing law enforcement agencies a bundle and no one appears to know how to address this growing problem. One local police station in the town of Vermilion, Ohio is taking a low tech path to deterring men from stalking under-aged girls. An officer with some pretty good computer skills is posing as a teenage girl and chatting it up with would be child molesters. The officer presents himself as a fourteen year old girl and chats on-line with the adult, male suitors. He agrees to meet with them and perform certain sexual favors, which were proposed by the suitors. When the men arrive for the rendezvous, they are apprehended and charged with a variety of sex crimes, depending on the content of the chat. To date, all of the evidence has proven to be admissible in court and the charges have stood in each case.*

Psychologist Dr. Samuel Jamison, an expert witness for the prosecution, questioned each of the alleged child molesters. In each case, the perpetrator admitted to being addicted to internet pornography and blamed their addiction for their actions. Dr. Jamison expressed his opinion that, unless drastic action is taken, more men will fall victim to internet pornography and start to exhibit the behaviors of these perpetrators further taxing law enforcement budgets, limiting their ability to address this growing problem.

Another area of concern is the number of internet pornography clubs. These clubs range from very low tech, low cost clubs ranging anywhere from $2.95 to $21.95 per month to exotic, posh clubs that are over $100 per month. Some very exclusive clubs are nearly one thousand dollars to join with a hefty monthly fee to maintain membership. These more expensive clubs cater to wealthy individuals who might be recognized and their businesses, professions, or reputations ruined by their exposure. Other clubs are set up so that couples can exchange videos of each other or they're paid to perform live. They have cameras in their bedrooms and are willing to share their performances with other couples. These clubs tend to have higher membership fees.

There's also been a huge increase in the use of cameras in our society. Traffic lights at thousands of intersections across the country have cameras that take photos of drivers running red lights. Security cameras in department stores and banks are commonplace. What isn't known is that many cameras are being used for apartment complex security in areas that most people don't know about or don't suspect. A very surprised couple recently sued a Laundromat operator for making a tape available on the internet. The couple was waiting for their clothes to dry and they got a little too frisky in the Laundromat storage room. What they didn't know is that the owner had recently been burglarized and had installed a security camera in the storage room. When he found the tape of the two having sex, he sold the tape to an internet porn site operator. The tape was duplicated hundreds, even thousands of times over and was shown on dozens of porn sites. Well, the couple had a friend who stumbled across the film and joked to them about it. They didn't think it was funny. They obtained a copy and confronted the Laundromat's owner who admitted to selling the tape. He told them it was their own fault for that kind of behavior in a public place. The case is still in court.

It's impossible to determine the number of internet pornography sites that are available to anyone with a few computer skills. Even with parental controls, children of most any age can stumble across a site displaying everything from heavy petting to hardcore sex including depictions of rape. Some of those images may not be staged.

The news anchor's female partner said, '*Jim, that's a very disturbing story.*'

'*Yes it is, Sheila.*'

The story ended. There was another brief pause as the anchorman took a moment to gather his composure after the report. He shook his head slightly then started on the next story on the teleprompter. '*In other news, a turnpike bridge is closed down when it is discovered that a stretch of the bridge was near collapse. Inspectors . . .*'

Joe muted the TV again. "Wow. I used to think porn was no big deal but it sounds like there are some pretty sick folks out there."

Lisa looked up from the classifieds. She'd kept looking at house ads but was half listening to the story on internet porn. Her face was serious, but she didn't say anything. Joe sensed that she wanted to say something but wasn't sure if she should.

"What's on your mind," he asked.

Lisa paused as if having second thoughts about saying anything. She took a deep breath then said, "I didn't want to say this because I know it will upset you but look what happened to your sister-in-law. Those bastards must have been sick to do that. What gets into someone's brain that they would abuse another human being like that?"

Joe looked back at Lisa, trying to keep a straight face. He'd seen a lot of misery in his life, mostly during wartime in Afghanistan. He also saw his sister-in-law in the hospital after she'd been beaten and raped. She was in a coma before she finally died from her injuries.

He said, "I've seen what people can do to each other and it makes me ill. I never equated pornography with violence, but after hearing that report I guess it's not just sex. Why some guy would take a chance on meeting up with a minor for sex is beyond me. I can't imagine what goes through someone's mind that would make them . . . ." Joe stopped without completing his thought.

Lisa stood and sat on Joe's lap. She hugged him and kissed him lightly on the lips. "I'm just glad I found you when I did. If I wouldn't have saved your life down there at the weight room, who knows where you'd be now? You'd probably be crushed under a thousand pounds of barbells."

They kissed lightly but with feeling. The story had obviously struck a chord with Joe. He wondered what Mike and Julie McKinney's life would be like now if they'd lived. But he put the thoughts out of his mind and put his arms around Lisa and held her tight. "Let's take a break from house hunting." He smiled at her with a hint of what he had in mind.

"Only if you promise me one thing."

"What's that?"

"That we buy a house soon. This apartment is getting smaller with every house we read about." She smiled and kissed him again, this time with a little light tongue and a little more passion.

Joe mumbled into her lips, "Whatever you want, you got it." He kissed her back. Within minutes they were in bed. Joe stopped for a moment and looked around the bedroom. He asked, "You don't have any hidden cameras rolling in here, do you?"

"If you recall, this is your old apartment. I'm the one who should be worried." Lisa smiled, her face showing mock concern with a raised eyebrow.

Moments later they were in each other's arms, hot passion radiating from every move. Nothing happening anywhere else in the world mattered to them.

Chapter 5

Bill Rollins yelled to his wife from his office down the hall, "Honey, what have you got left to do in the kitchen?" He was on his new computer, a Microvault 2000. The computer was a light laptop with a high speed internet access. It had all the latest advanced features including a Gruben Magic Graphics card and over two megabytes of SDRAM. The machine was so fast that the screens changed as if he were changing the channel on his Sony big screen TV. This was the first time he had a machine that actually had faster response than his high speed internet service.

His wife, Candace was just finishing loading the dishwasher with the dinner dishes. She hollered back to his office that she'd be just a few more minutes. She was getting excited because she knew what he had in mind. It was their two-year-and-six-month wedding anniversary and Bill wanted the sex to be electric. Candace had prepared for the evening by wearing her new thong with a heart shaped front over her pubic area. She'd trimmed her pubic hair in the shape of a heart to match her thong panties. She was sure that Bill would appreciate her creativity. He liked the special little things she did to keep their sex life interesting. So far there were no complaints.

Bill also liked to do special things for both of them to keep the sex interesting, if not intense. That's why he joined the Sensuous and Extreme Couples Club. The SExCClub was an internet porn site that catered to the wealthy. The club was very expensive, but the service provided was unique. The site had streaming video of over fifty amateur couples having sex live on the internet. Promotion for the site stated that the couples were volunteer participants who wanted to share their experiences with other couples. The information on the site read that, in order for them to appear on the SExCClub, they had to act natural, as if they were not on display; just act normal and ignore the cameras and microphones. The couple would just do what comes naturally. So far, Bill felt he was getting his money's worth.

At first, Candace was opposed to the idea of the club. Bill had visited porn sites before on his computer and she was not impressed. Most porn sites that he'd shown her before were classless, the content mostly trash that was degrading to women. She wasn't turned on by that at all. She told him that most women preferred sensual, exotic, and passionate activities. They weren't into the wham-bam-thank-you-ma'am, nearly abusive sex on most internet sites. *That's a guy thing*, she'd told him.

Being a couple very comfortable with their sex life, they talked openly about what would enhance their sexual experience and keep it fresh. Candace said she wouldn't accept anything that was degrading to woman or anything that displayed any violence. She also wasn't interested in any site that showed multiple partners or partner swapping. She wanted to see loving couples who liked to experiment with giving their partner maximum pleasure.

So Bill went on a search for a site that would be both exciting and acceptable to them both. Since he was a guy, the search took him to some very dicey sites with some pretty crude sex. He had to be careful to not get hung up on sleazy internet porn. Even he was surprised by some of the trash that was easily accessible to anyone with access to a computer and the internet. After viewing some of the graphic nature of the sexual abuse of these women, he wondered why they would allow themselves to be used like that. He figured it was all they knew or that they were making a few hundred bucks per film to perform. He could see why woman hated this class of porn and why some men, being the macho creatures that they are, would enjoy viewing that garbage.

After searching for weeks, Bill finally thought that he'd found the perfect site. The SExCClub site guaranteed that the sex was sensual, exotic, and loving. It also guaranteed privacy, confidentiality, and the ability to cancel any time the subscriber was not satisfied. The price for all this was an annual fee of $9,900. At first Bill left the site because the price seemed way out of line. But as he searched more and more for a site that offered a softer approach to porn, he found that another site didn't exist. This site filled a niche for the wealthy with a penchant for voyeurism that sparked their own sexual desires.

Finally, he decided that price really didn't matter. Money was not the object here. They were wealthy and set for life. They could afford the steep price and if it helped keep their love life alive and vibrant, it was worth the price tag. After just the first evening of viewing the SExCClub, Candace agreed. She was comfortable with the site's policy and the level of sophistication. Bill was rewarded with a very passionate night that lasted over two hours.

Candace finished in the kitchen and headed upstairs to the bedroom. She hollered to Bill that she would be upstairs whenever he finished in his office. He shouted back that he'd be up in a few minutes. He accessed the site for the club, entered his password, and his validation code. The site required two separate codes to enter the restricted, member's only area. This was where you could view live action. On the screen, he noticed that there was a yellow blinking light indicating that there were no live transmissions at this time. There were hundreds of archived performances, but Bill and Candace preferred to see couples live. You never knew what to expect and there was usually something new and exciting in the live action.

Bill yelled up to Candace that there was nothing live yet, but that he'd watch for a bit and let her know when something came on. She said okay, that he should take his time. When the live action came on, he would take his laptop upstairs and set it on the dresser next to the big screen TV. He had a connector that linked the computer to the TV so that the site was displayed on the massive sixty-six inch screen in their bedroom. The picture was so clear that they could make out fine details of the bedroom on the screen. They could easily make out the eye color of the couples. That was impressive considering the lighting in the room of the couple on screen was usually not studio quality. However it was done, the lighting was enhanced to provide a higher quality video stream than would normally be possible. *This must be some expensive cameras. No way would these couples live with video cameras and cables strewn about their bedrooms. I wonder how they do it?*

Just then, the light at the lower right of the laptop screen blinked green. He saw a young woman move into view of the camera. She appeared to be in her mid twenties and very fit. She was slender with dark hair and a light complexion. She was fully clothed in a white blouse and brown slacks. She looked as though she'd just gotten home from work at a law firm, accounting office, or some other such profession. She stood in front of her dresser mirror and removed her small earrings and hair clip then shook her head so that her brunette hair fell free onto her shoulders and back. She looked at herself in the mirror then lifted her hair up, let it fall and shook her head again. She scrunched up her face as if she wasn't satisfied with the look then shrugged her shoulders.

Bill waited to see what was next before running upstairs with the laptop. No sense setting up the big screen if there wasn't any action. He continued to monitor the screen which shifted to the closet. The brunette was now in the closet removing her blouse and pants. She wore a shear push up bra and matching panties. As Bill watched, she put on a light, silky tank top, removed her comfortable panties and put on a very tiny thong. Over these she pulled a silky pair of shorts. *Looking for some action tonight?* Bill thought as he watched. She finished in the closet, put on some slippers and headed out of site of the camera. The image on the screen froze and the light in the lower right of the screen blinked yellow. *False alarm.*

The light blinked green again. The scene shifted to a different home and a different bedroom, this one larger and more elegant. A young man, probably in his early twenties, was sitting on the edge of a king-sized bed pulling off his shoes and socks. He tossed them out of view of the screen. He'd already shed his tie and dress shirt and thrown them on a chair near the bed. He pulled off his pants and briefs and headed off camera.

The screen shifted to a large bathroom where the sound of a shower running could be heard. The camera showed a large offset entrance to a shower that must have been nearly five feet by seven feet. Tile covered the zig-zag walkway into the shower.   The built-in patterns on some of the tiles mimicked gods from Mayan or Aztec ruins. The man from the previous screen could be seen approaching the shower entrance

In a loud voice that carried over the sounds of the shower, the man asked, "Hey sweetie, would you like some company in there?"

A female voice sounded over the shower noise, "I'm almost done. I'm just finishing my hair."

"That's okay. You can start over. I'll help this time."

"Mmm. That sounds inviting. But why don't I finish and wait for you in bed." Her voice was seductive even over the sounds of the shower.

"I like that idea," he replied.

The water turned off and moments later a beautiful olive skinned woman emerged, her hair soaking wet and dripping. Water beaded on the surface of her skin. The man in the picture was obviously enjoying the view.

"Can you hand me a towel, please?"

"I think I like the view just the way it is now."

She gave him a look that said, you'd better hand me a towel, then said, "I'm catching pneumonia here. Let me dry off and you can warm me up when you get out."

He shook his head as if he were clearing the cobwebs. "Right." He handed her the towel and kissed her as he walked past her into the shower.

She wrapped herself in the towel and headed out to the bedroom. The sound of the shower starting could be heard as she made her way to the bedroom.

Bill took his laptop and headed upstairs. He was pretty sure that these two were going to put on a grand performance. He wondered how they could act as if they were alone when there had to be dozens, even hundreds of people watching. He thought that most folks would put on some kind of show for the cameras, but every couple they watched acted as if this happened every day. No big deal. They didn't even acknowledge that they were being watched. Obviously they knew. According to the club rules they were willing participants. If they knew, they were pretty darn good actors. How could they not know with cameras pointing at them from every angle?

Bill continued down the hall and up the stairs into their bedroom. He set up the laptop and connected the cable for the big screen. One tap on the F8 key and voila, the picture that was once on a laptop screen now filled the full sixty-six inch plasma screen. It was amazingly clear. He turned the volume up a bit and listened as the olive skinned woman finished drying her nearly perfect body. When she finished, she tossed the towel on a chair, leaned back on the bed and looked up at the ceiling. She closed her eyes. Her dark skin was accented by light skin where her bathing suit bottoms had covered her pubic mound and where spaghetti thin straps rode her hips. She stayed like that for several minutes until her husband came into the bedroom, still toweling off from his shower. He threw his towel on top of hers and moved to a spot at the foot of the bed, right between her knees. She looked up and smiled then closed her eyes again. Without a word he started caressing her knees. He moved his hands down to her ankles and rubbed her feet.

Bill yelled to Candace, "Honey, you better hurry up and get in here."

Candace was at the bathroom doorway. "I'm right here. You don't have to yell." She had a silky thin, short, light pink nightgown. She moved around to the front of the screen and saw the couple in the early stages of foreplay. Already Candace was turned on at the gentle movements of the man's hands over the gorgeous body of the woman lying on the bed. She sat next to Bill on the end of the bed. They both sat transfixed on the screen. The man's fingers slid softly over the young woman's thighs, causing her skin to prickle with goose bumps. She moaned softly and smiled, keeping her eyes closed while enjoying the expert touch. She inhaled sharply, arched her back then said softly and seductively, "Oh my, where did you learn how to do that?" He just smiled and continued.

After a full fifteen minutes of caressing the front of the woman's body, except her pubic area, he slowly turned her over and began massaging her back, starting at her neck, moving to her shoulders and working his way back down to her legs. Another ten minutes passed when she said, "I hate to say it, but I think it's my turn."

The action on the screen continued to emit the heat of the couple's body chemistry. She got onto her knees on the bed and directed him on to his stomach. She straddled his buttocks and began the ritual over again, this time, with her playing the masseuse. Twenty minutes passed before either partner directly touched each other's pubic area.

During this time, Bill and Candace were getting so turned on that they found it difficult to keep their hands off of each other. They cuddled and caressed each other. Each time one or the other ventured into the other's pubic area, a hand stopped the intrusion. Their rules were that there was no direct sexual contact until the action on the screen was completed. It was a difficult rule to follow, but one that they found increased their own sexual pleasure. They learned a lot from watching the internet couples, many of whom were very good at their love-making.

Finally the action on the screen got down to serious business. The couple performed in a number of positions. It was clear that they would be headed back to the shower because both were bathed in sweat as they held each other tight. They appeared to be falling asleep, entangled in each other arms and legs.

"Wow," Bill said as he turned to his wife and kissed her full on the mouth with passion. Candace was kissing back as her hands roamed his chest and back at the same time. He returned the favor by pulling her leg over the top of his and caressed her thigh.

"Wow yourself." Candace pushed him back onto the bed and straddled him, not letting him inside of her. She rubbed her whole body against his, sending sexual electricity through each of their bodies. Bill was near orgasm when Candace rolled off of him. She waited for several moments before she pulled him on top of her. He returned the favor by doing exactly what she had done, caressing and rubbing without intercourse. Then he stopped to keep himself from ejaculating.

After another twenty minutes of mutual stimulation, Bill finally entered her. They both came to an explosive climax within minutes. They stayed together, holding each other, panting and smiling. After several more minutes, Bill asked, "Want to do it again?"

Candace laughed. "We'll kill each other if we keep this up."

"But we'll die happy. Man, was that couple hot or what?"

Candace had to agree. Since they'd started watching the SExCClub together, their sex life had gotten better and better. They both felt it was worth every penny.

Chapter 6

"Damn." Jillian Rockledge cursed as she pulled her Volvo into the three car garage. The garage light was blown out again. "Thank God for delayed headlights." She was thankful that there at least would be some lights on as she fumbled with her keys and the grocery bags in her arms. Her husband, Nelson, told her that she should have her groceries delivered, especially while he was out of town at a legislative law convention. But she was bull headed and independent. She didn't like for others to do her work. She told him that she wanted to do this while she was still young. When they got older they could have their kids do the shopping. He replied that they didn't have any kids. She'd kissed him, smiled and said, "That'll give us something to work on when you're home."

She managed to get the groceries into the kitchen. She set the dozen eggs and milk in the refrigerator, put the cans of vegetables, boxes of cereal, and taco shells in the cupboards, and loaded the meat and frozen dinners in the freezer. Then she pulled out a bottle of merlot, retrieved a wine glass from the rack in the dining room, and poured a glass of the dark, red wine. She kicked off her shoes and sat back in her favorite recliner to relax. The living room was dark, the only light coming from the fluorescent fixture over the sink in the kitchen. The wine was cool and dry, just the way she liked it.

Her cat, Ginger, came up to her, putting her paws up on Jillian's leg, her nose sniffing the air, seeing if there was anything good to eat that she could coax away from her owner. Smelling only the wine and no food, Ginger reluctantly walked away, hopped up on the tan and burgundy love seat on the other side of the room and started washing a leg with her tongue.

Their dog, Fenton, was staying at her parents' house for a few days. He'd been whimpering ever since they moved into the new house a few weeks earlier. Nelson thought it might be the change from their old house to the new house that had him upset. Jillian wasn't convinced. But she decided that a few days away in a familiar setting couldn't hurt.

"So, little lady, would you like a few kitty treats?" Ginger paused as if to ask, *You talking to me?* Then she went back to washing her leg. Jillian walked into the kitchen and put a small handful of fish shaped cat treats in her food bowl. Ginger, hearing the treats hit the bowl, immediately stopped grooming and pranced to her food dish. She was trying to not look too anxious but it wasn't working. "I know you too well, miss. You look like you're gaining weight. We might have to put you on a diet." She watched her cat devour the treats in no time at all, then retrieved her wine and headed upstairs.

* * *

In the guest bedroom, Roger Tremper and Gerry Alberts were quietly waiting. They'd quickly put the master bedroom back in order as best they could. They'd been tearing into drawers and jewelry boxes trying to get their hands on as many valuables as they could. Then they were planning on leaving the beautiful home of Nelson and Jillian Rockledge with a boat load of marketable merchandise. As it turned out, Mr. Rockledge wasn't too loose with the cash when it came to expensive jewelry or other valuables. They had nice furniture to compliment the fabulous house, but he didn't buy lavish gifts for his beautiful wife. As they were getting ready to load a duffle bag with the few things that they did find, they saw the headlights of Jillian's car heading up the long driveway. They'd been in the guest bedroom for nearly half an hour waiting for Mrs. Rockledge to head into the master bedroom or to the bathroom for a shower, but she was taking her sweet time. They were getting antsy to get out of the house. They were both amazed that she hadn't heard them moving around upstairs but the house was a Messier home. It was solid and didn't make any creaking noises as they moved from the master bedroom to the guest room.

With a heavy southern drawl, Gerry whispered to his partner, "We got to get outta here, man." He was getting nervous. He was so shaken that he wanted to make a run for it, down the stairs and out the front door.

Roger was keeping his cool. He knew that if they made their move now, they'd get caught. This lady wasn't just beautiful, she was smart. And she was an attorney. He whispered back with his own Virginia accent, "Look, she's bound to head up here soon. Her old man won't be home 'til late tomorrow. She'll get tired and head for the shower before you know it." He paused then continued. "Besides, this house is isolated. You can't even see her neighbors. If we sit tight and don't get all freaked out, we'll be fine."

A few minutes later, they heard her moving around downstairs. Then they heard her footsteps in the entryway at the base of the stairs.

The phone rang, startling the two thieves. Jillian answered the call and headed back into the living room to her favorite recliner again.

"Damn," Roger whispered. "She was nearly on her way up." He paused. "Relax. When she's done on the phone, she's bound to call it a night."

Gerry whispered in a tense reply, "I hope you're right. I gotta pee."

Roger stifled a laugh.

* * *

Eve LaForest was on the phone checking on Jillian. She was Jillian's best friend. Like Jillian, she too was young and beautiful; born into wealth and married to wealth. Her home was another fabulous Messier creation. Eve recommended Messier Homes to Nelson and Jillian when they talked about buying a home. "No, no Dears," she'd said. "You build the home of your dreams. If you buy a home, it's someone else's dreams. You don't want to do that." The couple listened to Eve. They were very happy that they did. Jillian thanked Eve at least a dozen times over the last two months for the advice. Her home and her husband were everything to her.

With Nelson out of town, Eve hated for Jillian to be in that monstrous house alone. "It's in the middle of nowhere. That's the only thing I regret about recommending them to you. They built your home in the boonies," she told Jillian.

She replied, "It is not. Our neighbors are a mere quarter mile away. Besides, there are two Messier homes planned for the twelve acre lots to either side of us. It will only be about seven months and we'll have 'close' neighbors."

"So, when is Nelson coming home? If you want, I could come over for a visit. Just to keep you company."

"Eve, you don't have to baby-sit me. I'm fine. I'm going to finish this glass of wine, take a shower, and go to bed. Nelson will be home early tomorrow evening. We're going to have a late dinner, then a private welcome home party."

"Wonderful. Are Troy and I invited?"

Jillian paused a moment before answering, "I said a private party, if you know what I mean."

In a knowing voice Eve said, "Oh, that kind of party." She smiled to herself then said, "Can I watch?"

In faux shock, Jillian said, "No. What a pervert."

Eve laughed. "Are you sure you don't want company? I can be over in twenty minutes. We could have another glass of wine and I've got some good gossip to tell you about my sister-in-law. She is such a slut. I know she's cheating on my brother."

Jillian smiled as she asked, "How do you know this?"

"Because she told me," Eve said.

"No way!"

Jillian and Eve talked for another fifteen minutes until Jillian yawned loudly in Eve's ear. "You sure know how to give a hint that a person's boring you."

"You are so bad. I'm just very tired. I haven't slept well the last few nights with Nelson gone. I miss him."

"I told you I'd keep you company."

"But it wouldn't be the same."

"Gawd I hope not! Listen, you get to bed and rest. Sounds like you're going to need your strength tomorrow night. I want a blow by blow report the morning after."

"You are so bad, girl. Talk with you later."

"Night Sissy."

Jillian hung up the phone, shaking her head at the spoiled young woman who was her best friend in the world. She made a last check of all the downstairs doors to make sure that the locks were secure. She failed to check the French doors behind the curtain leading to the back yard deck. The door was closed but the latch was broken. Nobody used those doors so there was no need to check, or so she thought. She finally headed upstairs to get a good night's sleep. Talking with Eve put her at ease. Her body was feeling the drain from a busy day.

* * *

Roger and Gerry heard her footsteps lightly on the stairs. She walked right in to the master bedroom. Gerry was ready to make his move for the steps and out of the house but Roger put out an arm against his chest. He put a finger to his lips to make sure Gerry remained quiet. He whispered to Gerry, "Wait until she's settled down a bit. Only a few more minutes."

Gerry shook his head, pointed to his crotch and gritted his teeth. He'd needed to pee for over forty-five minutes. From the look on his face, he couldn't wait much longer. Roger smiled and nodded his head, assuring Gerry that he didn't have much longer to wait.

After a few minutes and no discernable noise coming from the master bedroom, Roger motioned with his head that they should make their move. Stepping lightly, they slowly made their way across the landing area at the top of the stairs. When they reached the stairs, Roger paused right by the door to the master bedroom. He slowly leaned towards the door so he could sneak a peak into the room. He saw Jillian in her panties and bra leaning over the dresser across the bedroom. She appeared to be inspecting her teeth closely in the mirror. He stopped leaning and straightened up to get into a more comfortable position. He watched as she backed away from the mirror, but kept her eyes on her own reflection. She turned her body sideways and looked herself over from top to bottom.

Roger was engrossed. He wasn't going anywhere with this show in front of him. Halfway down the stairs, trying to be as quiet as a mouse, Gerry turned and looked up the stairs at his partner. He couldn't believe Roger was looking into the master bedroom. He wanted to yell, but she would hear him for sure. He had to go back up the stairway to get Roger's attention. It would take nearly a minute to get back up the steps and remain quiet, but he had to get Roger out of the house before they both were caught. Slowly he turned back towards the top of the steps and took one slow, quiet step at a time. *Thank God these steps are carpeted.*

* * *

Jillian was turned sideways to the mirror inspecting her stomach for any sign of fat. There was none of course, but she wasn't taking any chances. Her belly was also smooth since she regularly shaved the thin line of hair that used to run from the top of her pubic mound up to her navel. Nelson said that he liked her hair line but he always made it a point during foreplay to run his hand over the now smooth skin below her navel.

Satisfied with her tummy inspection, she reached back and removed her bra which she tossed on a chair next to her dresser. She remained sideways to the mirror and arched her back to force her breasts outward. She wasn't small, but she thought she might try a little enhancement some day. Nelson told her she should wait until after she had children to make that decision. She just smirked and said, "What do you know about women?" She shook her head thinking about how little Nelson actually knew about her. He would sure be surprised about some of her antics in college, she thought. She reached up and cupped both her breasts, turning slightly as she looked in the mirror. She smiled.

* * *

So did Roger Tremper. He was becoming more excited by the second. The thrill of watching this beautiful woman while she undressed for him was almost too much to bear. He pressed himself against the wall next to the door and continued to watch. Gerry was just a few steps below him, trying to get his attention, but to no avail. Roger's full attention was on Jillian.

She turned towards the king sized bed and picked up her robe. She turned back towards the dresser, opened the top drawer and extracted a night gown. Turning again, she headed towards the bathroom and disappeared around the corner. There was no door on the bathroom and shower area. There was a small, separate room for the toilet and a long counter with a double sink. Another mirror ran the length of the counter.

Roger heard the water start in the shower. He waited until he heard the splashing of the water change as Jillian entered. He moved into the bedroom and positioned himself behind the bathroom entry. He watched her shower as best he could through the steamy shower door. His excitement grew with each minute. He knew he was going to take her once she exited the shower.

From the bedroom doorway Gerry watched Roger as he watched Jillian. He was shaking with fear and he really needed to pee. He ran into the bathroom off the guest bedroom and peed for what seemed like two full minutes. When he was done, he instinctively flushed the toilet. As soon as he did, he knew he'd made a mistake.

* * *

The drop in water pressure changed the flow of water in the shower in the master bath. Jillian stopped washing her hair. She was puzzled. *What was that? I didn't start the wash or the dishes. Nelson isn't home from his trip early or he'd have come straight up.* She quickly rinsed off and shut off the water. She reached out of the shower for her towel and toweled off the trunk of her body leaving her hair soaking wet.

She wrapped the towel around her back and tucked the end in between her breasts to hold it in place, then stepped out of the shower. She stood for a moment on the area rug by the shower and listened for any noise in the house. She heard nothing out of the ordinary; only the quiet hum of the bathroom vent fan and the drip from the shower head behind her. She shrugged her shoulders as if to dismiss the loss of pressure. She loosened the towel and leaned over to dry her legs and feet. Then she wrapped the towel around her hair and headed for her walk in closet.

* * *

Roger stood with his back tight against the wall outside the entrance to the bathroom. He was surprised when she suddenly shut off the water and stepped out of the shower. He had no time to move across the room and head down the stairs. Leaving wasn't on his mind anyway. A rush of sexual intoxication held him bound to the room. He waited as Jillian toweled off. His mind was filled with images of water running down over her body as she washed and rinsed. The scene played over and over in his mind even as he heard her on the other side of the wall. He willed his breathing to be deep, slow, and silent. He waited patiently for his prey. Then he heard steps heading out of the bathroom and she passed him heading towards the closet. She was naked except for a pink towel that was wrapped around her hair. *Perfect.* She only made it four steps into the bedroom. She was near the foot of the bed when Roger took two giants steps and grabbed her from behind, throwing her face-down on the bed. She started to scream but Roger grabbed her by the back of the neck and pushed her face hard into the dark-blue bedspread.

"It isn't going to matter if you scream. No one will hear you out here. It sure is a beautiful home but it's off all by itself. Nice and quiet. No neighbors to bother you . . . or me."

Jillian was petrified. She couldn't think straight. Her face was being pushed hard into the bedspread and the weight of this lunatic was full on her, nearly crushing her body. Even if she could get air into her nose or mouth, her lungs were being crushed. The man slowly relieved the pressure on her neck and lifted his body off of hers. She gulped in deep breaths as her face came up from the spread. He grabbed the towel and slowly removed it from her head. Her hair was still very wet, separating into thick, rope-like bundles. He was completely off of her now.

She started to turn her head but he said, "You just keep your face towards the bed. No sense you getting hurt because you seeing something that you shouldn't."

She was still taking deep breaths. Her heart was pounding rapidly in her chest. She heard a second man walk into her bedroom. Her mind raced, thinking first that she was going to die. *They're going to rape me and kill me.* Then she thought that maybe they were just a couple of thieves. *Maybe I can talk to them, reason with them. Thieves aren't murderers or rapists.*

She said in a quiet, shaky voice, "If you're here to rob us, why don't you just take whatever you want and leave? You don't want to hurt me." She stopped, hoping it would hit a cord with this guy. Then she heard a second voice.

"We're not going to hurt you, lady. We're going to make you feel real good, right Roger?"

Roger turned to his partner with an angry glare. He couldn't believe that Gerry used his real name. Then he turned back to Jillian and saw her naked body in front of him and his excitement rose again. "That's right."

Jillian heard the men start to disrobe. She reached a hand to her mouth and bit her finger trying to keep from crying. It did no good. One of the men took a tie from the Nelson's walk in closet and tied it around her eyes. They flipped her over and the two men took turns raping her. She smelled the foul stench of their breath, felt their rough, unshaven faces, and rough hands pawing at her body. It wasn't brutal. It wasn't physically painful. It was just totally degrading. Jillian felt helpless, dirty, and completely violated. Her skin crawled through the entire ordeal.

* * *

Candace and Bill Rollins sat upright in bed and watched in anger and horror at the obvious rape of Jillian Rockledge on the SExCClub. They felt helpless as the rape progressed and they wanted to disconnect from the site. Candace asked if there was anything that they could do to report the rape, but Bill was at a loss. The site's participants were supposed to be willing to share their sexual experiences via the internet, but their identities were also kept confidential for obvious reasons.

"Isn't there someone we can call? I mean this is a real time feed," Candace pleaded with her husband. "This is real. We've seen this woman and her husband before. Those bastards are really raping her. Just look at her. She's not into this. God, I wonder where her husband is?"

"I'm sorry, Babe. I just don't know what we can do. Maybe we should e-mail the club. I know they don't have a phone number. We could threaten to cancel our membership if they don't get the police over to this woman's place right away. Whoever is running the controls should know where this is coming from."

They both looked back at the large monitor with frustration, feeling helpless. After another minute, Bill disconnected the big screen and typed an e-mail to the club threatening to cancel their subscription if they didn't take action to assist this woman. He added in capital letters, "WE'RE APPALLED. WE DIDN'T SIGN UP FOR THIS!!" They signed off the computer not knowing if they would even get a response. They both lay back in bed feeling guilty, as if they were part of the assault on the poor woman. They didn't even know her name.

* * *

Across the United Stated and Canada hundreds of e-mails were pouring into the webmaster of the SExCClub, cancelling subscriptions or threatening to do so.

Chapter 7

It was just after 1:00 PM and the fish weren't biting on Lake Harris, south of Leesburg, Florida. The sun was bright, not quite directly overhead, but high enough to beat down on the shimmering lake waters. The reflection of light off the lake was enough to make the brothers squint their eyes as they talked, even with their ball caps pulled low. Pat wore a University of Georgia cap, with a pudgy bulldog sporting a menacing look. Joe wore a Cleveland Indians ball cap, Chief Wahoo smiling brightly. They were both loaded up with suntan lotion as they planned to spend the majority of the day on the water. They had half of a twelve pack of beer left, most of a twelve pack of water, and only a couple of sandwiches on ice. They'd been out on the lake since just before 8:00 AM.

They had enough bait to last at least through the end of the day without needing a trip to the marina, where they'd rented the boat. The twenty-three-foot Sea Ray Weekender was anchored within one hundred feet of shore. They could cast into the marshy, shallow water from this spot. They'd hoped to latch onto a few largemouth bass. So far, the bass were keeping to themselves. Pat remarked that it was probably too hot to land a bass. *They're taking their mid day siesta.* Looking back across the lake, they could see the tree-lined shore in the distance.

No, the fish weren't biting but Pat and Joe McKinney didn't mind. They were enjoying the day in the hot, October sun, having a few beers, reminiscing about the good old days. They'd decided those days weren't that good at all.

Pat sat thinking about their younger brother, Mike. As he did, he rubbed the white scar on his chin. It was a habit of his when he was in deep thought. He'd been injured in an accident, building greenhouses in Apopka, Florida. As he swung his hammer down on a sixteen-penny nail, the hammer's handle slipped in his sweaty hand. The hammer head hit the nail at an odd angle and sent the nail ricocheting right into Pat's chin, just to the left of his lower lip. The nail was embedded into his skin over an inch deep. It didn't hit any bones or teeth, but it did leave a rather ugly scar. Suddenly, he felt a sharp swat on his wrist that knocked his hand away from his face.

"Hey man, quit playing with that thing! You're going to rub another hole in your head." Joe was smiling, but Pat wasn't amused. Joe's slap on the wrist stung and left red fingerprints where the blow landed. "What are you thinking about now?"

"Do you remember when we first met Brian?" Pat was talking about Brian Purcer, a close friend of Pat's who'd recently signed a record contract and was now on tour promoting his first album. Brian's success had come quickly after being discovered in a small bar in Orlando. His band, *Brian Purcer and the Hot Licks,* was on a fast track to success in the music business, but it wasn't always a sure thing. He'd struggled as a laborer on the loading docks at the Orlando Sentinel while practicing with the band and playing gigs at local bars. He was perpetually exhausted, but still had a hard time sleeping. It all came together when he was signed by Atlantic Records.

At the same time he fell in love with a young woman named Ginny Parks. Ginny was a student at the University of Central Florida when they met. She was dating a guy named Danny Vallero, a small time dope dealer who was originally from Boston. Danny had done some business with the McKinney brothers when Pat, Joe, and their younger brother, Mike, were in the marijuana business. He was also part of a group of guys that had ripped off the McKinneys of tens of thousands of dollars. Those guys had paid the ultimate price, but Pat's mind was still filled with hatred when he thought of them.

Joe thought for a second, then said, "Yeah, but barely. That was what . . . eight years ago? Our state of mind was a bit foggy then. We went to that guy's house . . . hell, I forget his name now . . . Pete Hillman, Helmon . . . something like that. Pete was a friend of your buddy, Al Michaels. I remember that much. Anyway, they had a jam session going."

"Yep. Pete Hillerman. He and his wife were from up in Ohio, near Salem. Anyway, that was the first time I ever drank anything but American beer. Pete had Heini's on ice. We stayed there listening to the guys jam for at least a couple of hours and they ran out of beer. We were stoned and drunk pretty senseless by then, so we started looking for anything to drink. Pete had some Mad Dog 20-20. So I took a couple swigs of that. Man did I get sick the next day." Pat shook his head at his poor judgment back then.   "I think that was the worst hangover I've ever had. I prayed at the porcelain altar and swore to never drink again. I didn't feel human until the next night. So what did we do? We went back over there again the next night and drank and got stoned again." They both laughed a bit, then went silent again. Pat continued, "I can't believe we lived through all that crap. Not to mention everything that happened after. At least *we* made it."

Pat was talking about the drinking and the smoking, but he was also referring to something else far more dangerous; their former friends and business partners. He was also alluding to the fact that their brother Mike and his wife hadn't been so lucky.

Joe picked up on the reference right away. "Pat, we've got to get over it. We were kids. We didn't know anything about the real world except that it would be fun to get free weed and party.   We thought it would go on forever, remember? But shit happens and you have to grow up or you end up living a fantasy your whole life. We just had to do it quick. Mike got caught up in his grief and couldn't shake it.

You know, mentally he died when Julie was killed. It just took his body about seven years to catch up."

They both fell silent again. Joe's line jerked slightly. He could tell it was a nibble from a hungry fish because it was a sudden jerk, unlike the gentle movements of the rod caused by the boat swaying back and forth. They both watched Joe's line in silence, each deep in thought having nothing to do with fishing. The rod went back to its smooth rhythm. Joe picked up his beer and took a swig. Pat followed suit.

Pat spoke in a solemn voice, "You're right about Mikey. When those bastards killed Julie they killed Mike, too. They just didn't know it. They got what they had coming in the end. But what a price?" Pat paused as he and Joe watched their fishing rods. "Julie was such a wonderful girl. She could make everyone smile just by being around. She made our little brother so happy. I still can't believe that people can do that to each other." He went silent again.

Joe didn't have an answer for his older brother that he could share. But he'd seen worse in the Marine Corps in the sniper division. His Marine snipers would take bets on whether they could shoot a limb off of their targets before making the kill shot from over five hundred yards. When they did it, they'd laugh and high five each other as if they'd just hit a winning fowl shot or scored the winning touchdown. All this while a human being that they'd never seen close up was bleeding to death . . . bleeding to death until the kill shot was taken to put the poor bastard out of his misery. They would never know if the person they'd just killed was an enemy combatant or a kid hiding behind a shrub. But that was war. You couldn't mourn for the enemy and you couldn't second guess your decisions. Any hesitation meant that you were the one missing a limb. Joe never talked about his experiences on the battlefield. They were too grisly for the uninitiated. It was a time when men went temporarily insane and had a license to do so. It was no wonder many went to war as young boys, but came home as men, with deep mental scars.

"Hey man, let's not dwell on this crap. We're going to spoil a real nice day of fishing."

"So far this has been a real nice day of drinking. I think the fish are on strike . . ."

Just then, Joe's rod bent over in an exaggerated arc. The brothers looked at each other for a moment before Joe grabbed for his rod and yanked it out of the holding tube with both hands. Joe grunted as he fought to keep control of the rod and get his hand on the reel. He said, "I guess . . . the drinking's over for a little bit. He must have heard you talking and got insulted."

Joe worked the reel as he pulled the rod back over his left shoulder, let off and spun the reel as fast as he could. The line was tight in a straight line from the end of his pole to the surface of the water. Then the largemouth bass jumped above the surface of the water and struggled to free himself from Joe's line. Back underwater again the angry bass swam in exaggerated figure eights. The fight went on for a full two minutes until the great fish finally tired and surrendered. Pat netted the fish and laid him on the boat's deck. Joe grabbed the bass by one gill and reached in to remove the hook. The nineteen inch bass easily weighed over four pounds, probably approaching four and a half. Joe and Pat looked at each other and smiled.

"What do you think? Should we call it a day?" Pat, with his sunburned cheeks and ears, asked Joe, whose exposed shoulders were a bright red?

"Yeah. We better head back. We're gonna be toast by the time we hit the marina. We've got a bit of a drive ahead of us. I'm gonna toss ole tubby back in the lake. He can fight somebody else another day."

"He put up a pretty good fight."

"Yes he did." Joe leaned over the boat and shook the scaly fish one time then released him. The fish hesitated for a moment, then, with a couple quick flips of his tail, disappeared into the depths of Lake Harris. Joe scanned the surface of the lake and spotted a pair of eyes just above the surface.

"Look at the size of that gator."

Pat turned around to see the evil looking eyes glaring in their direction. "Wow, he's got to be a big one. Look how far apart his eyes are."

"He's a big dude, that's for sure." Pat's mind wandered. He was thinking about when he and Joe were at a county park not too far from Lake Harris. They were supposed to meet a couple of guys to talk about a truce to a big misunderstanding that they had with a major drug dealer. The dealer, Jason Roberts, thought that Pat and Joe were killing his hired help. He believed it, because Pat and Joe had every intention of doing just that. They were the bastards that had killed their sister-in-law. The meeting took place at Trimble Park in north Orange County late one evening. It was pitch black when Pat and Joe got out of their car and saw what looked like a muzzle flash from the woods. The two jumped back in their car and tore out of the park before they even knew what was happening. The next day they learned that a hit man was hiding in the trees surrounding the park. Before the assassin could carry out his mission, a friend of Pat's named Hatch, shot and killed the hit man. His body was thrown into Lake Beauclair where at least one gator made a meal of his carcass. It was a gruesome discovery by some poor fishermen.

Pat shook his head to clear his mind. He said to Joe, "I'm cranking this baby up. You want to get the anchor?"

Joe headed to the bow of the boat, pulled up the anchor and stowed it in its storage bin under the deck. The boat's outboard engine turned over and rumbled to life. Pat gave it some gas and the boat lurched forward. He steered the boat out away from shore then angled towards the marina. They had a good fifteen minute cruise across the lake to return the boat. From there they each had a half hour drive; Pat to Dunnellon, Joe to Pine Hills. Joe made his way back aft and stood next to Pat, holding on to the top of the windshield. He said, "You were thinking about Antonio . . . what's his name . . . the hit man. I could see it in your face. That gator made me think of that night, too. If Hatch hadn't been there, we'd most likely be dead."

Pat didn't say anything. He was embarrassed that his brother read his mind so easily.

Chapter 8

The instant message screen looked like code to everyone in the small conference room. As the lines came across the screen, they were projected on the white wall at one end of the room. The crowd consisted of law enforcement personnel from several cities and counties from around the country. They were in Vermilion, Ohio to learn how a small city was on the leading edge of finding and prosecuting internet-based sexual predators.

Officer Darrin Opfer was in a live chat session with a nineteen-year-old man. He called himself Lenny D. Lenny believed that he was chatting with a fifteen-year-old girl named Jewels. Opfer said that 'Jewels' was his bait name. He was explaining to the crowd that Lenny D. was typical of the young adult crowd looking to score with a young teenager. He was displaying a similar pattern of chat as most of the sexual predators he'd encountered in his nearly two years of on-line chat experience.

He said that he learned the chat lingo from his daughter. It was by coincidence that he learned his fourteen-year-old daughter was chatting on-line with a twenty-three year old man. The man was portraying himself as a high school football player. As he watched his daughter one evening, the 'football player' wrote some things that appeared to be a bit out of line for a high school student. He asked his daughter if she knew this person. When she said 'no' he became worried and started to ask more questions. One day while she was shopping with her mother, he logged on to her computer and opened the instant messenger. The 'football player' was on-line waiting for her. After several minutes of chatting as if he were his daughter, he asked if they could meet at the Sandusky Mall, and the 'football player' agreed.

Opfer asked what time, what he would be wearing, and where they should meet. With that information in hand, he contacted his Lieutenant and asked to set up a sting. They had to work quickly and find a young woman who would closely match the description of his daughter. They were running so close to the meeting time that he wasn't sure they could pull it off. But with cooperation from several local law enforcement agencies, they were able to have personnel in place at the mall ahead of the meeting time. The young woman used as their decoy looked to be about sixteen-years old, but from a distance the average person couldn't tell she was really twenty-four.

When everyone was in place, they immediately identified a young man loitering in the area of the meeting who fit the description of the football player. When the decoy detective arrived, the man walked over to her and asked if she was Jewels. She engaged him in a brief conversation where he revealed that he was her chat partner and that he wanted to meet her to see if she wanted to party. When she asked what he meant, he said, 'You know, have a few drinks and maybe a little sex.'

Six law officers converged on the man and arrested him. When they searched him, he had a number of drugs in his pockets, including GHB, a date rape drug. A search of his car uncovered more disturbing contraband. He had handcuffs, blindfolds, and a number of other sexual devices and a homemade DVD labeled 'Tanya'.

The man's name was Paul Pritchard. He was the son of a Methodist Minister. He lived in Mansfield, Ohio and was listed as a suspect in a number of open child abduction and rape cases in Ohio. When police searched his apartment they found video evidence of him with over a dozen minor girls.

When Officer Opfer talked to his daughter about what had happened, she was angry that he had invaded her privacy. He couldn't believe that she was defending this guy even after he showed her the danger she was in. He told his daughter that as long as she was living in his home, she had no such claim to privacy, especially if she was placing herself in life-threatening situations. Eventually she came to understand how naive she'd been, but it was a long process.

Paul Pritchard was charged with a host of felony and misdemeanor charges, including rape, gross sexual imposition, child endangering, solicitation of a minor, and tampering with evidence. The evidence was overwhelming and he was sentenced to fifteen years in prison. It was the first known prosecution of an internet solicitation case in Ohio. Officer Opfer was commended for his innovation in finding and arresting a sexual predator over the internet. Over the past two years he'd refined his skills at disguising himself as a teenager on the net. He started a program to give classes to law enforcement agencies on how to proactively pursue and apprehend these perpetrators.

"As you can see, the perp is loosening up and sharing more information as he becomes more comfortable with my responses. He's not concerned that I've identified myself as a minor. He appears to be a little drunk or high, but not necessarily. The shorthand chat language isn't a perfect one and many new abbreviations are regularly used. Most people who chat tend to type fast and not worry about spelling as long as it can be understood by others in the chat."

The dialogue was getting progressively more graphic in terms of what the perp wanted to do to 'Jewels'. Finally, Opfer asked if he wanted to meet her in person. He immediately agreed. Those in attendance were amazed at how brazen Lenny D. had become. 'Jewels' said that she had to be careful that her parents didn't find out. He agreed. 'Jewels' suggested that she set up a trip to the mall with one of her friends so she could tell her mom where she would be. 'Jewels' and Lenny D. set up a meeting at the Midway Mall in Elyria the next day around dinner time.

With the meeting set, 'Jewels' ended the chat. The crowd in the conference room clapped once 'Jewels' signed out of the IM chat room. They were impressed with the way

Officer Opfer handled the man and they felt confident that, with a little practice, they could set up a proactive sting operation of their own.

The attendee who'd traveled the furthest to attend the session was Detective Johnny Poleirmo of the Orange County, Florida Sheriff's Department. He asked, "How many of these perverts have you apprehended and how many convictions do you have over the last two years?"

Darrin Opfer answered, "Seventeen. The charges range from felony assault and rape to misdemeanor solicitation."

"How many cases have been thrown out of court?"

Opfer smiled a sly smile, "None, though one never went to trial. Seems we apprehended the son of the Mayor of Ashland. It's a medium sized city between here and Columbus. He threw a little political weight around and got the charges reduced to a misdemeanor. His kid pleaded No Contest and only got probation. But rumor has it that the Honorable Mayor kicked his ass pretty severely and made him move to Texas with his brother. He told his son that they execute people for that kind of thing down there."
This drew a chuckle from the crowd. "Just a rumor, of course. But they haven't seen the kid around Ashland since, so there may be some truth to it."

Johnny smiled. He was already thinking of ways to set up his own sting operation in Central Florida. He'd been given a decent budget to start a task force with the promise that, if he were successful, he'd be funded for years to come. A major part of the funding was coming from a grant from the Federal Government. Another part was from a local philanthropic trust. The trustee lost a daughter to an exceptionally violent rape and murder. When he heard about the idea, he was pleased to help in the funding of the task force and vowed to help fund it as long as it proved successful. Johnny's orders were clear; make at least a dozen arrests per year and have a successful prosecution rate. One stipulation was that he had to use mostly contracted help for the operation. He wasn't to make use of Orange County Sheriffs employees for the task force.

Johnny was fine with that. He felt he'd need some young talent to make it work. He needed young adults who were already skilled in Internet Instant Messaging. He also needed some computer weenies who could track messages from the server to the source. The thing he needed most was some folks who were experienced investigators. He had a couple of guys in mind. In fact, the first names that came to mind were brothers; Pat and Joe McKinney.

* * *

It was nearly 8:30 PM. Pat and Diane McKinney were sitting in the living room of their home in Dunnellon, Florida watching a DVD with their children. The Disney movie was one that Pat had seen a number of times before, but he actually enjoyed watching it again. It was fun to see the hidden adult humor in the movies supposedly made for children. Disney had some clever writers.

The phone rang as the scene switched to a small red crab with an oversized head, large eyes, and a Jamaican accent. He was trying to talk sense into a red headed mermaid, but it was no use. As with most teenagers, she already knew what she was going to do and there was no talking her out of it.

Diane grabbed the remote and asked, "Do you want me to pause it?"

Pat stood and headed for the kitchen to grab the phone, "Nope. I've seen this one about a dozen times."

He held the receiver to his ear and said, "McKinneys."

"Pat, how are you?"

Pat recognized Johnny Poleirmo immediately. "Great Johnny, how about you?"

"I'm good. I'm calling from near your old stomping grounds. When I say old, I mean real old."

"You mean Apopka?"

"Older than that, my friend. Try north Ohio. I'm in Vermilion."

"Vermilion. It's October. I hope you're wearing your thermal underwear. What is it, about twenty up there?"

They both laughed at the exaggeration. "No. It's actually pretty nice out right now. It's about fifty, last time I checked. It's supposed to get up into the sixties tomorrow, but I'm flying back to Orlando. My flight leaves Cleveland at about 10:45 tonight."

Pat said, "I know you didn't call to chat about the weather in the tundra. What can I do for you?"

Johnny paused for a second. Pat had a tinge of apprehension. Johnny told Pat the reason for his call. "I have a new job. I'm still with the sheriff's office but I've been given an assignment that I think will be a lot of fun. I've been given the go ahead to start an Internet Predator Task Force. The thing is, I need to recruit a team of people who have no ties to the department, but have investigative experience."

Pat wasn't sure he liked where this was going. He and Joe had just completed an investigation working for the Naval Criminal Investigative Service. Pat had nearly been killed. The only thing that saved him was his Kevlar Vest. He'd taken a bullet directly in the center of his chest. Had he not been wearing the vest, the bullet would most likely have pierced his heart. His chest was still slightly discolored from the bruise left by the impact of the bullet.

He said, "That sounds great, Johnny. I hope I can recommend some folks to you."

The silence on the other end of the phone told Pat all he needed to know.

He continued, "Johnny, you know I was nearly killed in Virginia, right?"

"Well, yeah, Pat. I knew that. But this would be a job sitting behind a computer screen and keyboard. You'd almost never have to go out in the field. You could do most of it from home. We'd buy you a new computer and pay for your high speed internet service."

Pat was starting to listen. He pulled the phone away from his ear to make sure Diane was still in the living room with the kids. "Okay, I'm listening."

Johnny continued to outline the plan, that Pat and others would try to make a connection with internet predators, acting as young teenage girls. He would train the computer teams on the lingo and what to look for in the responses that separate the perverts from legitimate teen chat. They would also be trained to run programs that trace the internet paths back to the suspected perverts. The more Johnny talked, the more interested Pat became.

Diane's voice came from the living room. "Pat, are you still on the phone?"

"Yes, Dear. I'll be just a minute."

"So, Johnny, who else did you have in mind for this task force?"

"Well, Joe's not busy right now, is he?"

Pat smiled. He knew that Joe and Lisa were looking at houses and making plans to be married. Lisa was also making plans for school in the spring. She had to have her classes picked out and the bill paid by early December, so she was busy. Joe, on the other hand, was free. Pat's reply was a very happy, "No, Joe's pretty much free. He has a few minor things to tend to, but nothing that would keep him from surfing the net all day and night."

Johnny heard the sarcastic tone in Pat's voice and said, "I'll give him a call to make sure. I'd hate for Lisa to be pissed at me. After she whipped Joe's ass, she'd come after me and I know she can kick my butt."

Pat chuckled. "Don't let on that I said he was free. She's going to be my sister-in-law, if all goes well."

"Really? When's the wedding?"

"I don't think they've set a date, yet. They want to get a few things finished before they do the deed. I told him to do it and get it over with. If he's not careful some other guy's gonna swoop in and snatch her. He'd be hard pressed to find another woman like her."

Johnny agreed.

"Listen, Johnny, when do you need me to decide? Are you on a tight schedule?"

"Not so tight that I can't give you a few days to think it over. I'll tell you what. You talk with Diane about it. If you need to talk more, I'm coming over for your barbeque. You can let me know then. In the mean time, I'll give Joe a call, and a few others that I have in mind. As soon as I have a team together, I have the go-ahead to get started. When I come over I'll tell you all about the session I just had in Vermilion. This guy, Darrin Opfer, really knows his stuff."

"Okay then. Let me talk with Diane. Then after she kills me, you can find someone else." Pat paused for effect. "I'm pulling your chain. I'll talk with Diane, see what she thinks. I'll see you in a few days. Good talking with you Johnny."

"You, too, Pat."

* * *

"He wants you to do what?" Diane's question was more of a statement. She was always apprehensive when Pat came to her with a guilty look on his face. Over the years, she'd learned to be skeptical of his ideas. She'd learned to spot the red flags in his face and manner when he was asking for her opinion on something that he already knew was dangerous. "And all you have to do is surf the web and engage perverts in instant message chat rooms? Then what, you run off to arrest these guys?"

"No, no. It's not like that. I just have to report the guys to the task force members and they do the apprehension. It'll be easy. And best of all, we get paid to do it."

"We?"

Oops. "Yeah, the team members."

"Your brother wouldn't happen to be involved with this, would he?"

Pat thought for a fraction of a second too long. Diane continued, "I knew it. You two are getting into another weirdo investigation. You'll be dealing with all sorts of dangerous, deranged people. Can't you leave this stuff for real law enforcement people? They have the training. You and Joe don't."

"I beg to differ. I've had six years of military training and . . ."

Diane cut him off with the wave of her hand. "Which one of these investigations involves a submarine?" Pat's silence spoke volumes. "That's what I thought. Pat, you were nearly killed last time. Pull your shirt back and let's look at the bruise on your chest from that bullet."

Pat just looked back at Diane. She was serious. She did not want Pat involved in any task force, but she was afraid that he was going to do it anyway.

Pat's face was solemn. He knew she was frightened that he'd get into another situation where bullets would fly and his life would, once again, be in danger. But he didn't see how this assignment would lead to a situation like that. It was all supposed to be from a computer terminal. How dangerous could it be?

"Listen Babe, Johnny said if we have any questions, he'll be here Friday night for the barbeque. If his answers still leave doubt in your mind, I won't do it. What do you say?"

Diane looked skeptical at her husband. He was making sense. She should talk with Johnny herself and get her own assurances that Pat would remain out of harm's way. If Johnny was convincing, she might go along with it.

She turned to Pat and said, "Okay. If Johnny can convince me, and that's a big if, then we'll consider it. And Pat, don't tell me you're doing this for the money. We don't need it. You're doing this for your ego."

Ouch, that hurt!

* * *

"So let me get this straight. He wants you to chat on line while acting like a little high school chick to try to lure adult perverts?" Lisa wasn't at all thrilled by the latest call which would occupy her fiancés time and energy. She knew Joe. When he put his mind to a task, he really focused on the task and nothing else. Just a few months ago, when he was called back to active duty, he hardly called her at all. He was so keyed into finding the bastards that were embezzling money from his former comrades in arms and his former employer that he would forget to call her. At the time, she was afraid that he'd fallen out of love with her. Nothing was further from the truth. Joe was just extremely focused. When he put his mind to something, nothing stood in his way of accomplishing the task. But he couldn't do one task and chew gum at the same time. That's why Lisa was afraid for Joe to get involved. This task appeared to have no finishing point. If he were to get on the task force, would he become consumed by the job?

"Well, yes. That's what the job involves. Remember that news story we saw yesterday about the explosion of internet porn? The city they mentioned was Vermilion, Ohio."

"I've been there. That's where they have the Wooly Bear Festival."

"Yeah. Well, there's a city cop who teaches other cops how to gain these pervs' confidence. Then they set up a sting operation and get the guy off the street. It would be a good thing, don't you think?"

"It's always good to get scum off the streets, but don't you see? There's no end to this task force. You know how intense you get. I want you to think this through before you make any commitments. Think a few years down the road when you've made a dozen arrests and convictions and the first guys are already back on the street. How are you going to react? You know you can't set up a hit squad just because you think that they should have been put away for life. You can't send in the sniper team."

He thought about that before he answered. "You're right. Can we at least talk more about it tomorrow? I don't have to answer Johnny for a few days. Maybe I can talk with Pat, too."

Lisa thought that was the last thing he needed. Pat would probably try to talk him into it. She could hear Diane trying to talk Pat out of it, just as Lisa was trying to do now with Joe. Maybe she should talk with Diane next. Together, they might be able to convince their men that this was a bad idea.

Chapter 9

The bright morning sun was just over the horizon to the southeast. The temperature in eastern Virginia was a cool 55 degrees. With heavy dew on the weeds and shrubs, the view from the second floor master bedroom was postcard-perfect. The trees threw long shadows towards the house as the sun slowly made its way into the morning sky just above the horizon. As the light shown over the landscape, hundreds of silky spider webs were illuminated in a silver glow. The dew-slicked webs showed nearly perfect construction by a creature that most people considered a nuisance, even a menace. But looking out this window, Tom Grayson knew that they were experts at an ancient craft. Just as he was a master electrician, they were master homebuilders. They used their webs as their lounge, their living room, and their pantry. As beautiful as the webs were to look at now, they were a death trap to unsuspecting insects, providing a convenient meal for the host. Tom marveled at their skills and wondered if his own skills would ever be able to measure up to their natural ability to construct a perfect habitat, every day of their existence.

Tom shifted his attention to the house where electrical wires protruded from the painted drywall all around the master bedroom and bath. This was the final room where electrical fixtures needed to be installed. The bedroom walls were painted a light blue with a contrasting overlay of sponged, slightly darker blue and a faint pattern of white. The effect was an exceptionally beautiful marble-like appearance. The drywall crew had cleaned the dust from the room and left it spotless. The painters had repeated that performance leaving the bedroom and the rest of the house in mint condition, ready for the next steps of the construction process. The room would be ready for wood trim once Tom Grayson finished his work. The floor was still raw wood. Soon after the finish carpenters completed their work, carpeting, tile, and wood flooring would be laid throughout the house to compete another fine Messier home. This home project was nearing completion. Only the landscaping remained after these few interior jobs and that would be completed before the end of October. The new owners would celebrate Thanksgiving in their new, fabulous Messier Custom Home.

Tom had the honor and pleasure of working for Theo Messier. He loved his work. He was paid well for supervising the installation of high end electrical devices in some of the most extravagant homes he'd ever seen. His work made these fabulous homes light up with bright chandeliers in entryways, modern fluorescent lights in the kitchens and baths and all sorts of modern electrical devices throughout the house. He installed motorized curtain rods on the oversized windows that opened to spectacular mountain or lake views. He installed the lights and timers for splash lighting that highlighted the homes' exteriors at night, turning them into showcases. The accent lighting made these already beautiful homes a true work of art to behold at night. It was his job to test every electrical device installed in the house before the finish carpenters were allowed to come in to install the wood trim. He was on a tight schedule but his small crew was finishing their job with time to spare.

Tom decided that he'd better take the time to inspect some of the work performed by his crew just to be sure no corners were cut. Sloppy work by one of his installers wouldn't be tolerated. He wasn't hard on his crew. Mistakes could be corrected. Fixing mistakes was easy and usually became a lesson for younger members of the crew. It's easier and less costly to do it right the first time. He would tell his crew before every job, 'Take the time necessary to do your job right. Let me worry about the schedule.'

His crew responded by doing top quality work. That was essential when working for Messier Custom Homes.

These were high end homes for wealthy, demanding people. Most of the couples purchasing Messier Custom Homes were young. Most had inherited their money and were spoiled, pampered people. Many of them complained even when no mistakes were made. They'd try to change the home design well into the project. Tom was glad that Theo Messier handled these issues. It was spelled out in the contract; no change orders were allowed after construction began. Theo almost always stuck to this policy. Somehow he'd manage to keep his clients happy even after turning them down for their request.

Tom started working for Messier Homes right out of the U.S. Navy. He'd met Theo on the U.S.S. *Enterprise.* When Theo got out, he started the home building business. Then when Tom was discharged, Theo hired him to do electrical work. Over the years he'd built a reputation for doing top quality work. He wasn't about to let that reputation get tarnished. Before he turned the house over to the finish carpenters, he inspected every electrical fixture installed in the home. If there was an electric device that had so much as a scratch on a finished surface, it would be replaced.

Each device had to perform perfectly. He knew that couples were paying serious money to buy a Messier Home and he wanted to make sure they got their money's worth. He never short changed the testing phase of the electrical installation.

Tom was a short, stocky man. At 52 years old, he was 5' 6" tall and weighed 220 pounds. His hands were dry and rough, the fingertips like sandpaper with flaking skin. On the home site, he always wore blue jeans and a pull over golf shirt which was tight around his muscular arms. He sported a faded blue tattoo of a naked woman on his left arm from his military days. When on leave in Rota, Spain he and a shipmate wound up in a tattoo parlor. They were both drunk. He woke up the next morning with a hangover and a multicolored senorita on his arm. Over the years he thought about having it removed, but as it faded, senorita looked less naked, so he left her alone. Tom also had a number of scars on his arms, face, and neck from moving in and out of house crawl spaces, attics, and other tight spots to install electrical wires and fixtures. The white streaks of the scars contrasted with his tanned, rough skin. One look at Tom Grayson and you knew he was a working man. He'd paid his dues to become the Electrical Superintendent for Theo Messier. He still did some installation work on each home but he'd turned most of the installation over to his crew. They were becoming quite skilled in their own right and would tell Tom to leave some work for them when he started to do more hands on work and less supervising.

"Hey Brad, how about installing these motors on the curtain rods. The diagram's on the floor by the window."

"Sure, Tom. Anything else left?"

Tom thought for a second then said, "Yea, the outlets in the bedroom and all the bathroom fixtures. I'm pretty sure they're in the bathroom vanity. Be careful to not scratch the finish on the vanity and . . ." He stopped when he noticed Brad rolling his eyes. "Okay. You've heard it a thousand times before. Just get it done and call me when you're finished."

With a big smile, Brad said, "Yes Mom."

Tom smiled, shook his head, and left the bedroom. He walked downstairs to the kitchen and started his inspection ritual. After three hours of looking over every electrical fixture in the sixty-five hundred square foot house, he was ready for the final test. Just as he headed for the steps, Brad hollered down to him that the installation was complete.

"Okay," Tom yelled back. "Go out to the garage and let's get started testing. You have your cell?"

"Yeah. I'll call you when I'm ready."

"We're starting with the downstairs rooms, so go ahead and flip on the breaker for the living room."

Brad and Tom worked through the time consuming process of testing each and every circuit in the house. This was no small task especially since the house had a number of specialty features, such as automatic accent lighting hooked to a combination of light sensors and timers. If either device was not activated, the lights would not be illuminated. The house also had dozens of three-way and four-way switches which had to be tested in every possible combination. Tom had to record the results of each of these tests as part of the standard checklist. There was a checklist for each phase of construction, twenty-three in all. These checklists were kept on file in Theo Messier's office.

After three hours, they were finishing the next to the last room when Tom flipped on the lights in one of the guest bedrooms. The lights didn't blink. Tom's face wrinkled into a frown. He tried again to be sure. Nothing.

"Brad, do you have the guest bedroom circuit breaker on?"

"Yeah, Tom. It's on."

"Check to make sure it didn't trip free."

"Nope. Breaker is still shut. I tested it and it's still hot and the connections solid. Is there a problem?"

"Yeah. The lights didn't even blink." Tom thought for a minute. *I did the wiring in here. I know I didn't miss anything.* "Hey Brad, open the breaker and take a brake. I'm going to pull the light fixture and see if I can figure out what the Sam Hill is going on here."

"Watch your language mister," came Brad's smart assed reply. "Okay Tom. Breaker's open. Call me if you need anything, I'll be standing by."

"Roger."

"I'm Brad."

"You're a real smart ass, too."

"I learned from the best."

Tom smiled. *Kids.*

He grabbed a ladder and loosened the bedroom light fixture. He inspected the wires and determined that the proper connections were made. *Nothing wrong here. Next to the attic.* He retightened the fixture and descended the ladder.

"Brad, I checked the light fixture and everything's in order. I'm heading up to the attic to check the wires. Maybe the insulators stepped on a wire and broke it."

"Roger, Tom."

Tom made his way to the master walk-in closet and hit the button for the electric retractable stairs. The stairway lowered down from the ceiling. Tom heard the stairs lock into place. At the same time the attic lights automatically turned on from the same switch assembly that locked the stairs in place. *Well at least this works.*

He climbed the steps into the attic. As he stepped onto the small landing at the top of the steps, he took a moment to get his bearings down. There was pink insulation as far as he could see. There were about a dozen light fixtures throughout the attic, all lit. The main area of the attic was tall enough for Tom to stand up straight with ease. He found the wire rack that ran from one end of the attic to the other, providing a convenient location for the main wire runs. From this rack the wires branched off to supply power to all of the upstairs rooms. Tom started what he hoped would be a short search for a broken wire. He suspected that one of the insulators had stepped on a wire and pinched it against a truss, breaking the connection. It had to be a clean break. If the hot wire inside the insulation touched the neutral or ground wire, the circuit breaker would have tripped. Since that didn't happen, Tom was afraid that the search might take a while.

As he carefully made his way around the attic, he began to sweat. The temperature was rising in the now mid-afternoon sun. He also had to be cautious where he stepped. Once he ventured away from the landing by the stairs, there were no planks to walk on. He had to walk on the truss cross members which were hidden by several layers of insulation. It was slow going finding the right wire leading to the light fixture or its switch. After nearly an hour of lifting and replacing insulation that covered his wires, Tom found the problem. He was right on the money. Someone had stepped on a roof truss but didn't realize that they'd stepped right on an electrical wire, breaking the copper line inside the insulating jacket. *Gotcha. Now I just have to figure out how to replace you, ya bastard.*

As Tom was making his way back to the stairs, a metallic reflection caught his eye. At first he ignored it and continued moving towards the stairs. Then a green blinking light was visible. *What the hell is that? It looks electrical. Whatever it is I should know about it.* He made his way to the blinking light. It appeared to be a small electronic box mounted against an exterior truss with a short antenna. It had been partially covered by insulation. An electrical cable ran into the box. Tom followed the cable back as far as he could and found where the cable had been crudely spliced into another power cable nearby. *Holy Toledo. What the hell is this?* He noticed a nameplate on the box. He pulled a pair of needle-nosed pliers from his tool pouch and carefully removed the wire splice. Ripping a piece of electrical tape from the role in his pocket, he covered the wire where the insulation had been crudely removed. He looked at the electronic box, noting the manufacturer, model number, and serial number before heading back to the landing. *Who the hell put this up here? Someone's head's going to role.*

Tom made his way out of the attic and into the main upstairs hallway. What was supposed to be a routine day to finish up a job had turned into two big time problems. First was the replacement of the electrical wire for the guest bedroom. That was an easy problem to solve even though there was real work to be done.

The other problem was a real mystery. His first thought was to go right to Theo Messier and tell him what he found. He was about to call Brad on his cell phone and discuss it with him when he thought that maybe Brad was involved. He settled on doing a little more investigative work on his own. He'd removed the electronic device from the attic. It had a nameplate with specifications, so he could look up information on the internet and find out exactly what it was.

"Brad."

"Yeah boss?"

"We need to head back to the shop and scare up some wire for the guest bedroom. Somebody stepped on it in the attic. Looks like a clean break."

"Okay Tom. I'll meet you at the truck."

* * *

Back at the shop, Tom sent Brad to track down the specs for the electrical wiring run to the guest bedroom while he got on the internet to look for information on the mystery box. It took just a few minutes to hit the jackpot. Tom's face reverted back to a frown once again. *Why would anyone put a transmitter-receiver in the attic? This house is equipped with cable and is satellite dish ready. That was such a shabby job of installation. It couldn't have been one of our guys. I've got to talk with Jeremy or Aaron about this. Theo's headed to France so I can't talk with him. At least I think his plane's taken off.* Tom scratched his head then rubbed his face. He wasn't sure just what to do. He finally decided that he should talk with the Messier boys, so he headed up the steps to the brothers' office. He knocked on the door but there was no answer. He knocked again. Silence. He tried the door handle. It was unlocked. He opened the door and took a step inside.

"Jeremy? Aaron? You in here?"

No response. The office was a large room with just the two large desks of the Messier brothers. The desks were in the middle of the room facing each other, the desk tops touching. A row of filing cabinets stood along the back wall of the office. To the left of Jeremy's desk was a large drawing table that long ago had been used to write out home designs. The table was now used to spread out the blue prints as the craftsmen reviewed the prints before heading to the building site each morning. The walls were painted a light, institutional green. To the right of the filing cabinets, a door with glass in the upper half separated the brothers' office from an old test lab. The door had Venetian blinds that were always closed. The office was well lit with six large fluorescent light fixtures that bathed the room in bright light. The ballasts of the lights gave off a hum which seemed louder with no other noise in the office.

Tom looked at the desks of the sons of Theo Messier. They were a mess but none of the clutter appeared to be related to the Messier Custom Home Building business. Tom stood over Aaron Messier's desk. He picked up some of the books, magazines, and catalogs. All of them were about computers and printers. He placed the papers back on the desk and walked around to Jeremy's desk. His desk was clean except for a day planner. Tom flipped the day planner open. There was not a single mark in it. The planner looked brand new. Tom's facial muscles tightened, his teeth clenched tighter. *Would telling these two about the transmitter accomplish anything at all?* It seemed like a waste of time. At least Jeremy appeared to have some interest in the business. Aaron, on the other hand, was never around.

Tom looked around the room again, then back at the door to the office. All was quiet. He slid the center drawer to Jeremy's desk open. The front tray contained the usual office junk; several stacks of Post-its, push pins, rubber bands, paper clips, a variety of screws, and some loose change. There was also a pair of scissors and other assorted junk. He slid open one of the file folder drawers. In one of the hanging folders, Tom noticed what appeared to be a magazine. He lifted the magazine and realized immediately that it was pornography. Tom shook his head at seeing the magazine then dropped it back in place. He was about to open another drawer when he heard steps in the warehouse outside the office. He closed the drawer, pulled out a note pad and pen and started to scribble a note to Jeremy about the short delay in completing the testing at the house. He was just finishing the note when the office door opened. It was Brad with a 250 foot box of wire and a diagram in his hands.

Brad asked, "You ready to head back to the house or do you want me to handle it?"

"I'll be just a second. I want to leave Jeremy a note about the short delay. Drop the stuff in the truck and I'll be right with you." He thought for a minute then changed his directions. "Better yet, take the new kid, Al Simmons, with you. Teach him how to fish out the old wire without damaging the walls and pull in the new cable. It'll be a good learning experience for him. Call me when you're ready to test it."

"Okay. I guess it'll take about two hours or so. Maybe more, depending on how tight we tacked down the cable inside the wall. Call you in a bit." Brad turned and headed out to find his helper.

Tom turned back to the task at hand. He headed back to Aaron's desk and opened the center drawer. The drawer contained a few manuals on network servers, wireless office systems, and mobile computing. There was also a stack of printed papers. Tom looked at the top page. It was from a mail order house that sold video and audio equipment for security. He picked up the stack of papers and thumbed through them. They were all mail order houses for electronic gadgets. Most of the companies advertised for spy equipment with military grade specifications. He looked at the stack specifications. He came across two spec sheets that had devices similar to the one he'd found in the attic, but not the same model. He wondered why Aaron Messier had any reason to have this information in his work desk. He shook his head and left the papers where they were, trying to leave them as he'd found them. He knew the Messier brothers were not as serious about the business as their father. That was a problem, now that Theo was gone. But he wondered what Aaron was up to with all the literature on electronic gadgets. And why would he put anything like this in the attic of any of the new houses?

He looked at the door to the test lab, hesitating before heading in that direction. He was about to try the door when he thought he heard footsteps on the stairs outside the office. He turned towards the office door and listened more closely. Nothing. *Come on, Tom, get hold of yourself.* Tom made a mental note to come back later and do a little more snooping. He was pretty confident that he'd found the source of the device. Now he just had to figure out why. Initially he was angry about someone screwing up his crew's work. Then his anger shifted to the deliberate act of splicing into a hot cable in the attic. Now he was curious about what Aaron Messier was doing. He wondered if Jeremy was involved, too. Whatever it was, their father was going to be outraged. He headed out the office door, but not before he quietly said, 'I'll be back.'

Chapter 10

E-mails to the Webmaster ranged from polite requests to cancel their membership to threats of legal action. The tone of most was terse and to the point. Whether the sexual assault was staged or not, it was inappropriate to be broadcast to club members. In all, seventeen percent of the total club membership cancelled. Nearly eight percent requested a full refund of their club dues and others threatened to do the same. It was a bad day for the Club.

In a wimpy voice that could barely be heard over the sound of cooling fans and electronic switches, the man at the controls asked, "Should we send out an apology? We could always claim that there was an error in programming or that another rival website hacked into our system." He waited for a reply and to see if his partner had any better ideas.

"Let's think about this for a minute. Number one, are there any legal issues? Could we be held liable for anything? I mean, this looked to be authentic. We've seen this couple in action before. They wouldn't stage anything like this." He paused for a moment in deep thought then asked, "Why didn't you cut it off?"

The controller's jaw tightened. He didn't want to admit that he'd left the control room to relieve himself, but he felt he had to come clean. No use lying about something so simple. In fact, he had gone to the rest room and the rape was already in progress when he arrived back at the control panel. He could have cut the transmission then, but he was aroused by the scene. He said, almost in a whisper, "I went to the can and it was over by the time I came back." *Close enough.* "Besides, the people watching were already pissed by the time I cut the feed. There was nothing I could do by then." *In the ballpark, anyway.*

The partner folded his arms across his chest, then raised his right hand to his chin in a thoughtful pose. He looked down at the controls as if searching for the correct answer to their minor dilemma. The air in the cramped room was dry and hot as the monitors and micro-electronics continued to generate heat. The whirring of fans was the only sound for the moment. A faint odor of hot electronic components filled the room even with the extra ventilation that was installed to keep the servers and other devices cool. The nine small monitors were playing reruns of archived amateur couples. The elder partner felt it best if they ceased all live feeds until they sorted out the risks of continuing business as usual. Finally he turned to his younger partner with an evil grin. "So who cares if we lose a few customers? Do you have the reports on the growth rate of memberships? Let's assume that this continues for at least the next twelve to eighteen months. How long will it take us to recover to existing membership numbers?"

It took less than a minute to display the figures on the large flat panel monitor. "It looks like seven percent growth rate per quarter."

"So in less than six months we're back where we were this morning? If this gets around a little, this might actually be good advertising as long as people don't come in expecting to see women getting raped," the older partner's smile widened. "So here's what we need to do. We create an apology header for the Home Page. We say that the couple staged the whole thing and that we had nothing to do with it. Put in there that we've contacted the couple. They agreed that they crossed the line and they've promised that it wouldn't happen again. Don't mention anything about losing subscribers or that we're willing to refund money. Screw them. What are they going to do? Call the police? Even if they try to come after us they'll never find us."

The controller sat and listened as the rough plan flowed from his partner. It was a sound approach. Nothing he heard appeared to be unreasonable. He could have the changes to the website ready in a matter of minutes.

The partner asked, "So, how soon can you get that posted?"

"It's almost there already. Give me ten minutes."

With that, the partner left the control room.

The controller was still worried about the rape. He didn't know anything about law, but it sure seemed to him that they'd done something illegal, even if they weren't directly involved. Somehow, even for a purveyor of pornography, he felt a little sleazier. But it didn't matter to him. He had plans of his own. This rinky-dink operation would soon be a part of his past if all went according to plan.

* * *

Tom Grayson needed information but he wasn't sure how to get it. Someone had installed the transmitter/receiver at the Keifer site, but how do you go about finding the culprit and what the purpose was? He figured the best way to find out was to ask some questions of his fellow workers and the bosses. He couldn't be so specific that he'd arouse suspicion. This wasn't going to be easy. On the other hand, maybe there was a logical explanation for the device being in place. *Right. Maybe pigs will fly, too.*

As Tom finished unloading the last of the remaining electrical supplies from his truck, he spotted Jeremy Messier leaving the main office heading for his truck. *Now's as good a time as any to get started.*

Tom shouted over the sound of a diesel truck leaving the lot, "Jeremy, wait up a second. I need to talk with you."

Jeremy turned towards Tom. He appeared annoyed that Tom would stop him from leaving work at 3:15 PM. He was usually on the road by now, but with his father being in Paris, someone had to run things. The truth was that the business ran pretty much on its own. The foreman for each craft knew how to handle most any situation that arose. But Tom wanted to make Jeremy feel like he was in charge. To Tom, it was almost a joke. He caught up with Jeremy as he closed the door to his Ford F250 heavy duty truck. He put his hands on the keys to show how much of a hurry he was in to leave, hoping Tom would get the hint. It didn't deter Tom in the least.

"Hey Jeremy, can anybody besides you and Aaron sign requisitions and change orders since your Dad's out of the business now?"

"No. Actually, it's just me. Aaron won't be singing them. What's this for?"

"Well, the Keifer property needs a change to the roof gable on the east end. They decided that they want an exhaust fan to cool the attic in the summer. It's also going to require a vent at the west end so the fan doesn't cause a vacuum in the attic. This kids an engineer, so he thinks he knows something about home design." Tom smiled at how easy the lie came out. He was sure Jeremy would have no idea how to check to see if there ever was a change order submitted. That's what he hoped, anyway.

Jeremy didn't hesitate. He said, "Sure. Do you have the order?"

"Nope, I have to write it up first and get Mr. Keifer to sign it. Will you be in the office later?" Tom knew that Jeremy was leaving for the day, so he wasn't surprised when Jeremy gave him a look as if to say, 'What, are you kidding?' Tom continued, "I'll have it drawn up and on your desk tomorrow morning. Just page me and let me know that it's signed."

"Okay, Tom." With that, Jeremy's truck window rolled up and the music from the truck cab started blasting. Jeremy pulled away and headed for home. Tom stood in deep thought. Jeremy hadn't even flinched when Tom mentioned the east end of the Keifer house attic. Maybe he wasn't involved. Maybe he was and was just a good poker player. Regardless, for now, Jeremy was off the short list. But Tom planned to keep him on the long list, just in case.

Tom turned towards the shop and saw Brad and Al, two of his crew members, leaving the building heading for the utility van. He headed to the van and shouted ahead, "Hey Brad."

Brad and Al both turned. Brad said, "Hey Tom. I was just heading back to the Keifer property to finish testing that wire we replaced. What's up?"

"Have you seen Aaron today?"

"Nope." He paused for a second then said, "Well, yeah. I saw him this morning in the shop. I haven't seen him since and probably won't. He never comes around anymore. Why, is there a problem?"

"Naw. Just needed to talk with him, that's all. If you see him, tell him I'm looking for him."

"Sure thing, Tom."

"Do you need any help with the final tests at Keifer's?"

"We got it under control. That wire we replaced today is the last thing we have to check." Brad waited for the usual, *"Are you sure?"* but none came. So he started the van and pulled away. Tom's lack of response surprised Brad. He was usually ready, willing, and able to help with any work, especially later in the day. He hated to see his crew work past their normal quitting time. It wasn't because of the overtime that Messier would have to pay. It was because he wanted his guys to have a life outside of work. But his lack of response puzzled Brad. Tom was obviously distracted.

Tom stood there for a moment watching the utility van head for the Keifer site. As he did, two more vans pulled away to other sites for last minute work at other home sites. He was in a quandary. Jeremy Messier was his first suspect, but didn't seem to know anything. Aaron Messier was also a suspect, but was never around. Was he capable of sneaking into a home and installing an electronic transmitter without being noticed? What were these things used for? Were the Messiers spying on their workers? Maybe some of the crews were stealing supplies. That didn't seem likely. If that were the case, surely Theo Messier would have confided in his supervisors to let them know.

No. This had Jeremy and Aaron Messier written all over it. Tom was determined to find the answer regardless of who got hurt.

* * *

The cell phone rang in one of those annoying new ringtones. It was a song by some boy band that was popular at the moment. The man at the control panel was even more annoyed because he was watching one of his favorite archived films. He clicked the mouse to turn off the sound and reached for the cell phone. He knew this couldn't be good news because only a handful of people had his cell. When he answered, there was noise in the background on the other end, like wind passing an open window. "Yes?"

The voice on the phone said to the controller, "We've got a problem. Tom Grayson found the transmitter at Keifer's. He's getting nosey. He's asking a lot of questions. I'm afraid he's going to figure it out."

The controller asked, "Are you sure?" He really didn't care but acted as if he shared his partner's concern.

"Yes, I'm sure. But I'll take care of Grayson. Just keep doing what you're doing and everything will be fine. Did you get the changes out that we talked about?"

"Yeah, about five minutes after you told me." He was indignant.

The elder partner smiled. "Good. You keep this up and you'll be able to retire before you're thirty."

There was no response and the phone went dead. As he drove along the road near the Messier Home Builder's office, the elder partner devised a plan to deal with the nosey electrician. *Electricity is a very dangerous thing. People should be very careful while they work with live circuits.* The smile grew wider and more sinister with each passing mile.

Chapter 11

Jillian Rockledge was seriously depressed. Since the rape a few days earlier, she'd been unable to concentrate at work. It had been a rough day. She spent the better part of her morning in deposition with a particularly tough witness. In her current state of mind, she couldn't concentrate, and had nearly botched the entire deposition. The witness was a highly polished man in his late twenties with a holier-than-thou attitude. He was a former friend of their client and a key witness for the prosecution.

Their client was accused of embezzling money from their employer. The theft was alleged to have taken place over a twelve year period. The total amount wasn't known, but was estimated to be nearly $750,000. Worse, their client lived a fairly lavish lifestyle compared with his income. He did have a large amount of debt which helped explain the standard of living. But he was in serious trouble. The firm knew it. The only reason that Jillian took the case was that a senior partner was a friend of her client's father. He offered to pay for the expenses. Jillian didn't care one way or the other. She knew she could win the case, but now, in her state of mind, it was going to be challenging.

She pulled her Volvo into the garage and closed the door. The lights inside the garage had been replaced. It still didn't make her feel any more secure. After the rape, she was constantly looking over her shoulder. She sat in her car for a moment, thinking about the rape, her mind in a fog. She shook her head, trying to shake off the fear and depression that seized her. She had to cook dinner. She had to try to act normal when Nelson came home from work. He could never know.

How will I ever keep this from him? She shook her head again. *Get a grip girl. Maybe I should call Eve and talk with her.*

She opened the car door and immediately heard an awful moan.   It sounded mournful, almost human, but primitive. The moaning turned to a loud whine. It was coming from inside the house.   Then a loud yelp pierced the door between the garage and the kitchen. Their dog, Fenton, now home from her parents, sounded like he was in a state of mourning. She'd never heard him like this. Quickly, she put the door key in the deadbolt, with a twist, the bolt slid back. Then she switched keys and tried to put the key in the lock on the door knob but she dropped them. She bent over, grabbed the keys and tried again. She turned the handle and opened the door.

When she opened the kitchen door, she flipped on the fluorescent kitchen lights.   Fenton was at the door to the basement again.   He was lying down with his paws at the base of the door. They were bloody.

"Fenton! Oh my God. What happened? Oh my baby!" Jillian ran to her precious Golden Retriever and wrapped her arms around his head. She looked him over and saw the blood on his paws. More blood drenched the beautiful golden fur on his chest. She looked for wounds around his head and chest but there were none. Then she held each paw and inspected them. They were both skinned raw and bloody. She continued to hold Fenton around the neck with one arm as she looked at the basement door. She noticed where Fenton tried to claw his way through the door.   The door was scratched badly and stained with blood. Fenton continued his mournful howl even as Jillian tried to comfort him. She tried to coerce him away from the basement door, but every time she moved him a few feet, he made his way back to the door.   He let out a loud, guttural groan once again.

Fear seized Jillian, and she wondered for a moment if someone might be in the house. Maybe the bastards that raped her came back and shot her poor dog. But other than the blood on his paws and fur, and the scratched basement door, there were no signs of disturbance in the kitchen. She was beside herself what to do next. It was a most bazaar situation. For the moment, she forgot about her depression as her precious pet's injuries displaced her own trauma.

She tried talking to her dog again, trying to calm him, but to no avail. She decided to call Nelson and see if he had any ideas. It was his decision to get the dog. Jillian didn't want a dog at first but she'd grown to love Fenton. He was like their first child. She grabbed her cell phone and hit the speed dial for Nelson's cell. He answered on the first ring.

"Hey, Babe. Miss me . . . What is that noise?" Nelson could hear the mournful sounds of their dog over the phone.

"It's Fenton. He's at the basement door again, but this time he's nearly scratched a hole in the door. His poor paws are a bloody mess, literally. He won't stop this . . . this mourning. He sounds like he's crying."

"I can hear him. What the hell could he be all wound up about?"

"I don't know, but I've got to get him to a vet. His paws are going to get infected if we don't do something. Can you meet me at Companion Care when you leave?"

"Sure. Can you get him in your car by yourself?" Nelson was worried that Fenton might turn on Jillian, thinking she might be trying to hurt him.

"Yes. Don't worry about that. Just get there as soon as you can. We have to figure out what's wrong with him, poor thing."

* * *

At the vet's office, Fenton's paws were cleaned and bandaged. Doctor Fulcrum gave Fenton a shot of antibiotics and prescribed additional antibiotic drops. He offered to keep Fenton overnight for observation, but Jillian insisted that he come home with them. She was sure he'd be fine. Dr. Fulcrum asked how he got the bloody paws. When they described his behavior to the doctor, he gave them a puzzled look.

"What do you have in the basement?"

"What do you mean? It's brand new. The only thing down there is a washer and dryer, the hot water heater, the geothermal unit and an empty storage room. There's nothing else there," Nelson said. He looked at Jillian for confirmation and she nodded.

"He's right. That's everything. We don't need the storage space so it's pretty much empty. And it's clean. We've only been in the house for a short while, maybe a month."

Dr. Fulcrum stood thinking for a moment then said, "I've only read about this in journals, mind you, but I think your dog may sense something in the basement that you can't see."

Jillian and Nelson looked at each other, then back at the doctor. Nelson said, "What, you think our house is haunted?"

The doctor smiled and shook his head slowly, then bent down and pet Fenton on the head. He held his hand under the dog's chin and looked into his eyes. He looked back up at Nelson, then at Jillian, then turned to Fenton again and said, "Did you do any work for the police, boy? Did you?"

The couple gave each other a puzzled look. "You think Fenton is a police dog? He's not even a German Sheppard. Besides, he wouldn't hurt a flea." Jillian was starting to put on her lawyer face, to protect her client, her child, her dog.

"No. Not that kind of police dog. Some police departments have dogs that perform lots of different things; sniff out drugs . . . find bodies . . ."

* * *

Fenton road with Jillian when they left the vets office. He'd calmed down since leaving the house earlier. He appeared exhausted and slept part of the way home, but not before licking Jillian's hand as she comforted him in the front seat. Her thoughts shifted between concern for Fenton and her own dilemma. She found it hard to concentrate on her driving. Nelson said that he had to make a call when they got home. He was going to pick up a couple of sub sandwiches on the way home, so Jillian didn't have to fix dinner and she could take care of her dog.

As Jillian pulled into the driveway, Fenton jerked. He sat upright in the passenger seat then started to moan. The farther into the driveway she pulled, the louder Fenton's moan became. Finally, it was a loud whale, followed by howls. The poor dog acted as if he'd lost his best friend. Jillian stopped the car abruptly, some thirty yards from the house. She backed out towards the street. The further away from the house she drove the lower the whaling from her precious pet. Fenton was scared to death of something in the house. Or was it fear? No, it was more like mourning. Could the vet be right? Could their precious pet have been through the trauma of finding dead bodies?

Jillian called Nelson on her cell. "Honey, I can't take him in the house."

"Wait until I get there and I'll help."

"No. It's not that. He's whaling again. I can't get the car near the house and he starts this awful crying." She waited for Nelson's response, but he was thinking and couldn't come up with any ideas. Finally, Jillian said, "Let's take him to my parents' house for the night. Maybe he'll be okay there until we can figure out what to do."

He agreed and said, "I'll call the Humane Society in the morning. Maybe they can tell us if he's had a history that will explain this. Maybe his previous owners were abusive. Heck, I don't know. It sure is strange though."

They disconnected. Jillian headed for her folks house, about a forty-five minute drive. Fenton was now calm. Again he licked her hand as if to say *thanks*.

"Don't worry, boy. Nobody's going to hurt you. I just wish you could tell me what's bothering you. I wish I could tell Nelson what's bothering me. We're a sad pair."

* * *

The next morning on the phone with the Humane Society, Nelson got his answer. It took him twenty minutes to convince the staff that this really was a serious matter. While the staff member on the phone looked for a senior staff member to field Nelson's questions he looked around his office. He had pictures of his beautiful wife on his desk, on the wall near his law degree and his license to practice law in Virginia. He noticed that in many of the recent snapshots of Jillian, she was hugging Fenton. They hadn't had him that long, but already he was part of the family. Fenton had hurt himself pretty badly and they needed to know why.

When the senior staff member came in, the story became clear. Over the past eight years, Fenton had been a cadaver dog with the City of Richmond Police Department. He had to be retired. Whenever he found a body he would go into a state of deep depression. That seemed like a normal reaction for any intelligent animal. But apparently Fenton's depression became acute.

Mrs. Mills of the Humane Society read from the file. "*Charlie*, that was your dog's original name, *can no longer handle the duties of a cadaver dog. His bouts of depression are getting longer and deeper. After successfully finding a body, he goes into a deep state of depression lasting as long as three weeks. When an attempt is made to press him into service, he refuses to eat and can't sleep. On his last assignment, he lost twenty-five pounds and . . .*"

"Stop. I've heard enough. You mean to tell me we have a dog that has almost human emotions when it comes to death?"

"Well, according to this file . . . yes."

"If that's true, what else would cause him to react like this? I mean, does he get depressed over other things? Was he mistreated when he was with the police? I mean was the training cruel?"

"Sir, I just work for the Humane Society. You'll have to talk with his former handler. If you'd like, I can call him and explain your situation."

"Please. Have him call me as soon as possible."

* * *

Later that morning, Nelson's phone rang. It was Lt. William Watts of the Richmond Police Department. "Mr. Rockledge, I understand that you're Charlie's owner. What can I do for you?"

Nelson again explained Fenton's behavior. Finally he asked, "What else could cause him to react this way?"

Lieutenant Watts didn't say a word. Finally Nelson thought that his call had been disconnected. "Lieutenant, are you there?"

"Yes sir." Another pause. "Mr. Rockledge, sir, what law enforcement agency has jurisdiction where you live?" Nelson said that they lived in Prince William County. "Sir, I'm going to call the sheriff's office and explain your situation to them. I'm sure someone from their office will be calling you."

Nelson was confused. He asked, "Why?"

"Because sir. You have a dead body in your basement."

Nelson was shocked at first. Then he became angry. How could this policeman who had no idea where he lived know that there was a body in his house based on the pitiful behavior of a retired police dog? "You're talking about a brand new house. We've been in the house for just over a month. This is some kind of joke, right?"

"I'm afraid not, sir. Charlie has never been wrong. He was our best cadaver dog. We've never found an adequate replacement for him. But I can tell you, if he is reacting the way you just described, I can tell you with near 100% certainty; you have a dead body in your basement. I'd bet my career on it."

Nelson hung up the phone. *How am I going to tell Jillian?*

Chapter 12

Jake O'Connor sat back in his overstuffed office chair and watched the 62 inch flat panel display across the room. It was the latest in TV technology and Jake had to have it. He had on a pair of chinos and a loose-fitting *Lands' End*, button up shirt with the sleeves rolled up over his bulging biceps. His shirt was unbuttoned nearly to his navel to show off his tight abs and muscular chest. His arms were tattooed with reptilian scales from his wrists to his shoulders. He had a Cobra snake tattoo on his chest. He was a genuine bad ass.

His office assistants, two exceedingly gorgeous young women, stood on either side of him rubbing over his arms, chest, thighs and crotch with their hands and breasts as he watched the latest episode of the SExClub. He loved the program. There was something about viewing people having sex that pressed all his buttons. What was even more titillating was that these were normal couples, not porn stars or models. They were definitely beautiful people; they had loads of money. But he could tell that they were not professionals. They were into each other and that was definitely a turn-on.

He looked up at his ladies and said, "Hey Babes. See that program on the screen? We're going to own that program." They both looked at Jake as if they were truly impressed. He continued, "That program brings in millions of dollars a year, all by itself. That'll double my company's income. I like it and I want it. Do you think I should have it?"

They both nodded in agreement without as much as a peep.

"Step back, ladies. I'm on a mission." With that, Jake stood, gave both of his eye-candy ladies a kiss and headed out the door, buttoning his shirt as he went. He found Shamus Kelly sitting in the outer room watching the same video.

"Shamus, do I pay you to sit around watching porn all day?"

In a gravelly, Irish accent, Shamus answered. "Well . . . yeah Jake. If there's nothing else to do, that's pretty much what I do. *Leave it to Beaver* reruns don't come on 'til later."

Jake put his hand on Shamus' cheek and said, "It's hard to get good help these days." He smiled and Shamus, his bodyguard and driver returned the smile.

"So where are we going, boss?"

"We're going to buy ourselves a porn website."

Shamus asked, "Don't we already own a couple of them?"

"Yeah, we do. But this one is special. It makes lots of money and we don't have to pay the actors. They do it for free."

"So where is this new porn business that we're buying?" Shamus' eyebrows lowered on his big, round face and his forehead wrinkled. He was wondering just where you shopped for a new porn business.

"See that screen?" He pointed to the action on the smaller TV set that his bodyguard was watching. "That's our new company. We just have to find the owners and make them an offer. First we have to go see the Geek. He'll know where to find the owners. Let's go."

They hopped into Jake's limousine and headed east on Interstate 66 towards the Washington DC beltway. Once on the beltway they sped north towards Maryland. The stereo was turned way up, blaring classic rock and roll on the black limousine's custom speakers. Jake loved classic rock, especially the *Doors, Led Zeppelin*, the *Beatles* and the *Stones*. He knew every tune in his collection by heart.

There were two other things in life that he loved; sex and Jake. He absolutely loved himself. He was handsome, muscular, and suave. He just knew that he was the smartest man on earth and that's why he was so successful. The ladies loved him because he knew how to treat them. He knew what they liked and he gave it to them. According to Jake, they didn't like to be pampered. They liked to be told what to do and when to do it. Jake was more than willing to oblige. According to Jake, all they needed was to do him.

Once on the beltway, heading north into Maryland, Jake sat back and smiled. He was about to learn who owned the most lucrative porn site on the web and he was going to make them an offer they couldn't refuse. The owners were like the bitches that he told what to do. And they were going to like it.

Shamus asked, "Jake, where to now?"

"Stay on the beltway until you get to exit 33. Then head north to Kensington. Let me know when we get just inside the city limits."

"So Jake, what the hell's in Kensington?"

"A little computer geek who's gonna make me rich."

* * *

When the car approached the city limits, Shamus turned the music down so that Jake could hear him. "We're at the city limits."

"See that welcome sign? Turn left at the first major intersection. Saul Road. Then turn left on Edgefield. You're looking for a green, two-story house, with a flagpole. I forget the address but the kid always has a green VW bug in the drive. This kid never leaves the house. He's as pale looking as a ghost. Wait 'til you meet him. Just don't laugh. It upsets him. This kid's going to find out where the computer feed is coming from for our new business, so don't piss him off. Got it?"

"Sure Jake." Shamus said it but without much enthusiasm. So Jake asked again, "Got it?"

"Yeah boss. Sure."

Jake went back to his music. The Doors were in a live performance of *When the Music's Over*. Jake started to sing along with Jim Morrison and shouted out, "Cancel my subscription to the resurrection. Send my credentials to the house of detention."

Shamus nearly laughed, but he knew better.

* * *

Clifford Rengel lived alone in a green, two-story house. It had three bedrooms and two baths, but could be considered a four bedroom home. He had a room that he used for an office and junk room that fit the real estate agent's criteria for a fourth bedroom. His kitchen was piled with pizza boxes and junk food bags. Some were empty; some had left-overs from days gone by. The kitchen reeked from the smell of mold on the abandoned food.

Clifford was a scrawny man. He was twenty-seven with greasy black hair and dark brown eyes. He was pale because he almost never went outside. He hated to meet people and he despised conversation of any kind, except instant messaging with other computer geeks on the internet.

He'd inherited a large sum of cash from his parents when they were killed in a boating accident on the Chesapeake Bay. They had owned a small chain of fast food restaurants. As part of the estate settlement, the business was sold and the profit put in trust to Clifford. He wouldn't have to worry about money for at least twenty years. With his computer skills, he wasn't worried about getting a job. He made money writing programs for friends and small businesses when he wasn't playing video games.

He heard the doorbell, but decided he wasn't answering it. He was in the middle of a video game called *The Dragon's Lair IV*. He was about to rescue a maiden. Once he did that, she would submit to him; which means that she would have video sex with him for saving her life. The bizarre part of this program was that the maiden would provide virtual sexual favors based on commands from the person at the controls. Clifford always killed the dragons and saved the maiden. He'd had lots of virtual sex. But he was still a real life virgin.

The doorbell rang again. This time it was followed by serious pounding on his front door. Damn. *Who the fuck is interrupting my battle? I'll wait and they'll go away.*

But the doorbell rang again and the pounding persisted. He yelled, "All right, already! Get off my nuts! I'll be right there!"

He paused the program and changed the channel on his TV so his guests couldn't see what he was playing, then went to the door. When he looked through the peep hole and saw Jake O'Connor and his burly looking body guard, he nearly wet his pants. He looked nervously around the room, wiped his mouth, and ran his hands through his greasy black hair. *What the hell does he want? What do I say?* The doorbell rang again and more pounding shook the door. He knew Jake wouldn't be happy standing at the door for so long.

Jake yelled, "Clifford, I know you're in there. Open up. I have a business proposition for you."

This got Clifford's attention. He smiled to himself and reached for the door handle. He turned the deadbolt and removed the chain. Slowly he opened the door and said, "Jake. Good to see you again. I was just in the back; couldn't hear you at first."

"Clifford, you're full of shit. Just let us in."

Clifford's eyes darted around the room, then back outside beyond his guests, then around the room again, with nervous jerks. He was searching his brain for something to say. Clifford was socially inept. He had a hard time communicating even in the best of circumstances. His communication took place with computer programs and video games and his virtual women, of course. Jake had him rattled, so his inability to talk was worse than usual.

He was about to speak and Jake cut him off. "Cliff, relax. I just need your help." Jake paused, then said, "Aren't you going to ask us in?"

"Uh, sure Jake. Come on in. Make yourself at home." He stepped aside and let Jake and Shamus into his house. As soon as they were inside, Shamus wrinkled his nose at the stench. He started to comment, but Jake elbowed him then turned his attention to Clifford.

"So Clifford, like I said, I need a favor. I'll pay you for the information." Clifford's right eyebrow rose. "I need you to find the address of an internet site. Can you do that for me?"

Clifford thought for a minute then smiled. "Is that all you want me to do?"

"Yeah. That's it."

Clifford put a finger to his lips then turned to Jake. His face appeared to be deep in thought, formulating some brilliant question. "How much are you paying me for this information?"

Shamus was surprised by the question. This goofy kid was daring to ask Jake a question like that? He figured Jake would just scare the kid into doing his bidding. But he was shocked to hear Jake's response.

"I'll give you $5,000 cash."

"You make it $10,000 and you've got a deal."

"Deal!" Jake extended his hand and they shook. Shamus was dumbfounded. He'd never seen his boss fold like that before. He'd just as soon punch a guy's face in for even suggesting that his information was worth more than Jake offered. But for some reason, Jake gave in to the kid. Maybe he'd learn why later, but right now they followed Clifford into another room. When they passed the doorway to the kitchen, Jake and Shamus literally had to hold their noses for fear that they'd toss their lunch. The stench was awful.

They made their way back to a room that was used for an office. It had two computers, a copier, a scanner, a printer, an expensive digital camera, and a video camera. There were three flat panel monitors and a large flat panel TV hanging on the wall. Half the room was a jungle of papers and files strewn all over. But the area around the computer was pristine. This appeared to be the center of Clifford's existence.

Shamus gave Jake a look as if to say, what a freak. He nodded his head in the direction of a poster of a very sexy cartoon woman. She was dressed in a very tight, very low cut, single piece costume. The poster was in neon green tones except the woman's lips. They were bright red. Her skin was an exaggerated tan. Her waist was extremely thin and her breasts were extremely large. Jake looked back at his body guard and shook his head. Shamus read his mind. *What a freaking nerd.*

Jake explained to Clifford what he was after. Within twenty minutes, Clifford had found the originating site's IP address. The screen displayed a small series of numbers separated by periods. 250.66.35.125.

"There you go. That'll be ten big ones."

Jake frowned. "Hold on Cliff. I can't use these numbers. That doesn't tell me shit. I need their real address."

Clifford looked around the room with a look of anxiety. In a timid voice he said, "Why didn't you tell me that little bit of information." He paused for a moment, then saw the look on Jake's face. He could see that Jake was getting angry and he didn't know what to do. Then he figured out what Jake needed. "Oh. I get it. You need the street address so you can contact them."

Shamus rolled his eyes and gave the kid the "duh" look.

Jake calmed down a bit then said in a calm voice, "That's right Cliff. I need their street address and phone number if you can get it. Can you get that for me?"

Clifford paused again, deep in thought. His face held a blank stare. Then he smiled as if a light bulb came on. "I've got it." With a few more clicks of the keys, Clifford had a whole page of information on the internet service. He frowned for a moment, hit a few more keys, then smiled.

He turned to Jake and said, "I had to do a little extra work there because the first address that came up is an empty lot. But that's because the owners of the site changed it from the real address several months ago. I guess they don't want anyone to know who the real owners are."

Jake looked at the information. He was floored when he figured out that the address was within thirty miles of his place. He smiled and turned to Clifford. "Way to go my man. You just earned $10,000. Print that page out for me, please." He turned to Shamus and said, "Pay my man Clifford."

"Sure, Boss. I have to go out to the car and I'll be right back."

Jake turned to Clifford and said, "What else can you do on this computer?"

Clifford frowned then said, "Play games, mostly."

Jake was speechless. He paused for a moment then turned away.

Shamus came back in the house with a small pouch. He opened it and showed Clifford the cash. "Count it if you like.

Clifford shook his head and said, "I trust Jake."

Shamus just shrugged his shoulders. Jake just smiled and took his printout. When they got into the limo, Jake said, "Let's go buy a porn business."

Chapter 13

Nelson Rockledge stood in his walk-in closet getting dressed for another day at the Capitol Building. He'd been home for two days now and he was increasingly worried about his wife. She'd greeted him happily when he came home from his trip to Texas, but her greeting appeared guarded and without passion. She simply hugged him, kissed him lightly then turned away. Ever since then she appeared to be avoiding him. Their only real emotional contact centered on Fenton, and the discovery that he was formerly a trained cadaver dog. He was starting to believe that maybe she'd been unfaithful while he was gone. He was afraid to bring it up for fear that he might be right. Or maybe she thought he'd met another woman while he was on his trip. Nothing could be further from the truth.

He always felt that she was too good for him. He'd come from a background of modest means, but had moved up the ladder quickly on the staff of Senator Barnhouse. He was one of the senator's most trusted advisors on legal matters and his draft legislation was rarely questioned regarding its legal accuracy.

He was always confident. He conducted business in a matter-of-fact manner. He made a very positive impression on his peers. At meetings he was known for having the facts at hand and he wasn't afraid to stand up to those who would try to keep him down. His style was professional and courteous. But when he made his point, he could back it up with data and facts. People learned early on that if you were going to challenge Nelson Rockledge, you'd better have your facts straight and at the ready. Nelson quickly gained the respect of his peers and superiors.

But when he met Jillian Markham a few years ago, his confidence was shaken. He was awestruck by her beauty and charm. She was articulate and witty. She was the only daughter of the CEO of one of the largest food distribution companies in the country. He was also nervous because of his mixed race background. In the upper crust of Virginian society, rich white girls weren't supposed to date black boys no matter how smart they were or how successful they may be; even if they were part white. But Jillian Markham didn't care. When she and Nelson met at a conference in Austin, Texas they fell for each other immediately.

Nelson was shy at first. He was aware of the obvious racial barrier between them. But Jillian wasn't deterred. She knew that Nelson was right for her. She encouraged Nelson to lighten up and forget color. And for a while, he did. But the barrier came back on the evening they went to meet her parents.

Andrew and June Markham were cordial and polite, but it was obvious that they already had a nice, young, white man picked out for their daughter. Jillian tolerated it for a while, but about an hour into the evening, she'd had enough. She explained to her parents that she wasn't interested in Winston Carlson Kendrick. She was in love with Nelson Rockledge. And if Nelson would have her, they were going to be married. Jillian's parents were stunned. They stayed that way for nearly six months, until Nelson finally won them over with his own brand of wit, charm, and intelligence. They had to admit, they were happy with the way he treated their daughter. Eventually they came to accept him for the accomplished man he'd become, even at his very young age.

But now, Nelson found himself in that awkward position again. He didn't know what to say to his wife. He was harboring those old feelings of insecurity that were present very early in their relationship. He knew he had to get up the nerve and just ask her the question. But what was the question? She hadn't given him many clues about what was wrong. Maybe it was as simple as asking her, *Honey, what's wrong?* He was about to open the door and ask her when the closet door opened. Jillian stood in front of her husband looking down towards the floor, with tears streaming down her face.

She finally looked up at Nelson, despair etched on her face, combined with terror. She said in a low, almost inaudible voice, "They raped me."

Nelson hardly knew what to say. The look on his face shifted quickly between surprise, horror, and rage. "Who raped you?" A pause. "How?" Another pause. "When? Where?" Nelson reached his hands out and ever so gently grabbed Jillian by the arms. He tried to pull her close to him and hug her, but she held her arms up to stop him. He then tried to steer her to the bedroom. He wanted to get her seated and calmed. He wanted to put his arms around her, but he didn't know what kind of physical and emotional train wreck she'd been through. Finally, she moved slowly back into the bedroom. He helped her slide into the chair by the bed.

She nodded her head towards the bed. "That's where they did it." Her face contorted into a wrinkled mass and she started to cry uncontrollably. Nelson held her hands now. He was still not sure what to do. He reached his hand behind her head and pulled her to his shoulder. He let her cry for several minutes before she slowed to a whimper. Then she continued, "They held me face down. I couldn't see them. There wasn't any use screaming. There was no one around. They ripped the phone cord from the wall. When they left I used my cell phone and called Eve. She came right over and I stayed at her house. I slept over there the night before you came home." Her whimpers were getting lighter now. "I can't stay in this bed alone. It's hard even with you here."

"We'll get rid of the bed. Hell, we'll sell the house. If you don't want to stay here, we can move." He paused for a moment. He had to say the next line, but he knew what her answer would be. "We have to call the police."

Her response was immediate and emphatic. "No! We can't call the police!" She paused then, through whimpers, she said, "They said they'd kill me and you if I called."

He tried to be calm and persuasive and said, "Honey, they all say that. They just want to scare you. They won't do anything like that. If they were killers they would have killed you." He began to lightly stroke the back of her neck hoping that would calm her but it didn't work.

She pushed his hand away and said, "Please don't touch me right now. I have to take a shower." She stood and headed for the bathroom. Even after she started the shower, Nelson could hear her sobs over the running water. She stayed in the shower until he left for work. He called to her and said he would stay home with her, but she insisted he go ahead to work. He told her that he was going to call Messier Homes and have the locks changed throughout the house. It took ten more minutes for him to leave her alone in the house, but he had to get to work. He had a full day's schedule of appointments. He also knew that Jillian's best friend, Eve, would be over to sit with her and get her out of the house if need be.

When he got to his office he called Messier homes. When Jeremy answered the phone Nelson ripped into him as if he were the rapist. He demanded that they change the locks on his home, because they had a break in and apparently Messier Homes uses inferior locks. He also said that they were not to go there until he was available to oversee the locksmith. In a calm voice Jeremy said he understood to which Nelson replied, "You couldn't possibly understand." Then Nelson slammed the phone down.

It was a rare moment when he lost control. He felt helpless for the first time in his life. He wasn't there to protect his wife. What kind of a husband was he? Should he quit his job? Maybe he could find a position which wouldn't require him to be away so much. It would certainly mean leaving the senator's staff. No executive position would allow him such a luxury. His work with the senator required that he travel several times a year and work long hours. How would he protect his wife? If they had children, how could he possibly protect them? He was angry and frustrated. He slammed his fist down on his desk and cursed out loud. The drive to the capital had allowed him too much time to think about the horrible ordeal his dear wife had endured. Sitting alone in his office didn't help. He couldn't concentrate on his work.

He slammed his fist down on his desk a second time and swore.

Chapter 14

Jody Williams parked her Mercedes in the second stall of their four stall garage. Charlie parked his own Mercedes in the first stall when he was home. She wasn't going to argue. After all, it was his brilliant mind that came up with the idea that made them millionaires at such a young age. She was still on cloud nine every time she turned into her long, winding driveway on the way to her fabulous, trophy home. The first few days, she would stop her car and simply gaze at the house and surrounding grounds. It was like a picture from *Home Digest* or some such magazine. *Maybe someday our home will be on the cover.* She grabbed the bag of dirty clothes from the trunk of her car and headed into the utility room. She dropped the bag on the floor in front of the washer, intending to start a load of clothes after her shower. She thought for a moment about where Charlie would be right now. The plan was for him to meet at the Pentagon with some Navy big wigs about some possible improvements to the noise elimination devices. Then he was heading back to the house. He didn't expect to be home before 7:30 PM.

She walked through the house to the main stairs off of the entryway. She could have used the back steps, but she was still getting used to the grandiose nature of the house. She felt like she was on a continuous tour of someone else's home. She was still coming to terms with the fact that it was all hers . . . and Charles' of course. She slowly walked up the stairs, looking up at the ceiling with its perfectly shaped rose bud pattern. Her eyes moved to the wood trim, carved with precision from solid oak. She stopped and leaned over to feel the soft carpet on the step in front of her. She smiled to herself.

Why am I so lucky? Do I really deserve this? She turned to look out the front window above the front double doors. As far as she could see, she and Charles owned the property. Her neighbors were out of site and out of mind. It was a far cry from their first apartment where the walls were so thin that you could hear every movement, every intimate encounter, every shout, and every argument. Those days were just a bad memory now. She turned again and headed for her bedroom and a nice hot shower.

The workout at the gym was vigorous and long, nearly forty-five full minutes. Her muscles were sore and she felt sticky from sweat. She intended to get a shower and read for an hour or so, then take a walk around the grounds. She still hadn't seen all of their property. It was so immense that it would take several trips to see all of it.

Charlie heard rumors that a small Civil War skirmish had taken place on the property some 135 years before. The battle left a number of artifacts. Other rumors were that a small fortune in gold was lost in the battle. Supposedly, a team of Confederate soldiers stole the payroll from a Union convoy and made off with the loot, intending to cripple the morale of the Yankee Army. When a team of Union soldiers caught up to the Rebels, they killed them and recovered the money. But instead of returning with the loot, they claimed to have lost track of the Rebels. The General in charge of the troops believed that the soldiers were lying and had them court marshaled. They were tried, convicted of treason, and hung on a tree on their property, near where the payroll was supposedly hidden.

Of course, that was all a rumor and no one had ever found the loot. But Jody figured that maybe she'd get lucky. Who knows; she was lucky enough to marry the guy who discovered a way to make submarines virtually silent.

She made her way to the top of the stairs and into the master bedroom where she stripped off her workout clothes, sports bra, and panties and headed to the shower. She turned on the shower and set the temperature to steaming hot. After a few moments she walked into the shower and winced at the hot stream of water as it ran over her head and down across her skin. After an uncomfortable moment, she became used to the heat. She washed her hair then started to soap up her neck, shoulders and breasts. She had an odd feeling that she was being watched. She looked out around the zig-zag entrance to the shower. She glanced around the bathroom, but saw nothing out of the ordinary, so she continued with her shower. After a few more minutes, she had a peculiar feeling, like being on display. Once again, she shook the feeling and continued. *I'm just not used to being in a place this size all alone. Silly of me.*

* * *

Across America, members of the SExClub were watching Jody take her less than private shower. They admired her beauty and grace as she thoroughly enjoyed washing away the sticky feeling of her workout. They knew something that Jody didn't know, but she was about to find out.

* * *

Charlie Williams was home, sneaking up the stairs and into the master bath. When Jody turned to look the next time, he was standing there, watching her soap up her buttocks, then lean over to clean her legs. He could hardly contain himself.

"Oh my!" He exclaimed.

Startled, Jody nearly fell over. "You bastard!" She yelled, but with a big smile on her face. "You nearly scared me to death!"

"When you bent over like that, I nearly had a heart attack, myself. All my blood left my brain and went to my head. Take a look." He looked down. There was no doubt, he'd enjoyed watching his wife's shower.

"Very funny. Guys only have one thing in mind." Jody turned the water off and threw her head back, gathering her long blond hair in both hands, wringing the water out. "Could you please come out of your trance and hand me that towel?"

"I can do better than that. How about if you let me dry you off?" Charlie's eyes never left her body.

"Well you have to dry off more than just my boobs. From the look on your face, you won't make it that far."

"We'll just have to see how far I go." Charlie pulled the towel off the rack and headed for the shower. He dried Jody off from top to bottom and managed to get a few hand slips in, along with a few tickles. "Now my lovely, let's retire to the bedroom. We have work to do."

Jody began to protest, "But I just took a shower."

"You can take another one. You'll be extra clean. But first, let's get a little dirty." Charlie smiled like a kid in a candy store with a pocket full of twenty dollar bills. He knew he was in for some great sex. He was already excited. His only fear was that he was too excited. But that didn't matter. They had all the time in the world. He'd just signed another contract with the Navy for $40 million dollars. The best part was that he didn't have to do any work. It was all in his head.

* * *

Jody and Charlie's performance that afternoon was a real crowd pleaser. The man at the control panel was excited as he watched the couple in action. He could hardly concentrate on controlling the cameras and microphones. He nearly forgot to record the scene when they started in the bathroom. But he remembered and the whole forty minutes was captured and downloaded to the server.

* * *

Back in the master bedroom as Jody and Charlie lay resting, she got that feeling again, like they were being watched. She couldn't shake it. She looked around the room but saw nothing but expensive woodwork and beautifully painted walls. Still, the feeling was there. Just then, her new kitten jumped up on the bed, purring. The kitten made her way over to Jody and rubbed against her elbow. Jody rolled over, pet her kitten on the head, scratched between her ears and asked, "Were you watching us? Is that why I feel like I'm on display?"

"What's that Sweety? Are we making porn movies now? We'd be good at it."

* * *

Across the country, hundreds of people chuckled at what they thought was a joke. But they had to agree, they'd be good at it.

Chapter 15

Johnny Poleirmo shook his head in disgust. He was in a private room at the Orange County Sheriff's Department in Orlando, Florida. He and another detective had a computer linked to the internet using a high speed broadband connection and a new flat-panel monitor. The investigation called for privacy for two reasons. First, the victims in some cases were juveniles, even very young children. Second, this investigation was being held close to the chest. Only a handful of members of the department knew the investigation was underway. The department didn't want any leaks to the press about their new experiment into fighting cyber-crime. They barely knew where to start and they didn't want to look foolish if they spent a lot of taxpayer money and came up empty. Johnny wasn't the pioneer in this field, so that helped. He learned a lot of tricks on his trip to Ohio.

The room was painted institutional beige with darker tan asphalt tile on the floor. The walls were made of cinder block. It had no windows and two heavy steel doors on opposite walls. The smell in the room was of heavy artificial pine cleaner with chemical floor wax mixed in. Johnny was convinced that he was going to die from chemical poisoning from all the cleaners that were used in the Sheriff's Office. There was a single table in the middle of the room made of heavy steel. It was bolted to the floor. The room was designed for interrogations, but in this case it was being used by the vice squad for the discreet investigation of sexual predators. The computer was a brand new, top of the line Microvault with the fastest processor available in a home computer. Of course, that was true when the Sheriff's Department ordered it a few months ago. By now it was on its way to obsolescence. The only two chairs in the room were occupied by Detective Poleirmo and his partner.

Johnny's partner was a young black man, twenty-five, just off of his first field assignment. He was moderately tall, at 6 feet 2 inches, and slender. His trim body resembled that of a long distance runner; not an ounce of fat on the young man. He held a criminal justice degree from the University of Central Florida and intended to get into the criminal law field. That was until his mother was sexually assaulted and killed by a known sex offender who had been released from prison after only six months. The perpetrator was placed on house arrest with an electronic ankle bracelet which he hacked off with a pair of tin snips. He'd been loose for two days before the Orlando Police Department found out he was on the prowl. Two days too late for Richard Herald's Mother. From that day on, he vowed to find out what made these sick bastards tick. He also vowed to put as many of them behind bars as possible.

"Holy crap. I can't stand to watch this shit. Can you skip to something where the girls are at least in their teens? This is killing me, these sick bastards." Johnny was disgusted. The girls being abused on the website were barely nine or ten years old, or at least they were made to look that way. Their internet chat sessions with some of the predators led them to a series of child pornography sites. Johnny spoke to his captain about adding the investigation of these sites to their duties. His captain agreed after seeing how young the victims were on the sites. "How do we find these bastards?"

Rick hit the keys on the computer and brought up a mining program that followed the signal of the website, hopefully back to its server. From the server he might be able to get enough information to determine its physical location.

He explained the process. "What we have to do is trace the signal through a number of routers and switch points. We do this by using a tracking software program called SearchPoint Source Finder. The host server where this program originates can send the program out over any number of repeater servers. Plus they're sure to go through a number of one way firewalls, kind of like a diode in electronics. The signal can come out, but no signals can come in. That's the bad news. The good news is all firewalls have to let some signals through because that's how programs check for a successful transmission. They have to get feedback so that the owner of the website is sure the broadcast is getting out successfully. So we have to figure out how to piggyback on those feedback signals; kind of trick the firewall."

"Is that easy to do?"

"That depends on the experience level of the site owners and the complexity of their firewall software. We'll have some successes and we'll have some challenges. Let's get started. We'll see how well this mining software works."

The screen was divided into halves with the web broadcast on the top half and text on the bottom. Johnny could see feedback coming from the server as Rick read the text. It looked like gibberish to Johnny, but Rick was smiling as he read.

Rick hit a few more key strokes and Johnny heard the printer hum. He leaned back for a moment and loosened his tie. He reached behind the computer and grabbed the printouts from the small ink jet printer.

"I think we may be off to a good start. See the fourth line of the printout? That's the location of the server, the physical location, I mean." Johnny looked at the line Rick pointed out and was disappointed. The address was in California near Los Angeles.

"How is this good news? They're in another state all the way across the country. How does that help?"

"Well, we've proven that the tracking software works, for one thing. Second, I think we can do some targeted searches based on the physical location. In other words, instead of searching for a specific site, we can search for sites in a given location. You give me an hour to play with this and I'll tell you when we're ready to get serious about busting some of these creeps."

Johnny thought about it for a moment then nodded his head slowly. "Okay, you get started. But I want to know as soon as you think we're making headway. Can you really narrow down the location to a specific area?"

Rick didn't hesitate. "I know I can. Where would you like me to start?"

"How about within a mile radius of the department building. Then if you don't get any hits, expand it in five mile chunks. I'd like to clean up our neighborhood first. Maybe we can make some quick scores, make some examples out of them. Get a few successes and then build on them." Johnny thought for a moment, looked around the beige walls and said, "And I'd like to make a trophy wall in this room." He looked back at Rick. "What do you think about that?"

"Hey Johnny, whatever floats your boat. I'm more in it to make sure what happened to my mom, doesn't happen to others."

Rick turned back to the computer and the keys started to rattle at an amazing speed. Johnny shook his head. *This kid must spend hours at the computer at a time. What a life!* "You want anything from the machine? Candy bar? Soda?"

"Sure. How about a Snickers and a Coca-Cola?"

"You got it." Johnny headed out making sure no one was passing the door. He closed it behind him. Johnny had no sooner left the room when Rick received his first website search results. He'd expanded the search criteria to ten miles and got seventeen hits. He reviewed the descriptions on the printout and quickly determined that they had several good leads. He was certain that there was a big future in busting perverts. There were just too many of them for him and Johnny to make a dent in the juvenile skin trafficking business. But he was willing to do his part. Maybe they could show other departments how to set up their own programs. It would take a massive effort to slow down the child porn business.

He began signing on to the websites most likely to be using child porn stars. He was rewarded with a winner on the second site he entered. The site obviously catered to pedophiles. Busting these guys was going to be real satisfying. *I couldn't help you, Mom. But I'm going to help these poor kids or I'll die trying.* He recorded the information from the site and went on to the next. Of the seventeen hits, at least three were marketing kiddy porn. Two others were questionable. Rick figured that they'd make the first few busts and that would send out a strong message; stop and pull up stakes or we're going to hunt you down.

Johnny came back with Rick's Snickers and Coca-Cola. He looked over the printouts and Rick's notes as Rick continued his search of the web for local website operators. He came up with twenty-seven more by expanding the search another twenty miles. He looked up at Johnny and said, "We're going to be busy for years to come."

The disgusted look on Johnny's face said it all. "Yeah. And that sucks."

* * *

Later in the day, Johnny called his friend, Pat McKinney. They discussed Johnny's new assignment, his partner, and what they found. Pat was incensed at what he heard. He thought about his daughter, Anna, and his son, Sean. He thought about what he'd do to anyone who even thought of hurting his children. The vivid picture in his mind wasn't pretty.

"So, Johnny, what's the plan? Are you going to set up a team to just bust in and catch these guys in the act?"

"I wish it were that easy. We have to gather evidence and it has to be air-tight. Then we'll go to a judge and get a warrant and then when the timing is right, we'll set up a sting or a SWAT raid, depending on what the situation warrants. If we know that they have so much evidence laying around that they can't clean it up before we bust the doors down, then a SWAT raid is the best way to go. If they run a tight operation and it's mobile, then we set up a sting, which takes a lot longer." There was a pause. "Okay, I can hear the squirrels running around in that head of yours. What are you thinking?"

Pat paused before answering. He had been thinking of a way to help his buddy, Johnny. As his plan developed in his head, he rubbed the scar on his chin. It was a habit that he couldn't seem to break. Finally he said, "Oh, I don't know. I have a few computer skills, you know. Maybe I could do a little surveillance on these perverts before you get the official go ahead to set up wiretaps and whatever else is in your plan. How about it?"

Johnny thought for a moment. If the department were to set up illegal surveillance then the whole case could be thrown out of court on a technicality. But if someone else provided useful information unsolicited, that was another story completely. He had to give this some thought and he'd have to know exactly what Pat had in mind, mainly so he could deny any involvement by the Sheriff's Department.

"Pat, let's talk more, later, face to face. Can you meet me for lunch tomorrow?"

"Sure, what are you buying?"

"How about a Stromboli at Luigi's off John Young and Lee Road? Say, 12:30?"

"You're on. See you then."

Johnny hung up the phone and headed back to the converted computer room. Rick had a mountain of information that they'd have to sift through over the next few days. They were both floored at the number of porn shops on the web that originated from Central Florida. Rick looked at Johnny and said, "What can you say, sex sells."

"This isn't sex. This is perverse. These . . . animals are sick. If I have anything to do with it, we're going to send these guys to the chair. They deserve nothing less, sick or not."

Johnny sat down and started through the papers, categorizing and prioritizing them. The more likely they were dealing in child pornography, the higher the priority. They would be the first on the hit list.

Chapter 16

Sheila Demarca was thirty-four and short, with straight, brunette hair that hung to her shoulders. Today, she wore a light green blouse and dark green skirt that finished just above the knees. Her earrings were small, simple hoops, and her necklace was a thin chain with a three-quarter carat, star-shaped diamond. She was smart, articulate, and very organized. She was a perfect secretary for Nelson Rockledge. She helped make a very effective Staff Adviser an outstanding Staff Adviser. Whatever Nelson did well, which included most everything he did, she helped him do them more efficient. Sheila had worked for Nelson for the last three years.

She watched Nelson from where she stood at his office door. She'd never seen him so agitated. Never before had she seen him slam his fist on his desk. He was always calm and in control. Even in situations where his boss was giving him a hard time or his subordinates seemed to be failing to produce the results he expected, he always remained calm. He always focused on the situation, not on the individual. His belief was, people would perform at their best if provided with the right tools and a clear path for success. He was usually right. There was always the exception where a person just didn't want to do the required job, and on occasion an employee would have to either be reassigned or let go. Sheila remembered only one employee, in the three years working for Nelson, who had to be fired. He usually found another position to which the employee was better suited. Three years of steady calm. Now Nelson was out of sorts.

"Hey, Boss, is there something wrong?" Sheila's question caught Nelson off guard. He looked up from his uncommonly messy desk with a surprised look. It took a moment for him to gather his thoughts.

"Hey, Sheila, can you get me the Hilliard report? I have to review it for a presentation tomorrow."

"Well I could, but I'd have to move your elbow. You're leaning on it."

Nelson looked under his left elbow and sure enough, it was right where Sheila said. He shook his head slightly then gave her a look of defeat. He placed both elbows on his desk and rubbed his face with both hands. When he looked up again, she could see the stress in his face. Something was definitely wrong.

She took a step into his office and closed the door behind her. "Okay, Nelson. Let's have it. What's going on?"

Nelson kept his silence a few moments longer while he contemplated his answer. He decided to tell Sheila the plain, unabridged truth. "Jillian was raped the other night by two guys. They broke into our house while I was in Texas."

Sheila gasped. "Oh my God, is she alright?"

"Yes . . . and no. They didn't physically hurt her, but she's emotionally freaked out. She won't let me touch her. She's walking around, sitting around, laying around like a zombie. She did let me take her to the hospital for a blood test. We told the doctor that she was feeling run down. They did a pregnancy test and took the standard battery of blood tests plus HIV. It all came back negative. She's going to be tested again in a few months, this time by a different lab, just to make sure these creeps didn't give her AIDS. So, at least we know she's not pregnant or infected with anything."

Sheila's face showed the compassion that she had for Jillian and Nelson. She'd met Jillian at a number of work related functions and really liked her. She was easy to get to know and was fun to be with. She also knew what Jillian was going through. She'd been raped when she was nineteen. She knew that Jillian had a long road ahead, dealing with fear, anger, pain, and doubt. She also knew that Nelson was going to have a hard time coping with what would seem like rejection from his wife.

"Nelson, maybe I can help. Did you go to the police?"

"No. She said she couldn't. The bastards threatened to kill both of us if she did. I told her it was just talk, that if they were killers, they would have killed her. She wouldn't budge."

"You know, Nelson, the company offers confidential counseling for things like this. It could help you both. This isn't going to be easy."

Nelson didn't hesitate to answer this offering. "Jillian wouldn't go, at least not yet. I'll keep that in mind, though. It might be an option later."

Then Sheila offered, "Maybe I can talk her into it. You see, I went through this when I was younger. I think I know what she's going through."

With a pained expression, he said, "Oh, my God. I had no idea. I don't know what to say. When did it happen?"

"It was years ago. I was a senior in high school."

He paused, then said, "I can't imagine how you must have felt . . . how Jillian feels now."

He was deep in thought while he looked back at his secretary. He leaned back in his chair and folded his hands across his chest. When he spoke, it was quiet, just above a whisper. "Sheila, I'll do anything to have my wife back the way she was before this happened. If you think you can help, I'll talk with Jillian tonight. She might be mad that I told you about this, but it can't get much worse. We barely speak. I don't know what to say. Maybe you do?"

"I can't make any promises, but I know how I felt. I wish someone would have been there for me; a woman, not a man. This kind of thing breaks your trust in men for a while. You're guilty by association. You may have to give her the space she needs, at least for now."

"I can do that as long as I know it will help in the long run." Nelson paused. "You know what? I feel guilty because I wasn't there to protect her. I couldn't stop them. I put her in a vulnerable position by building that house in the middle of nowhere. She could have screamed and nobody would have heard her cries. What kind of a man does that to his wife?" "Nelson. You didn't do this. You built her a dream house. You both love that house. You said it was all she talked about for almost a year before it was built. It isn't your fault. You couldn't possibly have known anything like this would happen!" Sheila stopped and sighed then continued in a calming voice, "Before Jillian can get better, you have to forgive yourself. You have to know that there was nothing you could have known or done that would change what happened. You have to be the strong one here. And you have to make sure she knows you'll always be there for her."

Nelson nodded his head in agreement. She was absolutely right and he knew it. This wasn't going to be easy, but he was the one who had to set the path to recovery.

Nelson asked, "So, do you think we should go to the police?"

Without hesitation, Sheila answered, "Yes. It may be too late to gather any evidence, but at least she can give a description of the bastards to the police. They may have other cases that are similar. The guy that raped me was on the prowl for months before they got him. He spent time, got out, did it again to some poor high school girl, but she clawed his face. Pretty much marked him, plus they found his skin under her nails. They got him again and he's still in prison."

Nelson again was deep in thought. He reached across the desk and touched Sheila's hand. He said, "Thanks for listening. I'll talk with Jillian and see if she'll talk with you. I think I can get myself together." After a moment he spoke more forcefully, "I know I can get myself together. I'm not going to let these bastards ruin our lives. We're going to be fine. We're going to be better than fine. It may take time, but we're starting tonight when I get home." Nelson didn't quite smile, but it was the first sign of confidence that Sheila had seen since she walked in his office.

"Nelson, just take it slow. She's had a very traumatic experience. Be firm, but gentle with her." She nodded and

Nelson nodded along with her. "Your best remedy right now is to bury yourself in your work right after you call her and tell her how much you adore her. She needs that now. Trust me."

Nelson nodded to Sheila then gave her a genuine smile, filled with gratitude. It wasn't much of a smile, but considering the task ahead, it was a huge step.

As Sheila headed for the door, she turned and said, "Be sure to call me and let me know when I should come over. I'm pretty much free all week."

In a quiet, choked up voice, Nelson said, "You're the best, Sheila. Thanks."

Her smile was cautiously optimistic. She said, "No problem, Boss."

Chapter 17

It was a warm evening for October in Virginia. The day had been cool, near sixty-five degrees, but as the afternoon wore on, the temperature rose. The humidity rose along with the temperature as the night sky darkened. The moon shined brightly, though it was only at first quarter.

Tom Grayson looked around the parking lot at Messier Homes' construction office west of Stafford, Virginia. He could see vague shadows from the moonlight. He sat in his truck in a dark corner of the lot long after the work crews were gone. The bright copper glow of the mercury vapor lights cast eerie islands of light near the two story building. The office windows were now dark, the last foreman having left nearly an hour before. He wanted to be sure that he'd be alone as he rifled through desks and cabinets. As the most senior man at Messiers, he could stay at the offices as long as he liked. He thought it might look suspicious if he were caught looking through Jeremy and Aaron Messier's space after hours. He figured that Jeremy would be off to his favorite bar, chasing women. No one knew where Aaron was during the day, much less where he went at night, but Tom knew he wouldn't show up at the office. He was confident that the Messier brothers were behind the placement of the transmitter in the attic of their newest construction job. He just needed the proof before he started throwing accusations around.

Tom scanned the area. From his vantage point he could see the entire gravel lot. No cars were within sight. The angle of the parking lot lights made the low points in the gravel look like puddles of rain. Tom knew the day had been dry. It was just the moonlight and the shadows of the mercury lights playing tricks on his eyes.

Finally it was time to move. He opened the truck door. The dome light came on and a warning tone sounded. He immediately shut the door, cursing himself for leaving the keys in the ignition. His heart was pounding. He brushed the back of his hand across his forehead, feeling the sweat. Pulling the keys out of the ignition, he thought to himself, *Some kind of detective you are?* Now, expecting the dome light to come on, he opened the door again, exited the truck and headed for the office. *Remember, you're supposed to be here. You can't act like a crook. If anyone sees you act this way, they'll think you are a crook.*

Tom took a couple of deep breaths. Using his keys, he opened the office door. He decided to leave the downstairs lights off and only turn on the lights when he was in the inner offices. He closed the door behind him and paused to get his bearings. His eyes began to adjust to the dark. The main room of Messier construction offices was an open area, twenty-four feet deep and thirty-six feet across. There was a small desk near the front door where a receptionist used to sit. But when Theo Messier built a sales office nearly a mile down the road, the receptionist desk went unoccupied. Dust covered the desk, disturbed only by a few empty coffee cups, a doughnut box, few papers and a couple of stray tools. The foremen's offices, including Tom's, were on the main floor to the left of the door. To the far right was the workers' lounge. It was also used as a meeting room. Above the foreman's offices on the second floor were Jeremy and Aaron's shared office. Theo's old office was above the worker's lounge to the right. No one had entered his office since his departure to France.

Tom moved to his left, towards the stairs to the brothers' offices. In the dark, his foot caught a heavy plastic trash can and knocked it over. He lost his balance for a moment, but his hand caught the back of a chair, and he regained his balance. The contents of the trash can spilled out over the floor. A couple of empty soda cans rattled across the floor, sending Tom's nerves into overdrive. He cringed. He paused for what seemed like ten minutes. In reality it was only 12 seconds. *What am I doing here? I'm no detective.* He again took a couple deep breaths, then continued on towards the stairs. He moved up the stairs to the office door. He listened at the door to see if he could hear anything in the office. Thinking aloud, he spoke to himself in a soft tone, "You idiot. If someone were here, they'd have heard the noise already." Shaking his head he said, "Get a grip, Tommy."

He tried the door to the Messiers' office but it was locked. He reached in his pocket and pulled out a key. He'd gotten it from Theo many years ago. He knew it would come in handy someday. It still worked. The door slid open and Tom walked in. He flipped on the light and headed across the room for the door to a private workshop that was next to the brother's office. This would be tricky because he didn't have a key for the workshop. He tried the door knob. To his surprise and relief, the door was unlocked. He moved inside, found the light switch and turned on the workshop fluorescent lights.

The workshop was a narrow room, only eight feet from the door to the outside wall. The room was twenty-four feet across. A workbench ran the length of the twenty-four foot room. Like the old receptionists desk at the front door, the workbench was covered with dust, disposable coffee cups and assorted other junk. There was a pile of electronic gadgets. Some were in pieces but others appeared to be new out of the box. Nothing on the bench looked as if it had been touched in months. Could this be where the brothers tested their transmitters? Based on the amount of dust and trash lying around, there was no way Jeremy and Aaron used this room for anything but a junk room.

Tom was bummed. He was sure that he'd find an elaborate testing lab in the room. He threw up his arms and headed out to the outer office, closing the door behind him.

Tom stopped and looked around in frustration. He came into the offices looking for clues about electronic gadgets and their purpose and he was striking out. How could he have been so wrong? He decided to go back into the workshop again.   Maybe he'd missed something.   He entered the workshop and turned the lights on. He looked slowly from one end of the room to the other.   It still appeared that the workshop was nothing but a junk room. As he looked from one end to the other, something seemed out of proportion. What was it?   From the doorway, he looked back out into Jeremy and Aaron's office.   Then he looked back into the workshop. *Odd. It looks like the workshop isn't as deep as the office area.*   Tom looked again.   He couldn't be sure but it looked like there was about a four foot difference in the depth.

He went into the brothers' office and began to pace the distance from the door to the back of the office. *Nine regular steps.*   Then he went into the workshop. *Seven steps.*   He looked at the wall from top to bottom. He looked at the floor in front of the wall. The wall had no baseboard. He looked at the wall more closely.   There was a small gap, no more than an eighth of an inch wide. He felt along the gap, trying to pull at it. He thought the wall might move. It didn't. He backed away from the wall, inspecting every inch. He began to push against it, moving from top to bottom hoping to find a magic button, making the wall swing open. But the more he probed, the more frustrated he became. He looked to the left and noticed a slight overlap in the plywood. He pushed on a point to the right of the overlap. The wall moved slightly.   He pushed harder and the wall began to swing open at the right side. He continued to push until he was able to grab the wall as it swung away from the corner. A four-foot section of the wall opened up.

As the wall swung open, Tom looked in. The space was indeed about four feet deep and eight feet wide. The walls were made of drywall with holes about a quarter inch in diameter.   The drywall had not been painted but there were numerous vertical and horizontal indentations where something had been hung then removed. Tom saw a number of empty electrical conduits coming out of the floor near the wall. On closer inspection, a number of spiral pieces of black, yellow, and white plastic were on the floor near the conduit openings. Tom recognized these as remnants from where wires were pulled out of conduit and a thin layer of insulation was stripped from the wire.

By the number of conduits in the room, he figured that there had to have been at least eighteen power cables coming into the room. There may have been other types of cable as well. He'd seen yellow power cables before, but they were rare. It was more likely computer cables. But why would a small hidden room need all this power? Maybe it was just a cable room to pass through and distribute power throughout the building. But that didn't make sense. The power supply to this building was at the opposite end of the building. Tom continued to think through the puzzle. He decided to follow the conduit runs and see where they originated. He walked back out into the workshop and closed the wall, making sure that not trace of his intrusion was evident. He left the room and turned off the lights, then left Jeremy and Aaron's office, again shutting off the lights. He was now in the main room at the top of the stairs. He paused to allow his eyes to once again adjust to the dark. He heard the floor creaking behind him. He froze.

He waited for another few seconds in the dark. Finally he could pretty much see around the entire room from his second floor vantage point. He didn't hear another sound so he took a step towards the stairs. When he was at the top step he heard two quick steps behind him then he felt hands at his back. He was shoved hard from behind and he toppled down the steps, head over heals. On the way down, he caught his head on a beam that held the railing. He ended up at the base of the stairs, unconscious.

The man walked calmly down the stairs past the heap that was Tom Grayson. For good measure he kicked Tom's arm. He heard Tom groan as the kick hit his ribs as well, knocking the wind out of his lungs. The man smiled to himself and walked out the front door of Messier Homes construction offices.

* * *

Half an hour later, the man at the controls shifted his attention between the action on six of the nine monitors and the other three at the bottom. The top six showed different views of a very active couple in the middle of some very hot sex. It was difficult for the man to concentrate on the bottom three monitors which showed a digital recording of Tom Grayson walking around the Messier Brothers' office, looking through the old workshop. He was obviously getting frustrated at not finding whatever he was searching for. The controller was watching the recording from half an hour earlier because he'd fallen asleep while Tom Grayson had searched the construction offices.   Luckily, the system had a built in feature to automatically start recording on a signal from a motion sensor at the office. The entire event was captured on the server.

The taller partner walked into the control room and said, "Keep your eyes on him. If he found anything, we need to know."

"But what could he have found? There's nothing there," the control man said.

"You'd be surprised. Did he go into the workshop?"

"Yep. Took a quick look around then went back into the outer offices."

"Good. It's a good thing we moved the control room out of there. It was only a matter of time before someone figured out what was going on in there. We're safe for now. I'm sure we'll have to make another move within a year or so. By then we might want to go offshore with the control station or maybe shut down altogether." He paused then burst out laughing. "We're never shutting this down. This is like the goose that's laying gold bricks. Screw eggs. They're too small."

The man at the controls smiled at his partner's joke. He looked at his bank account just this morning. Money was starting to come in fast. He had no idea what to spend it on. He was always in the control room in the evening. And he was quite content with the arrangement.

"Looks like he got frustrated. Do you think he'll try again later?"

The tall partner put a hand to his chin and rested his elbow in his other hand. He looked thoughtful for a moment. "No, I don't think so. Let's see if he decides to quit after this evening. I suspect Mr. Grayson will stay frustrated and give up."

The man at the controls nodded his head in agreement. He wasn't completely convinced.

The tall partner looked at his young partner. *Is this kid going to keep his shit together? I think so. If not, computer nerds are a dime a dozen. For now, this arrangement works.*

The two men watched the recorded version of Tom Grayson being pushed down the stairs.

"Oh my God! Did you see that?" The man at the controls was frantic.

The older partner, in a calm voice said, "Yes, I saw it. Just keep watching. He's okay. Maybe a little banged up, but that's what he gets for snooping around."

"But what if he's dead?"

"I said keep watching. He's not dead. Look at his chest."

On the monitor, the green night vision image was very clear and showed that Tom was breathing. It also showed quite a bit of blood. He was in a position where the blood looked like it was draining from his mouth. The tall man pointed out that it was coming from the bump on his head. He told his partner to stop worrying. They'd find him in the morning if he didn't come to sooner, and leave on his own.

"Okay. I trust you. But I'm still going to check the live feed and see if he's still there."

The tall man rolled his eyes and left the room. His younger partner went back to the six monitors where the couple was just erupting in a simultaneous climax.

"Damn, I missed it." He hit the back button to view the scene over again.

Chapter 18

It was just before 5:00 PM on Friday. The sun was angled to the west in the Florida sky with the temperature hovering around 88 degrees. The usual afternoon showers had drenched the western part of the state, but the roads were already dry. The passing shower raised the high humidity to nearly unbearable levels.

"So, Pat, how's your mom holding up?"

Johnny Poleirmo's question hung in the air for a moment. Pat was a bit ashamed that he really hadn't talked to his mom much recently. It had only been eleven weeks since Daniel McKinney, Pat and Joe's father, passed away from a fatal heart attack. It was the second family crisis in less than a year. The other was the death of Pat and Joe's brother, Mike. The McKinney Family had seen more than their fair share of grief. As Pat and Joe knew, some of it they'd brought on themselves, but the rest just seemed to find them. They needed a streak of good luck. But more than anything, they needed time to heal. Pat and Joe had been on a whirlwind case tracking a couple of fugitives across the Southeastern United States. With the combined stress of the travel, the manhunt, and family tragedy, they were exhausted.

Pat came out of his momentary trance and looked at his friend. "She's been doing okay, but we haven't talked in a few weeks. She's traveling with Lisa's Mom. They've become fast friends. I think they're helping to prop each other up. Misery loves company, I guess."

Pat was referring to Ann Goddard's husband, Lisa's dad, who died the same week as Pat and Joe's dad. It was a double slam to the families. They should have been celebrating Joe and Lisa's engagement. Joe and Lisa were able to find strength in the midst of all the adversity and finally got engaged, though they hadn't yet set a date for the wedding.

"Mom and Ann are supposed to be here in an hour or so. They flew into Tampa International today, but decided that they had to stop at one of the malls down there." Pat smiled. "I guess she's grieving gracefully. Having Ann with her helps them both, I think." Pat took a swig of his beer then said, "So life goes on."

Johnny asked, "So how's that bruise on your chest? Is the pain finally gone?"

Pat put his finger to his lips and moved his head slightly in Diane's direction to let Johnny know that this subject was off limits in front of her. She was just out of earshot. The bruise was in the center of Pat's chest. He was lucky that he was wearing a Kevlar vest or that bullet would have put a hole through his heart. The bullet had dented the vest but didn't penetrate. Oddly, the bruise was in the shape of a heart, which Pat took to mean his time wasn't up yet, but that he was spending his life credits. He'd misspent a number of those credits in his youth. How many more did he have? Only God knew. He said to Johnny, "We can talk later."

From back on the patio behind the house, Pat heard the doorbell ring. He shouted out, "We're all around back." He hoped whoever it was could hear him over the music. The barbeque at their Dunnellon, Florida home was for Pat and Diane's family and a handful of their closest friends. Pat expected that Joe and Lisa would be there any moment. He told Joe that he and Lisa needed to announce their wedding date so Pat and Diane could make vacation plans. Joe just laughed. Pat wasn't amused.

Also on the guest list was Brian Purcer and his fiancé, Ginny Parks. Brian was on a break from his band's Blue and Gray Tour. The band, Brian Purcer and the Hot Licks, was playing in a northern city one week then playing in a southern city the next week. Since they were from Florida and had a hard-pounding southern sound, their producers were trying to gin up publicity using a *War Between the States* theme. So far, the first half of the tour was an overwhelming success. Their first album had five hits in the top fifty songs on the Billboard charts. Their biggest hit, *I Know You Better than You Think*, was number one and looked to be a fixture in that position for some time.

Brian's personal wealth was also shooting up the charts. Pat had given him the name of a financial adviser and Brian was taking his advice. His investments were growing quickly. As more profits from concerts and compact disc sales came rolling in, Brian was moving more money into his portfolio. He told Pat early on, "I'm not going to end up like some of these rock stars and piss it all away on parties and dope." He was following through on that promise.

Ginny was also helping to keep Brian's head on straight. She made sure his eyes were on her and not a bunch of under-aged groupies. Brian and Ginny were head over heels for each other and their future looked bright indeed.

Like Lisa and Joe, they hadn't set a date for their wedding. Part of their dilemma was Brian's tour. It had already been extended once and more dates were being considered. The producers figured as long as the money was rolling in, might as well keep the money machine running. They were keeping a close eye on Brian and the rest of the band. They wanted to be sure that they didn't burn them out on their first tour. So the producers promised an extended break after the end of the Blue and Gray Tour. Brian was counting on it. He wanted to take Ginny on a long vacation and honeymoon, but he couldn't even plan past the next couple of weeks. But the tour would be over before too long, he was sure of it.

Lisa and Joe appeared from around the side of the house. Lisa went right over to Diane and gave her a hug. Pat, Joe, and Johnny shook hands and exchanged greetings. Anna and Sean McKinney came running out of the house to see their Uncle Joe and Aunt Lisa, even though she wasn't officially their aunt, yet.

Within minutes, Brian and Ginny joined the party. Brian waved at the guys and gave a drinking motion, indicating that he could use a beer. Pat nodded and headed for the cooler. He handed Brian his beer and gave Ginny a peck on the cheek. Only Emma and Ann were still missing. But the drinks were flowing, the grill was started and the music was playing. Joe joined Lisa, Diane, Brian and Ginny, sitting at the patio table. Brian started to tell stories about life on the road. At the grill, Pat and Johnny were talking about Johnny's new assignment. He was still in vice at the Orange County Sheriff's office.

"So what's it like looking at porn on the job all day? Sounds like a tough gig. Most people get fired for that." Pat's joke didn't play well with Johnny. He didn't crack even a hint of a smile.

"It sucks. There are some real sick dudes out there." Johnny paused and took a swig from his beer. "We've been tracking almost thirty kiddie porn sites just in central Florida. There's probably a hundred more that are questionable. The girls on those sites are probably underage, but they're close enough that we can't prove it . . . yet. But the ones we're sure of, you just wouldn't believe. These kids, girls and boys, are no more than ten or twelve years old. If I'm in on the bust it's gonna be real hard for me to keep from killing these folks on the spot." Another pause. Johnny's eyes glossed over. He looked both angry and sad.

"Hey man, snap out of it. Sorry I brought it up." Pat looked at Johnny's bottle, which was nearly empty. "You need a refill?"

"Sure." Johnny put on a weak smile, finished his beer and handed the empty to Pat. He couldn't get some of the horrid images out of his mind. Maybe this assignment was too much for him. He was a law and order kind of guy. He believed in the criminal justice system. But he was wondering if there were better ways to deal with these creeps. He shook his head to clear the evil thoughts as Pat returned from the cooler with a full, cold brew.

Johnny said, "There is one bright spot. That sting operation I told you about, where the guy goes into chat rooms and acts like a teenage girl, is working. We've already had one successful bust and we're setting up for more."

"That sounds promising. Is that what you had in mind for me when we talked?

"Yeah. We'd like to have people doing both the sting and the child porn cases. So, what are you doing with your free time now that the military case is over?"

"Relax. Spend time with Diane and the kids. Relax some more. Drink beer. And maybe I'll relax some." Pat smiled. He lifted his beer and the two men clinked bottles. Pat flipped the steaks on the grill and sprinkled them with some seasoning mix. The smell of the smoke coming from the grill immediately took on the aroma of the spices. Pat took a deep breath of the air and smiled.

"Do you think you could help me with this investigation?"

"What, so I can drive myself crazy like you? Let me tell you something; I've met people in lots of professions. Nurses, for instance. They are great people and we can't do without them. But when you talk with them and hear their stories? I mean, they're really telling the stories of their patients. You can see the pain in their eyes and their body language. It is torturing them inside." He stopped and took another drink. He picked up the tongs and pressed each steak as if he were looking for some sign that the steaks were getting done. He looked around his back yard for a moment, then turned back to Johnny. "I just saw that same look in your eyes. This job is killing you. You have to deal with the scum of the earth. I don't know how you can do it."

Johnny's eyes got hard again. His jaw tightened. He looked directly at Pat. "Somebody has got to stop this crap. If we don't get this filth under control, I hate to think what our society is going to be like in twenty years. What's it gonna be like for your kids? Aren't you worried about Sean and Anna?"

"Yeah, I am. And if I could solve every problem, I would. But you and me, we can't round up every bad guy and sock 'em away. Or better yet, save the courts some time and blow their brains out. We're supposed to be the good guys here." Pat had to watch his words. Johnny was still an Orange County Sheriff and Pat had some skeletons in the closet. For some of his misdeeds, the statute of limitations would run out some day. For at least one, there was no legal protection. Pat had turned over a new leaf, but the past would always be on his heels.

"Since taking on this task force I've been wondering if those young cops on that Dirty Harry movie didn't have the right idea. You know, the ones that were killing the drug dealers and pimps? They took out a lot of bad characters."

"Johnny, just think about how that movie turned out."

"Yeah, but that was the movies. Maybe real life would be different." Johnny gave Pat another weak smile.

"Right."

Joe left Lisa, Ginny, and Diane and came over to visit with Pat and Johnny. He shook Johnny's hand and punched Pat in the shoulder. Pat put down the tongs and rubbed his shoulder. He pointed to the cooler nearby. Joe took the hint and grabbed a beer. He hollered to Lisa and asked if she wanted one. Lisa shook her head and turned back to talk with Diane.

"So Johnny, how's the porn business going? That's gotta suck looking at sex all day."

Pat rolled his eyes as Joe unknowingly poured salt on the fresh wounds. Pat punched Joe in the arm as he gave him a stern look. "You insensitive prick."

"What ?" Joe looked from Pat to Johnny in surprise.

"Don't worry about it. Pat and I just had this talk. It sucks, no pun intended. It's just that I have to look at kids . . ." Johnny stopped, shook his head and took a long pull off of his beer.

Brian left the women and joined the men at the grill. He wore a big smile.

"I guess I don't have to ask how the tour is going." Pat said with a big grin.

"I don't know how to describe it. A few months ago we were playing to bar crowds of what, fifty people? Now we're filling concert halls and sports arenas. I'm afraid that one day I'll wake up and realize it was all a dream." Brian's smile beamed wide.

"It is a dream, my man. You just happen to be living it. How's Steve treatin' you?" Steve Trevino was Pat and Diane's financial adviser. He'd recommended that Brian talk with Steve about his new financial situation and see if he could help. Brian was real pleased to date.

"I gotta tell you man, he's one sharp dude. If things keep going like they are now, the sky's the limit. He sure knows his stuff." Steve had Brian's portfolio on the move. He promised Brian that they would have meetings every quarter to make sure he was happy with the direction of his investments. So far, Brian had no complaints. Pat and Diane agreed with Brian on Steve's competence as a financial adviser. Steve had taken Pat's questionable income and turned it into legitimate investments. Since over seven years had passed, all the old records had been destroyed and no paper trail existed back to Pat's past business dealings. Brian had no such issues. His success was more recent. He was always frugal but never had money to invest in a meaningful way. Now he had a growing empire to protect and nourish.

"That's excellent, Brian. Now, the next big question; When are you and Ginny tying the knot?"

"I can't tell you until I get the okay from Ginny, but I think we're heading to Vegas right after the tour. But the tour's been extended for a couple more weeks so that's on hold until we know the final gig date. I think the first week in November, maybe?"

The four men held their bottles towards each other and clinked long necks again. Each took a pull from their beers.

"Congrats, Brian," Joe said. Johnny followed with his own congrats and a pat on the back.

Pat looked over at Diane.   She and the ladies were having their own talk.   He asked, "Are we ready?   The steaks are just about done."

"As usual, waiting on you, Dear."

Pat sighed. *The story of my life.*

Chapter 19

"Just thirty miles from my place." *How convenient. I'll just drop by with my offer and that will be that.* Jake shook his head in the back seat of his limo, thinking that the new owners of the exclusive Messier Homes were also the owners of the classy porn site. You just don't know about people and their secrets. Theo Messier was well respected in the Washington, DC area, especially to the west of town. But his sons were another matter. Jeremy was known as a playboy and Aaron was thought to be autistic or at least an extreme introvert. No one who knew the Messier family expected the sons to be able to handle the business now that Theo was retiring. Jake gave Cliff the Geek an extra $5000 for his work finding out the trash on the Messier brothers. It's amazing what a little work on the computer can dig up.

But that wasn't Jake's concern. His only interest was to get the boys to sell him the porn business. He figured that a lowball offer and a few, well placed threats would force them to sell. Their daddy wouldn't like it much if the boys dragged his cherished family name through the mud. The press would have a field day, with their high brow clients, finding out that Messiers were linked to a porn business? That would be quite a scandal. Nobody would buy a Messier home again. Jake knew he held all the right cards. He didn't really want to play them. He just wanted a clean transfer of the ownership of the business. He was confident that he had the upper hand.

The ride to Messier homes offices was easy enough. Jake hardly had time to listen to the Doors' LA Woman. He yelled the ending lines so far out of tune that Shamus scrunched his face up, like he was eating lemons.

Shamus turned the stereo down as they turned into the dusty gravel parking lot for Messier Homes. It was nearing 5:30 PM and the lot was clearing out fast. Only about half a dozen cars remained. The few workers who were there turned and stared at the limo pulling into the lot. They were used to seeing fancy cars in the lot, but not this late in the day. The only people left at the office were tradesmen. The Messier Brothers were long gone. The senior man on the site was Tom Grayson. He was busy wrapping up his review of timecards when the limo came to a stop in front of the office.

When Jake, wearing a black, silk shirt with no sleeves, swaggered into the office building with his thug behind him, Tom stopped and looked through the office window. He saw Jake looking around as if he owned the place. Jake's eyes roamed the interior of the office, looking for someone to wait on him. He spotted Tom and headed directly towards the office. Tom stood, looking at this guy with tattoos all up and down his arms. As he made his way to meet Jake and Shamus at the office door, Jake grabbed the door knob and walked right in.

Without a greeting, Jake said, "Where's your boss?"

Tom's look was incredulous. What made this guy think that he wasn't the boss? Tom said, "I'm the shift foreman today. What can I do for you?"

"I got no time for no shift foreman. I want to see the boss. So where is he?"

Tom hesitated again then asked, "Who are you and what do you want?"

Shamus moved a little closer to Jake. The look on his face was a bit sinister. At six feet, five inches tall, and the look of an NFL linebacker, he was intimidating.

Tom figured he'd better not make too much of a fuss or this bozo was going to beat his ass. He wasn't in the mood to get beat up. He already had bruises from his fall down the stairs the previous night. He wondered if these guys had anything to do with that.

A couple of Messier employees hadn't left yet and two of them watched the scene from the parking lot. They slowly made their way to the front door of the office building, keeping an eye on Jake and Shamus. Tom saw them out of the corner of his eyes and figured he could relax a bit. But he was still wary. The guy in the front was obviously the leader and the other guy was just hired muscle, but he didn't need the situation to escalate. He tried a calm approach.

"The owners have left for the day. Is there something I can do for you?"

"Yeah. You can get them on the phone and tell them I want to talk to 'em about a business deal."

"What, you want to buy a home or something?"

Jake snickered as he turned to Shamus. He shook his head, "No, I don't want no damn house. I already got a house. I want to talk with your boss, the owner of this here business. Now, hook us up."

Tom raised his eyebrows in surprise at this cocky, obnoxious punk. He thought he might as well call Jeremy and let him deal with this asshole. He had better things to do. Maybe while Jeremy was busy with this character he could do a little more snooping around and figure out who was putting electronic transmitters in his houses.

"Okay, Mr. . . . what was your name?"

"Jake."

"Okay, Jake. I'll get Mr. Messier on the phone. We'll see if he has time to come talk to you."

With a smile and not just a little arrogance, Jake said, "Oh, he'll come and talk to me. You tell him I have a business proposition that he's gonna love. He'll be here."

Tom sat down at the desk, moved the timecards aside, pulled out his cell phone and tapped out Jeremy's cell number. After four rings, his voicemail picked up. Tom left a message that Jeremy had a visitor at the office and hung up.

"What, that's it?" Jake asked.

"Just give it a minute. Jeremy never answers his cell without screening his calls."

True to Tom's word, his cell rang out an odd chirping tone. Shamus made a face as if Tom's cell ringtone was a bit feminine for a barrel-chested guy like him. Tom answered. "Hey Jeremy, there's a gentleman named Jake here at the office to see you." A pause. "I explained to him that you were gone for the day, but he insisted that I call you. He says he would like to talk with you about a business transaction." Another pause. "I don't think he wants to buy a . . ."

Jake reached out and ripped the cell out of Tom's hand. Tom stood and was about to reach for his phone when Shamus moved between him and his boss. His ribs still hurt like hell from his tumble down the steps and he winced with pain. Tom stopped short then backed up a step. Jake smiled as he looked directly at Tom. In a fake, friendly voice, Jake said, "Hi Jeremy. This is Jake."

By the look on Jake's face, he was enjoying the moment. He listened as Jeremy apparently asked him who the hell he thought he was. Jake let him go on for a few more seconds before he finally said, "Jeremy, are you finished?" Jeremy went on another tirade as Jake held the phone away from his ear and smiled, moving his lips, mocking Jeremy's protests. When Jeremy finally took another breath Jake said into the phone, "Jeremy, listen. I really have a deal for you, but I need to talk with you in person. Can you come back into your office today? Cause if you don't, you're not gonna like the alternative to making a lot of money." Jake held the phone away from his ear again, but there was no protest from the other end.

"Jeremy, my man, you still with us?" A pause. "How soon will you get here?" Another pause. "Great. See you in a bit."

Jake turned to Tom. "You look tired. Go home and get some rest. I don't want to see your face any more tonight. Ya dig?"

Tom just shrugged his shoulders and stood again. As he started to leave, Shamus said, "Mr. O'Connor asked you a question."

In a sarcastic, mocking voice, Tom said, "Sorry, Mr. O'Connor, I was just heading home." He walked past Jake and purposely bumped into Shamus. It was a senseless show of manhood, especially with his sore ribs and bruised arm, but he figured he wouldn't do anything unless Jake gave the order. Shamus flinched as if he was going to take a swing at Tom, but he stopped short. Tom left the office and drove down the road. He made a U-turn and parked off the side of the road in a wooded area on the property next to Messier's property. He walked back towards the offices. He didn't know what he was going to see, but he was going to try to find out what kind of business Jake had in mind.

* * *

It was another twenty minutes before Jeremy Messier pulled his pickup truck into the lot. He took his time. He was in no hurry to talk with this Jake character, whoever he was. He watched the two men through the office building windows. Jake had to be the guy with the bald head and tattoos. The other guy must be his hired muscle. What the hell would this guy want at dinner time on a Tuesday night? Jeremy figured the only way to find out was to ask. So he got out of his truck and walked right in as if he owned the place, which, unlike Jake, he did.

With determined strides and a stern face he said, "I'm Jeremy Messier. Which one of you . . ."

Before he could finish, Jake walked up to him and stood face-to-face with Jeremy. Without cracking a smile he said, "I'm Jake O'Connor and I want to buy your movie business."

Jeremy stared back for as long as he could keep a straight face, then started to smile. After a few seconds his face twisted into dismay. He looked from Jake, to Shamus, then back to Jake. Their faces were stone serious. "Is this some kind of joke?"

"Do I look like I'm the jokin' kind of guy? I want in and I'll make you a fair offer. I'm not gonna go broke payin' for it, but like I said, I'll give you a fair price."

"Well that's mighty white of ya there . . . what was your name again?"

Jake's shoulders sagged a bit as he looked away from Jeremy around the room. His face started to get tight. His hands balled into fists at his side. Then his arms tensed. Shamus thought his boss was going to hit Jeremy.

Jeremy had the same thought as he watched Jake's whole body tense up. He didn't know what to do. If he tried to run, his goon would grab him and hold him while Jake pummeled his face. He was on the verge of turning and dashing for the door when Jake said in a remarkably calm voice, "Look Jeremy. You got a family name to uphold. You don't want to be in the porn business. If you get caught, there'll be hell to pay. You'll lose all that fancy, tight-assed clientele that you have for your home business. Your old man would kill you."

"What do you know about our business?" Jeremy was talking about the home building business. He truly had no idea what other business Jake was offering to buy.

"I've seen it with my own eyes. That high class porn site you guys have. All you have to do is sell it to me and I'm outta here. So, what's it worth to ya to turn it over to me. I'm telling ya it'll be better for all of us. You clean up your act. I get a new business venture that will fit well with my other business ventures."

Jeremy's head was spinning. He had no idea what to say or do. How could he sell a business that he didn't own, especially an internet pornography business? He frequented many sites. Hell, he figured most men in America did, too. But he didn't know anyone who actually ran a site. But that didn't matter. This guy, Jake O'Connor, thought he did and that was an immediate problem. He had to think fast. These guys meant business.

"You want to make an offer? Let's hear it."

Jake smiled, his one gold tooth contrasting against the rest of his whitened chops. "Now we're talking. I did a little research, you see. Your site takes in about one million, five a year." He paused and smiled, thinking that Jeremy would be impressed with his knowledge. Jeremy just listened with a poker face, not a muscle flinching. Jake continued. "But you need to get out of this business real fast, so I'm prepared to give you five hundred G's cash. You hand over all the equipment and admin access to the site. Then you promise to stay out of my business."

Now Jeremy was intrigued. He was being offered half a million dollars cash for a business that he didn't own, had no idea who did, or if it even existed. But the guy was going to cheat him. The "business" supposedly took in over one $1.5 million dollars a year, yet Jake was only offering a third that amount. Obviously this was his first low ball offer. Jake didn't look like a guy who did a lot of negotiating, though.

"So Jake, can I at least take a day or so to think about your offer? I have partners. We'd have to talk about it and see if your offer's good enough."

Jake's smile broadened. He looked at Shamus. He turned back to Jeremy. "I'll give you 48 hours. That means I'll be back Wednesday, right here. You have a decision by then. Make sure it's the right decision. Understand?"

Jake nodded to his body guard to head for the door. Just before they exited Jake turned to Jeremy and said, "I don't like disappointment. Don't disappoint me, Jeremy." He raised his finger in a pistol shape, smiled and jerked his hand back like a recoiling gun. The message was clear.

Chapter 20

Pat was on his first assignment. It wasn't easy, even though he didn't have to do anything physical. He sat in front of a computer in a twelve foot by twelve foot room. It was painted institutional pale green. The only furniture was a table, two chairs and a computer. His job was to watch internet porn. *How tough could it be?* He was no stranger to pornographic movies. When he was stationed aboard the USS *Alabama*, the crew used to regularly watch porn movies on their off-watch time. That was until a number of crew members complained to the captain and the executive officer that they were offended. So the decree came down. No movies containing explicit sex were allowed to be viewed in common areas of the ship. Punishment for offenders would be swift and expensive. To Pat's knowledge, nobody violated the rule.

Pornographic movies were one thing. But what filled the screen in front of Pat was far beyond anything he'd ever seen. The cute little girl in the movie barely had bumps for breasts and no pubic hair. She couldn't have been over twelve. It made him sick to his stomach. The good news was that he only had to connect to the site. Once connected, he started the recording software program. The program was designed to capture the on-screen action as well as the transmission data associated with the host site. The source data was usually blocked by some kind of firewall, but this program had the ability to get through most firewalls. Some porn site owners were less sophisticated than most website designers. Many were coming to the realization that they had the same hacker issues that most site owners had. Someone was always trying to plant a virus or worm in their system.

As Pat clicked the 'Acquire' button to commence the recording portion of the program, Johnny Poleirmo walked into the office. With a straight, serious face he asked, "So how's your first venture into child porn going?"

Pat shook his head. He took a deep breath before he answered. "There are some really sick folks out there."

"Yeah. We've got a lot of work ahead of us. My partner, Rick, has already identified over eight hundred individual sites. Most are located in California."

Pat turned to face Johnny. "So, let's say I get a dozen good, local leads. What's next?"

Johnny had to think. Their plans were pretty sketchy at this early stage of the task force. He had some good notes from Ohio, but this was all new territory for the Orange County Sheriff's Office. The next steps were still not solid. His gut was telling him to just gather the information on the sites and make a raid. Whatever happened they'd learn from it. Then they could adjust and the next raid should go better. But in this business you didn't get brownie points for trial and error. If it didn't go well the first time out, your operation sometimes got bad publicity within the department, and your program was shut down. There was always some liberal, legal group looking to make a name for itself, protecting the first amendment rights of some rich sleaze-ball.

Johnny said, "Here's what I think we're going to do. We get the data and set up surveillance. Then we gather as much evidence as possible. We might have to try to infiltrate the operation to get more evidence first hand. Then we go for the bust."

"Sounds simple enough. How long does all that take?"

"Maybe months. Maybe weeks if we're lucky."

Pat's eyes grew wide. He hadn't thought that it would take that long to get kiddie-porn dealers off the street. "And while we're trying to build this case, some poor little kid's life is destroyed. That's justice for you."

"At least we're starting to do something. We didn't even know where to start a year ago. Now at least we know about the problem and realize how much of a problem it is. But the bigger problem is that this business is growing faster than we can even imagine. If there weren't a bunch of freaks out there willing to pay for this shit, we wouldn't have a problem." Johnny shook his head. "Same thing with drugs, Pat. You've gotta have a market to sell your product."

Pat knew that all too well. He was part of the problem at one time. It had cost him and his family dearly.

As he thought about what Johnny said, the computer made an electronic 'ding'. The recording program was finished. Pat reviewed the instructions for retrieving the file and brought up the screen. It was filled with an electronic form showing the file number assigned to the recording. Other data, like the date and time of the recording, the name of the website with IP address, were also on the form. It had the company name, the owner of the site, and the location of the server. There was additional data such as the number of hits on the site which was in the tens of thousands and the IP addresses of the computers used to visit the site. It had a link to the site and another link to the recorded film. The program worked perfectly.

"Wow. That's awesome. It's also a bit scary. I know we're using this to hunt down bad guys, but it seems to me that this could be used against every day good guys."

Johnny smiled. "Actually, this program was adapted from another program that does just that. It's like a market research tool. It gathers a lot of data on personal shopping and internet usage habits. Law enforcement just recognized that there was a need for this in fighting internet crime." He put his hand on Pat's shoulder and said, "Don't worry, I won't tell your wife about the time you spend on the net."

Pat shook his head. His first step into fighting kiddie-porn was a success. He only had about fifty more sites to visit over the next ten hours. He was already floored at the extent of the problem and they were only scratching the surface.

* * *

Later that evening after Sean and Anna McKinney were tucked away safely in bed, Pat sat down next to Diane on their living room couch. He stretched and yawned. He leaned his head back and stared at the ceiling, noticing the patterns left by some soft bristled brush.   The rosebud pattern always impressed him for some reason. Each rosebud looked like the next, but each had its own slight differences, like snowflakes. He closed his eyes. His mind immediately wandered to some of the images that he saw earlier in the day.   After just a moment of the shocking scene his body jerked and his eyes flew open.

"What's wrong with you?" Diane was staring at Pat with a surprised expression. "You jerked. It shook the whole couch."

Pat gave Diane a worried look. "I have to check on Anna."

"She just got to sleep a few minutes ago. She's fine." Diane put her hand on Pat's left arm and moved closer to him. "You know, you can't let this job get you all wound up. Remember the last time you got too involved?"

Pat didn't want to think about that. It almost got him killed. He said, "This isn't like that case at all. I saw films of the most . . . perverse . . . I can't describe it. Little kids being used like sex toys. How can people be so . . . sick?"

Diane watched Pat agonize over the images. They must have been horrific to be affecting him this way. She said, "Can I fix you anything, glass of iced tea, something stronger maybe?"

"Iced tea would be great as long as its decaf." Pat smiled weakly at his wife. She knew how to distract him when his mind worked overtime. Tonight was going to be a real challenge. He hoped he could get the images out of his head. If not, it was going to be a long night.

* * *

Back in Orlando, Johnny and Rachel Poleirmo were talking about the same subject. The small, three bedroom house with a bath and a half had plenty of room for the two of them. They were saving for a down payment on a larger house, just in case they needed more room. The family room was his favorite place to relax after work, with its wide opening to the lanai. The screened in area off the family room usually allowed a nice breeze to flow through the house and out the front windows. Tonight, the air was a bit stagnant and humid, even for October. The many indoor plants hanging in the screened porch didn't move a bit. It made everything that Johnny and his wife, Rachael touch feel sticky.

He looked across the family room with a blank stare. Johnny had warned his wife that his new assignment was going to be rough. He was afraid it would screw up his brain. During his time in vice he'd seen his share of the underbelly of society. Now, he was diving head-first into the muck.

"It makes you think twice about bringing a baby into a world so full of scum. I'd be petrified to let a child out of my sight."

Rachael brushed a strand of her light blond hair behind her ear. Her expression was tight with concern. "Honey, we've talked about this. Are you changing your mind? If you are, I think you should ask to get out of this assignment. I mean, you've just started and look at what it's doing to you."

Johnny sighed. She was right, as usual. He did promise that they would try to have a baby within the next year. He knew she was ready to be a mom. He also knew that both their parents were bugging them about 'their grandchildren.' He had to change his frame of mind. He had to figure out a way to leave work at work and at least pretend to be normal at home.

He turned towards her on the couch and looked her directly in the eyes. "Baby, I haven't changed my mind. That's just me talking before I think. It'll be okay." He paused. "I just have to remember that I'm doing this to protect the kids." He paused again, then said, "And our kids, when the time is right."

"Well, Johnny Poleirmo, you better get it together."

Rachel took him by the hand and led him to the master bath. The high gloss, peach-colored walls reflected the bright fluorescent light. On the countertop between the double sink sat a home pregnancy kit. The pane in the little window on the handle of the kit clearly showed a plus sign. Rachel picked up the test kit and said, "You're going to be a dad in about eight months."

Johnny's face turned to a broad smile. He hugged his wife tight, kissed her and hugged her again. "When did you find out for sure?"

"Well, I'm not absolutely sure even now. These test kits are pretty accurate, but I'm making an appointment to see the doctor next week. I've been feeling nauseous in the morning for about the last week. I haven't had any flu symptoms or anything else so I figured . . ."

"Rachael Poleirmo. I love you." They hugged and kissed passionately. They made their way into bed and out of their clothes. "Let's make another one," Johnny said, his breathing getting deeper.

"I'm pretty sure we have to have this one first," Rachael giggled a bit. "But I guess we can practice."

And they did, off and on for the next two hours. Later as Johnny relaxed, he watched his wife sleeping. He worried about what the future held for their baby. He didn't like the images playing over and over in his mind. He had one more reason to get these sick bastards off the street. He didn't know if he was up to the task.

He also worried about what kind of father he would be. *Welcome to fatherhood.*

Chapter 21

"Hey Tom, what happened to your arm?" Jeremy noticed that Tom had been holding his arm close to his stomach. He tried hard to keep it in one place as if it were in a sling. Jeremy saw him grimace with obvious pain when he bumped it against a file cabinet. He walked over to his desk and sat down, being careful not to let his arm hit anything else.

"It's nothing. I lost my balance at home the other night. Fell against the wall in the garage. It just hurts when I try to lift too much. No big deal." The truth was, it had been growing steadily more painful since he was pushed down the stairs several nights earlier. The bump on his head was not as noticeable but it still hurt like hell. He wondered whether Jeremy had anything to do with the assault.

"If you need a few days off, don't sweat it. We're not real busy right now. We're between projects since you finished the electrical work on the Paulson house. What was it you were trying to tell me the other day when I was heading out?"

Tom looked at Jeremy and thought *What the hell? What better time to confront him than now?* He took a deep breath and plowed right in. "I found a transmitter in the attic of the Paulson house the other day."

Jeremy frowned. "A transmitter? For what?"

"I don't know. I was hoping you could tell me."

Jeremy's stare became more intense now. He was getting pissed at Tom's innuendo. Tom continued. "This transmitter was spliced into an electric wire. A real sloppy job, I might add. No connection box or wire nuts, just wrapped around the hot and common wires, and taped. None of my electricians would have done that." Tom's stare left no doubt who he thought was behind the work. Jeremy and Aaron were always leaving work early. Tom had no idea where they were going, but he suspected that they might be going to job sites to rig up these transmitters. Even though he only knew of this one, he figured that there were others.

"So you think that I'm behind this?"

Tom shrugged his bulky shoulders. He still had an accusatory stare fixed on Jeremy. "I don't know, Jeremy. Convince me otherwise." After a few seconds of silence, while Jeremy was thinking of a response, Tom continued, "What did that thug, Jake, last night. I asked if I could help him, but he wanted to talk with the boss. He made it perfectly clear that he didn't want to buy a house. He was here for something else." Another pause. "Then there's this transmitter thing. I still can't figure out what it was doing up there. I figured that you would know. I thought maybe Aaron had something to do with it, but I can't even get him to a home site. He is an electronics geek, but I think he's too lazy to do anything like this."

"Maybe the new owners put the thing in. How would I know?"

"Are you guys into anything illegal?"

Jeremy's face turned red as anger seized him. Tom had known him for years, since he was in elementary school. He'd watched the brothers grow up. He'd even helped Jeremy learn about the Electrical Code in Virginia. He'd practically raised Jeremy and Aaron for about a year after their mother, Theo's first wife, disappeared when they were toddlers.

"How can you even ask a question like that? I'm not putting in eighty hour weeks or anything, but I'm not risking my business over something stupid." His stare became even more intense. "Where did you get an idea like that?"

"Because, that Jake guy looks like a slime ball. And he was here to see you. Why else would he be here? Like I said, he wasn't buying a house."

Jeremy had to decide quickly if he'd tell Tom the truth. If he mentioned that it was pornography, would Tom go to the police? Or worse, would he go to Theo? Jeremy broke the intense gaze he'd had on his foreman. He had to choose his next words carefully. He backed away from Tom and sat at the carpentry foreman's desk, several feet from where Tom sat. He drummed his fingers as he looked around the shop floor.

"Here's the deal. Jake, whom I've never met before, wanted to buy my porn business. It sounded like a great offer, but I don't own a porn business. Never have. But he was insistent that I did. So I let him think that I did 'cause of the hired thug he had with him. I figured if I started arguing with him, he'd have the guy beat the shit out of me."

Tom looked at him as if he were hearing a fairy tale. *Like, 'yeah, right.'*

Jeremy continued. "What did you do with the transmitter?"

"I've got it at my house. I haven't touched it since removing it."

"Can I look at it?" Tom gave Jeremy another doubtful look. "Okay, can you describe it to me?"

Tom described the unit to Jeremy and the way it was tied into the electrical wiring at the house. Jeremy seemed to be listening intently. His interest appeared to be genuine. Maybe Tom was wrong about him. He knew Jeremy was kind of a playboy. But being a playboy didn't mean anything criminal.

Jeremy asked, "Do you know what the transmitter was being used for?"

"Nope. I don't have that kind of knowledge. I know electricity, not electronic gadgets."

Jeremy leaned his elbows on the desk and put one hand to his chin, deep in thought. *What the hell is going on? I wonder if this is Aaron's doing? If it is, I'm going to kick his ass. He's putting Dad's whole company, our company, at risk.* He turned to Tom, "We have to figure out if the transmitter and the visit from this Jake character are connected. I know you don't trust me right now, but I have too much to lose if this company's reputation is hurt. Something like this could put us out of business."

Tom was beginning to believe Jeremy. But he wasn't totally convinced. He asked, "Where were you the night before last, a few hours after the shop closed?"

"I was at Tina Jensen's house. We spent the entire evening together. Why?"

"The reason I'm holding my arm like this is somebody pushed me down these steps. It was dark and I didn't see who it was. They left in a big hurry. I thought it might be you."

"What were you doing walking around here in the dark?"   Then he realized that Tom was doing a little investigative work on his own. Someone didn't want him to be snooping around. Then this Jake character shows up wanting to buy a porn business. Something was happening at Messier Homes and Jeremy didn't like it. He had to start paying closer attention to the business and his employees.

"Tom, it isn't me. Whatever is happening here, I'm just as much in the dark as you. Maybe we can work together to figure this out. What do you say?"

Tom gave his boss a look that was less than enthusiastic. But after a moment he agreed. Jeremy reached over to shake his hand, but Tom couldn't straighten his sore arm. He just nodded to indicate that the deal was made. He still had many unanswered questions about the Messier brothers.

* * *

In the control room, the older man frowned. He was listening to the recording of the conversation between Jeremy and Tom. This new partnership might become a problem. Tom had some technical knowledge and wasn't afraid to get dirty. Jeremy was a pretty smart guy even if he was young and liked to party. When he set his mind to something, he usually got what he wanted. The combination of the two was a threat to the business. Then there was this new problem with Jake O'Connor entering the picture. Who could have anticipated that? *Just another obstacle to overcome.*

The young man at the controls looked at his more experienced partner. In a quiet voice, he asked, "What now? What if they figure out what the transmitter's for? We're in trouble."

With an incredulous look, the older man said, "This is just another challenge on the road to great riches. We'll handle these minor problems and learn from the experience. Don't get all excited. You just continue to work those controls. I'll handle Jake, Jeremy, and Tom." The older man's voice exuded confidence. Outwardly, he was calm. But his brain was working overtime to figure out how to address the three problems. Since Tom worked with electricity, that would be the easy one. Jake was a thug. They're always killing each other. His body guard would have to be taken out at the same time. No big loss there.

Jeremy was a different story. He was the owner of a prominent business. Anything that happened to him would be big news. There would surely be an investigation. The story would be on all the major news networks. He'd have to ponder this for a bit. Every problem has a solution. Some are more drastic than others.

"Key up the recording of Jake O'Connor when he visited Jeremy." It took a minute, but the audio of Jake making the offer to Jeremy for the porn business played. Jeremy seemed to be playing along as if he did own an internet porn site. *There's my answer. We just have to arrange a meeting where Jake turns over the money to buy the business. When he finds out there is no business to buy, he's going to be awfully pissed. Pissed enough to kill? A guy like this . . . sure. We'll kill two birds with one stone.*

He looked over at the younger man at the controls. He'd already lost interest in the audio of Jake and Jeremy. He was busy watching a recording. A young, professional couple was having a little afternoon delight on a long lunch break. The live action was being fed out across the country. One thousand one hundred and thirty-nine people were watching the live action. It was a hot afternoon on the SExClub.

* * *

Pat McKinney was given the okay to work on the investigation from home. The door to his office was closed and locked. The sound on the computer was muted. He came across a website that had a particularly difficult firewall. He couldn't get around it no matter which of the tricks he applied. He was hesitant to call Johnny Poleirmo's partner for assistance, but it really bugged him that he couldn't get into the SExClub site. If they had this much protection, what were they hiding? He was about to start over with the firewall defeating software when the phone rang. It was his brother Joe.

"Hey Pat. What are you doing at home?"

"I'm trying to get into a porn site."

"You're a sick bastard."

"It's work, man. You wouldn't believe how sick some of this stuff is. I'll tell you about it sometime, but I don't want to say anything in the house. I don't want the kids to hear."

"I'll bet not."

"I'm a little frustrated with this one site, though. I can't get around their firewall. I was just going to start over with the different firewall busting programs and see if I missed something that should have worked."

"Go ahead. But real quick, the reason I called. Lisa and I are looking at a house in Winter Garden tomorrow. Can you and Diane join us? We could use your help in pointing out things we should avoid."

Pat thought about his schedule. Except for trying to bust porn site operators, his schedule was pretty open. He had a few clients for his consulting business early next week, but nothing tomorrow. "I'll have to check with Diane, but I think we can make it. I'll call you back."

While he was talking, he applied the first firewall busting application to the SExClub site. To Pat's surprise, it worked immediately. The first page gave an elaborate welcome message. It also explained that all the people involved in the movies were willing participants and only wanted to share their experiences with paying customers.

There were three buttons on the screen with mini video displays above each. They were set to provide thirty second samples of the live action. One of the buttons was green, the others were yellow. Pat clicked on the green button and immediately his screen was filled with a couple in the throes of passionate sex. They were both adults, so Pat didn't record the action, but he was mesmerized. He thought about the message that these were not actors, but real people, willing participants. He shook his head and wondered how anyone could willingly expose this very private and personal part of their relationship to total strangers.

"Pat? Are you still with me?" Joe's voice came over the phone.

"Would you and Lisa ever consider going on the internet in a live sex show?"

On Joe's end of the phone, he pulled the receiver away from his ear and stared at it. He couldn't believe Pat's question. "Did I just hear you ask if Lisa and I would be porn stars on the internet?"

"That's not exactly what I meant. I'm looking at a web site right now. It's called the SExClub. Supposedly these couples are willing participants. Their sex is beamed, live, all over the internet. The site is real expensive to join, like almost a thousand bucks a month. They have to be paying these couples to be that expensive. But are people really that crazy?"

Joe knew that people were definitely crazy. When it came to war, they were insane. But if people could be that insane in wartime, what's to say that they couldn't be insane in other ways. "Pat, people are certifiably insane. Now the internet gives them an outlet for their insanity and they think that it's a game. They believe that there's some level of protection by being on the net. Fact is, everyone on the net is real. You're finding out how easy it is to find people with a strange view of reality.

Pat's attention was again drawn to the screen. The couple was changing positions. The action resumed from a different camera, which was slowly zooming in for a close-up. "Man, I've got to get off this case."

"We'll have to put you in sex detox. Don't forget to talk with Diane about tomorrow."

"Tomorrow? Oh yeah, the house. I'll talk with Diane and call you for directions later." Pat's attention was again drawn to the screen. "Wow. I didn't see that coming."

"Go take a cold shower, dude." The phone went to a dial tone.

Chapter 22

"Candy! Look at this! Hurry!" There was an angry edge in Bill Rollins' voice. Candace hadn't heard her husband yell at her like this in ages. He was so easy going that she wondered if he ever got angry about anything. As she entered the room, she could see that his face was red. His whole body was tense. She walked into the master bedroom to see what had Bill so worked up. When she looked at the big screen television, she knew. She gasped.

"She can't be fifteen years old!" She held her hand to her mouth as she viewed the girl on the screen. "She can't be his wife. He's got to be nearly thirty." They looked at each other, wondering what to do next. They were big fans of the SExClub internet site. They were planning another night of hot, passionate sex, but this would send the evening in a completely different direction. Finally they looked back at the screen. Bill's shoulders sagged. He was still angry, but he felt cheated. His emotions were on a roller coaster ride. He was outraged that a young girl was being abused, live on the internet. And there wasn't a thing he could do to stop it. He sat on the edge of their bed and looked around their bedroom, feeling helpless.

In a voice filled with futility, Candace asked, "Honey, what can we do?"

Bill looked back at his wife. For a moment he looked defeated. Then his expression turned to the look he gets when trying to solve a problem. He put his hands on the back of his head as he looked up at the ceiling and took a deep breath. He lowered his eyes, stood, and met his wife's stare. Finally she could see resolve in his gaze. "We're cancelling our subscription and we're threatening legal action, that's what. There's no way that poor girl knows she's on an internet site. Look at her. She doesn't even want to be with this guy."

As they watched, the man on the screen said, "Come on, this'll be fun. Your mom won't be around for a few days. Don't worry about that."

"I'm not worried about that," she said in a nasty tone as she sat on her knees on the bed. She held her arms across her chest, trying to hide her small breasts. All she had on was her panties. Her blouse and pants were thrown over the end of the bed. As she knelt there, she kept her eyes on the man. He was circling the bed slowly, holding a video camera, apparently wanting to get the young girl on film. He obviously intended to record the two of them. "I don't want to do it! You're not going to get me to agree to do this. I especially don't want to do it with you! You're my mom's boyfriend, for God's sake! I can't believe you followed me in here, you sick bastard!"

"Look, Frannie, it'll be fun. You've had sex before, I know you have. I've heard you in your room with Jimmy." This made the girls cheeks flush red with embarrassment and anger.

Bill was still fuming. He said to Candace, "Jimmy must be her boyfriend. I'll bet he doesn't know about this!"

On the screen, Bill and Candace heard the man say, "Just relax and we can both have some fun. You know you want it. Your mom doesn't have to know about it. Just lie back and . . ."

At that moment Bill hit the power button on the huge projection TV and the screen went blank. He turned to Candace and said in a strained voice, "That's it. We're cancelling our membership. There's something going wrong with the management at this site. This is the second time in just a week that they've shown this kind of crap. It's one thing to stage a rape. That's already over the line, but to show an underage girl and her mom's boyfriend?" Bill's voice was getting louder by the minute. He pulled a chair up to the laptop computer. He immediately went to the home page for the

SExClub, clicked on the 'Contact Us' link and typed out a scathing letter. He announced that he and his wife were cancelling their membership. He also wrote that they may seek legal action to have the site shut down. *We didn't sign up for rape and child pornography.* He finished with a second threat of legal action. Then he shut down Internet Explorer and turned off his computer. The mood was blown for the evening.

Around the country, more than seven hundred other members cancelled their membership and threatened the owners of the site with legal action. It would put a significant dent in the income of the owners of the SExClub.

* * *

The mood in the control room was somber. The air was stale, and reeked of moldy food. The trash can was overflowing with garbage, from candy bar wrappers and empty pizza boxes, to used tissues. The older man looked in disgust at the young man at the controls. "Why didn't you shut down the feed? You knew that was outside the rules."

The young controller just sat there and stared at the blank, main screen. The nine smaller screens were filled with a number of prerecorded, popular films. He started to speak, then changed his mind, and didn't say anything. His inaction at the controls was indefensible. He knew that he should have cut the transmission, but he was mesmerized by the young girl. She was beautiful and so innocent. He wanted to reach out to her and help. Of course, there was no way to do that. She was over forty-five miles away in an expensive Messier Home. Her mother was the director of a hugely successful fashion magazine. She was at least eight years senior to her 'boyfriend'. She was also too busy to notice that her boyfriend had lustful eyes for her teenage daughter.

"Are you just going to sit there, or are you going to answer me?" A pause. "Never mind. I want a total count on the number of cancellations by tomorrow. We have to see if this is going to affect our plans, long term." He kept staring at the younger man. "You have to follow the rules! You have to pay attention! I can get a dozen pimple-faced geeks in here to do what you do! I should fire you!"

The young man looked down at the dusty floor of the control room. He still hadn't said a word. He wasn't about to argue.

The older man said in a quiet but stern voice, "Now, clean up this mess. And don't put up any more live feeds tonight. Let's let this simmer down a bit. We'll see if we need to do a sales campaign to build up the clientele again."

With that, the older man opened the door to the control room. He turned one last time to give his young operator a disgusted look and a subtle shake of his head. He closed the door behind him.

The younger man gave the closed door a snarl and the finger. He didn't care what the old man said. He had plans of his own that didn't include him.

He turned back to the screens and selected one of his favorites from those playing. He pressed a few buttons and the video was suddenly playing on the larger screen. He put on a headset and turned the volume up loud. The moans of ecstasy filled his head. He began to rub his crotch through his jeans. His mood immediately improved. Maybe he'd have a nice night after all.

* * *

Pat McKinney had the recording program running when the scene on his computer cut off. He wondered if he got enough information to locate the site and its owners. He watched the computer screen, hoping that he'd acted fast enough to capture the needed data to start tracking these sick bastards. Through his office door he could hear his wife talking to Anna about how pretty her Barbie Doll looked in her new dress. He smiled to himself thinking what a great life he had and wondered what he'd done to deserve it. He also wondered what he'd do if anyone were to take advantage of his daughter. No way would he let a filthy prick like the guy on the screen get away with what he'd done to his girlfriend's daughter.

The monitor changed and the form filled the screen with the website, its owner, address, IP address, and other information. The link to the recording was at the bottom of the form. He clicked the link and hoped that he got enough of the recording to make a case, or at least start an investigation. He noticed the city; Stafford, Virginia. That was as close as he could get. There was no street address listed. He had no idea where that was, so he pulled out his handy Rand McNally Atlas and opened to the index. He found Stafford and took note of the coordinates. When he flipped forward several pages to the map of Virginia, it took just a few seconds to find the small town. The map was too small to show any road details other than Interstate 95 and several state highways. Then Pat remembered a computer website called *Mapquest.com*. He launched the site, typed in the city name and state and a nice map of the city of Stafford was displayed, complete with tools to zoom in and out. He noticed that Courthouse Road was the main, east-west road through Stafford. But it appeared that Stafford covered a fairly large area near the Quantico Marine Corps Base. He realized he'd have to get a better address for this website or they'd never be able to locate the servers and their owners.

Pat picked up the receiver and dialed Johnny Poleirmo's number. Johnny picked up on the second ring. "Poleirmo."

"Johnny, I've got a line on a website that's started to show underage girls being forced to have sex. This site's really different than others I've been watching."

"How's that?"

"For one, the site's expensive. I mean real expensive." Pat emphasized 'real.' "We're talking thousands of dollars a year for a membership." Johnny whistled on the other end of the phone. Pat continued, "The site usually features attractive couples in very tasteful scenes. Supposedly these folks are willingly being watched and transmitted out to the internet."

Johnny frowned. What sane person would allow themselves to be viewed by thousands of complete strangers?

Nothing good could ever come from that. Well, letting people watch you having sex wasn't a crime, at least none that he could think of.

Pat continued. "But tonight, a scene came on where a young girl, maybe fourteen or fifteen came on the screen. She was naked except for panties. From what she was saying, her mom's boyfriend was trying to get her to have sex with him . . . on film. He was chasing her around the bed with a video camera. It didn't look like either of them knew they were being watched by a much larger audience. Then the feed got interrupted, like someone knew that they shouldn't be airing the two of them."

"Did you get anything on recording software?"

"Yeah, I did, but it's from up in Virginia south of DC. Town called Stafford."

Johnny couldn't place the town, but he figured it was a start. He'd have to see if his buddy in Vermilion had any contacts in Eastern Virginia. He wasn't sure if he had the time and energy to spend chasing perverts all along the eastern seaboard, but maybe it would be worth the trip.

"Okay, Pat. Can you e-mail me the file? I'll get on it first thing in the morning."

"Done." Pat had already e-mailed the file. He didn't like this assignment anymore. He thought he'd found a decent site with simple erotic, sensual love-making. Then the site dips into the gutter. It made him feel dirty and he didn't like it.

* * *

Johnny was already dialing the phone for his contact at the Vermilion Police Department. He hoped that he could pass the information along and give some other department a leg up on the site's owner. The sooner these guys were out of business the better.

Chapter 23

"Aaron, where have you been the last couple of days? We have a company to run."

Aaron was looking down at the kitchen floor. He didn't want to work with his brother. He didn't like the home building business. He didn't like being around people. He just wanted to collect his share of the money from the business and be left alone. He continued to ignore his brother.

They were in the kitchen at Aaron's house about 300 yards behind Messier Homes construction offices. The home was separated from the offices by a heavily wooded area and a steep hill. The house was some 200 yards off the access road, which was also hidden by a thick stand of trees. It was isolated from civilization, which was how Aaron liked it.

Jeremy stood, leaning against the kitchen counter. He stared straight at his younger brother, waiting for him to look up. He was getting more pissed as he watched Aaron's body language. He knew his brother was shy. Actually he was an introvert. He rarely spoke with anyone. When he did, it was almost inaudible. It wasn't that he was stupid. On the contrary, he was highly intelligent. His IQ was much higher than his older brother's. But he had no social skills, and no ambition. He was content sitting around the office, looking through magazines and technical manuals on air conditioning units or other household appliances. He would look at the exploded view of the machines, mentally putting the units together in his mind. Once in a while he would laugh out loud at one of his own thoughts. He'd make a suggestion on what would make a dishwasher last longer or work quieter. Jeremy used to watch him read the manuals. He wondered if he really could make these things work better.

"Aaron, are you with me? Earth to Aaron."

"Cut it out, Jeremy. Stop making fun of me."

"Then talk with me, little brother. What's got you so bummed out? Why haven't you been to the office?"

"Because."

"Because why?"

"You'll laugh at me if I tell you."

"Aaron, I promise I won't laugh. Tell me. What's got you so bummed?"

Aaron finally looked up at his brother, then immediately looked away. His gaze lazily wandered around the kitchen, looking at the faded wallpaper, and the dirty stove. He finally stopped looking around when his eyes settled on a picture on the refrigerator. Jeremy followed his stare. The picture was of their mom. It was an old snapshot from nearly twenty-three years before. The picture was faded and cracked. The corners were dog-eared. The colors were mostly gone. Jeremy walked over to the refrigerator to get a closer look. He took the picture off the refrigerator and turned back to Aaron.

"This is what's got you all depressed?" Jeremy had to turn his head and grit his teeth to keep from laughing. He promised he wouldn't, so he thought back on the pain he felt when he read the note that she left. His mood quickly changed to indifference. "Mom's gone, little brother. She didn't want either of us. She didn't want Dad. She was only thinking of herself when she left. Why are you getting worked up over her?"

Aaron's face flushed red with anger, but the color of his cheeks was the only sign. He looked back down at the floor. Without looking up he said, "She didn't leave. Dad made her go away." His quiet voice was tense. "Dad treated her like trash. He forced her to go away." His eyes remained glued to the old, dingy tile.

"Look, Aaron." He held the picture in front of his brother. "Look at this picture. Look at Mom's face. She's happy. I remember when this picture was taken at the park in town. She was happy to be with us." He set the picture on the counter next to Aaron. "Then something happened, and she wasn't happy anymore. Maybe she found another man. Who knows?"

"Don't say that. She wouldn't have gone away with a man. She was happy to be with us. But when Dad was around her, he always made her feel like she wasn't doing enough to help him. Remember? It was always the business. She had to do everything so he could get the business going. She never did enough for him. I think she finally had enough." He looked up at Jeremy for a moment, then back down at the floor. "He made her leave. It was his fault."

"You've got to get over this, man. She's gone. She's not coming back. Just get over it, would ya?" Jeremy turned and walked towards the living room. "Hey. I'm going out for a drink. Want to come along? Maybe you'll meet a girl."

"I don't want to," Aaron mumbled.

"Suit yourself. Be at work in the morning. It'll help you get your mind off Mom."

Aaron looked up and watched as Jeremy left the kitchen, heading towards the front door. He snarled and gave him the finger when he was out of sight. He waited until he heard the door shut then he got up and stretched. He put the picture of his mother back on the refrigerator. He stretched and walked to the living room, looking out the window to make sure his brother was gone. When the taillights of Jeremy's truck were beyond the trees, he headed to the basement of the house to a small room. He had his own work to do.

* * *

Pat moaned at Diane's touch. She was very practiced at running her fingernails over his back with just the right pressure. It was more than a tickle but not quite a scratch. Her nails stopped at a rough spot on his back. It was a familiar spot that she always seemed to find and flick with her fingernail. To Pat it felt good. He moaned again with a low guttural sound. She continued down the middle of his back and stopped at the dimples at the small of his back. With her thumbs she put pressure on the dimples then made a circular motion with both thumbs. After a few minutes, she worked her way up his back again.

"Okay, mister, my turn."

Diane lay down next to Pat, extending her hands above her head. She was naked except her bikini panties. As Pat sat on the lower part of her butt, he began to massage her shoulders and neck. His touch was soft and warm. This time it was Diane's turn to moan. He was being so gentle and sensuous. It had been quite a while since he took this long to get her completely naked. They'd been touching and caressing each other for nearly half an hour now. They were both aroused, their body heat rising with each new stroke of a hand. Pat bent down and kissed her at the base of her neck then slowly traced a path down her backbone to a spot between her shoulder blades. As he lightly licked at her lower backbone, she moaned even deeper.

For the next forty-five minutes, Pat and Diane made love. The intensity and intimacy of the sex was like nothing either of them had ever experienced in their seven years of marriage. They lay next to each other, breathing hard, bathed in sweat, and totally spent.

"When and where did you learn how to do that?" Diane had never experienced an orgasm like that before in her life. She never dreamed making love could be so explosive.

"I can't tell you. My girlfriends will get mad."

Diane tried to look angry as she slapped Pat on the arm. Her smile gave her away. "You tell your girlfriends that I'm going to kick their asses if they come near you." She rolled on her side, facing Pat, placing her hand on his chest. "That was unbelievable. Have you been reading up on how to please a woman or something?"

Pat was hesitant to tell her that he learned it from watching the couples on the SExClub website. But he figured he may as well come clean. He took a deep breath and said, "Well, do you really want to know?"

"Yeah. I really do."

"You know I'm hunting these pervs on the internet. Well, one of the sites I found isn't a kiddie porn site. It's a site where couples are actually sharing their love making on the internet."

Diane frowned. She was thinking that maybe she didn't want to hear anymore. It was one thing to share your sex life with your husband, but to share with complete strangers? And Pat was watching this while he was supposed to be tracking down child molesters. "I'm not sure I like this."

"What do you mean? You said you loved it."

"I'm not talking about the sex. That was something else." She smiled and blushed. "I'm talking about you watching this . . . this stuff . . . on the internet. It can't be good for you. Are you sure you won't become one of those sex addicts?"

Pat smiled. "If I do, I know where to come and get my fix."

Diane smiled but it was strained. "I'm serious. What if you can't stop? What if you end up getting more excited about surfing porn sites than you do about making love with me? I think it happens. Haven't you seen the shows about this on TV? Besides, it's not like you have a real job that takes up your spare time. Remember, idle hands are the devil's playground."

"You don't have to worry about that. Once I finish this assignment I'm not looking at any more of this crap. There's a pretty fine line between erotic and sick. But some folks leap across the line with both feet. There are some pretty sick dudes out there."

Diane looked serious at Pat. "I want you to promise me that you'll quit if you start to feel like you can't stop." She paused and waited for him to answer, then said, "I'm serious."

Pat's playful expression turned serious, too. "I promise."

Diane rested her head on Pat's shoulder and fell asleep in minutes. Pat thought about what Diane said. He could see how men got hooked on porn. It was clearly as addictive as the most powerful drugs on the market. But if you had to overdose on something, this was Pat's drug of choice. He drifted off to sleep with Diane in his arms.

* * *

Joe and Lisa were showering together after an evening of intense love making. They'd spent the evening going over the details of the contract counter offer that they'd received. When they finished and couldn't think of anything else to ask their realtor, they fell into each others' arms. They were pretty sure that they were about to buy a house. Lisa loved the house. Joe liked the house, but he loved Lisa so he would learn to love the house. Pat and Diane were very supportive and helpful during their walkthrough. They made a few recommendations. They thought it might be a good idea to request that the current owners pay for a roof replacement or knock several thousand dollars off the price of the house. In the end, they knew they were going to get a great house for a good price.

Soaking wet, they kissed slowly. They'd been in the shower for so long that the water was getting cool. Finally, they made their way out of the shower. Joe offered to help Lisa towel off, but she declined. They got their robes on and made their way to the apartment living room. They both looked around the apartment with its white walls and dark blue carpet. They both got a sad look on their faces as they realized, if all went well, in a few weeks, they'd be leaving the apartment for good. It was where they had their first kiss. It was where they made love the first time. It was where Joe had proposed.

Joe said, "You know, I think I'm actually going to miss this place."

Lisa leaned over and rested her head on his shoulder. In a quiet voice she said, "Me too. We have so many memories in such a short time." She put her hand inside his robe and rubbed his chest. "Let's go make a few more memories."

Joe leaned over and kissed her on the mouth, the passion rising quickly. They stood and embraced. Lisa stepped on Joe's feet and wrapped her arms around his waist. In small steps, he made his way to the bedroom with Lisa riding his feet. They made love again, for the second time that night.

* * *

The circle was large. Light filtered in and an image was visible though there was no definition to it. The image went black, then came back. After a moment, the image in the circle began to gain definition. It was a person walking back and forth, pacing like a caged animal. As the image became more defined, it changed from varying shades of gray to bright colors. Finally, a face came into view. The face smiled directly at the circle. Several fine lines appeared in the circle, forming a plus sign across the image.

Pat recognized the face. His own smile grew. Then his smile turned to anger and his own face twisted into an ugly snarl. His animal-like emotions took over. He felt the stock of the assault rifle against his shoulder. He felt his finger lightly press on the trigger. As he looked at the face in the circle, it started to laugh, as if mocking Pat. Then he heard a voice.

At first it sounded like an echo in a cave from a great distance. Then the words got louder, clearer. He saw the face of Danny Vallero speaking the words, "Go ahead. What are you waiting for? This is what you've wanted for the past eight years!" The face of Danny Vallero laughed out loud.

The laughing was so loud it began to hurt Pat's ears. He wanted to silence that laughter. He put more pressure on the trigger, but it wouldn't budge. He pulled the stock harder against his shoulder until it hurt. Again he applied more pressure. The gun still would not fire. He looked at the face in the circle again to make sure his aim was still true but the image started to shake, as if his nerves were making the gun barrel vibrate. He took a deep breath and tightened his grip on the gun one more time. He pulled on the trigger with all his might. This time, the hair-pin trigger released with ease. He wondered what caused it to work this time. He looked back in the circle and watched as the bullet sailed slowly towards Danny Vallero's face. It was taking forever. Why wouldn't it speed up? Danny would be able to simply step out of the way at this rate.

But as Pat watched, Danny continued to laugh until the bullet was right in front of his forehead. Only then did he say with cartoon-like alarm, "Uh-oh." In an instant, Danny's head exploded. It was no longer in slow motion. The sudden shift back to real time startled Pat. He sat bolt upright in bed, sweat pouring from his body, his skin, pasty white. Dazed, it took him a moment to realize that he was still in bed, next to Diane. His head throbbed from the tension of the dream.

Pat got out of bed and made his way to the bathroom. He quietly closed the door and flipped on the light. From the medicine cabinet, he grabbed a bottle of pills. When he noticed that they were aspirin, he put them back and reached for the next bottle. He popped open the bottle of Excedrin PM, shook two out into his hand, then washed them down with a cup of water. He stared at his image in the mirror. He was alarmed at the ghostly image looking back at him. He finally understood that professional help was his only real option. It was just a matter of time before these dreams would drive him insane, or worse, to his grave.

This time, Diane remained asleep through the entire episode. But this wouldn't be the last dream. They were becoming more frequent and more vivid.

* * *

They slept in the next morning until the phone rang. It was Pat.

"Hey, Joe, rise and shine. You're sleeping the whole day away."

"Pat, we don't have kids. We don't have to get up at the crack of dawn."

"Well, you have to get up, because we have to make plans. We're going to be perv busters. So put your thinking cap on. I'm coming over."

"Great. What time will you be getting here?"

Pat yawned after his rough night, then smiled to himself and said, "In about two minutes. I'm calling from my new cell phone. I'm just down the street."

"Bastard. Take your time. We have to get dressed."

Chapter 24

"Nelson, I'm sorry." Jillian Rockledge's face was drawn. The dark circles under her eyes were pronounced. Even with the liberal amount of make-up that she'd applied, the lines of anxiety were etched around her eyes.

Nelson's expression was sympathetic. "Oh, Baby. You don't have anything to be sorry about." Nelson stood up from the overstuffed lounge chair where he'd been watching the news. He'd been watching the television, but it was just a distraction in an attempt to relieve his own tension. He'd been trying to think of anything that he could do to remove his wife's cloud of shame and guilt. None of this was her fault. She didn't ask to be raped. If anything, Nelson felt it was his fault for not being home to protect her. He closed the space between them and slowly, cautiously, put his arms around his wife. He felt her tension, but he also felt her begin to relax for the first time in nearly two weeks. They were making progress.

As he lightly stroked Jillian's back he repeated, "You don't have anything to be sorry about. If anyone is to blame, it's me. I should never have left you home alone. We're in the middle of nowhere. We don't have any neighbors." He paused but she remained silent. Then he continued, "I've been thinking, maybe we should sell the house and . . ."

She started to protest but Nelson stopped her. "Hear me out, sweetheart. I love the house, too, but this thing; this mood. It will always haunt us as long as we live out here. Why don't we get a condo closer to town? We can find a gated community with a guard. Everyone would have to have a password or a keycard to get in."

Jillian lifted her head off of his shoulder and looked her husband in the eyes. "You'd do that for me?"

"I'd do that for us." They looked lovingly into each other's eyes for a long moment then hugged tighter. Jillian started to quietly cry onto Nelson's shoulder and held him tighter. Nelson could again feel her tension and anxiety melt away. She kissed him lightly on the lips. She again rested her head back on his shoulder. He wanted so much to kiss her hard on the lips. He could feel his own passion building. He was fearful that if he pushed too hard, she'd tense up again, and move back into her mental shell. He held her tight for a long while, still stroking her hair and back ever so lightly.

Then she slowly lifted her head and kissed Nelson again. It was still a light kiss but this time, with more passion. He kissed her back with intensity. They were soon moving their hands over one another like starved lovers. Nelson's fear of her retreating to the dark recesses of her mind was now gone. He was still trying to make sure their progress down this road was slow and methodical, but she would have none of it. Her kisses were deeper and more passionate with each passing moment. The next few minutes were a blur as they found themselves in the master bedroom. Jillian hesitated for just a second as they made their way to the king sized bed.

The room had been totally remodeled over the past week. A new bed was in place and the furniture was placed in a totally different arrangement. It looked like a completely different room from the one in which Jillian had been raped. Still, Nelson was afraid of the ghosts that might assault her mind. He didn't know if she could get past such a traumatic violation of her life.

If Jillian had any such thoughts, they were being suppressed deep in her mind. She helped her husband undress and tossed his clothes, one by one, across the room in an uncaring manner. When he was down to his boxers, she stood up in front of him and said, "Your turn."

Nelson slowly undressed his wife, stopping to lightly kiss, lick, and caress every inch of flesh. When she was finally down to her panties, they both lay down on the bed, their passion replacing their fears.

* * *

Roger Tremper and Gerry Alberts waited for Aaron Messier in the kitchen of his ranch style house. The place was a mess. There was a strong odor of burned grease mixed with spoiled food throughout the house. The counter was strewn with food crumbs and stains from coffee or soda. The sink was stacked high with dirty dishes. Aaron said that they should make themselves at home, so they grabbed a couple of beers from the refrigerator. They sat on stools and watched television. There was nothing on but bad comedies with canned laughter. Once in a while Roger would chuckle at a one-liner but they mostly sat quietly and drank.

"What's taking him so damn long? We said we'd be here at 9:00 and we're here. Where the hell is he?" Roger was growing impatient. He was thinking about leaving, but then thought about the amount of money they made from these rich folks. Fencing the stuff was easy, too. So he finished one beer and went to the refrigerator for another.

Gerry was getting antsy, too. "Grab me another one while you're up. I'll sit here all night and drink his beer, but he needs to get his ass out here. What's taking him so long?"

"Planning takes time." Aaron came into the kitchen from the basement stairs in the hallway. He must have been in the basement the entire time. He looked at the empty beer bottles and said, "Looks like you guys have been passing the time alright."

"Yeah. Well you said 9:00 and we've been here since 9:00. Where've you been?"

"I told you, doing research." Aaron looked from one to the other. He was a different person around Roger and Gerry. He felt superior to them. He felt confident. It wasn't like being around his dad or Jeremy. They always looked down on him. Not so with these two losers. He was in charge now. He was giving the orders. He said, "Let's get to work."

They were at the kitchen table drinking beer and taking notes.   Aaron was talking, describing the layout of the Kirkwood home. The Kirkwoods were planning a three week trip around the country. They had no animals, no kids, and no relatives in the immediate area. They depended on a security company from North Carolina who had very little local support, and therefore, very slow response times. Besides, the Messiers installed the security devices for the company. Aaron knew all the details about the system's strengths and weaknesses. It would be a piece of cake to break into the house, undetected, even for the likes of Roger and Gerry.

"So you're telling me that all we have to do is go around back, set this magnet by the keypad at the back door and the alarm won't sound. I'm not sure I'm buying this." Roger's tone was skeptical, at best.

"Look, have I ever steered you wrong?"

"Well, now that you mention it, yeah. That last deal was a real screw-up. That lady almost caught us red handed. We almost didn't get out before she saw us." Roger managed to keep a straight face. He told a bold-faced lie, and Aaron knew it. He had it on tape. Not only did Jillian Rockledge see them, she felt them in the most degrading way possible.

"You made it out without her knowing, right?"

"Well, yeah. I don't think she suspected a thing. Ain't that right Gerry?"

Gerry turned his head away from Roger and Aaron. He couldn't stand Roger lying. They were professional thieves. Gerry hated Roger for taking them to a whole new criminal level. Sure, stealing was bad. But that was just stuff. All that expensive junk can be replaced. Those rich folks always have plenty of insurance. They probably got more from insurance than the stuff was worth in the first place. But rape? That's a whole new ballgame. He actually felt bad for the woman. He felt guilty for taking part in the rape. But he was so damned excited at the time that he couldn't help himself. He'd never seen a naked woman that perfect in real life. She could have been a centerfold in any of those magazines he liked. Plus, Roger egged him on. It was his fault.

"That's right. She never suspected a thing." The lie came out smooth as silk. Gerry was committed. He would always have to remember that he swore the woman never saw either of them. "Let's get back to this job. We have a lot to do and not much time. So, just how rich are these Kirkwoods?"

Aaron smiled. This was unusual for him. He normally didn't show any emotion during these planning sessions. If he was smiling, then there was something special about this job. "The Kirkwoods are, what you call, filthy rich. They have a lot of stuff, but we're not going after that crap. They have a safe in the house that is loaded with cash."

Roger and Gerry's faces lit up. They liked the sound of cash. It would be easier to handle and it would be impossible to trace. Roger sat up straight on the bar stool, took a pull on his long neck beer bottle, and rubbed his hands together. "When can we do this job?"

Aaron set his own beer bottle down and said, "They left this afternoon. We can get started this evening. I think it might take two trips to haul all the cash out."

"Wait a minute. Isn't that risky? I mean, what if someone sees us go in the first time? They might be waiting for us the second trip in." Gerry was worried about the two trip plan. He knew that just about anything could go wrong, even in a simple job. Making two trips just multiplied the chances of getting caught.

"Hey, twice the risk, twice the reward. Trust me. This isn't going to be risky. It's a piece of cake. This house is so isolated that nobody's going to know about it. We could camp out there for days and no one would be the wiser." Aaron looked at his two accomplices. "Relax, fellas. This is going to be our best job yet."

The smiles slowly returned to Roger and Gerry's faces. They were counting their money before they even finished their third beer.

* * *

Nelson and Jillian made love for over an hour. They built up each other's confidence, taking their passion to levels that even they'd never achieved before. Nelson's fears about his wife's mental state had faded very early in the heat of their lovemaking. At first, he was cautious. Then he was relieved. Now he was confident. He had his wife back.

Jillian was feeling passion again for the first time in nearly two weeks. She'd been afraid to approach Nelson, fearful that she might not be able to perform without shrinking away in fear. Nelson had been so gentle, taking his time, not trying to move too fast. He was firm, but in a way that made her feel protected, shielded from harm. He was her knight. He assured her that she was safe. Her body and mind released emotions and energy that had been bottled up. The result was like a chemical reaction that built up tremendous energy. It was a sustained reaction that emitted heat, but didn't burn itself out.

After they both climaxed for the second time, they lay back exhausted, still holding each other tight. Their eyes glazed over, their smiles wide in post sexual bliss, Nelson started to speak. Jillian put her finger up to his lips. She wanted the first words.

"You saved my life tonight. I mean, I wasn't sure I would ever be able to make love again. You fixed that. You made me feel whole again. I can't . . . I can't thank you enough." Tears formed in Jillian's eyes. They fell on the pillow as Nelson tried to wipe them away with his thumbs. She smiled through her tears.

Nelson embraced her and held her tight, wishing to put a force-field around her. He wished he could stay with her and protect her twenty-four hours a day, but he knew that wasn't to be. He said, "I thought I'd lost you. I can't imagine what you've been through. I can promise you this though; I'll do everything in my power to protect you. If that means we have to move, then we'll move. If that means leaving the state, or the country, then we will. All this stuff," he made a gesture with his arm, "it can be replaced." He held her a bit tighter.

"You can't be replaced. Ever. Whatever it takes, we're going to make sure nothing like this ever happens again."

With that, they kissed. Then the kiss became more passionate. Before they knew it, they were making love a third time.

* * *

Tears of joy were falling. Their love making was passionate. Hundreds of couples across the country were cheering out loud in their own bedrooms. Nelson and Jillian's most private triumph was shared with thousands of people across the country on the internet. Jillian was still being violated. She just didn't know it.

Chapter 25

Joe sat on the leather couch in Pat's home office. They were discussing the kiddie porn case. He was leaning back, looking up at the ceiling, frustration plastered on his face. Pat had turned off the loaner computer that he was using for the investigation. He couldn't stand to look at any more sites for the time being. The images of children being abused were too depressing.

"I know that the law says everybody deserves due process, but this is ridiculous. By the time you gather all this evidence, these sick bastards are closing up shop and moving on."

Joe was agitated. Pat had gone through the plan that Johnny Poleirmo said they needed to follow in order to build a case against the operators of kiddie porn sites. Joe couldn't believe it. No wonder the porn business was exploding. There wasn't much risk of getting caught. By the time the cops find out who the site operators are, they shut down their websites and move on. With the kind of money they made, it was nothing at all to abandon the site, erase any tracks that led to them and start anew. Heaven knows, there's plenty of material out there in cyber-land to sell. Apparently there were plenty of customers, too.

Joe was red in the face. His temples were pulsing, and his square jaw was jutted out. It had been a while since Pat had seen him this angry. "So what would you do?" Pat's question didn't help calm Joe. He knew it would only serve to anger him even more.

After a moment, Joe said, "Right now? I'm afraid I'd just kill 'em myself. That would be quicker and more efficient.

It'd save a lot of time and taxpayer's money, and probably save some kids' lives."

Pat smiled slightly as he said, "And it would make you a murderer. So how are we any better than them? What if the anti-drug people took that attitude with us when we were dealing? We might not be having this conversation, 'cause we'd be dead."

"True, but at least we weren't using little kids as sex toys. We sold a little grass, Pat. That's a whole lot different than what these pricks are doing. They're destroying little kids lives."

"Some folks would say that we did, too."

Pat agreed with his younger brother, but he knew that not everyone else felt that way. There were plenty of people who viewed drug use, even marijuana use, in the same light as child pornography. Pat and Joe got out of the drug trade and got their lives back on track. It wasn't easy and people died, including their own brother and sister-in-law. They had intended to take the law into their own hands, but fate intervened. Pat still had blood on his hands. He lived with the knowledge that there was no statute of limitations on murder, though he considered his actions to be self defense. He had to protect his family. If he'd have let those monsters who betrayed his family live, he wouldn't have been able to look himself in the mirror. He was only directly responsible for one death. It haunted his nights. Even though the score was settled, he still had nightmares. He would see one of his former enemy's faces through the scope of a rifle. The face would appear in the crosshairs of the scope. Then he'd feel the recoil of the powerful rifle. The scene in the scope was always the same. The head would explode as if a bomb had detonated. Pat would wake up yelling, his body drenched in sweat.

Usually, Diane would sleep through the episode, but on a number of occasions she would wake up and ask Pat what was wrong. He'd try to explain with a half truth, that he was having a nightmare. When she pressed for details he would always say that he couldn't remember. He knew that if the dreams continued, he'd have to get professional help. Worse, he knew he couldn't tell Diane about the source of his nightmare. She knew about the pot dealing, but the rest of the story would have to go with him to his grave.

Joe broke into his thoughts. "You know, when we had those problems with our old business partners, we planned to take care of them ourselves. What's so different about this? Why shouldn't we shoot these bastards and be done with it?"

"For one thing, this isn't personal. These people, no matter how sick they are, haven't done anything to us." Joe shrugged his shoulders as if to say '*So what*'. "Second, we've got a clean slate. We don't want to screw that up. Third, we're not paid killers. We both may have killed in the past, but we're not in the past."

"Okay. But there's got to be a better way than this. We'll spend too much time building a case. These guys will pack up shop and head for another town. Hell, they don't even have to leave town. They just set up business under a different name. They'd probably be back in business before the ink dried on the investigation."

Pat listened to Joe's reasoning and had to agree. There had to be a better way to nail these guys. A long, drawn out investigation just wasn't going to cut it. Besides, he wasn't sure how long Diane would put up with him being on this investigative team. Even worse, he didn't know how long he could stand looking at these poor children being abused.

Pat asked, "Alright, what's your idea to sting these guys? How do you make it short and make it stick in court?"

"I don't know. I'm no legal scholar, but I know we can come up with something. There's got to be some law that we can throw at them to put them out of business for good. But we also have to protect these kids. It must kill you to have to see these kids on these websites."

Without saying a word, Pat nodded his head. The vivid images invaded his mind even when he wasn't performing searches for the illegal sites. What Diane had warned him about, was happening very quickly. He knew he wouldn't be able to last long on this job. It was like a virus invading his mind.

He shook his head and said, "We'd better put a plan together fast. My brain can't take this much longer. Do you have any ideas at all?"

Joe thought for a minute, but no flashes of brilliance hit him. He asked, "Is the prosecuting attorney on the investigative team?"

"Not officially. He does get advised of any progress. He was the one who set the minimum requirements for a bust."

"Somebody should tell him that he'll never bust anyone with these guidelines." Joe thought for a moment then said, "Maybe that's it. They're just guidelines. If you can make arrests, show the perps the overwhelming evidence, and get confessions, maybe we can show the prosecuting attorney that he doesn't need this drawn out process."

Pat raised an eyebrow at Joe's logic. It might work. But the powers that be have been doing this for a long time. If they felt an over-abundance of evidence was needed, then maybe it was. It just seemed like overkill. In the mean time, kids were being exploited. What a balancing act between the rights of honest citizens, and protecting those citizens from thugs who are abusing the system. No wonder vigilante groups sprung up from time to time.

Pat said, "All we can do is talk to Johnny. It's his investigation. Maybe he'll run the idea up the chain of command and see what the higher ups think. My guess is that they'll shrug it off and go with the original plan." Pat's expression didn't give Joe much reason for optimism. But he didn't have any better ideas at the moment.

He said, "I've gotta go. I'm meeting Lisa at the apartment. We've made the final counter offer on the house. We're so close that it's pretty much a done deal. We're just waiting to see if the owners will accept it. If they come back and turn down the counter, we can live with it. I'm getting a little nervous. So is Lisa." He paused and looked off into space as if he were thinking of the details of the contract.

"Listen, Joe. You just have to take the plunge. Trust me, you're getting a great deal and it'll work out fine." He stood and walked over to his younger brother, put a hand on his shoulder, and said, "Let me know how everything goes with the counter offer. Relax, Lisa is gonna love you for this."

Joe nodded, then stood and headed for the office door. Pat stopped him saying, "If you get any other ideas on how to bust these guys, call me. I'm with you. There's got to be a better way."

"I keep coming back to the easy solution." Joe made a pistol shape with his right hand and made a fake shot at Pat's computer. He smiled and walked out. Pat heard him say goodbye to Diane. He then heard him say to Sean and Anna, "Come here, kids. Give Uncle Joe a big hug." As Pat looked down the hallway, Anna jumped into Joe's waiting arms.

Sean walked over to his uncle and while smiling said, "Here's your hug, mister." He punched Joe's arm.

Joe made a face with an exaggerated look of pain. "Hey, watch it, Mr. Tough Guy. You might hurt somebody with those fists. Are they registered as lethal weapons?"

Sean laughed.

Pat's eyes watered slightly watching his brother and his kids. He wondered what he'd ever do to anyone who took advantage of his children. Then he thought, *'Maybe Joe's right. Maybe we should all take this personally.'*

* * *

Later that evening, when the kids were in bed, Diane and Pat were sitting alone in the living room, watching television. Diane was wearing shorts and a tank top. Pat wore jeans and a *Brian Purcer and the Hot Licks* tee shirt. The air in the room was a comfortable seventy-two degrees. Pat's attention wasn't on the TV program because he was also reading notes from some of the websites that he'd found. He wanted to make sure the paperwork was in order before he turned it over to Johnny Poleirmo the next day.

Diane was watching Pat as he frowned from page to page. As he read through the papers he subconsciously rubbed the scar on his chin. She knew he was deep in thought and not paying attention to the TV show at all. She was worried that Pat was, once again, getting too personal with another investigation. It frightened her.

She got up and walked over to the couch where he was working. He looked up from the paper he was holding with a quizzical look. Diane asked in a soothing voice, "Can I get you anything? Glass of iced tea, cup of coffee?"

"A tall glass of tea would be nice. Thanks."

"Is there anything else? I don't want to disturb you, but you didn't eat much at supper. Can I fix you a sandwich or a piece of that apple pie?"

Pat set the papers down. He stopped rubbing his scar and looked at Diane. "Sit down for a second." Pat's face remained serious, the lines on his forehead pronounced. "I'm not sure I can stay on this case much longer."

Diane's heart and mind gave a sigh, while her outward expression remained unchanged. Pat continued, "I can't believe how big this problem is. I feel like it doesn't matter what I do, the problem won't go away. It's like trying to drain the ocean with a sump pump." The look of frustration on Pat's face intensified. He sat back on the couch and let out a long sigh.

Diane stood directly in front of him. She picked up the stack of papers and dropped them on the floor next to the couch. She put a knee on either side of his legs and straddled him. She put her arms around his neck and lightly kissed him on the lips. She ran her hands through his thinning hair then rubbed his tense shoulders.

"You can't fix everything, even though you'd like to. There are some problems that even the mighty Pat McKinney can't fix."

Pat smiled up at Diane. He put his hands on her legs and rubbed lightly. He knew she was trying to distract him, to relieve some of the tension.

"Is it that obvious? Am I really that stressed?"

"Oh, yeah. When you start rubbing that damn scar and your forehead looks like a washboard, it is that obvious. Besides I've got another sign. When were you going to tell me that Joe and Lisa are in the final stages of buying that house?"

Pat looked confused. "Didn't I tell you? Joe told me this morning right before he left."

"Well, after Joe left this morning, Lisa called. She said that the realtor was coming over with the signed papers when Joe got back to the apartment. Lisa called a little over an hour ago and said they signed the agreement. They're prequalified, so it's pretty much a done deal." She leaned in closer to Pat's face and whispered, "I can't believe you didn't hear the phone."

Pat frowned. He didn't remember the phone ringing earlier, but he was searching child porn websites after Joe left. Was he so engrossed that he didn't hear the phone ring? That was a scary thought.

Pat looked back at Diane and asked, "So did you get any other details?"

"Nothing big, just that they want us to take another tour. This time to help them pick out paint, wallpaper, appliances, stuff like that." Diane held Pat's face in both hands and asked, "Can you tear yourself away from your investigation long enough to go do that?"

"Sure. I need a break anyway."

"Ready for that pie and iced tea?" Diane started to get up but Pat held onto her legs.

With a broad, devious smile Pat asked, "Why don't we have a different treat first? I need to relax, remember? I'm supposed to eat less and get more exercise. Your orders, right?"

"Maybe we can hold off on the pie." Diane leaned over and kissed Pat lightly on the lips and lingered there. Within minutes, their kisses were molten hot.

Diane whispered, "We either need to move to the bedroom or risk getting caught by the kids."

With that, Pat clicked off the television with the remote and stood, picking Diane up as he did. She giggled quietly and wrapped her legs around his waist. Somehow, they made it to the bedroom. They skipped iced tea and apple pie, and they did burn a lot of calories.

Chapter 26

Even though they'd threatened to cancel their membership twice, Bill and Candace were back on the SExClub looking for action. They talked about their threat and decided that they'd give the company one last chance to get their act together. After all, everyone makes mistakes. So Bill opened up the site, half expecting it to be closed down. To his surprise, the site was operating, business as usual.

"Candy, are you coming up? It looks like there are several great choices tonight." Bill was laying on his stomach, screening the live streaming sex options for tonight's love making on the SeXClub. The bedroom lights were already turned down low. Bill wanted the mood to be smoldering hot. He was afraid the evening would be awkward. He and Candace were skeptical about whether the site would go back to their advertised classy air or if they'd continue the slide into common smut. But they were ready to give it another chance. They'd always enjoyed the stimulation that the internet site provided.

Bill was already in a dark-colored, thin robe with nothing on underneath. He was relaxed as he tapped his finger on the touchpad, moving the pointer around the screen, selecting different previews. He turned his head and was about to yell to Candace again when she appeared at the bedroom door. Apparently she was ready, too. She wore a very sheer, short negligee, matching thong panties, and a smile.

Bill looked her over from head to toe, and everything in between. His attention was now completely focused on his wife. His wide, sly smile told Candace that he approved of her choice of evening wear. She slowly moved towards the bed.

When she laid down beside him, she lightly rubbed a shoulder against his. "Are you sure you want to watch this tonight?" Bill nodded towards the image on the big screen.

"I'm pretty horny already, but I'll bet we can make this the hottest night ever." She reached back and ran a finger softly up one leg from just behind his knee. She stopped just short of his rear end.

A shiver of anticipation ran down Bill's spine. His smile widened. He said, "Well let me show you the candidates. First we have a lovely, thin brunette and her muscular husband. These two have to be professionals. Just look at them. They have perfect bodies."

Candace looked them over as they started to slowly caress each other. There was no doubt that they'd put on quite a show, but Candace wanted to see the other couples. Bill went through two more before he came to a blond woman and her tall partner. He seemed a bit awkward as they moved towards their bed. She was shorter and beautiful. She threw her hair back, and a close up of her face shown on the screen. Candace thought that she recognized the woman just as Bill tapped on the touchpad to switch to another couple.

"Wait, back up to the last couple."

"Why, you like the tall dorky guy?"

With a bit of annoyance in her voice she said, "No. Just do it."

"Okay." Bill did as requested, wondering what had grabbed his wife's attention.

The couple on the screen was completely naked. They were just getting into serious foreplay when Candace saw the woman's face again, this time just briefly. "It can't be." Candace was concentrating on the screen more intently. Her face was an odd combination of a smile with disbelief. She'd stopped touching Bill altogether. She got out of bed and approached the big screen TV to get a closer look. She got too close and had to back off so the image didn't appear distorted. Finally, the young blond lay on her back and looked almost directly at the camera. "It is! That's Jody Owen! I don't believe it."

Bill looked closely at the screen. Candace was right. It was Jody Owen and her boyfriend. He thought they were probably married by now. Candace and Jody were classmates in college at The Ohio State University. Jody was in love with this nerd, Charlie Williams. Charlie was a computer whiz, and a tinkerer. He would toy with different things, and tell you how something could be improved. Everybody used to tease him about it, but they could see that he was probably right about the different ideas he had. He took everyone's ribbing with a smile and a shrug of his shoulders. More than one of Charlie's friends said that he was going to be a millionaire one day. From the looks of the bedroom, he must have made his mark.

But here he was, on the internet, with his girlfriend, or wife, treating everybody to a night of sex. Bill looked at his wife as she stared at the screen. She turned to Bill and said, "This isn't right. There's no way that Jody would agree to this. She was so shy in college that she wouldn't even change into her bathing suit in front of us at the gym. That was in the girl's locker room." She turned again and looked at the screen. "I'll bet she doesn't know."

"How could she not know? I mean, the cameras have to be right in front of her." Bill looked at his wife as if she had two heads. "I mean, look at the different angles. There has to be at least six cameras in the room."

"I don't care if there are a hundred. She wouldn't do this. Hell, look at us. We're wilder than any of our friends, and we wouldn't do this." Bill slyly smiled at his wife, as if maybe he might. She said, "Sure, you think you would now when there're no cameras around. You put a couple of cameras in here and see how open and free we are." Bill's smile faded a bit, and he shrugged his shoulders. She was right. He was all talk in private, but no way would he expose himself and his wife, like the couples on the SExClub.

"I have an idea." Candace left the bedroom and grabbed her purse. She came back in with her cell phone.

"Candy, what are you up to?"

"I'm calling her right now."

"You have her phone number?"

"Yep. I've had it since college. I called her a couple of years ago. I was going to be in Ohio for work, remember? I hoped we could meet for dinner. She'd already left for Georgia. She was living with Charlie by the sub base just north of Jacksonville. She gave me her new cell number and said to call anytime. This is anytime, isn't it?"

Candace dialed Jody's number. There was a delay. She thought that she might not have the right number, or maybe Jody's phone was off. Then she heard the phone ring in her ear. A moment later, an electronic sound could be heard coming from the big screen's speakers. Candace let the phone ring six times when voice mail kicked in. She hung up and immediately dialed again. Once again the phone rang in her ear, followed by the electronic ring on the screen.

On the big screen, Jody paused for a moment, then ignored the annoying sound. But Candace was not to be deterred. She dialed a third time.

This time, Jody stopped. She said to Charles, "I have to get that. It might be Mom. She said she wasn't feeling well earlier."

Charles rolled off Jody and lay on his back. He moaned, expressing his disappointment. He rolled his eyes and said, "Okay. Just remember where we were." He stared at the ceiling, as if he were analyzing something.

Jody grabbed her purse and pulled her cell phone out. Just then the phone went to voice mail. Candace swore. She quickly dialed again. Jody was about to turn her phone off when it rang for the forth time. She looked at the display and didn't immediately recognize the incoming number. Then she smiled and flipped the phone open.

"This better be good, girl."

"Oh, believe me, it is. I'd ask what you were up to but I already know." She paused for so long that Jody thought she disconnected. "So what's a nice girl like you doing on the internet?"

Jody was puzzled by the question. She asked, "What do you mean?"

Candace paused again, not knowing exactly what to say. Bill said, "You better just tell her. You've gone this far."

She took a deep breath and said, "Jody, Dear, I'm watching you on the internet right now. Bill and I both are."

Jody still didn't understand. She asked, "What, am I on the news or something? You know, Charlie invented this thing for submarines and . . ."

Candace cut her off. "No, Dear. We're watching you live . . . on a porn website. You and Charlie."

Jody's expression turned to bewilderment. Then she smiled. "You're kidding, right? This is a joke. Good one, Candy."

"Jody, do something. Hold up a couple of fingers, or whatever you want. I'll tell you what you're doing." In the background, Bill and Candace could see Charlie turn on his side and look towards Jody. He was frowning. He didn't know what was going on, but he could tell that the call was getting serious.

Jody held up her hand and displayed five fingers. She said into the phone, "How many fingers am I holding up?"

"Five." There was no hesitation in Candace's answer. Jody turned around to face Charlie with a look of alarm. "Now you're facing Charlie." Candace told Jody each move she made over the next fifteen seconds, including walking over to the dresser and picking up a gold necklace.

"How are you seeing this? There aren't any cameras in here."

Candace said, "Look up and to the right." Jody did. "Too far to the right. Look left about a foot." Jody appeared to be looking right into the camera. "What do you see?"

"Nothing. Just the ceiling, the wall, and the ceiling molding. Charlie, come over here and help me."

"What are we looking for, Dear?"

"A camera." Charlie looked at his wife in disbelief. "Are you serious?"

"Deadly."

* * *

The control room sat empty while the operator went to take a bathroom break. He was gone for a full fifteen minutes. He was reaching for the control room door when the doorbell rang. He stopped and looked at the security monitor. It was Jeremy Messier. *What the hell does he want?* The controller thought for a minute and decided that he needed to let him in. He bounded up the steps of the basement and headed for the front door. He opened it and said, "Hey, what's up?"

"Nothing much, little brother. I just wanted to see if you were planning to come into work tomorrow. I also wanted to apologize for some of my comments the other night."

Aaron Messier, the controller, didn't want to spend a lot of time chatting with Jeremy, but he really had little choice. He couldn't think of anything that would send him away. He couldn't say he was going out, because he never went out. So, he decided to make as little conversation as possible. Maybe that would bore Jeremy, and he'd leave.

But Jeremy brought a bag out from behind him. "How about a beer, as a peace offering. I said some pretty harsh things about Mom the other night. I've been thinking about her, and I shouldn't have said that stuff."

Aaron looked down at the carpet in the living room, and quietly said, "Don't worry about it. I know you didn't mean that crap."

Jeremy thought for a minute. He said, "It's not that I didn't mean it. I just shouldn't have said it. I know you think Mom was some kind of angel." He realized that Aaron was becoming agitated so he quickly added, "Look, I'm sorry. I don't want to start another fight. Let's just shake, and agree to disagree. Okay?"

Jeremy held out an open beer to his brother. He grabbed the bottle, and took a deep pull on the beer. It tasted good, and went down easy. Jeremy held out his bottle for a toast. They clinked bottlenecks. They both took deep drinks. As they drank, Aaron worried about what was happening on the SExClub. He'd already screwed up twice in the last week. He couldn't afford another mistake. His partner would have his ass.

* * *

Charlie stood on a chair in the bedroom, trying to find the camera that was supposed to be right in front of him. All he saw was dark ceiling molding. The deep grooves were intricately carved. The overlap of one piece to another was so well done that the seams were barely visible.

Then Charlie moved his fingers across the molding. The picture disappeared on Bill and Candace's TV. "Stop!" Candace yelled into the phone. But the picture came back on. "Tell Charlie to move his hand back to his left. Tell him to do it slowly."

Jody said, "It's just to your left." She paused as she waited for Candace' signal. "Stop! Right there. She says you're blocking the camera right now." This time the picture stayed black.

"No way," Charlie said in a matter of fact voice. He looked closer. Then he smiled. "I think I found it. This lens is like the head of a finishing nail. It's dark so that's what it looks like. It's tiny."

"Oh my." Jody realized that she and Charlie were still completely naked. "Put your hand over the camera."

"But why?"

"Because, Dear. We're still on the internet."

Charlie looked down at his now totally relaxed penis. He immediately put his hand over the camera. "Jody, Darling, can you please get my robe?"

Jody was already handing him the robe, but he had to uncover the camera to put it on. Over one thousand people watched the entire scene in complete disbelief. Up to now, they weren't sure if the website was a scam. Now there was no doubt. Many couples were already writing in to cancel their memberships. Others were scratching their heads, not sure what to do.

Bill, Candace, Jody and Charlie were discussing what to do next. Charlie wanted to get a lawyer and sue the owners of the site. Bill and Candace weren't sure. Getting a lawyer might be a good idea, but how would they find the owners of the site? They might be offshore somewhere. What good would a lawyer do?

Jody was completely humiliated. She was getting angrier by the minute. She wasn't thinking about a lawyer. She wanted to kill the bastards. What if someone taped them and sent a tape to her parents? What about Charlie's contracts with the military? Would they continue to do business with him if they found out about this? He would be easy prey for blackmail.

A lawyer wouldn't do. Jody was thinking about a more permanent fix.

Chapter 27

The office door was locked to make sure that Sean or Anna didn't sneak in quietly while Pat was cruising porn sites. The last thing he needed was for his children to be exposed to this trash. Diane would never forgive him. She still didn't like the idea that he was working on this case, especially at home, but Pat was making good progress identifying the operators of many sites. His argument was that he was making a positive difference. In reality, he knew that they couldn't keep up with the proliferation of child pornography. He wondered if the solution really was to resort to vigilante tactics. He thought back to a short time ago when he and Joe had to take matters into their own hands. He briefly had a mental image of the face of Danny Vallero through a rifle scope. This was followed by an explosion of blood and brain matter against a white wall in the background.

He lurched in his leather seat at the mental image. He'd taken care of that problem. Still, other problems followed. A major drug lord in Central Florida put a hit out on them, but they handled that problem, too. *Maybe there is an end to it all. Maybe you have to take matters into your own hands when the system fails you.*

Pat turned his attention to the computer monitor on his desk. He had the sound on low, even though he was using headphones. He opened a search page and entered the site address of the SExClub. The files he'd sent to Johnny Poleirmo didn't contain enough data to build an air tight case against the site operators. So Pat was back at the site to get more recordings of them broadcasting kiddie porn. The young girl in the last broadcast wasn't a young child, like so many he'd recently seen, but she was still a child according to the law.

The opening page had a stately looking home with southern mansion style pillars. The fancy scripted font below the porch of the mansion said "Welcome to the Sensual and Exotic Couples Club. The front windows of the mansion opened and closed quickly showing naked couples embracing, but nothing graphic. A disclaimer at the bottom of the page explained that anyone under eighteen years of age should not enter the site. Pat smiled at the irony of the statement, as if teenage boys would leave the site. *That just tells them they've hit pay-dirt.* It also claimed that, while the sex in the site was graphic, it was only of loving couples. No threesomes, homosexual acts, or group sex were allowed. The couples were willing participants, but were not compensated. They just wanted to share their love with other loving couples.

Pat clicked the "Enter" button below the message. The home page opened with an explanation of the rules of the site. It also stated that all the couples appearing on the site were willing participants and of legal age. Pat was still amazed that people were paying the large annual fee for the site. He shook his head, and set up the program to defeat the site's firewall.

As the program began to work its magic, Pat stood up, removed the headset, and walked around his home office. He picked up a picture of his three year old daughter, Anna, and smiled. She was only two years old in the picture. Her bright smile and round little face filled the frame, showing only a few baby teeth in the front. He wondered what he would do if someone abused his daughter. He already knew the answer. He'd already dealt with his enemies for a much less severe offense.

After the program worked for nearly fifteen minutes, he was in. He sat back down, put the headphone back over his head, and scrolled through the small windows of live feeds. Several of the windows were dark with no images showing, just a red light. Pat figured that this meant there were no live feeds from that location. Another window had a yellow light.

He could see a young woman undressing, but she was obviously over eighteen. Another window showed the image of a couple completely naked and in the heat of intercourse. Pat scrolled down to several more live videos, but he couldn't find any with women who appeared to be minors. He was becoming aroused watching these couples in various sexual acts. He noted that all the windows contained couples, not threesomes or anything bizarre.

Then he came across a video where the couple was looking directly at the camera. They appeared to be searching, trying to find something. He clicked on the video and turned up the volume.

The woman was on a cell phone. She was giving the tall man instructions on where to look. The man's face was so close to the camera it looked comical, like looking through the peep hole in a hotel room door.

The woman said, "It's just to your left." A pause. "Stop! Right there. She says you're blocking the camera right now."

His monitor was black but the audio still came through. Pat frowned at the monitor. *What were they looking for?* He continued to watch as the picture of the couple came back into view. They were both naked, looking for . . . what . . . a camera? If they were willing participants, why would they be looking for a camera? And why would the camera need to be hidden? *Maybe these folks aren't as willing as the site says.*

Finally the man said, "I think I found it. This lens is like the head of a finishing nail. It's dark so that's what it looks like. It's tiny."

"Charlie, keep your hand over the camera."

Pat watched the woman as she finally realized that they were naked, and they were on the internet. She ran from the room. She came back in a robe. She handed the tall man a robe as well.

The woman continued to talk on the phone. The man blushed, got down from the chair he'd been standing on, and put on his dark-blue robe. He turned to his wife and said, "What if there are more cameras?

The woman was still on her cell phone. Pat heard her say, "Oh my God. You're kidding. Oh, God. Tell me you're kidding." She held the phone to her chest. "She said there are probably about six cameras in the room. And there's got to be microphones, too."

"How does she know that?" Charlie looked at the woman.

"They can hear us over the computer. They've seen other couples on this website. It's a porn site. She said to look at points from different angles in the room. There may even be some in the bathrooms. Oh God, Charlie. We can't stay here tonight." The woman began to cry. Then her face turned red with anger.

Pat watched the entire scene. Then he remembered to start the recording software and capture the data from the site again. Maybe they couldn't get these guys for kiddie porn, but they could get them on other charges. Within a few minutes, Pat had the date and the recording.

Once Charlie moved away from the camera, Pat thought he recognized the man. After a moment, he was sure of it. Charlie Williams, the dorky, boy-genius from the USS *Nevada*. *Holy crap!*

All of a sudden, the screen went blank.

* * *

By the time Aaron Messier made his way back to the control room and disconnected the feed from Charlie and Jody Williams' house, the damage was done. He'd made his third serious error in less than a couple of weeks. His partner would be furious. He might order the site shut down. It didn't matter to Aaron. This was Plan 'B'. Plan 'A' was just about ready to execute.

As he looked around the cramped space, he tried to think of a way to hide any evidence of his failure. *If I erase the recording and the code for the recording, no one has to know this even happened. The only problem would be if another flood of people canceled their memberships. But if I delete their e-mails, who would know? I control the e-mails. The only time he even knows about them is when I forward them to him. It's settled. This never happened.*

* * *

Pat made two quick phone calls. The first was to Johnny Poleirmo. He told Johnny about how the couple obviously had no idea that they were being recorded. They also certainly didn't know that their love making was being broadcast over the internet.

"I'm pretty sure that I know the guy. His name's Charlie Williams. He was on the USS *Nevada* with me. He's some kind of boy genius. But that's another story."

On the other end of the phone, Johnny listened to this amazing coincidence. "So how does an ex-sailor end up in an expensive house on an expensive porn site? I mean, the house must be huge by your description."

"Well, that's the boy genius part. He's kind of an inventor. He came up with this improvement to sound dampening equipment for submarines. It improved the efficiency of the sound mounting devices by some huge percentage. He patented the idea when he got out. The Navy paid him a ton of money for the idea. Within a year of getting out of the Navy, he's a multi-millionaire. He can afford the huge house, and more."

"Why the hell can't I come up with something ingenious like that? At this rate, I'll never retire."

"You love it too much anyway."

Johnny pulled the phone away from his ear, and rolled his eyes. He returned the phone to his ear and said, "Oh, yeah, I just love this crap. It's great risking my neck every day for peanuts, hanging out with the underbelly of society. What fun?" He shook his head.

"Working on this case has opened my eyes. I thought that I knew the lowest of the low. But seeing how some of these poor little kids are abused, I just can't believe it. What makes these sick bastards tick?"

"I don't know, Pat, but I'd like to make their tickers stop. I've been in this business for a while and I've never seen anything like it." He took a deep breath, then continued. "But we're at least trying to do some good. Maybe we can pop a few of them, make examples of them. If we can get a few prosecutions and prison terms, we'll at least have done something for the good of society."

"Yeah. And maybe we can protect a few kids in the process. Anyway, Johnny, I'll send you the new file of the site. Maybe we can get them on a number of charges."

"We have to find them first. Good job, Pat. Keep it up, no pun intended."

"Boy, that's a riot. If this cop thing doesn't work out, there's always room on the comedy tour."

Johnny chuckled. "I thought it was funny."

"I'll bet you did. Talk to you tomorrow."

They both disconnected.

Pat's next call was to Moniac, Georgia, home of the southern end of "The Swamp." Moniac sat on the very southern edge of the Okeefenokee Swamp near the Florida – Georgia border. It was also home to William 'Hatch' Hatcher. He answered on the third ring.

"Yep."

"Hatch."

"Pat. How's that bruise on your chest?"

"Healed. But once in a while it hurts. I think it's a reminder to be more careful. But, you won't believe what I'm about to tell you."

"Try me."

"Do you remember Charlie Williams?"

"Yeah. Smart, tall, dorky dude from the *Nevada*? He's rich you know."

"Yeah, but this is even more freaky than that."

"What, is he a big porn star now?"

Now it was Pat's turn to hold the phone away from his ear and stare at the receiver. "Wow. That was a great guess."

Pat proceeded to tell Hatch about his freelance work for the Orange County Sheriff's Office. He knew the part about child pornography would anger his friend. Hatch's little sister was raped and killed a number of years before. He finally got to the part about where he saw Charlie Williams looking for the camera. Pat could hear Hatch chuckle, which was about as much emotion as he ever showed.

"So this is kind of funny, but it really isn't. Do you know how to get in touch with Charlie?"

Hatch paused for so long that Pat thought he lost the connection. Finally he piped up and said, "Pat, my man, today is your lucky day. Charlie just called me."

Pat was shocked. He had no idea that Hatch and Charlie kept in touch after each of them left the Navy. They had nothing in common. More to the point, they had the least in common of any two people that Pat knew. Hatch was from the deep south, the backwoods of Georgia. He barely finished high school and he loved weapons, especially guns, knives, and explosives. He especially loved military grade, small arms. Hatch was agile, quick, and smooth. He could run for ten miles without too much effort. His training area was the swamp, and it served him well.

Charlie didn't care for any kind of weapons unless he could take them apart and analyze them. He figured he could find a way to make them more efficient. But he tinkered with so many other things that guns weren't of real interest to him. He was from Newton Falls, Ohio. His family worked in factories until Charlie came along. When he told his dad that he wanted to join the Navy, he was stunned. Charlie was so uncoordinated that he was sure he wouldn't pass the physical. People described him as a geek. He was tall enough to play basketball, but he didn't have the motor skills needed to play sports. Somehow, he passed his physical, made it through boot camp, and volunteered for submarines. As tall as he was, and with his coordination problems, he banged his head on pipes, doorways, and cabinets all over the sub. Luckily, all his head knocks were superficial.

"So, did he tell you about the movie business?"

"Yeah. He said he might need someone with my skills. He wasn't sure how, but he said he was going to find out who did this. His wife was fit to be tied. He offered to pay me. I told him I wasn't a hit-man or nothing like that."

Pat raised an eyebrow, knowing Hatch's past. He said, "Well, from what I saw, I'd agree. If I were running that site, I'd be more afraid of his wife."

* * *

Jody Owen Williams was packing enough clothes for a week's stay away from home. The idea that her home was invaded by cameras was too much to handle. Whoever did this was one sick person. The idea that they weren't safe and secure in their own home was beyond imagination, especially after paying well over a million dollars for the house and property. Theo Messier was going to hear about this. She told Charlie that they needed to find a good lawyer and sue Messier Homes into bankruptcy. He told her to calm down, but she was beyond that.

They were in the guest bedroom after quickly grabbing clothes from their dressers and closets. As far as Jody was concerned, the master bedroom was off limits. Who knows what was being transmitted across the United States, or the rest of the world for that matter.

"Are you ready?" Jody's question was short and full of venom. She knew this wasn't Charlie's fault, but she needed an outlet for her anger.

"Jody, can you please calm down."

"Calm down? Not only 'No' but hell no. Don't you get it? Our lives could be ruined by this. Who knows how long this has been going on? For all we know, people could be buying DVDs in porn shops with us as the stars! And you want me to calm down?"

Charlie smiled, trying to ease the tension. "I know I'm good, but a porn star? Don't you think that's a stretch?"

"That isn't funny. Maybe in about twenty years, when we know we're in the clear, and the bastard who did this is dead, it might be." Jody looked at Charlie with an angry expression. "You've got to get mad about this, Honey. Don't you feel . . . violated? Dirty? I feel like I need a shower but I'm afraid to . . . in my own house!"

"Alright. I know, dear. But we have to calm down and think this through so we make good decisions. Let's get out of here. Can you think of anything else that you'll need for the next few days?"

"I've just got one more thing." Jody headed to the walk in closet and came back with a Glock 9 mm and a box of shells. She set them in her suitcase and zipped it up. "I'm ready now."

Charlie looked at her with a dumbfounded expression. They left without another word.

The evening was dark, the result of clouds covering the sky as far as the eye could see. There had been a light rain that made the roadways wet and slick, causing a spray from the cars and trucks as they passed. The air smelled cleaner now than it did earlier in the day, the result of the rain cleaning away the impurities. They rode in silence until they were heading north on the western leg of the Washington, DC beltway.

Finally, Charlie broke the silence. "I called a friend of mine before we left." Jody looked over at him, wondering where he was going with this. "He does a lot of interesting things, but he specializes in finding out information. He also knows how to help people even the score." He briefly looked over at his wife, who was paying close attention. "I think he might be able to help us."

The corner of Jody's mouth turned up slightly, just the hint of a wicked smile. She turned her head back towards the road. In her mind, she could see a man pulling the trigger of a pistol, shooting a bad guy as he watched porn on the computer. She felt a touch of satisfaction as the imaginary bullet killed the imaginary bad guy.

She said, "When can I meet him?"

Chapter 28

The mansion sat isolated from the nearest property by at least a quarter of a mile. The long drive down the winding entry road took forever with the vans lights off. Roger nearly drove the old van into a tree that was very close to the drive at a fairly sharp turn. Once his eyes adjusted to the dark of the evening he was better able to maneuver on the road back to the Kirkwood mansion.

After they parked the van in front of the five car garage, they made their way around the back of the house. Aaron said that entry into the back of the house would work better because of the tall pine trees that surrounded the back and both sides of the stately brick home. It was designed in the likeness of a southern mansion. Roger and Gerry were in awe. They were a bit intimidated by the mere size of the house and grounds. But the lure of millions in cash was too much to keep them away.

The motion-sensitive lights came on as expected. It made their approach to the back patio door easier. The magnet appeared to work, just as Aaron said it would. The light on the keypad stayed green. Nothing changed to indicate that Roger and Gerry had forced open the back patio door. They both held their breath as they watched for signs that an attack dog was in the house or that an alarm was going off. After a full five minutes of waiting outside the opened door, they figured that their plan must be working.

They made their way through the house to the second floor. The master bedroom was to the right at the top of the stairs and down a short hallway. Double doors opened into a room that was supposed to be 24 feet wide by 30 feet deep. It looked as large as a gymnasium. The two thieves stood inside the doorway for several seconds looking around at the rich-looking decor of the room.   They felt intimidated again, wondering to themselves if they'd bitten off more than they could chew. Roger was the first to break free of the trance.

"Snap out of it, man. We've got to move. The closet's straight ahead." He looked over at Gerry who was still glossy-eyed. He yelled, "Hey! Snap out of it! This ain't no dream! There's over a million bucks waitin' for us if we get our asses movin'."

Gerry finally took one hesitant step towards the closet where the safe was supposed to be located. Roger was there already opening the door. The light in the closet turned on automatically when he opened the door. They both, again, were awestruck. The safe door was at the far end of the closet. It took up the entire wall. It was a simple looking door despite its size.

Roger moved to the safe with his mouth hanging open. There was nothing hiding the safe. There were no clothes to move. Roger thought back on what Aaron said. *This is going to be easy. All cash.'* So far, Aaron's description of the house, the alarm system, and the location of the safe, were all exactly as he'd described. The next test was opening the safe. Aaron gave them the combination with step by step instructions. Roger pulled the instructions out of his pocket, held them up to the light and read. *Five steps. No more complicated than a small safe except the step to disarm the alarm. Aaron's right. This is going to be a cakewalk.*

* * *

Back at the control panel, Aaron watched the progress that his accomplices were making. He snickered as they looked like a couple of kids in a candy store when they entered the bedroom. *Trailer trash. These guys are nothing but trailer trash. They wouldn't be able to handle becoming millionaires.* He watched the monitor as Roger started to work on the safe. He wasn't in direct contact with his thieves, so he couldn't help them if they made a mistake. But mistakes were going to be forgiving in this case. Security for this house was almost nonexistent. Considering the wealth that the Kirkwoods' had, they sure weren't security conscious. But how were they to know that Aaron was watching them for the last six months, monitoring their moves and habits. When he overheard them talking about an extended vacation to Dubai, he doubled his efforts to create the plan that he now had in motion.

A fool and his money are soon parted. And it's going to be all mine . . . These two fools won't even know that they've been scammed.

Aaron turned his attention back to the screen where Roger was spinning the dial on the safe. He appeared to be on the final spin back to zero. He stopped, grabbed the handle and . . . nothing happened. The handle didn't budge. Aaron shook his head in surprise. *What did that idiot do wrong?*

* * *

Back at the safe, Roger's face took on an expression of irritation. He stopped, looked back at the instructions, then smiled. He grabbed the dial again and spun it one more time. He reached for the handle and this time it worked. Apparently he hadn't taken the dial to zero. Roger took a deep breath and pulled the door open. For the third time in less than ten minutes, Roger and Gerry stood with their mouths wide opened. Their mouths soon took on wide smiles as they moved slowly into the interior of the safe. Stacked on shelves on the left and right side of the safe were bundles of bills. They'd never seen so much cash in real life.

"Oh my god. Oh my god." Roger repeated the phrase over and over again. Gerry hadn't uttered a word. He simply stood at the safe's entry with his mouth hanging open. Roger continued, this time in a shout, "Oh . . . my . . . god!!"

"Roger, we got to get to work. This might take us more than two trips." Gerry stood gawking without moving a muscle. The smile that had formed on his opened mouth was starting to vanish. He was reasoning that people with this much money had to be ruthless with anyone trying to steal it. Maybe this was drug money. Maybe it was from illegal gambling or prostitution. Maybe it was mob money. Wherever it came from, there was a ton of it; all cash. Gerry wondered if this crime would ever be reported to the cops. He was now starting to get scared.

"Hey Roger, are you thinking that maybe we should just get the hell out of here?"

Roger looked incredulously at his partner. He was standing in a safe filled with cash. There was no way he was walking out of here empty handed. "Are you nuts? We've come this far. If this is mob money, we're dead anyway. But if it were, don't you think security would be a bit tighter? We'd have been killed in the driveway. This is just some rich slob who doesn't know how to cover his ass. Get your bags out and let's get to work. We need to fill at least four bags each. Before we move the cash, we'll make sure the room looks exactly like it did when we got here. We'll take the bags down to the truck and get the hell out of here. Then we can watch the news and see if anything gets reported. If not, then we come back tomorrow night, just like Aaron said."

Gerry seemed to calm down. He pulled out several large trash bags and headed to the right side of the safe. He nervously reached for the first stack of bills. He looked at them, smelled them, then placed them in the bag as if the bills would shatter. Roger turned to him and said, "Move it, man. They won't break."

Gerry started getting into a rhythm. Before he knew it, he'd filled four trash bags with cash and tied them off with a twisty. At about the same time, Roger finished filling and securing his bags. They were both sweating. They moved the bags out into the bedroom and closed the safe door.

Now came the hard part. Trash bags filled with money were heavy. They had to carry the bags down the hall, down a flight of steps, through the house and around to the garage. It was hard work, but somebody had to do it.

* * *

In the control room, Aaron smiled as he watched Roger and Gerry carry the heavy bags of money through the house. He was smiling to himself when he heard movement outside the control room. He quickly changed the feeds on the various screens to either archived porn scenes or live feeds from some rich couples' bedroom.   Just as he finished switching the screens around, his partner entered the room.

"Aaron, what are you watching?"

Aaron was worried that his partner knew something about the robbery scheme. He looked down at the floor in front of the control panel. His personality changed from the controlling man in charge to the introverted, silent man, unsure of his own judgment. He was intimidated once again by his partner. His response was so quiet that his partner had to strain to hear. "I'm making sure that I don't let stuff go out that will get us in trouble." He continued to stare at the floor.

The older man was looking directly at Aaron. He thought he detected something different in his manner, a bit more confidence, maybe. Normally he would have stuttered at least once. But maybe he was reading more into it than was really there.

"That's good, Aaron. We can't afford to have you making any more mistakes. You keep a good watch on these screens and make sure you follow our rules. I'm going to be gone for a few days. I'll be back Thursday evening. Can you handle it?"

"Yes, I think so," came the almost inaudible response.

"Good. I'll call to check on things tomorrow."

Aaron just wished he'd leave. He wanted to get one of his screens switched back to check on Roger and Gerry's progress. If his partner didn't leave soon, they'd already have the money loaded and be gone. That wouldn't be too bad but he liked to keep tabs on the progress. *The sooner I get my money, the sooner I can get out of here and away from this controlling freak. Not to mention my stupid brother.*

Finally, his partner turned and walked out the door of the control room. Aaron immediately gave the departing man the finger. He waited a few seconds, then switched one of the monitors to watch his partner as he left. The camera showed him walking out the front door, heading to his car. Aaron switched a second camera back to the Kirkwood mansion just in time to see Roger and Gerry picking up the last two bags of money from the bedroom. His face broke out into a wide smile. Within the week, his plans would be complete. Nobody would look at him like the village idiot again.

* * *

Roger drove the old van to an abandoned drive-through convenience store at the edge of Centerville. He had the keys to the store which had gone out of business several years ago. The store was now owned by Aaron Messier. Roger and Gerry's orders were to unload the money in the walk-in cooler and lock it. They were to leave the store before dawn, then get a hotel room and get some sleep. The plan was for them to do some surveillance on the Kirkwood home the next day before their return trip the next night. If there were no signs of the Kirkwoods, the next load was on. If the property was swarmed by cops or other activity then the second haul would be called off.

Roger and Gerry completed unloading the last bag of money into the cooler, but not before Roger opened the bag and grabbed a large stack of bills.

"What are you doing, man? We're not supposed to take any of the money. Aaron said we'd split it up this weekend when things are quiet."

"Well what Aaron don't know won't hurt him. There's more money than we could even count in there. He won't even know this is gone. Hell, this little wad won't even be missed."

Gerry thought for a minute then went and grabbed a handful for himself. "I like your way of thinkin'. Hell, we're doing all the work and taking all the risk. All he's doing is sitting at home. He's lucky we don't take off with all of it.

Just then, a voice filled the store. Roger and Gerry jumped, looking all around at the ceiling. The voice was coming from a number of speakers in the ceiling, but they couldn't see them. It was Aaron. "You boys go ahead and take what you got in your hands. It'll be a bonus for doing a good job tonight." There was a pause. Aaron wanted to give them time to think. He wanted them to realize that he'd planned ahead and if they were thinking of double-crossing him, they'd better think twice. "You just make sure that the plan stays on schedule. And guys . . . don't ever try to cheat me out of my money." Just then a stream of liquid sprayed down from the ceiling. Just as quickly as it started, the water stopped. Both men nearly wet their pants. "That could have just as easily been a bullet. Remember, we're partners. Partners don't screw each other. Understand?"

Gerry answered in a shaky voice, "Yeah, Aaron. We understand."

"How about you Roger? You understand, too?"

"Yeah, Aaron, I mean partner."

"Good. Then we're going to make a lot of money. Now get out of there and get some rest."

They locked up the money in the cooler. Then they locked up the drive-through. When they felt they were a safe distance from the cameras and microphones, Roger said, "That prick ain't gonna see any of this money. Who the fuck does he think he is, spying on us like that. We'll see who gets the last laugh."

Gerry didn't like it at all. He wasn't sure he had the stomach for this business. He was a simple thief. He wanted a big score, but his idea of a big score was a couple thousand bucks. These last two jobs were taking him places he didn't want to go. His mind raced as Roger babbled on about ditching Aaron as a partner.

Aaron recorded every word from the van. He knew it might come in handy later when he had to deal with Roger and Gerry. He hoped they enjoyed the handful of cash that they took. It would be their last reward.

Chapter 29

The sky was gray, with low clouds rapidly moving west to east, pushed along by twenty-five mile per hour winds. The air was damp, making it feel colder than sixty degrees. The group of people beside the roped-off hole were standing close to each other, their windbreaker collars pulled up to protect their faces from the chilly wind.

The large, yellow backhoe dropped another scoop full of earth onto the large pile at the corner of Jillian and Nelson's house. According to the supervisor on the job, the hole appeared to be about six feet deep. They should be near the footer supporting the basement wall.

The supervisor, Jim Carson, wore blue jeans and a brown, Carhartt jacket over his large, beer-belly midsection. He had a Tidewater Tides ball cap that was stained with sweat lines, propped on his head. A hint of a short-cropped haircut was visible at the sides of the hat. He came over to the small group and said in a heavy Virginia accent, "We should start to see stones in the dirt with the next few scoops. Once we see that we'll slow down. We'll put the shield plate in so that the dirt won't cave in on our guys. Once that's in we'll have them climb down and use shovels."

Deputy Lyons nodded. "How long do you figure it'll be before the plate is in place?"

"I'd give it another thirty minutes or so." He paused. "So, what exactly are we looking for?"

Lyons took a deep breath. "A body." He looked at Jim Carson, then at Jillian and Nelson Rockledge.

Carson's face turned to a frown. He saw the tense looks on the home owners' faces then turned back to Lyons.

"Should my guys have any kind of protective clothes on before they go down there?"

"It isn't necessary. If they find anything, we'll have them stop where they are and we'll bring in a crime scene team to take over. We don't know exactly what we're looking for at this point." He paused to see if Carson had any questions before he went on. "We'll brief the guys before they go in. If they find anything at all, they should stop immediately. Our guys are standing by and will be here within half an hour once we hear from you."

Carson asked, "How do you know there's a body down there?"

"We don't, but we're about ninety-nine percent sure. We have pretty solid information that we'll find a body. I'd rather not go into details because as soon as we confirm that there's a body, this will become a crime scene." He looked at Jillian and Nelson again. "We'll probably have to rope off this area for a few days. We may even erect a protective cover, but with your secluded location, and this being on the back side of the house, it shouldn't attract too much attention."

Jillian pulled up her windbreaker collar even tighter, covering her face with her hands. She didn't know what to think. Should they sell the house and move? If they found a body, would they be suspects? Could they even sell the house? Surely the neighbors and the entire region would know that a body was found under their house. It would be in all the papers. She leaned into Nelson who put his arm around his wife's shoulders.

Nelson said, "Let's go inside, honey. Deputy Lyons will get us if they find anything." He turned to Lyons and Carson and asked, "Can I get you and your guys anything?"

Carson nodded, "Sure. Coffee would be great." Just as Nelson and Jillian turned, one of the workers at the edge of the hole shouted over the backhoe engine, "We've got something, Jim. Looks like a piece of plastic trash bag."

"Tell your backhoe operator to stop right there. Have them put in the shielding plate and put a ladder in the hole. We'll take it from there."

"Okay." Jim Carson turned and started shouting orders to the backhoe operator and his crew. They began making preparations to get the huge steel shielding plate off the flatbed truck.

Deputy Lyons turned and walked away from the backhoe and hit speed dial on his cell phone while Jillian and Nelson looked on. When he finished, he spoke to the distraught couple. "The crime scene folks are on their way. They should be here soon. In the mean time, maybe you should get that coffee and try not to worry about this. When we verify what's down there, we're probably going to have some questions for you. It may take a while, so try to relax now. It may be a long afternoon."

This revelation made Jillian tense. Even though she was an attorney in the firm's criminal division, she was surprised when Lyons suggested that they might be questioned. Then she reasoned that it was just standard procedure to question the property owners where a body was found.

Nelson said, "No problem, Deputy. Let us know when and where. We'll get that coffee."

Inside the house, Nelson started the coffee while Jillian sat at the kitchen table with her face in her hands. She was worrying about her precious golden retriever. He'd suffered such depression when he sensed the body from the basement. She wondered about the emotional stress that the dog must have felt. Even now, it must be difficult for the animal to be away from them, though he was in good, familiar hands with Jillian's parents. She was starting to feel a headache coming on and figured that she'd head it off by taking a migraine tablet and lie down for a bit. With the rollercoaster of emotion she'd been on for the past two weeks, the strain on her mind and body was overwhelming. Her life had been turned upside-down and there appeared to be no end in sight. She felt selfish thinking only of herself, but she figured Nelson was coping well, on his own.

She told Nelson her plan. He stood behind her and rubbed her shoulders. He could feel her tension and agreed it would be a good idea. She stood, kissed Nelson lightly on the cheek, and headed upstairs for the bedroom. She took her pain pills, stripped down to her underwear and crawled into bed.

She tossed and turned for several minutes before finding a comfortable position. Outside she heard the backhoe start up again as the workers put the cave-in shield in place. When the engine stopped, Jillian was fast asleep.

* * *

In the control room, Aaron watched the monitor as Jillian climbed into bed. He was hoping to see more action, but when she fell asleep, he shook his head in disappointment. He switched the monitor to another bedroom on the outskirts of the nation's capital.

* * *

The foul odor of human decomposition filled the air in the vicinity of the hole. It took the crime scene investigative team less than two minutes in the hole to determine that there was a body. Within two hours, they'd removed enough material from around the body to relocate it from its concrete tomb to a vinyl body bag. They already determined that the body had been cut up before being stuffed in the trash bag. Another bag of material was also removed from the scene. It contained what appeared to be a power miter saw, but positive identification would have to wait for reconstruction in the lab. Another small bag contained a 9mm Glock, probably the murder weapon. Ballistics tests would have to confirm that as well. The team took more than one hundred pictures of the body and the rest of the crime scene. The photos would be enlarged to look for minute details of evidence.

As processing of what was now a crime scene progressed, the weather deteriorated even more. Rain was now a real threat. The team constructed a protective tent over the hole and roped off the area with crime scene tape. Deputy

Lyons stayed on the scene the entire afternoon. The lead crime scene investigator, Ted Griffin, said that the body appeared to be a young woman. He said that the body had been there for about three to four months, based on the level of decomposition, which was slowed by the body being bagged and in the cool ground.

From comments that Nelson and Jillian made earlier, Lyons calculated that the home was under construction about that time. He'd confirm that when he talked with the couple in a few minutes.

"So, Ted, I hear that you may be retiring in a few months. How can you give up the glory and prestige of such a great job?" Lyon's broad smile made it clear he was pulling the senior Crime Scene Investigator's leg. Ted was one of the pioneer's of modern forensics in eastern Virginia. The number of new forensics school graduates invading the job market made him decide, that at age sixty-seven, he'd had enough. He'd seen violent crime spread from the inner city of the capital to the surrounding suburbs. The nature of the crimes was becoming more violent and was taking its toll on his psyche. It was time to let the know-it-all graduates take over. After all, they'd grown up watching crime scene investigators on TV dramas and didn't need his archaic methods of forensics.

"Yep. I've climbed into these holes too many times. My knees can't take it anymore. Besides, I've got grandkids. I'm even going to have a great grandchild in a few months. Arlene and I are going to get an RV and travel around, pestering our kids, and spoiling our grandkids. We've earned it."

Ted's wife had just recovered from a lung infection that nearly killed her. The recovery had been tough. But he figured they needed to spend their remaining years enjoying themselves. He'd seen enough death for ten lifetimes. He wanted to be among the living from now on. His wife's illness and long recovery only drove home the point more forcefully.

Lyons patted him on the shoulder and voiced his congratulations. The Crime Scene Unit would miss a true professional. Now he had to figure out how to work with the incoming CSU lead. That might be tough. It was rumored that Ted's replacement was a forty-five year old woman named Shirley Williams. She had a reputation of being one of the most unpleasant people on the force. Like most CSUs, she was strict about maintaining control over the crime scene. Unlike her counterparts, she had no qualms about writing up complaints about improper handling of the scene, regardless of whether it was warranted or not.

Lyons took a deep breath and sighed. He could smell rain in the air. His thoughts drifted to his own wife. She'd succumbed to leukemia several years ago. He knew the pain of seeing a loved one suffer and die, while you had no alternative but to watch and pray that the chemical concoction that the doctors fed her would work. You hoped that the hours that you spent praying would cause a greater power to intervene. In the end, she'd suffered for less than six months. The pain she'd endured must have been unbearable, for in the end, he wasn't sure it was the disease that killed her or the massive amount of pain killers being injected into her system to keep her "comfortable."

He broke out of his momentary trance and shook his head. He had work to do and no dwelling on the past was going to bring her back. He headed to the back door of the Rockledge home just as Nelson was bringing a tray of steaming coffee out to the workers. He said, "When you get through passing out coffee, I need to talk with you and your wife for a bit."

"Jillian went upstairs for a rest. She might be out for a while. Can it wait?"

Lyons thought for a second then replied, "It might be better if I talk with you first, alone, anyway. I'll wait here for you."

"Go ahead in and grab a cup of coffee. I'll be right in."

"Sure."

Lyons sat at the table with a mug of coffee. He looked around at the newly finished kitchen. The smell of the home was that of brand new construction. You could still smell a hint of paint, tile glue, and new carpet in the air. The woodwork still had a glossy sheen from the new varnish. The cabinets looked expensive. The kitchen looked as if it had just been used for a layout in *Better Homes and Gardens* or *Kitchens and Baths* magazine. The only thing out of place was a half filled coffee pot.

He turned in his chair as he heard the kitchen door open. He stood to greet Nelson, now holding the empty tray at his side.

"Please Deputy, sit. Can I offer you anything else?"

"No, I'm fine. Let's get to it. I don't want to keep you longer than necessary." He reached inside his coat and pulled out a notepad and pen. He flipped several pages and made a note of the date and time, then added Nelson's name, home address and the circumstances of the interview.

"Mr. Rockledge, I want to start by telling you that you and your wife are not suspects in this investigation, though you are not ruled out. But based on the circumstances, your dog's reactions, the fact that you didn't even know he was trained in locating cadavers . . . what I'm trying to say is, you're very low on our list right now."

Nelson didn't have any apparent reaction to this news. His face remained without emotion. He had his courtroom face on now. "Deputy, how can I help? My wife is going to go through some serious emotional trauma from this. I'd like to provide whatever information I can to help find whoever did this."

Lyons stared back at Nelson, seeing, and feeling, that he was sincere in his desire to make this investigation short. He started out with a series of basic questions about his relationship with his wife, her family, his family, their jobs, income, and habits. He asked if any family members or friends had come up missing in the last six months to which Nelson responded "No." The questions went on for about forty-five minutes. All of the questions seemed to be answered to Lyons' satisfaction as he scribbled in his notebook.

Finally, he asked, "When did construction start on the house? Specifically, when was the basement dug and poured?"

"Well, this is October 14. We moved in on September 30th. The contract said the house would be built and ready for occupancy in less than one hundred days. Construction went almost exactly as planned. Thinking back, they started digging the basement the last week in June and poured the footer the Monday after digging was finished. It was June 23rd when the footer was poured. I remember because Jillian and I met out here at the site to toast the first real bit of construction. We took pictures. As a matter of fact, the builder met us here and took our picture in front of the hole. Or it was actually the builder's son."

"Who was your builder?"

"Messier Homes. Jeremy Messier happened to be here inspecting the progress and took the shot."

Lyons' eyebrows rose. He asked, "Do you still have that picture?"

"Oh yeah. We have pictures of the progress on the house almost every day. We've got two full albums of pictures of the construction. I wanted to make sure I knew where every water-pipe and drain, every electrical wire, and every board went in this house. That way if we want to mount a picture, we know where not to put the nails, among other things."

He couldn't contain his smile. He asked, "Do any of the pictures have any of the construction workers in them?"

"Sure, most do in fact."

"Can I see these pictures? They might be very handy."

Just as Nelson stood to get the photo albums, Jillian came down the steps. Nelson met her at the foot of the stairs, kissed her on the cheek, and asked how she was feeling. She yawned and said fine in a sleepy voice.

"Deputy Lyons wants to ask you some questions."

She tensed, but nodded her head, reassuring herself that she was up to the task. She was wearing jeans and a baby blue turtleneck sweater even though the temperature in the house was quite comfortable.

She entered the kitchen and greeted Lyons, "Hello Deputy." She sat in the same chair that her husband had just vacated. "Nelson said you wanted to talk with me?"

Lyons had to make an effort to keep his eyes on her face. The sweater she wore, even though high around her neck, framed her body perfectly. He forced his mind back to business. "Yes, Mrs. Rockledge. First, I just wanted to verify a few things that your husband said. You started construction in June of this year?"

"Yes. Nelson is getting the photo album. It will be easy to tell because all of the pictures are dated on the back." As she finished, Nelson walked into the kitchen with two large photo albums. He set the first album on the table and opened it to the first page of pictures. It was of unspoiled land that was very picturesque. Great pine trees towered above a small clearing. On closer inspection, Lyons could see small stakes in the ground with red ribbons. He figured that this was the outline of the house foundation. Nelson flipped the page and a backhoe was busy digging the hole for the basement. A few pictures later, men were setting up forms in the floor of the hole where the footer would be poured. At least eight men were busy carrying boards and pounding stakes into the ground. The next picture was of the completed footer, though the concrete still appeared to be wet.

Lyons looked closer at the picture, trying to get his bearings down. He determined where the front of the house was oriented and moved his finger along the footer where the body was found. There were no body parts sticking out, no black garbage bags ready to stuff under the footer. No apparent evidence at all. He looked closer at the picture but nothing obvious jumped out at him.

He looked at Nelson and Jillian and asked, "May I?" At the same time he made a gesture with his hand indicating that he'd like to remove one of the pictures from the album.

Nelson said, "Sure, whatever you need. We have negatives so if you need any of these, they can be replaced. Or you can get prints made from the negatives if that would help."

Lyons lifted the picture and turned it over. Just as Jillian said, a date was in the top right hand corner on the back. It was dated June 23rd, 5:45 PM. He didn't think that the pictures would reveal anything obvious, bet he decided that he should take the originals to the CSU and see if they could make out anything. Jillian and Nelson didn't protest. It was obvious to him that they wanted to help the investigation in any way they could. He was glad of that, because, with a three-and-a-half -month old corpse and little else to go on, this case was going to need all the help it could get.

Chapter 30

Jake O'Connor slammed the phone down on the receiver so hard that it sounded like a gunshot from the room outside his office. His body guard ran into the office half expecting to see Jake with his head blown off. After seeing his boss sitting in his high-back leather seat, seething with anger, he knew everything was okay. He also knew that Jake received bad news about his latest attempt to buy the new, high-class porn network.

"Shit, Boss, you scared the hell out of me. I thought somebody broke in and shot you."

"How in the hell would somebody get past you, you fricking idiot, without you seeing them. There's no back door to the office, so you tell me why you thought that! Were you sleeping out there or something?"

As usual, Jake was wearing chinos and a buttoned shirt with the sleeves rolled up past his biceps. His face was still beet-red. Shamus didn't know what to say. He looked around the room, hoping that he would come up with something brilliant to say to calm Jake down. The looks on his face made Jake even angrier.

"What the fuck do I pay you for? You're supposed to protect me. You didn't even know I was in here alone? Get the fuck outta here! Make sure nobody comes in here, like you're supposed to be doing! What am I paying you? Whatever it is, it's too much!"

Shamus stopped for a minute, thinking of something to say to explain himself, but after a moment of staring opened mouthed at Jake, he turned and left his office. When the door was closed, he shook his head, smiled to himself, and shrugged.

Jake sat and stewed at his desk. He was outraged that Jeremy Messier hadn't returned his calls. *Who does he think he is, not answering me like this? I'll show his ass.* Jake rubbed his bald head with his hand several times before placing his hands face down on his desk. He was putting his plan together on how to convince Jeremy that he needed to sell him the porn business. The plan was pretty simple. He would take care of business right after closing time at Messier Homes. *Nobody ignores Jake O'Connor.*

* * *

Across Stafford County at the construction offices of Messier Homes, Jeremy Messier was finishing up the day's business. His foremen were reporting crew's hours and handing in their plans for the next day. As he sat in his office, he felt a strange sensation. His foremen were all tense as they turned in their reports. There was none of the usual banter about meeting for drinks or getting together for a friendly game of eight ball after work. Faces were tight and grim. When Tom Grayson came in, his arm was in a sling from the fall he'd taken a few days earlier. His shoulder had stiffened. His doctor recommended that he immobilize the arm for a few days and give the swelling a chance to go down. Tom also had a grim expression and wasn't in the mood for small talk. Jeremy felt like he was the only one who wasn't in on a secret, so he stopped Tom before he could leave the office.

"Tom, how's the arm? When are you supposed to get out of that sling?"

Tom wanted to get out of the office and head for home, but he turned to face Jeremy. He said, "I've got an appointment day after tomorrow. Doc says it depends on how my shoulder feels and if there's any restriction in movement. So far it feels pretty good. I'll probably still have to take it easy for a while." He looked at Jeremy for a second and started to turn towards the door again.

Jeremy said, "Can you sit for a minute? I need to talk with you."

Tom hesitated, then turned and sat in a chair across from Jeremy. "Sure. I hope this won't be long. I've got to get home."

Jeremy knew this was a lie, but didn't pursue it. He asked, "What's going on? I mean, it seems like everyone's walking on eggshells. Even you."

The look on Tom's round face was a combination of a frown and a question. He waited for Jeremy to continue. When he didn't, he asked, "Haven't you heard?"

Jeremy threw his arms out to his side, palms up. "Heard what?"

Tom leaned forward as if telling a secret, then said in a normal voice, "The County Sheriff found a body under the Rockledge house earlier today. I thought you knew."

Jeremy's jaw dropped, his eyes went wide. "Why didn't anyone tell me this? I had no idea. Tell me you're kidding." When Tom shook his head slightly, the gravely serious look remained on his face. Jeremy knew it had to be true. He leaned forward, elbows on his desk, and put his face in his hands. He remained that way for several long seconds as time seemed to stand still. Finally, he dropped his arms down to his desk and stared back at Tom. "Does everybody but me know about this?"

Tom said, "I don't think Aaron knows . . ." as he made a gesture with his head towards Aaron's empty desk ". . . unless someone's gone to his house and told him. He hasn't been in for days, and even when he's here, he might as well not be. He keeps his damn nose buried in those electronic gadget magazines." He stopped and wondered if he'd gone too far, making fun of Jeremy's brother. But Jeremy rolled his eyes and nodded his head in agreement.

"Have the police contacted you or anybody else?"

"Nope. Hank Willis' brother works for the sheriff's office. He called Hank as soon as he heard the news. Thought maybe he should get a heads up. I can't imagine anyone here being involved. Hank's brother said the body was under the footer; looked like it was buried just before the footer was poured. Might just be some drug murder and the construction site was a convenient place to dump a body. Who knows?"

Jeremy thought about that for a few seconds. At the time the house was under construction, no one could have seen the building site from the road. It was very secluded, except for the gravel construction road going into the woods. Jeremy doubted that it was a random body drop.

As Jeremy continued to think, Tom asked, "Anything else? I've really got to run." Before he stood up, he asked, "Have you heard anything else from that Jake O'Connor punk since he stopped the other day?"

Jeremy winced. He was supposed to call him with more information about what he was willing to take for the porn site, which he didn't even know existed. That was another problem without any clear solution. "No, I haven't. Maybe he'll just go away."

Tom still had his doubts about Jeremy. He was pretty sure that they hadn't heard the last from Jake. He stood and said, "I hope you're right. That guy had trouble written all over him. The last thing we need right now is a gangster type hanging around." Then Tom thought maybe there was a connection between this Jake character turning up in the offices and the body that turned up under the Rockledge house. But why would he show his face now, just when there was sure to be trouble? It didn't make any sense. *I'll think about it later over a beer.* Tom stood and headed for the door again. He said over his sore shoulder, "You should talk to your lawyer. If the cops contact you for an interview, he should at least know what it's about. He may be able to tell you what not to say."

Jeremy looked surprised. He hadn't considered that he or anyone else with the company needed to talk with a lawyer. But now, thinking about it, the sheriff's office was almost certainly going to talk to anyone who worked on the Rockledge house, especially the concrete crew. As Tom left the office, Jeremy's mind raced. *They'll probably want to talk with everybody who works here. I'll have to have a meeting with the crew first thing in the morning, let them know what's going on. Hell, they probably know more than I do by now. But it still needs to happen.* He turned back to the paperwork on his desk, but his mind kept going back to the body. *How had anyone been able to plant a body under the footer of that house? Bizarre.*

* * *

Shamus pulled the limo into the parking lot of Messier Homes just as the last of the workers was pulling out. The sun was just edging behind the hill at the west side of the construction offices and the air was cool for a mid-October afternoon. The sky was crystal clear, allowing a chill to invade the air. He pulled the limo right up to the front door of the offices.

Shamus and Jake stayed in the car for a full two minutes. Jake said he wanted Jeremy to see them outside and sweat a bit. Shamus wondered if Jeremy was even at the office.

"Hit the horn a couple of times. I want to let him know I'm here."

Shamus hesitated for a second, apparently too long for Jake's liking. He yelled, "Lay on that horn for a few seconds, now!"

Shamus hit the horn as he said, "Sure, Boss."

The limo's horn let out a loud trumpet of noise, blasting loud against the building. It sounded even louder than Shamus had expected, especially with the empty parking lot and the sound bouncing off the buildings. After five seconds, Shamus let off the horn. They sat again for several seconds before Jake decided that he'd waited long enough.

"Let's go. Just stay behind me. No matter what I do, you keep your cool. I'll do the talking and anything else I need to do to convince this punk I mean business."

Shamus said, "Sure, Boss."

They got out of the limo and looked around for anyone else at the site. The lot was abandoned. They headed for the door, Jake in the lead.

* * *

Tom saw the limo as he was leaving the office parking lot. When he saw it turn into the parking lot in his rearview mirror, he knew who it was. He turned around at the first driveway and headed back to the offices. As he slowly passed the parking lot he heard the blare of the limo's horn. He also noticed that no one had left the car. He continued past the lot and parked his truck in a stone path off the road, about fifty yards from the offices. He sat for a moment, trying to decide what to do. Should he call the Sheriff's office? Or call for help from some of the workers? He could call Aaron, but he'd be useless. For that matter, what could he do with his arm tied up in a sling? Well, at least he could call the sheriff if things got out of hand.

He turned his truck ignition off, got out, and locked it. He headed down the side of the road until he came to a path that he knew led to the offices. As he neared the building, Jake and Shamus got out of the car and headed for the office door. *Damn. What now?* Tom moved in closer when the door to the office closed. It was only in the mid fifties, with a cold, brisk wind, but Tom was sweating. He could feel his heart pound as he approached the office window. Since Jeremy's office was on the second floor, he didn't know how he was going to see or hear anything that went on inside. He figured that he better take a chance and try to sneak inside. He looked through the glass of the office door and saw that Jake and his goon were already in Jeremy's office and the door was closed. Since the office wall that looks out over the office was all glass, he could see Jake, Jeremy, and Shamus clearly. He crept inside the door and let it close quietly behind him. He lightly stepped behind a support beam, for all the good it did. His shoulders and stomach stuck out on all sides of the narrow beam. He managed to work his way across the office very close to the stairs that went up to Jeremy and Aaron's office. He was now out of sight. He could hear the conversation, though their voices were muffled.

But what he heard made his heart sink. Jeremy was talking about selling an internet porn business. He didn't want to believe it, but it was right from the horse's mouth.

* * *

"Look, I don't even want to sell it, so that's my price. I won't take anything less."

Jake was already mad, but the idea that this Boy Scout was dictating the terms to him sent him over the edge. He walked closer to Jeremy, who was standing next to his desk and got right in his face. "Fuck you! Here's my price. I give you half a million in cash and you get to live. If you don't want to play, I'll kill you where you stand, right now. I got an alibi, too. I'm at a bar right now. Right Shamus?"

He turned to Shamus who said, "Right, Boss."

"So you see, hotshot, you're kind of in a tight spot. Either you agree or you're dead. That ain't so hard to understand, is it?"

Jeremy looked directly at Jake's eyes. He could feel the heat of his breath which had a distinct onion and garlic odor. His breath, mixed with his cheap aftershave, made for a nauseating mixture. Behind those eyes was a cold-blooded killer, he was sure of it. But he still didn't know how he was going to pull off selling something he didn't have. He thought he'd try pressing one more time.

"Look. I'd sell the site to you right now, but I have to talk with my partners. They think that it's worth a lot more than you're offering. So, it isn't that simple."

Jake's face turned a deep red. He reached behind his back and pulled out a Glock 9mm. Before Jeremy could move, the pistol was at his throat and Jakes fist held his collar. He gritted his teeth and spat as he spoke. "I don't give a fuck about your partners. You tell them you're selling the site. They can either go along or get buried with you."

* * *

Below the offices, Tom moved towards a closet to try to get into a better position to hear the conversation. When he did, he kicked a trash can and it spilled pop cans and disposable coffee cups all over the floor. He quickly ducked in the closet and locked the door from the inside. He stood silently, trying to control his breathing. He figured he was a dead man.

* * *

Jake shouted at Shamus, "Go."

Shamus pulled his gun as he left the office and scrambled downstairs. When he got to the bottom, he saw the overturned trashcan, pop and coffee running on the floor. Slowly walking towards the can, looking around the office, he didn't see anyone or anything else out of place. He noticed the closet door. Shamus approached the door and reached for the handle. He turned the knob. The door didn't budge. Suddenly, he heard a loud thud. The ceiling shook and he headed back upstairs to the office. Jeremy was trying to pick himself up off the floor as Jake stood over him. As he opened the office door, Jake gave Jeremy a vicious kick to the ribs. The sound of cracking told them that he had at least one broken rib. Air rushed out of Jeremy's lungs and he collapsed on the floor, fighting for air.

Jake leaned over him and said, "You're gonna sell me the site or this will seem like a pat on the back. Next time I see you, make sure you have all the information for the site ready to hand over to me. Understand? I'll see you in a couple days." He gave Jeremy a pat on the shoulder, then straightened up and signaled for Shamus to head out.

As they reached the bottom of the stairs, he asked, "What did you find?"

"Nothing, boss."

He was about to tell him to look again when he thought he heard sirens in the distance. He nodded his head towards the front door. They got in the limo and left. After a moment, an ambulance sped past in the opposite direction.

Jeremy stayed on the floor of the office, trying to catch his breath. His rib cage throbbed. He felt like he'd been stabbed. Each time he tried to move, he felt a sharp pain on his left side.

But that pain was the least of his troubles. Why was this lunatic trying to buy a website that he didn't own? It turned out to be a pretty bad day. Just when he thought it couldn't get worse, Tom Grayson walked into his office.

Jeremy was bleeding from the top of his head. It looked like he'd been pistol-whipped. But Tom couldn't feel sorry for him right now. "I thought you said you weren't doing business with that thug."

Jeremy managed to get up on his knees, then with great effort, tried to get to one knee. Tom, with his one good arm, came around to help him. He put his powerful hand up under Jeremy's armpit and helped him get to a standing position. Jeremy lowered himself into his seat. He thought about trying to explain, but when he drew a breath to talk, the pain shot up his chest and he passed out.

Tom waited to make sure he was breathing, then sat down at Aaron's little-used desk. He looked Jeremy over for a while, wondering what he'd gotten himself into. He figured he was owed an explanation. He'd wait until Jeremy woke again, then he was going to get some answers. Maybe it was Jake or his thug that pushed him down the stairs? But why attack him in the dark? They didn't seem to have any problem being seen at the office. It didn't add up. Maybe Jeremy could help him do the math . . . when he came to.

Chapter 31

Pat McKinney hung up the phone and stared at the screen, disgusted and angry. The poor little girl on the computer monitor couldn't have been more than eleven years old. She'd just been raped by a man who had to be nearly sixty. It made Pat nauseous and he grabbed the trash can next to his desk. He heaved several times, but stopped short of actually tossing his dinner. His head was still spinning and his vision blurred. For a moment, he wondered if he'd had a stroke. He tried to sit back in his office chair and get his bearings, but it was taking way too much time. The last time he remembered his mind being this scrambled was when he was a teenager. He'd smoked some powerful pot from a one hit bong. When his lungs filled with the potent weed, the inrush of THC into his system caused him to black out. It wasn't long after that experience that he figured being a pot head wasn't the right career path for him. He cleaned up his act. Unfortunately, not before the troubles began for him and his family.

His vision started to clear and the room stopped spinning. After a few minutes, he felt almost normal again. He looked at the computer monitor again and his feelings of dread came rushing back.

He'd just run the capture program to get as much information as he could from the website. Unfortunately, the site was located on a server out of California. *Damn. This is just too damn big. We'd need a task force of thousands of agents across the country. Who would pay to look at this trash?* Pat's mind churned along, trying to figure out a way to catch and prosecute these guys. But he didn't even know who 'these guys' were.

Right after he started the capture program he had called Johnny Poleirmo. He wanted Johnny to know that he wasn't sure he could continue with the investigation much longer. He couldn't take seeing these children being brutalized. These poor kids had no one to protect them. No matter what Pat did, he couldn't save them. It was a chilling reality. This evil would continue no matter what he did or how many of these creeps he rounded up. He felt another wave of nausea role across his stomach. He heaved again, this time a small bit of vomit escaped into the trash can. He clicked the mouse and closed the website. *I'll have to clean that up.*

The ringing of his desk phone brought him out of his fog. He reached for the receiver and nearly knocked over an empty beer bottle. "Hello?"

A slow drawl filled Pat's ear. It wasn't so much deep-south but it was definitely south of the Mason-Dixon Line. "Hey there, Mr. McKinney. I understand that you might need a hand tracking down some bad guys. Thought I might offer my services. They're priced right, too. Free."

Pat recognized the voice of William Hatcher immediately. "Hatch, didn't I just talk to you yesterday?"

"You may have. I'm in the area, and thought I might stop by if you're not too busy."

"Hell yeah. How long will it take you to get here?"

"Bout thirty seconds. I'm in your driveway. I bought one of these fancy new cell phone thingies. I just have to learn to press the right buttons now."

Pat pulled back the curtains that looked out of his office to the driveway and sure enough, Hatch's bright red 1996 Corvette was sitting there. To Pat's knowledge, the 'Vette cost more than his log cabin in the Okeefenokee Swamp, north of Moniac, Georgia. It was the only luxury that Hatch owned . . . except for his extensive gun collection, new cell phone and a very expensive computer.

Diane met Hatch at the front door and gave him a big hug. "Come on in, Mr. Hatcher."

"What? Is my uncle here or something? What's this 'mister' stuff?"

Diane giggled a bit at Hatch's little joke. He always knew what to say to cheer her up. She took his arm and escorted him back to Pat's office where the door unlocked and opened. Pat looked out at his wife locked arm in arm with his friend.

"So, Pat, do you spend all your time locked in that room while your beautiful wife here sits alone?" He turned to Diane and said, "If he ignores you too long, you let me know. I've got a spare bedroom at the Okefenokee Swamp, Spa, and Resort."

Diane's eyebrows shot up. In mock surprise she said, "Wow. That's some offer. What kind of activities does the resort have?"

Pat was looking at Hatch and Diane with a smirk. "This ought to be good."

"Well, ma'am, we do a lot of fishin, and gator wrestlin' and snake chasin'. Then of course there's the big skeeter hunt."

Diane frowned. "Skeeter hunt?"

"Yes, ma'am. The skeeters are so big down there we hunt 'em with shotguns."

Pat smiled. He'd already heard Hatch's routine about the mosquitoes in the Okefenokee Swamp. He'd been to the swamp several times on business. Though Hatch exaggerated, the size of the pesky bugs in the swamp was incredible. And they came in large swarms. The best solution was to avoid being out at dusk.

Diane smiled at Hatch's attempt at humor and turned him over to Pat saying, "He's all yours, Dear. You two deserve each other. Before I leave you two to your vices, is there anything I can get for you? Beer, iced tea, coffee?"

"Miss Diane, I sure would appreciate a tall glass of lightly sweetened iced tea. If you could dip your finger in it to sweeten it up a bit, I'd appreciate that." He smiled and she winked as she turned and headed for the kitchen.

He turned to Pat and asked, "How in the hell did God bless you with that woman? You certainly don't deserve it." His smile was mixed with a mock frown.

"I ask myself that every day."

"I'll bet you do."

"Anyway, it's good that you're here. Joe and Johnny Poleirmo are coming over in about twenty minutes. We're going to put a plan together for tracking down and prosecuting these internet perverts."

Hatch and Pat moved out of the hall and into his office. He looked at Pat's eyes and noticed the dark circles and pronounced wrinkles. He'd seen Pat in tense situations where he wasn't sleeping well. He knew the look all too well. The office was a mess and the trash was nearly overflowing with coffee cups, computer paper and . . . *what the hell is that? Looks like left over lunch.*

"Hey Pat, I hope you don't mind me saying, but you look like shit. Before Joe and Johnny get here, you want to fill me in? This doesn't have to do with old Danny Vallero, does it?"

The name Danny Vallero caused Pat's body to tense. Danny was a small time drug dealer and philanderer. He'd stolen a pretty large sum of money from the McKinneys when they were dealing grass. Pat and Joe took offense to that and Pat blew his brains out with a high powered rifle. To him, it was self defense. Others, who went strictly by the law, might have considered it cold-blooded murder. Danny was the main source of his recent nightmares. Hearing Hatch ask him about it made the dreams all too real.

He turned to Hatch and said, "No. I can live with that. That was just taking out the trash." Pat paused. "Now we're dealing with a landfill. Wait 'til you see this garbage. You won't believe it. These porn sites are sick, and anyone can access them. I mean, kids could accidentally stumble onto them." Pat stopped, his eyes on the verge of tearing, and stared at his computer monitor, which was off. He was imagining one of the scenes he'd watched earlier. A chill ran down his spine.

Hatch shook his head. "Pat, my man, you can't save the world. I know this is tough, but there are all kinds of bad things happening out there in this great big world. You need to pull in your sphere of influence." As he said this, Diane knocked on the door and entered the office with a glass of iced tea and a cup of coffee for Pat. She set them down on a couple of ceramic coasters of lighthouses of the Great Lakes.

"I think that's great advice. He's killing himself with tension and worry. I keep reminding him that if he comes home dead, I'm going to kill him." Looking at Hatch, she said, "Maybe you can talk some sense into him." Diane smiled, but the worry lines showed on her face, too. Looking at Pat with an intense stare she said, "You know how I feel about this."

Pat looked up, but there was no intensity in his face. Only fatigue. In order to end the inquisition he said, "Thanks for the tea and coffee, honey." He kept looking at her and she returned his stare. After a tense moment, she turned and left the room, closing the door behind her.

Pat felt exhausted. He needed a break. He looked back at Hatch who had a half smile on his face.

Pat asked, "What?"

"I'm glad I'm not in your shoes. I would hate to see that woman get riled up, especially if she was gunnin' for me." He watched Pat's expression for understanding then continued. "I don't normally get involved in domestic situations. It usually never works well, plus I'm not married, so I'm not the best qualified person to dispense marital advice . . ."

"Could you hurry this along a bit? My brain is getting numb."

"Oh, sure. Well, like I was sayin', I'd recommend that you take your wife's advice and get the hell away from this kiddie porn case. It's whippin' your ass, man. I can tell. If you don't believe me, look in the mirror. That should tell you what you need to know."

Pat knew Hatch was right. He knew Diane was right. But Joe and Johnny were on their way over, so he couldn't quit this minute. He had to pull the plug soon or he was dooming his brain to an eternity of torment.

Pat told Hatch that he'd end his time on the case as soon as he could. He knew it was the right thing to do for his family, and for his own sanity. Hatch did Pat a favor and changed the subject. They reminisced about a few of their exploits while on liberty from the submarine. The time went by quickly and before they knew it, Diane was showing Joe and Johnny into Pat's office.

Pat's computer went to work. They found the high priced website based in Stafford, Virginia. Pat worked the keys and the firewall bypass program did its magic. He made sure they were on a stable screen on the site and ran the capture program. It worked smoothly this time and within five minutes they had not only the city, but the street address for the service provider.

"Wow, that's some program," Joe commented. "Are we sure this thing is accurate?"

Johnny smiled, "Oh yeah. I wish the rest of the process were this easy."

"Me too," Pat chimed in. "So where do we go from here? At least this server is in this half of the continent. Most of these websites originate in California."

Johnny looked around at the other three. He said, "I made contact with a guy in Stafford County, Deputy Lyons. The sheriff there has given him permission to use our information and dig a little deeper. I guess he doesn't much like the idea that there might be a kiddie porn site in his county. He's hand-selected four guys who he trusts. They'll get us set up with equipment. Officially, we're there to assist them. If we make a bust, he wants the collar, of course."

Joe shrugged and said, "Everybody wants the glory and it is their territory."

Pat asked, "When will they be ready for us?"

Johnny looked around the room at each of them before answering, "Tomorrow. But I told them it might be Friday before we can get there. That gives us about thirty-six to forty-eight hours. Can you all make it?"

He was asking all three of them, but he looked most intently at Pat. He wasn't sure Pat was up to the task after nearly being killed in Virginia a few months ago. Hatch and Joe nodded right away. Pat said, "I'm ready," though his response was a bit tentative.

Joe's jaw tightened. He said, "Pat, are you sure you want to make this trip? Don't you think you're in enough hot water with Diane? Remember what she said last time?"

Pat wanted to show these guys who wore the pants in his house, but he was sure they wouldn't buy it anyway. He said, "Look, I'll talk it over with Diane. I'll let you know tomorrow. Plan on me being there." He looked around the room at the stern faces. They didn't look too confident that he could pull it off. And they weren't sure that he should make the trip. No one voiced opposition, though.

Joe asked, "Are we driving or flying?"

Johnny smiled. "Only the best for you guys. We're driving. I get to use a rental."

Joe said, "Oh great."

Pat and Hatch rolled their eyes.

Johnny smiled. "Hey, it'll be fun, like a big road trip."

"Yeah," Hatch said. "The road trip from hell."

Pat said, "Let's just hope it isn't the road trip to hell."

Everyone stopped smiling and stared at Pat.

Chapter 32

Jeremy's ribs hurt like hell. He played football in high school and had been hit hard before. But this pain was far greater than anything he'd ever felt before. It took him forty-five minutes to fully get his breath back. Still, he was breathing more shallow than normal due to the pain. Each intake of breath meant a sharp piercing stab to his side. Shallower, steadier breaths helped avoid the debilitating pains that he felt immediately following his beating. As he sat in his office chair, going over the last hour in his mind, he couldn't believe his life was in danger. Why was this Jake character so hell bent on buying a porn site from him . . . especially since he didn't know anything about it. For all he knew it didn't even exist. Maybe he should try to find this website so at least he knew why he was getting his ass kicked.

Then there was Tom prying into his business. Why the hell was he so interested in this? Sure, these thugs hanging out at the office was a bit scary, but they weren't after him. *Why can't he let me handle this? That punk, Jake wouldn't be anything if he was alone.* The pain on the left ribcage was throbbing. He tried not to move, but just breathing was painful. Thinking straight was out of the question. He relaxed and tried to smooth out his breathing. *There, that's better.* He turned slightly to his left to take pressure off his ribs and that seemed to help a bit. Then he noticed the first aid kit hanging on the wall. *Aspirin, Tylenol, Ibuprofen. There has to be some kind of pain killer in there.* He got up ever so slowly and headed to the cabinet. He managed to down four Extra Strength Tylenol. *There. Maybe it'll help in an hour or so.*

He got back to his chair and assumed the least painful position he could. Then he tried to think about the events of the evening again. *Who are all the players here?* This Jake character and his hired muscle sure weren't playing. He ran his right hand down across his left rib cage and felt the swelling at the point of most intense pain. He should've put ice on his ribs, but it was too late for that. *Focus.* Then there's Tom. *He found that transmitter gadget at the one house. What the hell was it doing there? Tom was one of the few people who knew about electricity. Maybe he planted it there? But why would he bring it up if he was the one who . . . can't be him. Tom's been a part of the family business almost from the beginning. He wouldn't do this. I'm not thinking straight at all. Damn this hurts.*

He thought about his brother, Aaron. He always had his nose in those electronics magazines. He knew a lot about electronics, but it was mostly what he'd read in the magazines. Jeremy thought he'd be too lazy to plant a transmitter in somebody's attic . . . *wouldn't he? Why the hell would someone put a transmitter in someone's attic? Tom said it wasn't wired to code.* Then it hit him. *Oh shit. It is Aaron.*

Jeremy rose slowly and moved to Aaron's desk. He lowered himself into Aaron's seat and opened his middle drawer. There was a bunch of office junk; loose paper clips, rubber bands, push pins, a box of staples, and Post It's scattered around in the drawer. He reached in and pulled out a stack of electronics supply catalogs. He leafed through them until he found one that said, *Special on short range transmitters. Great for audio and video signals up to 500 feet through walls, 1500 feet in open line of sight transmission. Military grade specifications.*

He continued to look through the catalogs and found a longer range transmitter-repeater station. The more Jeremy looked, the angrier he got. What was his little brother getting himself into? Was Jake really looking for Aaron?

Another light came on in his head. He realized that the transmission wasn't coming into the houses, it was going out.

Was Aaron really spying on their customers? Was he that stupid and brazen? *No way. Everybody thinks he's the village idiot, he's so damned introverted. He was always so afraid to do anything, now it looked like he was a high tech peeping Tom.*

Jeremy decided he had to confront his brother about the transmitter. He wasn't sure if Aaron knew who this Jake character was, but he was sure he wouldn't want to find out. He had to talk to Aaron and get to the bottom of this.

It took Jeremy a full ten minutes to get down the stairs and out to his truck. When he opened the office doors, the cool air hit him. It felt great on his face which was wet with sweat from the pain. It took five more minutes before he felt he could drive two miles to Aaron's house, even though it was just down the hill from the offices. He turned left out of the office parking lot and headed down to the first intersection. He took another left and headed towards Aaron's driveway. He didn't notice Tom's truck pull out of the secluded driveway along the road and follow him from a distance.

Jeremy also didn't notice the black limo that pulled out behind his truck well in front of Tom. Tom noticed though. Jake was on Jeremy's tail.

Jeremy made the turn towards Aaron's house. He was still not fully alert and he started to drift to the side of the road. His front right tire went off the shoulder and jerked the truck, jostling Jeremy in the driver's seat. His ribs lightly hit the steering wheel but it felt like a heavyweight punch to the ribs. The pain shot up through his rib cage. He felt nauseous and slowed his truck, easing it to the side of the road. He threw the truck into park and nearly blacked out. The limo sped past and kept going. Jeremy didn't even notice.

Tom turned into a driveway about one hundred yards behind Jeremy's truck and waited. He hoped nobody was home. The house looked dark, so he sat and waited. It took nearly five minutes, but Jeremy finally pulled back out onto the road. A minute later he turned left into Aaron's driveway. Tom drove past once, did a u-turn down the road, and drove back to Aaron's gravel drive. He couldn't see the house from the road. The leaves on the trees were bright with fall colors. Brilliant red, orange, and yellow leaves covered the hillside, making it look as if it was on fire. The leaves were starting to drop, but most trees still held their thick canopies.

Tom turned into the drive and eased his truck closer to the house. Finally, Jeremy's truck came into view. Aaron's truck, a green Ford F150 was parked outside the garage. The house sat at the foot of a gently sloping hill. The hill, Tom knew, led to the back side of the offices of Messier Homes. Even though it was nearly two miles by road, the house was actually less than 400 yards through the wooded area and up the hill. The terrain was rocky, but not too steep.

As he watched Jeremy approach the house, favoring his ribs, Tom thought about why Aaron never came into work anymore. Being this close he could walk to work. But he never was into the business even when Theo still ran the show. His biggest contribution was the electronic controls for the curtains in some of their most expensive homes. The curtains were controlled by computer and a light sensor. It was pretty ingenious, but only a handful of clients wanted the luxury item.

As Tom sat in the driveway, just out of sight behind a stand of trees, Jeremy walked through the front door of Aaron's house without knocking. He was red in the face. Tom wasn't sure if it was from pain or anger. Moving in closer would put him at risk of being seen. He didn't see any way to get more information, so he decided he'd better get home. He also didn't want Jake to drive by and see him sitting in Aaron's drive. It would be a dead giveaway, maybe in more ways than one. Tom pulled back out onto the road and headed for home. He went past the offices again just to make sure Jake wasn't there trashing the place. To his relief, the office looked quiet. The sun was setting and it was getting dark. Tom headed for home, hoping for some peace and quiet, especially after all the surprises of the day.

He didn't know what to think. Was Jeremy really in the porn business? Why was he so hell bent on seeing Aaron?

Maybe Aaron was in on it, too. It all seemed too surreal to Tom. These kids were instant millionaires, taking over the business from their dad. Or they soon would be. Messier Homes had orders stacking up. They were almost to the point where they might have to turn people away. But if this office drama kept up, the business was in trouble. It wouldn't matter how many people wanted a Messier Home. The company would be dead, along with at least one owner. Where the hell was Theo? Surely, he'd want to know about this. Maybe he could get this mess straightened out. But he was somewhere in the French Alps with his young, sexy wife, Natashia. He'd been gone for several weeks now. Why hadn't he called to see how business was going, or to check on his boys? It wasn't like Theo to just drop it all and disappear.

* * *

Aaron finished watching the recording of Jeremy getting his ass whipped when he heard the front door close. He quickly turned off the recording and left the control room. He slipped through the fake door that doubled as a wall in the basement. He secured the wall, making his way up the basement stairs. Then he walked out into the hall to the kitchen, spotting Jeremy easing himself down onto a bar stool. He looked like hell, and Aaron knew, for good reason.

He asked, "What happened to you? Some jealous husband kick your ass?"

Jeremy didn't appreciate the comment and stared back at his little brother. He felt a brief wave of nausea then said, "For your information, I was negotiating a deal to sell a porn site. I don't even own one, but somebody thinks I do. Any idea why someone might think that?" He stared at Aaron and was surprised to see him staring straight back at him. He wasn't looking at the floor or the ceiling. He wasn't even trying to avoid his stare.

He replied, "No. I wouldn't." He paused. "You still haven't said what happened." He waited as they continued to stare at each other.

Finally, Aaron walked over to the refrigerator, pulled out two beers and handed one to Jeremy. Aaron opened his and took a deep pull. Jeremy tried to open his, but the pain would not let him put any pressure on the cap. Aaron held out his hand, offering to help. Jeremy hesitated, then figured he'd better hand it over, or he wouldn't be drinking beer tonight.

The silence continued for several minutes, then Jeremy said, "Look, a guy named Jake came to see me a week or so ago. He said he wanted to buy my porn site. This dude had some muscle with him. Just a little bit ago he came back to the office and put a gun to my head. Said he really wanted the porn business. When I stalled, he knocked me down and kicked the shit out of my ribs."

The whole time Jeremy was telling his story Aaron was only half listening. He already knew the story. He'd watched it live and saw the replay. He almost smiled while listening to his brother, but caught himself. Finally, Jeremy finished talking, still looking at Aaron for a reaction. When he didn't get one, he asked, "Are you listening, Aaron?"

"Yeah. I just don't know how this has anything to do with me. Why are you telling me this? Sounds to me like it's your problem."

Jeremy's anger started to rise. His face turned red again, this time not from pain. He was obviously going to have to explain it to Aaron in simple terms. "I'm telling you this because I don't have a porn site, but obviously somebody does, and they're using our business address. This Jake character is bad news." He again noticed that Aaron didn't look the least bit disturbed by his comments. He was still holding Jeremy's stare, not wavering.

Finally, Aaron said, "What do you want me to do? I don't have a porn business. Neither do you. You want to put a hit out on this guy?"

Jeremy's jaw dropped in stunned amazement. He couldn't believe what his little brother said. He asked, "Are you kidding? Ever heard of prison?"

"Ever heard of dead? Sounds like this guy's gonna kill you if you don't do something first."

Aaron's words struck a chord. Jake said he was going to kill him if he didn't complete the deal for the site. Maybe he should strike first. Jake probably didn't think Jeremy had the balls to do it. But after the beating he took tonight, he was wondering how far he would go to protect himself.

Aaron said, "I don't see any other way, bro'. Either you do him, or he's gonna do you. It would be better if you did him, at least in my opinion."

Jeremy took another short sip of his beer. He couldn't drink more than a quick hit without his ribs feeling like a knife cutting into his side.

As Jeremy thought about his situation, Aaron's mind was miles away. He was thinking about the money sitting in a walk in cooler at a vacant drive-through store. He had boxes lined up to package the cash and ship it to the Cayman Islands. His own plan was coming together. He really could care less about what happened to Jeremy. After all, it was his carelessness that screwed up their lives. If it wasn't for Jeremy, their mother would still be alive. Aaron knew another one of Jeremy's secrets. He had the evidence to prove it. The DVD of Jeremy and Natashia having sex at one of the nearly finished Messier Homes was going to be Aaron's parting gift to his brother.

Chapter 33

"Candie said the site was an expensive club. She knows 'cause her and her husband are members."

The look on Charlie Williams' face almost made Jody laugh. The lines on his forehead were pronounced as he tried to make sense of illogical behavior. She could see his mind working, trying to figure out why anyone would want to allow themselves to be seen having sex over the internet.

"Do people really do that?"

Jody shook her head. Her husband was brilliant and handsome, but he was so naïve about some things. His shelter was his own mind. He saw mechanical and electrical devices with such clarity. Yet he didn't realize that there were sleazy, slimy bastards in the world who would sell their own mothers for a buck.

"Charlie, sometimes I think you're the blond in this relationship. Of course there are jerks that do this. That's why our prisons are full. That's why the courts are full. That's why somebody hid cameras in our house. The world is full of bad people." She looked at him for some understanding, but he was still trying to calculate this new information.

"Look, let's just try to get into the website and look around. Maybe we can find a way to locate these bastards." Jody shook her blond hair, pulled it behind her head with both hands and wrapped a hair tie around it to make a pony tail. She typed in the web address of the site; www.sensualexoticcouples.com. Jody worked her way to the home page. It was well designed and intended to show a touch of class. She was impressed. It took her a moment to get angry again. She looked around the page for a way to enter the site without paying. See paused then tried a couple of links.

Charlie looked at her and smiled. He asked, "Can I try?"

"Sure."

She slid her chair away from the computer and let Charlie move in. He took a few seconds to look over the home page then went to work, clicking keys. After a few minutes, they were at the screen selection page of the site. In unison, their jaws dropped. They were looking at nine screens on their monitor, with different couples in action on each screen. Instructions at the top of the page told club members how to bring up any one of the scenes for full screen viewing. It also had indicating lights that were different colors to show which screens were displaying live, versus recorded, action. There was also a link that let you go back into the site's archives and select previously recorded sessions.

"Let's see if we're in the archives." He looked over at Jody to see if she had any objections. Her face was pale. Her only response was a look of fear and a slight shrug of her shoulders. He took that for a yes. "Here we go."

Jody didn't like the sound of Charlie's voice. It sounded like he expected to find a video of them making love. She took a deep breath as he started tapping keys again, clicking links and watching couples. Sometimes the couples were just getting undressed. In others, they were intertwined in the heat of intercourse. After nearly half an hour of going through the links, Jody was starting to relax, thinking that they wouldn't find themselves on film. Charlie was about to click the next link when he hesitated. He looked over at Jody with a worried expression. Again, she tensed.

When the screen popped up, she looked on in horror as she watched herself, naked on the bed, looking off camera with a smile on her face. As the scene progressed, she realized it was one of the first nights in their new home. She and Charlie watched, their mouths wide open, barely comprehending that this was them, filmed in their own home without their knowledge.   Subconsciously, Jody grabbed the lapel of her collar and pulled it tight over her neck.   Tears formed in her eyes as the reality of the situation sank in.

"Turn it off."

Charlie hesitated.

A little more loudly she said, "Charlie, I said turn it off."

"Just a minute, Pumpkin. I can't believe the quality of the . . ."

Jody screamed, "Turn the damned thing off!"

She felt violated, like she'd been gang raped in public. How could anyone get away with this? Why didn't anyone know that their house had hidden cameras? It was so far-fetched that she still thought she might wake up from a nightmare. The whole thing would be nothing more than a bad dream. But as Charlie exited the site, she knew it wasn't a dream at all.   Someone, with knowledge of their home's construction, must have placed the cameras in the ceiling molding and other locations in the house – their house. She looked over at the suitcase sitting on the bed. She knew the Glock 9mm was in there.   She just didn't know who she needed to kill.

Charlie saw his wife looking at the suitcase. He wasn't sure what she was thinking, so he offered, "Honey, we'll get to the bottom of this. We'll be back in the house in no time. Trust me."

Jody looked Charlie in the eyes. Her face was getting redder by the second as her anger boiled to the top again. "I'm not worried about getting back into the house. All I want right now is to find out who did this to us and string them up by their balls." She paused. "So, the friend that you called. What was his name?"

"You mean Hatch?"

"Yeah . . . Hatch. When is he supposed to get back with you?"

"I expect to hear from him anytime now."

As if on cue, Charlie's cell phone rang. He answered before the second ring finished. "Hatch. Jody and I were just talking about you."

Hatch didn't like people talking about him, especially in public. He asked, "Where are you and Mrs. Williams now?"

"We're at the Ritz Carlton in Tysons Corners."

Hatch breathed a sigh of relief. He figured that they were insulated enough from anyone trying to listen in on their conversation. Still, he preferred that they talk face to face. That wasn't possible until at least the next morning when the car pool of team members rolled into town. "Can I interest you both in a nice, private lunch? And it'll be with three other guys. I'll even provide the room service. You tell me what you want and I'll bring it to you."

"Sure Hatch. That sounds like a good idea." Hatch heard Charlie cover the phone and explain to Jody what Hatch had in mind. When Charlie got back on the line he said, "Can you stop at O'Malley's Sports Pub tomorrow before you get here and get two Philly Cheese Steak Subs for us and get whatever you guys want for yourselves. We have whatever you want to drink, here, so don't worry about that."

Hatch shook his head. Charlie could have Filet Mignon brought to his door at the hotel and he was ordering a cheese steak sub. The man knew his roots. Hatch got directions to the restaurant and the hotel, and disconnected the call.

* * *

The next day, Hatch, Johnny Poleirmo, and the McKinneys met at Jody and Charlie's hotel room. After small talk and eating, the six talked candidly about the website. Johnny told them the server was in Virginia near Quantico Marine Base. They still didn't have an exact address but were zeroing in on the server location even as they met. Charlie offered to assist and explained that he had a high level of computer skills. But he also had a staff of people who were even more skilled than he was. One in particular was a former hacker who learned his skills as a young teen. When he got into serious trouble hacking into one of the defense department's main computers, he quickly learned the costs of being on the wrong side of the law and the benefits of joining the good guys.   He was one of Charlie's highest paid technicians.

Johnny asked, "Can we trust him? It sounds like he has a cowboy streak in him."

Charlie explained, "All that happened before he turned fourteen. He's nearly twenty-four now. He has a wife and two kids. He knows he can't afford to stray to the dark side."

Johnny glanced over at Pat and Joe. They both knew where this kid was coming from. One day they woke up and they were in deep. Pat's mind wandered. He started to rub the scar on his chin, deep in thought. *You have to recognize that you're in too deep and find the path back. If you don't, you end up dead or wishing you were. Apparently Charlie's man's figured that out.* Pat felt Joe's stare. He and Joe looked first at each other, then at Johnny. They both nodded their approval.

Johnny said to Charlie, "Okay, let's bring in your guy and put him to work."

Jody gripped Charlie's arm. She whispered to him, "Will he see those pictures of us?"

He whispered back, "I'm afraid so, Babe. It can't be helped. The sooner we find these creeps, the sooner they're out of business. We'll make sure the files are destroyed. These guys will be discreet."

Charlie called his computer guy and explained what he needed. He came right over to the hotel. When he was told he was hacking into a porn site, he cracked a half smile, then made a face as if to say, you're kidding, right? When Charlie shook his head with a stone-cold serious look, he said, "Let's get started."

Jeff, the former hacker, looked at the computer and did a few quick checks on the available memory. It was Charlie's computer and had been purchased in the last month. It was purchased specifically to perform advanced calculations with the sound signature software used for Charlie's research into sound dampening. The hard drive had lots of storage space for new programs.

Jeff said, "This should work fine." He took a small rectangular device from his pocket and plugged it in to the back of the computer. "This is a jump drive. It's just a storage device. I'm downloading a program that I've developed to hack into servers and bypass firewalls. It works pretty fast, much faster than most programs available on the black market. Since these programs are generally illegal, I usually don't let anyone know I have it."

Johnny spoke up. "Don't worry, Jeff. We're not here to bust you for hacking. Just get us what we need. No repercussions, we promise you."

Jeff worked for Charlie so he felt like he needed his approval before he went on. He looked over at Charlie who nodded.

He took a deep breath and entered the website. When he reached the page with nine different choices, he smiled slightly, then stroked a few keys again. Suddenly, the graphics disappeared and the screen was filled with code. The men in the room stared in awe. They had no idea what the symbols on the screen meant.

"This is the code behind what you see on the screen. If you read and understand this particular programming language, you can pretty much do whatever you want. This is one of the ways that hackers pirate websites."

Another twenty minutes went by without a word. Finally Jeff said, "Okay. Here's what we're looking for." He pointed to a section of code that still looked foreign to the rest of the people in the room. "All I have to do is correlate this information with a few databases and . . ."

An hour later, Jody, Charlie and the team were sitting back, trying to relax. Jeff was trying to figure out why his search turned up a vacant field west of Stafford, Virginia. It was in the general area of where the original team thought it would be. There should be a building on the grounds somewhere. But the Internet satellite search turned up the empty field. Pat suggested that any buildings might be blocked out of the satellite image by trees. That was quickly disproved by zooming in and searching areas adjacent to the site where trees were clearly visible.

"I think we should go to the site and walk the field. Maybe we'll see something that will point us in the right direction." Pat's suggestion wasn't getting rave reviews. Finally he said with some force, "Anybody got any better ideas?"

There was silence in the room. Finally, Jody spoke up, "It's better than sitting here on our asses. Let's go."

Charlie looked at his wife with an odd expression. "You're not going, are you?"

"I'm not going to sit here and do nothing. You're going, too."

Charlie started to shake his head in protest. The look on his wife's face made him switch to a nod.

Joe spoke up, "Before we go, we'd better get a good idea of what we're looking for. We can't go out there blind."

Jody said again in a more forceful tone, "We also can't sit here all day. It's a good hour's drive and it's getting late already. We're burning sunshine here."

Hatch said, "Charlie, you are one lucky man to have a woman like Miss Jody, here." He looked at Jody and said, "Miss Jody, you can be on my team anytime." Hatch looked around and said, "You heard the woman. Let's get crackin'!"

Chapter 34

"I never thought I'd . . . be able to . . . make love again." Jillian's words were punctuated by the heat of passionate intercourse. She and Nelson were twenty minutes into another intensely sensual love-making session. Jillian was relaxed and enjoying sex again. She wasn't looking around in a panic. She wasn't crying. She wasn't afraid of intruders. And she wasn't afraid of being violated. She was like a new woman. She had renewed faith in her husband. It was his strength and compassion that pulled her through and made her feel whole again.

"It wasn't me . . . Babe. You were so strong . . . we helped each other. We make . . . a great team." They continued to say what they were feeling. It appeared to make their passion build more with the sound of each other's voice. "Oh, yes. That's fantastic."

Nearly three thousand couples around the United States were watching as Nelson and Jillian were becoming their internet heroes. Many of the couples watching cheered in their own bedrooms. The ability of Jillian to overcome the stigma of the rape, with the help of her husband, was truly inspirational. They didn't know that they unintentionally violated her as they watched. The SExClub assured them that Jillian and Nelson were willing participants. None of them stopped to consider why this woman, who was forcibly raped, would be willing to remain on camera, sharing her horrific experience. It never occurred to them that they were party to a crime, regardless of her miraculous recovery.

Nelson and Jillian continued what they thought was a private, intimate act, giving themselves fully to each other.

They moved closer and closer to the pinnacle of their passion. Nelson suddenly stopped and made an odd face. Jillian continued to work herself until Nelson said, "Honey, stop."

She stopped and asked, "What is it?"

"Do you smell something burning?

Jillian sniffed and said, "Yeah, I do. It's getting stronger." She rolled off Nelson and they both sat up in bed and looked around.

Across America, thousands of viewers were becoming confused. Just as they were cheering on the couple, they stopped. Then their internet feed was interrupted. Most tried to reset the connection but discovered that other websites were available. They tried to sign back into the SExClub site, but it was suddenly unavailable. The disappointment was real, but most couples went on with their own love-making.

As Nelson and Jillian sat in bed, they looked around the room, trying to find the source of the burning. Nelson stood when the smell got even stronger. He put his robe on and handed Jillian hers. She also put her robe on and walked around the room.

"There," she said, "along the ceiling, near the wall." She pointed to a spot on the ceiling where the wood molding was smoking.

"What the hell?" Nelson couldn't believe what he was seeing. How could a piece of ceiling molding be burning? There were no electrical wires passing through that area. He knew that because he watched the electricians route the wiring throughout the house. Jillian saw his expression and asked, "What's wrong?"

Nelson hesitated. He turned to Jillian and said, "There's nothing up there. I mean . . . I should check the attic. Maybe it started up there and is spreading." Even as he said it, he didn't believe it. While they watched, a small, intense flame shot out of the fancy molding then stopped. The smoke was briefly more intense. After the flame stopped, the smoke started to dissipate. The confused look on Nelson's face grew more intense. He got a chair and pushed it over beneath the burnt woodwork. He climbed in the chair but couldn't get close enough to see anything.

Jillian said, "Shouldn't we call the fire department? I mean, this could spread."

Nelson went to his wife, held her in his arms and said, "Whatever it was, it isn't smoking anymore." They both watched as the smoke thinned. "You can see the smoke clearing, but it's gonna smell bad in here for a bit. Check out the other rooms for me and see if you can smell anything, anywhere else in the house." Jillian walked into each bedroom and the spare bath. Nelson was right. The smoke was confined to their bedroom.

Jillian was starting to get a bad feeling. Nelson met her in the hall at the top of the stairs. He was on his way to get a step ladder.

When he returned and set up the ladder, he used a magnifying glass to inspect the damage. He wasn't sure but it looked like some kind of electronic device in the burned out hole. He decided to be more aggressive. Using a screwdriver and claw hammer, he pulled an eight foot stretch of molding from the ceiling. Several small wires pulled out of the ceiling as he pulled the finishing nails from the ceiling and wall. He carefully walked down the ladder and laid the molding face-down on the floor. There were two more devices. Nelson looked puzzled again. Could they be some kind of embedded thermostat? The lights in the room were adjustable but the adjustment was manual so they were most likely not light sensors. He shook his head as he eliminated the possibilities, one by one.

Finally, he pulled on the back of one of the devices. It appeared to be mounted in place somehow. He pulled harder and the electronic gadget pulled out of the trim. He held it close as he examined the device. He wasn't sure, but it appeared to be a miniature microphone. Again, his mind raced, wondering why a microphone would be mounted in the ceiling. The device further down in the molding looked a bit larger. As Jillian watched, Nelson pulled the other device from the board.

He repeated the process on this device. There were two sets of wires attached to the electronic gadget and what appeared to be a small wire sticking out the back. *An antenna? If that's true, this must be a transmitter or receiver. And what is this?* He looked closer. The lens of the camera was so small that at first, he didn't recognize it as a lens. But the more he looked, the more certain he became. And that meant only one thing. Someone was watching them. He didn't know how to tell Jillian the bad news. But the expression on his face said it all.

"What is it Nelson? What are these things?"

"Jillian, we need to pack some clothes for at least a few nights. I don't think it's safe for us to stay here."

Jillian looked around. Her fear started to rise. "Not safe? What are those things?"

"Let's just get packed and I'll tell you in the car. We can stay at your folks for a few nights, right?"

Jillian started to tremble. The strength and resolve that she'd built up over the last few days was rapidly breaking down. Nelson reached out and put his arms around her to calm her. He hoped he could work a little magic and keep her from a complete breakdown. He couldn't tell her about the cameras and microphone now. She'd lose it completely. He held her tight and said, "Let's get dressed and packed. We need to get moving. Once we get you settled at your folks, I'll come back over and call for help.

"What kind of help? What's going on?"

"Jillian, sweetie, let's just get packed. Okay? Everything's going to be fine." He stroked her hair and continued to whisper reassurances. He only wished he believed it himself.

* * *

Jillian was at her parent's house, safe from the ghosts and real life perverts. She was still in shock, wondering why she couldn't be safe even in her own home. Her words rang in Nelson's ears. "If I can't be safe in my own home, where can I be safe?" He swore to her that they would find out who did this, who invaded their lives. It was such a total violation of their lives, even Nelson wondered if they'd ever really feel safe again.

When he returned to the house, he called his attorney at home and asked him to prepare a lawsuit against Messier Homes on the grounds of invasion of privacy. He explained what he'd found. He needed a private investigator, someone who knew electronics. His attorney recommended a guy that worked for his firm, Anderson Gershwin.

Anderson met Nelson at his house just after 10:00 PM. He was tall and lanky, about six foot three, in his early thirties. He couldn't have weighed more than one hundred sixty-five pounds. He wore a navy blue windbreaker, blue jeans and dark soft-top shoes. He had no facial hair. His face was pale and covered in pock marks, apparently from a bad case of acne in his youth.

Nelson's attorney advised him that Gershwin's fee was already pricey and that a late-night, emergency meeting would cost a lot more. Nelson assured him that money was not an issue.

"Mr. Gershwin, thanks for meeting me so late and on short notice."

"Please, call me Andy, Mr. Rockledge."

"That's Nelson. Now that the BS is out of the way, let me show you why you're here."

They walked upstairs in silence. It gave Andy a chance to take in the surroundings. The house, he knew immediately, was a Messier Home. He'd been in several of the custom built homes. There was something about them that made them stand out. It was obvious that Nelson Rockledge could afford his fee, but he wasn't worried about that. At the base of the stairs, the house still had that new house smell, even though Nelson and Jillian had lived here for several months. As they made their way to the master bedroom, Andy could smell the burnt electronics. It wasn't overpowering, but it was definitely in the air. It got a bit stronger as he passed through the bedroom doorway. Nelson stood next to the piece of molding that he'd taken down earlier and presented it like a game show host, extending his hand as if saying, the winner takes home this beautiful piece of ornate molding. But his face held a different expression. He was frowning, his facial muscles tense.

"Andy, I think someone planted cameras and microphones in my house. I want to know who, and why. But mostly, I want to know where they are. I think it has to be an employee of Messier's. But I don't have any way to prove it. That's where you come in. How can you help us?"

"Let's start with the devices. They usually have serial numbers on them. Of course, whoever is doing this would have to be a complete idiot to register them in their name and then use them for something as obviously illegal as spying on someone. Hey, criminals aren't known for their intelligence."

Andy took the two devices that Nelson had removed. He looked at the camera first. He didn't look long then switched to the microphone. He mouthed the word *Wow*. He looked back at the camera again, rubbed the tiny nameplate with his fingertip. "The serial numbers are intact so we can find out where they were purchased. It might be a little harder to find out who purchased them, but if you're willing to spend a little payola, then we can get a name."

Nelson nodded. He smiled slightly as he thought about the gun in his dresser drawer. "How soon can you get me that information?"

"If I get these back to my office tonight, I think I can have an answer for you first thing in the morning." Nelson nodded his approval. "Also, do you mind if I take down another piece of molding to see if I can find another pair of these? Maybe I can get a set of prints off them. These," he held up the ones that Nelson had pulled, "are probably no good for prints since we've both handled them."

"Sure." It never occurred to him that there might be more cameras around the room. "Do you think there are others?"

"Oh yeah. I have a feeling there are plenty. But let's take this one step at a time. We'll be quick, but we have to be thorough."

What do I tell Jillian? She'll be devastated.

Chapter 35

Aaron was getting sick of the smell in the old walk in cooler at the drive-through. The cooler hadn't been used in over two years. The lingering, musty smell was bad when he first entered the cooler, but got worse the longer he stayed inside. He was glad that he was down to the last box, though there was still enough cash left in the last bag for at least one more, full box. He figured he had enough money packed to last at least one lifetime and that's all he'd need. Maybe if there was time he'd come back and grab the rest, but he doubted the risk would be worth the reward.

He finished assembling the last box. He lined the inside of the box with plain paper and started loading stacks of cash in the box. The boxes weighed about 45 pounds each. He didn't know how much cash was in each. The bills were wrapped in such a way that the hundreds, fifties, twenties, tens and fives were together, but the stacks were randomly grouped. It would take hours to get even an estimate. As he dropped the last stack of bills into place, a siren sounded outside of the building. Aaron was startled. He froze and didn't make a sound. He carefully looked out the cooler door and watched as an ambulance roared past. He drew in a deep breath, then headed back to the task of sealing the last box and putting it in the stack.

Next, he slapped premade labels on each box. The delivery service would be there the next day. His instructions to them were to deliver the boxes to a private marina in Miami, Florida. From there, Aaron was planning a little boat trip to the Cayman Islands. He already had the account set up. He already had a condominium leased. And he already had an alias created with a new identity. Aaron smiled as he put the last label in place.

* * *

"I told you he was double-crossing us! That son-of-a-bitch! We should go over there right now and kick his ass! We'll leave him in that cooler and take all the money. That fuckin' son-of-a-bitch!" Gerry was livid. He continued to vent, spitting out off-the-cuff ideas about how they should dispose of Aaron Messier and take all the money.

Roger just sat in the truck and listened. He was pissed, too. But he knew they had time. Hell, they were supposed to go back to the house and make another haul tomorrow night. For that matter, they could go there right now and finish the job. Plus they could find their own hide out and split the remainder 50-50. That would be plenty of money for the two of them. They wouldn't need to bother with Aaron. And maybe they could spring a trap that would teach Aaron a lesson. By the time he figured out who'd stung him, they'd be long gone.

Roger looked at Gerry and said, "Would you stop with the whining already."

Gerry was insulted that Roger would call this whining. He was plotting, figuring out a way to get that Messier bastard. Roger continued, "I want to get back at him just as much as you do. We just have to think this through, that's all." He paused and looked back through the field glasses at the drive through. They didn't know what Aaron was doing inside, but they figured he was stealing their money. It didn't matter that they'd stolen it in the first place.

Gerry was getting antsy. "He's been in there for over an hour. What the hell is he doing?"

"We'll see. Maybe he's just counting it or something. It could be all night if that's what he's doing. Hell, there's at least a couple million bucks in there." Roger was about to tell Gerry his plan to go back to the Kirkwood house when the back door of the drive through opened. Aaron walked out and headed for his truck. As far as Roger could see, he was empty

handed. So the money stayed put for now. That was good.
But Aaron didn't go there just to look at the cash. There was
something going on. He'd carried a bundle of what looked like
boxes into the store, but came out with nothing.

As they watched, Aaron started his truck and drove off,
heading towards his house. Roger and Gerry waited a few
minutes and fell in behind Aaron's truck. They followed at a
distance all the way to Aaron's. When his truck disappeared
into the drive, they kept driving past.

Gerry asked, "What now?"

"Let's give Aaron a call and ask him about tomorrow
night. Maybe he'll slip up and tell us what he was doing at the
drive through tonight."

"Good thinking. If we don't like his answers, we can
go do the rest of the Kirkwood house tonight."

Roger nodded. They were just a night away from being
millionaires, one way or another.

* * *

Aaron chuckled to himself. *What morons. They didn't
think I saw them behind the drive-through? Why do I even pay
these guys? Idiots. Fools.* Aaron was smiling as he drove
towards his house. *They'll be rotting in a jail cell when the
police get the film of the rape. Or better yet, I'll send their
names and addresses to her husband. I'll put a note in there
about how they enjoyed his wife's company. That should send
him over the edge. I won't have to worry about these two
anymore.*

He looked in his rear view mirror at the old pick-up
truck that Roger and Gerry were following in. *Ha! Come on
fellas. Come on over if you want. It won't matter. You fools
will probably go over to the Kirkwoods. If you only knew
where they got their money and where they sent it. You'd think
you were doing your patriotic duty stealing it. But all you want
is a big score. You jackasses would be caught within a week of
having all that cash 'cause you don't know how to keep your
cool.* Aaron shook his head at the irony. He was going to fool
them all.

He turned into his driveway and watched to see if his stooges would follow him in. When he saw the truck drive past, he smiled. *Time to crank up the video cams.* I'll bet they show up at the Kirkwood's within two hours. They can't help themselves.

Aaron parked and went straight to the control room. He keyed up the cameras at the Kirkwood residence on one of the small screens then brought up several of his favorite archived videos. He watched the video for about ten minutes then headed upstairs for a beer.

When he got his beer he sat on a bar stool in the kitchen. He had to decide what he would do about the camera failure at the Rockledge residence. That was unfortunate. It was also bad for business. They were becoming the most popular couple on the network. After the rape and now the recovery, people seemed truly interested in the Rockledge woman's well being. *Strange.* It was almost like a soap opera. They were into the sex, for sure. But they also seemed to be responding to the drama. Their motivation didn't matter to Aaron. It was all money. Their subscription numbers were on the rise again in just a few days. He was happy. His partner was getting off his back a little, not that it mattered. Within twenty-four hours this was all going to be history. He had going away presents for all of them. *We'll get them back, Mom. You'll be proud of me.*

His house phone rang, startling him. He shook his head and answered. "Hello?"

"Hey, little brother. Are you up and about? I wanted to talk with you about this Jake character. I think you might be right about hitting him first."

Aaron hesitated. He hadn't expected to hear from Jeremy again so soon. "Yeah, well, he did threaten to kill you. It only makes sense to protect yourself. How are the ribs?"

Jeremy was again taken aback by Aaron's change of personality. What changed in the last few days to make him come out of his shell? "The ribs are still sore as hell. I can hardly move without a pain running all over my body." He

266 P. J. Grondin

paused. "Aaron, are you feeling alright? Are you on some kind of new meds? You seem . . . different. You never used to be so opinionated."

"What, can't I help my big brother? After all you've done for me?"

Jeremy didn't know where that last comment came from. He'd never really done anything for Aaron. He mostly stayed away from him. They were so different. But he played along to see where Aaron was headed. "Well, I guess. Any ideas on how I should do it? I mean, he's always got his bodyguard with him. How can I even get to him?"

"I might be able to help you with that. This Jake character likes to hang out at a lady friends' house near Tysons Corner. He goes alone. You could nail him after he leaves in the early morning when the least number of people are around. Fewer chances for witnesses. Just get a gun with a silencer. But you can't think too much about it. You'll lose your nerve."

Jeremy held the phone away from his ear and stared at it for several long seconds. Who was this person with all this advice? "Okay . . . Aaron. This is Aaron right?"

"Look man, I've gotta go. If you want to drop by for a beer it has to be in the next twenty minutes. I'm getting a little tired."

"We can skip it for tonight. Maybe tomorrow. I'll call. Maybe my body will start to recover by then."

"Sure." The phone disconnected. Aaron headed down to the basement and let himself into the control room.

He stopped in his tracks. "Hello Aaron."

"Hi." Aaron's eyes immediately went to the floor. Just like that, he was back to his introverted self again.

His older partner asked, "When were you going to tell me about the problem at the Rockledge house? You know, the little fire and the fact that they know about the cameras and microphones." His partner's expression was a patient, probing look. It was a sinister look because Aaron knew how explosive his temper could be. He'd seen it in action twice before. He didn't want to be the recipient of the third such event.

* * *

Almost an hour later, Roger and Gerry were about ten minutes away from the Kirkwood's. They were going to break back in and get their share of cash. Screw Aaron. They called Aaron's home phone and got no answer. So much for trying to get him to slip up. No matter. They had plenty of black trash bags that would soon be filled with cash. They wouldn't be headed to the drive-through this time. Roger and Gerry had a different destination in mind. Plus they added a new twist. They planned to drop some evidence in the Kirkwood vault that would point the finger right at Aaron Messier. They'll teach that bastard to fuck with them.

As they approached the Kirkwood driveway, they saw flashing lights. The driveway to the Kirkwood's was blocked by a county sheriff's car. Stunned, Roger kept driving past. Neither man drew a breath or looked at the sheriff's car as they went by. Their plans were instantly flushed. After they passed the house, Roger kept looking in the rear-view mirror, expecting the sheriff's car to chase them down. Roger made a left turn and headed towards Interstate 95.

"So what the fuck are we going to do now?" Gerry was pissed off again. Aaron had screwed them out of their take on the initial haul. Now the cops were crawling all over the Kirkwood residence.

Roger didn't answer for almost a full minute. Then he said, "We're going to grab the money when Aaron tries to move it. We just have to keep a close eye on that drive-through." He paused. "So we should probably start watching it about 4:30 AM. He's gonna want to move it soon."

"Okay. But we've been up all day. How are we gonna stay awake?"

"We'll just have to take turns watching. Let's go get cleaned up and then we can start. You can take the first watch."

"Great. So when I fall asleep you can blame me."

"You are such a crybaby."

* * *

The sheriff received an all clear. Apparently it was a prank call that a bomb was spotted near the driveway of the Kirkwood residence. He shut off his lights and headed out on his regular patrol.

Chapter 36

"Get outta here! Now!" Jake chased his ladies out of his office. They'd tried to get him to relax by offering to perform a little ménage a trois, but he wasn't in the mood. The girls barely got their clothes together when he shut the door to his office behind them. Once again, he hadn't heard from Jeremy Messier. He was through playing nice guy with this punk. His time was running out.

A drink. That's what I need. He grabbed a bottle of Green Spot Irish Whiskey from the liquor cabinet and poured a generous glass. He took a drink and savored the taste before swallowing the mouthful down in one quick gulp. He took a few seconds to let his throat soothe a bit, then took another drink. He let this mouthful swish around a bit before swallowing. He loved Green Spot. Once he started drinking the top shelf brand, he never touched another brand of whiskey. He couldn't believe that he drank the cheap booze all those years. But that was before he made his fortune in porn and flesh peddling. Even after he could afford the expensive stuff, he kept drinking cheap liquor. Then a friend told him he needed to upgrade. *Stop acting like a low-rent hood. You're a wealthy man now. Act like one.*

Jake started spending like a rich man but he still dressed and acted like a hood. It was in his blood. He'd never be a suit. And the friend that told him how to be classy? Dead. Someone blew his brains all over his expensive suit. *Too bad. He was a jackass anyway.*

He finished his second Green Spot and poured another. He was calm, but still mad as hell. He was smiling now. He knew that he was going to have his new porn site today or

Jeremy was a dead man. He looked around his office and smiled. *I got all the class I need. I got babes. I got big toys.* He smiled in the direction of his new, big-screen TV. *I got a couple expensive cars. I got a great gun. But I'm not gonna waste killing that punk with my good gun. I'll do it with a throw away.* He took another drink of whiskey and swallowed it straight down. No time to savor the taste. He had to take care of business. He slammed the glass down on his desk, reached into the bottom drawer, and pulled out a Smith and Wesson .357. *This ought to do the trick.* He checked to make sure it was loaded and stuck it in the waistband of his pants. *Time to go to work.*

He headed out the office door. He yelled, "Hey! Let's get the fuckin' lead out."

Shamus jumped up trying to catch up with his boss. He knew Jake was through playing with the Messier kid. It was going to be a dangerous night.

* * *

Jeremy hung up the phone. His talk with Aaron left him scared. He'd washed down a couple more Ibuprofen with a couple bottles of Bud Light, trying to stop the continuously throbbing pain in his side. He had no doubt that he had at least one broken rib. The bruising was unbelievable. It covered most of his torso on his left side. He was trying to think through the pain, figuring out what he should do next. He had a feeling that this Jake character wasn't going to wait much longer. Jeremy never called him with the answer that he wanted, the one that he couldn't give because he couldn't sell something he didn't have.

He took another big gulp of Bud Light then looked at the gun sitting on the table. Was he going to have to use it in self defense? If he went out and killed Jake now, would that be considered self defense or premeditated murder? Should he go on the offensive and knock Jake off before he knew what hit him? *It might be my only chance. If I have to face him while Shamus is there, my chances of getting away alive are slim.*

That guy looks like a paid killer. He wouldn't bat an eye before he killed someone. Especially me!

Well, that narrows things down quite a bit. Jeremy thought back to his encounter with Aaron at his house; Aaron acting strange. All of a sudden he was mister motor-mouth. He never used to say anything unless you drug an answer out of him. Now he was running his mouth and looking Jeremy straight in the eyes. He wondered if he'd been on medications all these years and decided he didn't need them anymore. Their mother's disappearance did hit Aaron particularly hard. He still got extremely depressed talking about her. *Screw that. She left. Dad had to do all this on his own, for the most part anyway. Tom was a big help to him, but other than that, he had to run the business and raise us.* Jeremy shook his head to get back to the task at hand. *Must be the beer and pain killers.*

Jeremy finally decided he had to be the aggressor. It was time to shit or get off the pot. He picked up the gun and dropped it in his jacket pocket. He pulled it back out and checked the clip for bullets. It was loaded and ready to go. He looked at it again to make sure the safety was on. It was a good thing he checked because the safety showed a red dot. He flipped the switch and put the safety on before he dropped it in his pocket again. *Hell, I can hardly stand to have this gun on me much less use it on somebody, even if it is a bastard like Jake. Guess I better have another bottle of courage before I leave.*

Tysons Corner. So Jake the mad man has a girlfriend. I wonder if she's a nut case like him? She'd have to be. If I have another beer I might not be able to make it to his girlfriend's tonight. Maybe I will swing by Aaron's for that beer. The beer and the pain killers were taking their toll. With that, Jeremy closed his eyes and fell asleep.

* * *

Jake and Shamus drove past Messier's offices. They were dark and locked. Jake was more pissed now than ever. He yelled at Shamus, "We're coming back here at closing tomorrow! That fucker'll be here! He's done! We'll just kill him and take the site for ourselves. I'll get geek boy to hack in and take over. The cops ain't gonna give half a shit about a stolen porn site. Jake's face twisted into a wicked smile. Shamus was thinking that Jake had finally gone off the deep end. He headed the car back towards the interstate.

* * *

Pat, Joe, Hatch, and Johnny were checked in at the Holiday Inn Express north of Stafford. They wanted to be close to the empty lot so that they could get an early start. Pat called Diane to let her know that they made the trip without any problems, except that Joe snored so loud, he kept Pat and Hatch awake. Plus Johnny wouldn't stop most of the trip so they could use the rest room. Finally, Joe threatened to pee out the window. Johnny didn't want to get stopped by a fellow officer, so he relented and stopped for a whole ten minutes for a pit stop.

Pat said to Diane, "It's a good thing you packed those sandwiches for us. We'd be starving by now. We're heading up to a Subway for dinner. It's within walking distance, thank God. I couldn't stand another ten minutes in that miniature jail on wheels."

Diane said, "You are such a wimp when it comes to traveling. You never could make it more than a couple hours without stopping for food or a bathroom break."

"Me? You're the one with the teeny, tiny bladder. We always had to stop on road trips because you couldn't hold it."

"That's because I was seven months pregnant. There's not much room for a full bladder when you have a child growing inside." Diane was smiling at the thought. She remembered the trip around Lake Erie in July when the temperature was near ninety degrees. Their car's air conditioner went out about half way around the lake, near Lemington, Ontario. Diane suffered in the heat as Sean, then unborn, was making a soccer ball out of her bladder. "I remember that you had to stop at McDonalds, supposedly to get a milkshake. I also remember you beating me to the bathroom."

It was Pat's turn to smile on his end of the phone. He remembered it well. It wasn't one of their most pleasant trips, but it was memorable. They were at Niagara Falls the night before when an electric storm blew in. A lightning bolt hit a tree that was less than fifty feet away. It sounded like a bomb went off. The lights in the park at the American Falls went out. It was pitch black as they tried to find their way back to their hotel. They still had a good time, but it was mostly because they had several stories to tell at parties.

Diane's voice became more solemn. "Pat, you be careful. Use your head and stay away from trouble. You hear me?"

"I will, Dear. I miss you already. I'll be home soon. I love you."

"I love you, too."

"Kiss the kids for me."

"I will."

Pat held the phone a little longer, heard the click, then a dial tone. With his eyes watering slightly, he set the receiver down.

Joe came out of the bathroom and asked, "Are you done yet? I've got to call Lisa. We're not even in the house and she's already got plans for making over every room in the place."

"Get used to it. It never stops. Diane is still trying to get me to remodel the bedroom. Hell, its perfect already."

Joe was deep in thought. When he broke out of his trance he said, "I don't think Lisa was ready to buy a house."

Pat's jaw nearly hit the floor. Lisa said several times that she wanted the house. It was Joe who was hesitant to put in a bid. "Wow. I must have missed something, 'cause I'm sure Lisa said, "Let's buy it" about four times. I recall you saying, "Maybe we should look at one or two more." Then she said, "I really like this one." And you said . . ."

"Okay. Alright. I get it. I wasn't sure. Buying a house is a big step. I wanted to make sure we made the right decision." Joe looked away. Pat was trying to read his face but Joe wouldn't even look at him.

"You aren't having second thoughts about Lisa, are you? 'Cause if you are, I'm going to kick your ass all the way back to Florida."

Joe looked back at Pat and laughed, but it was a forced laugh. Then he said, "First off, you couldn't kick my ass on your best day. Second, I'm not having second thoughts about Lisa. I'm just . . . well . . . this is a big commitment. I mean, it's like we'd . . . hell, I don't know. I felt funny about house shopping and all."

Joe's square jaw jutted out in a nervous gesture. Pat had only seen him like this once before. It was when he was preparing to leave for Marine boot camp. He was committed but he was still unsure of himself. After boot camp he wreaked confidence. Even now he was sure of himself in almost everything he did. Until now.

"Joe, what's the problem? You look like a scared little kid."

Joe sat down on the edge of the hotel room bed. His shoulders slumped as he thought about what to say. He looked up at the ceiling, gathering his thoughts then said, "Ever since Dad died and then Lisa's dad died, I've been feeling a little vulnerable. You know, when I got out of boot camp, I felt invincible; almost immortal. Now that I'm about to be discharged from the reserves, I feel alone. You know, the Marines are a part of me, but I'm giving that up, I guess for Lisa. I'm not sure I want to."

Pat looked at his younger brother. What he'd just said made perfect sense. The military builds a strong bond, whether you like it or not. He felt it in the Navy, though he was happy to get out. But he knew the Marine Corps forged a stronger bond. Joe was his brother, but he knew Joe had a brother-like bond with his fellow Marines. That bond was forged in the blood of fellow Marines. Once a Marine, always a Marine.

He said, "Look Joe, I know you love the Marines. I can't possibly know how it feels to give up being in the reserves. It's part of your life and always will be. But Lisa is part of your life, too. She'll be a bigger part of your life than you'll ever know. Just don't let the Marines get in the way of a happy life together. You'll regret it later." Pat paused then added, "Trust me on this."

Joe looked at his older brother. He did have more experience in this department. He thought for a few moments then said, "I know Lisa's the only one for me. I don't have any doubt about that. I'm just scared to leave part of my life behind. The Corps was great for me; still is."

"Have you and Lisa talked about this? Does she know that you don't really want to give up your reserve status?"

"Nope. I told her I would without even discussing it. When we came back from Virginia and my arm was grazed by that bullet, the fear in her eyes when she saw that was all I needed to make up my mind. I made the commitment to get out right then and there. In the heat of the moment, it was an easy decision. Now, with some afterthought, I'm not sure it was the right decision. Not for me, anyway."

Pat sat on the bed across from Joe. He looked at his brother and smiled. "Then you'd better have another talk with her about this, and soon. If you don't think you can leave the reserves, then you better find out if she can stand you staying in. If she can't, then one of you is going to be miserable your entire lives. You don't want that. Talk to her and find out if that fear was just a shock reaction. That was a pretty intense night."

Pat pulled his own shirt up to show Joe his chest. The heart shaped bruise where the bullet hit against the Kevlar vest on Pat's chest was still visible, almost two months later. It was a yellowish discoloration now, but it left a lasting impression on Diane. She hated to let Pat out of her sight.

"See this? I think Diane beats on it while I'm sleeping to make sure it doesn't go away. She never wants me to forget that I could have died. I think that's what Lisa was feeling. She may still feel that way. Diane and I talked about it. We know how each other feels.   You and Lisa need to be absolutely honest with each other."

"So are you absolutely honest with Diane?"

They both knew the answer to this question. There was one thing that Pat could never tell Diane. That he had killed another man in cold blood would go with him to his grave. The expression on his face was reflected in Joe's own expression. It was their bond. Only they, and Hatch, knew the whole story. The three would never speak of it, even in private.

"I have to call Lisa."

"Okay. I have to take a shower. I'll be in there a while so take your time."

Joe nodded his appreciation and Pat headed for the bathroom.

Joe dialed and Lisa answered on the first ring. "Hey, Babe. I miss you."

"I miss you, too."   There was a silence on the line as Joe took a deep breath. Lisa was afraid he was having second thoughts about the house in Winter Garden.   "You haven't changed your mind on the house, have you?"

"No, absolutely not. But I have decided a few other things. First, I love you more than anything."

"I love you, too."

"Second, whatever you want to do to the house is fine with me. If you want a new kitchen, bath, whatever. You decide and we'll make it happen."

Lisa's smile lit up the entire apartment living room. She was nearly giddy with excitement. "Are you sure?"

"Absolutely. I love the house. We'll love it even more when we make it the way we want it."

"Oh, Joe. I love you."

Joe was silent for several seconds. Lisa thought they'd disconnected. "Joe, are you still there?"

Joe took a deep breath. "Lisa, we do have something else we need to talk about. But I don't want to do it over the phone."

"You want to stay in the reserves."

Joe was stunned. He didn't know what to say for a few seconds. Then he said, "Well . . . uh . . . yeah. How'd you know? I mean, I haven't said anything about it."

"I know, but I could see it in your eyes, in your manner, in your heart. I know you love the Corps. If it means that much to you, you have to stay in. I'll love you no matter where you go or what you do."

Joe was choking up on his end of the phone. He said, "It was that obvious, huh?

"Oh, yeah. But that's okay. At least you're being honest with me. I mean, if you'd have kept this from me for years, then sprung it on me about how miserable you are because of me, I don't know what I'd do. As long as we're honest with each other, we can make it through anything."

They talked for a while longer about their new house and the things Lisa wanted to change. The talk was light. Then Joe said, "Lisa, I've got to get to bed. I'll call tomorrow when I know more about when we're gonna finish up here."

"Joe, we're really homeowners. "

"Your first house is going to be your dream house."

They exchanged more love talk, then disconnected. Joe smiled to himself just as Pat exited the bathroom.

"Looks to me like everything went well."

"You bet your ass it did." Joe's smile broadened.

Chapter 37

Nelson was sitting alone in the master bedroom where he'd removed every length of ceiling molding and placed it on the floor. The small wires ran up through the ceiling into the attic at one end of the bedroom. They were easily concealed behind the intricate ceiling molding. The slight smell of burned electronics still hung in the air. He was astonished at the number of cameras and microphones mounted in the fancy trim. Someone spent a lot of money on the installation and wiring of the cameras. Nelson surmised that someone was making a lot of money by filming him and his wife. That was the only plausible explanation he could think of why they would go to this much expense. Besides, there was a lot of risk planting these devices permanently in a home. There was bound to be a malfunction eventually.

"Is she alright?" He called and asked Jillian's mother how his beautiful, young wife was doing. She'd been through two very traumatic, personal attacks in the last few weeks. The first was physical. The second might as well have been. The issue with their dog, Fenton, seemed trivial by comparison. She felt completely vulnerable, not sure where to turn for the privacy that she so desperately needed. She told Nelson that it was her fault. She said that if they'd only bought a less expensive, less extravagant home, this wouldn't have happened. Nelson tried his best to assure her that none of this was her fault. It was the work of a few sick bastards and they would find them and prosecute them.

Jillian's mother felt sorry for Nelson. She knew he was doing his best to take care of her daughter. "She needs to rest, but I'm not sure she'll sleep well. She's in her old room curled

up in bed. She won't take anything to help her calm down."
She paused then said, "Nelson, I'm sorry."

On the other end of the phone, Nelson gave a puzzled
look towards the receiver. "Sorry for what, June?"

In a guilty tone, she said, "Well, I told Jillian that you
two should build that . . ."

Nelson cut her off and said more forcefully than he
intended, "June, this isn't your fault. It isn't Jillian's fault. It
isn't anyone's fault except the son-of-a-bitch that planted those
cameras. We're going to find whoever did this and they're
going to be locked up for a long time. Then they can have
cameras watching them all the time, in prison. Don't blame
yourself. That's the way these people want you to feel. Then
they can get away with it and do it again to others. We're not
going to let that happen."

June was silent on the other end of the line. Even
though she knew Nelson was right, she still felt a tinge of guilt
course through her mind. "Nelson, thank you for taking care of
Jillian. You're a good man."

"Thank you, June. When will Andrew be back?"

"He should be back tomorrow."

"I'd like to talk with him. We need to find someone
who has special skills in home security. It's the only way
Jillian will ever be able to trust anyone again." He took a deep
breath and continued. "This is going to be a long recovery. I'll
be over later this evening. Don't wait up. I have a few people
I have to talk with tonight."

"Alright. You have the key. Nelson, please be careful.
These people seem awfully bold."

"I will. Good night June."

Nelson sat back in the cushioned chair trying to relax,
waiting for his visitor. After hanging up the receiver, he
thought about what June said. *These people seem awfully bold.*
There was no doubt about that. How could anyone think that
they could get away with planting cameras in someone's
home? It was obvious that they were filming their most
intimate moments, but where were they recording them and

selling them? Was there really a market for this kind of trash? It was mind boggling. And what if people they knew saw them on the internet? Would they think they were in on it willingly? Nelson just shook his head, wondering where this was going to end.

He knew one thing for sure. Someone at Messier Homes had to be involved. It was the only way those cameras could have been planted during the construction of the house. Someone on the inside was one sick bastard.

As Nelson sat in the corner chair and looked around their bedroom, where all the molding was removed, he knew that they would never be able to continue to live in this house. He also knew that the source of the problem was at Messiers. He thought about Jillian. She would always wonder if they missed a camera or two. She'd never feel like this was her home ever again. This fabulous home was ruined for her. They put their lives into making sure that this was their dream home, the only home they would ever want to own. And it was . . . until now. Someone had taken that dream and turned it into a nightmare. He wondered if the two rapists had anything to do with this. Maybe they were in on it from the beginning. But were they willing to have themselves caught on film raping a woman? It didn't seem likely. But having unknown cameras in your million dollar home wasn't likely either.

Nelson was startled when he heard the doorbell ring. He shook his head and went down to greet his old friend, Samuel "Sammy" Jones.

Sammy and Nelson were friends all the way through high school. Sammy played football and had a promising career. He'd signed a letter of intent to play for The Ohio State University to play linebacker, but a freak injury during practice stopped his career in its tracks.

His football career was over. But he had other talents. He could solve problems. He could read people like a book. He also had an interest in computers and electronic devices, mainly video and audio devices. He also had an IQ that was off the charts. He could remember details from conversations forever that most people forgot within minutes. He was also one of the most articulate speakers Nelson had ever met.

He started a small private investigations office, specializing in surveillance for industrial companies. Employee theft prevention was his most lucrative line of work. Many large corporations had a hard time keeping their employees honest. Sammy helped them stay honest by giving seminars to employees on the cost of theft from employers. When that didn't work, he helped employers catch dishonest employees. Nelson trusted the man his lawyer recommended but he wanted Sammy to give his opinion and verify what he was being told.

"Sammy my man, how are you?" Nelson's smile, though genuine, was obviously strained. He shook his friend's hand and showed him into the entryway.

Sammy Jones stood nearly a half a head taller than Nelson's six-feet two-inches and outweighed him by at least forty pounds. Sammy was muscular and broad. His thick neck tapered down to his shoulders and was squared with the sides of his head. His short cropped hair was flat on top and squared down the sides which made his head look like a block. His skin was dark black from his Jamaican ancestry. He had handsome features. Sammy looked around the house and whistled. "Fabulous place you have here, Nelson. You must be doing well, a bit better than when we were in high school."

Nelson's jaw again tightened at the thought that he and Jillian would have to move out of their dream home. That's why Sammy was here. He wanted to know just how professional these creeps were. He also wanted to know what it would take to plant this many cameras without being spotted during home construction. After an hour, he had his answer.

Sammy explained to Nelson that the equipment was expensive, military grade electronics. And the installation was pretty good. The cameras were concealed well. The way the lenses were hidden by the fancy ceiling molding was pretty ingenious and difficult to detect. But he also said the transmitter that Nelson discovered in the attic was a hatchet job. Sammy said rhetorically, "After spending all that money on high end cameras, they spliced the central transmitter into some live wires without an electrical box? Just a quick splice and some electrical tape. Pretty shoddy work from that standpoint."

"So this isn't a professional job?" Nelson's face was twisted into a frown.

"I'd say that, whoever installed the transmitter had to do it as a rush job. It wasn't well thought out. It could have been put any number of places. A house this big has a lot of room where false walls or wire channels could be used to hide a device like this." He held up the transmitter that Nelson found in the attic under a small piece of insulation. He couldn't believe that the splice was done so poorly in a house that had such high quality workmanship in every other aspect. "I'm not sure that anyone from Messiers did this, at least not the transmitter install."

Nelson looked puzzled now. If this wasn't someone from the Messier's crews then who could have had access to the site while it was under construction? He asked Sammy that question.

"Nelson, this house is isolated. Anyone could have come out here at night and done this job. I bet that this didn't take twenty minutes. The splice job was so poor I'm surprised that the wires had electrical contact. It was probably done at night with a flashlight, meaning poor visibility. But it had to be someone who knows something about electricity. They had to know what wires were hot all the time."

Nelson looked puzzled again.

Sammy continued. "Some wires run from light fixtures down to switches and back. When the switch is off, the wire won't have power. But wires that run directly from the power panel have power all the time, as long as the circuit breaker is on. So your installer had to know what wire to pick or they had to at least know how to use a proximity voltage tester. They can detect hot lines without breaching the insulation."

Nelson's face registered understanding. He thought about members of the building crew that he'd met during construction. He tried to think about the electricians. The only name that came to mind was Tom Grayson. He didn't appear to be the type to plant illegal cameras and transmitters in new homes. But who knows what goes on in some people's minds?

"Sammy. If this were your house, where would you start?"

"I'd start with the Messiers, the owners I mean. Confront them and let them know you mean business. Put the responsibility on them to find this bastard. It is in their best interest to find this creep and fire him, maybe even help in the prosecution.   They can't afford the bad publicity and the lawsuits that their bound to get. Plus, your house probably isn't the only one wired up like this. There may be dozens."

Nelson's jaw dropped in surprise.   He hadn't considered that there might be more homes wired with cameras and microphones.

"The other thing you need to figure out, with my help, of course, is where the transmitter was sending the signal. I'll have to look up the specs on this model. It could be sending a signal as close as five hundred yards to many miles. It could be transmitting to a satellite, then who knows where it's going from there.

Nelson's surprise was turning to anger once again. "Do you mean to tell me people all over the world could have been watching while we . . ." His voice trailed off. The more he thought about that possibility, the angrier he became.

He and Sammy talked strategy for the next forty-five minutes. Sammy was trying to keep his friend level headed, but the entire time Nelson was thinking of his own plan. The slight scent of the burned electronic camera invaded his senses. He thought of Jillian, curled up on her childhood bed at her parent's house. He'd brought her back from one intense physical violation, but could he bring her back from a virtual invasion of their home? Your home was supposed to be your refuge, the place you could come to find protection from the outside world when things were tough. Now that layer of protection had been breached. There was nowhere for her to hide. Worse, Nelson felt violated as much as Jillian. He was supposed to provide the home where they could be safe. Had he failed? His mind was starting to play tricks on his psyche. The words he spoke to Jillian and Jillian's mother came back to him. *It isn't your fault, it isn't Jillian's fault. It isn't anyone's fault except the son-of-a-bitch that planted those cameras.* He thought, *It isn't my fault either.*

He had to be strong for them. He had to get back the feeling of security. He had to restore his poor wife's confidence in him, in his ability to provide protection and security. He hoped he could, but this time, it would be much more difficult.

After Sammy went over the main points of their discussion, they shook hands, agreeing to keep in touch. Sammy headed to his car and left. As his tail lights hit the end of the drive, some 200 yards away, Nelson headed up to the bedroom. He had to make sure his gun was loaded.

Chapter 38

The predawn, October air was chilly and damp. The northeastern sky, only moments ago a dark gray, began to turn blue, with wisps of pink clouds high above. There was very little air moving as a high pressure system gripped the region, keeping the cold rains at bay. That was good news for Hatch, Johnny Poleirmo, and the McKinney brothers. They'd just come from central Florida the previous day and weren't prepared for the shock of the crisp air between the Potomac River and the Blue Ridge Mountains. The thin jackets that each wore couldn't fight the chilled air that invaded their bodies.

"I guess we should have listened to Diane, eh Pat?" Johnny was the first to point out that Pat's wife said they should take warmer clothes, particularly warmer jackets, with them on their journey to Virginia.

Hatch chimed in, "Yeah, but Pat knows better than to think it might be in the forties here in Virginia. Hell, it was seventy-two when we left Dunnellon. Right, Pat?"

Standing by the side of the car with his arms crossed over his chest, shivering, Pat didn't say a word. His teeth were chattering though. He wasn't looking forward to walking around the ten-plus acres in his tennis shoes, especially since the dew on the weeds and grass was heavy. He was already thinking ahead, knowing that his feet would be getting soaked to the bone and frozen.

He knew what it was like to have frozen feet. When he and Joe were young, living in Port Clinton, Ohio, Daniel McKinney, their dad, took them ice fishing out on Lake Erie. Pat hated it. The entire time on the ice, all he did was complain. He didn't even drop his line through the hole cut in the ice. Joe caught three perch and their dad caught four. Then before they left, they threw them back in and headed for home. All that time on the ice and they didn't have a thing to show for it.

When they got home, Pat complained more as he took off his shoes and three layers of socks. They were soaked through to the skin. His feet felt like they were being stabbed with daggers as warmth returned. He swore that he'd never go ice fishing again. What was the point if you couldn't even eat the fish that you caught?

Joe loved it. He asked his dad when he could go out again. Joe and his dad went out several more times that year and the next. Then they moved to Indiana and never went out on the ice again.

Pat was already dreading the idea of his feet getting soaked with icy cold dew. But it was that feeling of needles penetrating his feet that he hated the most. He shook his head at the thought.

A bright glow illuminated the hilltop as the sun rose, now fully up over the horizon. The team couldn't see it because they were at the foot of a south-facing rise to the hill. The majority of the acreage that they planned to search was on the south slope. Only about four acres was beyond the rise. Johnny and Hatch were discussing the best way to cover the ground. They were also waiting on a team from the local sheriff's office to join in the search. Officially, Johnny, Hatch, Pat and Joe were there to assist the sheriff. In reality, they would lead. They weren't sure yet what they were looking for, but they figured they'd know when they found it.

Joe had been scanning the terrain as if trying to locate Iraqi insurgents. He had field glasses raised to his eyes and was meticulously moving up and down the hill. It was like he'd divided the hill into blocks and was searching each block thoroughly before moving on. He turned to Pat after mentally marking the spot where he left off.

"Does this remind you of ice fishing on the lake?" His smile was broad, knowing that it would hit a nerve with Pat.

He gave Joe a surprised look with a touch of annoyance. "How the hell did you know I was thinking about that?"

Joe continued smiling and said, "It was written in big, bold letters on your face. It was the same look you had while you watched me and Dad catch those puny perch. You were so pissed when we threw them back."

"Hell yes, I was pissed. I froze my ass off. I thought they were going to have to amputate my feet. When the feeling came back in them, I wanted to cut them off. Man that hurt."

Pat started to smile at the memory. He thought about his dad. He was only trying to do something any father would want to do; spend time with his boys. Pat's mind drifted for a moment as he thought about his son, Sean. He took Sean fishing in Florida on Lake Harris. It was quite the opposite experience between him and Sean. His son caught a nice-sized large-mouth bass. When Pat said that they would take it home and eat it, Sean nearly gagged. He said he'd rather throw him back. It was then that Pat got the call from Diane that Pat and Joe's dad had suffered a heart attack.

As Pat stood thinking about the two similar, but very different father-son experiences, a feeling of homesickness washed over him. He suddenly felt like he needed to go home and spend more time with Sean. He didn't want to miss a moment of Sean growing up. He sensed that he'd already missed too much. Being out on the submarine during Sean's early years, Pat missed several birthdays, his first day at school, his first step, and first words. He didn't want to miss another life event.

Just as he was going to turn and tell Joe what he was feeling, two sheriff's cars pulled in behind the rental car. It was time to put their search plan into action. Pat shook his head and shivered one more time. *Maybe when we start walking up this hill I'll warm up a bit.*

Johnny greeted the four sheriff's deputies and introductions were made all around. One of the deputies commented that they probably should have dressed warmer. Pat took an immediate dislike to this guy, though he knew it was only in fun. Without a lot of fanfare, they pulled out a topical drawing of the lot and laid it on the hood of the first cruiser. Pat placed his hand on one corner and others followed suit to keep the drawing flat.

Deputy Lyons was apparently the senior member of the four. He spoke in a deep southern voice that carried well even in the damp morning air. As he spoke, he pointed out the boundaries of the parcel. As Pat listened, he noticed the name of the owner on the drawing. Freemen Trust. No real names.

When Deputy Lyons stopped to ask if anyone had any questions, Pat asked, "Do we know the names of the trustees for Freemen Trust?"

Deputy Lyons smiled in Pat's direction. He said in that deep southern voice, "We have some staff folks workin' on that now. We have a contact at the county office who does some investigatin' when we need 'em to, so I'm thinkin' that we'll have a name real soon."

That seemed to satisfy Pat. Joe asked the next question. "Are we going to have any problems if we stray onto the property that borders the search area? Do you know who owns the land on either side and in back?"

Lyons looked back down at the map then turned back to Joe. "The land to the right," he pointed to the land to the back side of his cruisers, "belongs to another trust. But we know who the trustees are. That's William and Ethel Horton. They've owned the property for ages. It's about 200 acres that runs along the road. They sell some timber from it occasionally. I think they plan to leave it to their kids. That ought to be fun. They have eleven and they're all over forty. I'd hate to be the executor of that will."

He pointed to the back-right corner of the parcel. "At the back corner of the lot there is a short stretch of land with 'bout a hundred fifty feet of common boundary. That land is owned by the City of Stafford. They use it for leaf disposal but are thinkin' 'bout puttin' in a compostin' facility. It's gettin' opposed by most of the locals."

"Next to that," He pointed to the top of the hill, "is an empty treed lot owned by Melissa Grand. She's a local writer. I guess you'd call her an author. She writes murder books that happen in eastern Virginia. Fiction, but she comes in and talks to us, on occasion, to get ideas. Some of her stories get a little too close to real life, at times."

"Next to that, and the last parcel that borders that back property line, is a small home on a big piece of property. That is owned by Aaron Messier."

"Finally, the property to the left is owned by Messier Homes. Aaron is one of the brothers who now own Messier Homes. Used to be owned by Theo Messier. Rumor has it that he moved to France with his young bride and left the business to the kids." He looked around at his audience. "Any other questions?"

When Deputy Lyons said Messier Homes, Pat looked over at Hatch who was rubbing his chin and squinting in the direction of construction company property. The name Messier seemed familiar, but where had he heard it before? He didn't have time to worry about it. They were getting ready to start the search. Pat let go of the corner of the drawing and headed to where Hatch was still looking over towards Messiers' land.

"Why the look?" Pat posed the question, then stood back to let Hatch think.

"You recognized the name, too, didn't ya?"

"Yeah, but I can't place it." He thought hard for a moment but nothing came to him.

"Messier Homes is the outfit that built a home for one Charlie Williams and his beautiful wife, Jody. Speaking of the Williams, I thought they were coming out here with us."

Pat said, "The sheriff advised them to not be here. Johnny delivered the call last night. Charlie was understanding, even pleased. Jody was not a happy woman. Charlie probably did not get lucky last night."

Hatch replied, "I still wouldn't want to be the guy who has to face Jody if she finds out who planted those cameras."

The rest of the team was starting to walk down the road towards the Messier Builders property line. Hatch and Pat fell in line. When the team got to the boundaries, Johnny asked each man to fall in a line about a full arm's length apart. They were going to walk up the hill slowly combing the ground as they went. Johnny explained that they didn't know what they were looking for, but if they came across anything that shouldn't be on an empty lot, they should tell everyone to stop. They would investigate each find on the spot.

They set off, heading up the hill, trying to follow the property line as best they could. Since there were no clear identifying markers for where the trust property ended and Messier's started, they didn't know if they were staying within the property line of the trust. The uphill walk seemed easy enough until the team came to a few boulders sticking out of the ground. Then they had to work their way around the boulders and reassemble the line. About half way up the rise, Messier's property sloped down. Pat could see the construction offices, storage buildings, and the gravel parking lot. It was early but there were several pickup trucks and utility vans already in the lot. Pat could see a couple employees loading supplies, getting ready to head out to a home site. He wondered what it would be like to build a home. He took another step and tripped on a tree root sticking up, just above ground level.

"Damn. I better watch where I'm going."

Joe turned and laughed when he heard Pat trip. Just as he did, he tripped and fell forward, breaking his fall with his hands. He got back up and brushed off his hands, noting a slight break in the skin where a spot of blood appeared.

"Damn. I guess I deserved that."

Pat agreed. The entire team looked where Joe tripped. Sticking out of the ground, hidden by brightly colored leaves, was a white PVC gooseneck pipe. It was an air vent. The puzzled looks on each man's face begged the same question; what was buried on this empty lot that would require an air vent?

Deputy Lyons police radio crackled to life. The female dispatcher on the radio said a few words that were inaudible to most everyone in the group, but Lyons appeared to have understood. He said a few words back to the dispatcher and the conversation continued. He took out a notepad and made a few notes before he said, "10-4. Out." That was the only thing the team understood.

"Hey Johnny, we got a few names for you on this lot. Frank Butcher, Welston Anthony, and Theo Messier." He paused to gage the reaction of the team. He continued, "It appears that the three bought this land using a trust. Our contact at the county did a little research. It appears that the three of them were in business together building homes. The trust specifies, like most trusts do, that the surviving trustees get the property of the trust upon the death of a trustee."

That was nothing earth shattering. The only other consideration was if there were family members involved, such as wives or children. Lyons continued. "It appears that Mr. Butcher and Mr. Anthony are deceased. They died together in an accident at a jobsite. They were blasting rock out for a building site. They thought they had a bad fuse when the dynamite didn't ignite. They went to investigate and BOOM! Killed 'em both. Mr. Theo Messier is now the sole trustee."

The team raised their eyebrows at that. The story sounded just a bit suspicious.

Pat asked, "Was Theo Messier investigated for possible wrongdoing?"

"According to our source, yes."

Johnny cleared his throat to get everyone's attention and pointed to the vent pipe. "We can look into the files on the accident later. But what do you make of this?" Joe and Pat shrugged their shoulders. They had no idea.

Hatch said, "Come on you two. You should recognize this. There's some kind of vault under here. This is an air vent for the vault." Hatch was talking about the underground vault that Pat and Joe had on property they owned in Florida. Their vault had vents similar to the one in front of them.

But what was in this vault in the middle of an empty lot and how were they going to find out?

Chapter 39

Tom Grayson sat in his office trying to finish the day's report. It wasn't happening. His mind kept going back to Jeremy's dilemma. He just didn't want to believe that Jeremy was stupid enough to get into the porn business. He also didn't want to believe that Messier Homes' very existence might be in jeopardy because of its connection to this trash. It was apparent that Jeremy was into something he couldn't handle, but what could he do to help?

Then there was this electronic device that he'd found in one of Messier's houses. Was that tied to this porn business? If it was, should he go to the police? Surely that would hit the news. And just as surely, Messier Homes would be out of business. No one would ever trust the Messier name again. Tom and his coworkers would be out of work. And no one would hire them if they were under suspicion of placing that transmitter in the attic. They'd be blacklisted from every construction business in the eastern United States. Not to mention that his own reputation would be mud.

Then there was the possibility that they'd be prosecuted for breaking some law. Who knows what laws were broken, but it couldn't be legal to spy on someone in their own home.

Then there was the question of Theo Messier, why no one had heard from him or Natasha since leaving the company to his boys. Surely Theo would have called Jeremy and Aaron to see how the business was running. Well, he'd call Jeremy anyway. *I can't believe he hasn't called me, just to ask my opinion of how they're handling the company.* Tom shook his head slowly. This was getting to be a complicated mess.

Then, today, when the crews were getting ready to head out, they saw a bunch of guys searching the lot next door. It turned out to be at least four deputy sheriffs and some plain-clothes guys. He had no idea what that was all about. They didn't even come over and ask permission. They just walked the entire property. He wondered what the hell they were looking for.

As Tom was trying to get refocused, Jeremy walked up the steps to the offices. He was still moving slow, obviously sore from the beating he took the other night. He looked terrible and shouldn't have come in at all. But he was here, so Tom decided it was time to clear the air, once and for all.

He asked, "How're the ribs?"

Jeremy slowly sat at his desk before answering. He was still taking shallow breaths to keep the pain to a minimum. Tom couldn't see the goose egg on Jeremy's head from where Jake had nailed him with the butt of his gun. But it was easy to see that he was still in bad shape.

Jeremy moved slowly in his seat, trying to get comfortable. He looked at Tom with an apologetic expression. "Sore. My whole freakin' body is sore. I'm taking a couple different pain meds and I'm still . . ." he paused to readjust his position. "I'm still so sore I can't think straight." Then he looked back at Tom.

Tom took a deep breath then said, "Listen, I've gotta know. Are you selling porn on the side? I mean, are you setting up cameras and transmitters in our houses?"

Jeremy looked at Tom, his expression serious. "Tom, I am not in the porn business, never have been, and never will be. I've got enough problems. We've got two houses that are behind schedule and . . ."

Jeremy stopped as one of the crew knocked on the office door. Jeremy and Tom both looked over to see a young man, probably in his early twenties, in a suit and tie, walk into the office carrying a large envelope. He had the slick look of an attorney, but the suit looked cheap. He looked completely out of place in the construction office. He walked up to Jeremy and asked, "Jeremy Messier?"

"Yes."

He handed Jeremy the envelope and said, "You've been served." He didn't say another word, turned and left the office. Jeremy and Tom, both speechless, stared at the man as he walked down the steps. The crew member just shrugged his shoulders and headed down the stairs to the workshop. He headed out the front door, right behind the suit.

Jeremy looked at the envelope. It was from the Prince William County Court. He ripped the package open and pulled out the document. It was a lawsuit initiated by Nelson and Jillian Rockledge, Plaintiffs versus Messier Homes, Theo Messier, Jeremy Messier, and Aaron Messier, defendants. Jeremy read through the lawsuit. It sounded like legal mumbo-jumbo to him until he got to the paragraph about the home being defective because of the discovery of the dead body under the foundation.

A few paragraphs later, the plaintiffs allege that the defendant placed cameras and microphones in the home. The purpose of the cameras and microphones was to violate the privacy of the homeowners. The lawsuit went on to allege a number of other illegal activities by Messier Homes, all in connection with the planting of the electronic devices.

Tom saw the change in expression as Jeremy's face turned pale and his jaw dropped.   His chest must have tightened, too, because he grabbed his ribs as another sharp pain ripped up his side.

"What is it now?"

Sweat was now forming on Jeremy's forehead and he started to shake. He looked up at Tom and tossed the papers across the desk in his direction. Tom read down to the part about the body. So the rumors that they'd heard were true. There was a dead body found and Nelson Rockledge and his wife blame Messiers. He reread the paragraph several times. No doubt about it.   The presence of a dead body was confirmed. Their bad day just got worse. Then he skimmed down to the section where cameras and microphones were found in the home. He looked hard at Jeremy. He couldn't tell if Jeremy's ribs were getting worse with the rising tension level or if the information about the cameras and microphones caused him more distress. He looked genuinely distraught at this revelation.

They didn't have time to discuss the lawsuit when another young man entered the office. He was short, about five feet seven, and appeared to be about twenty years old. He had on a dark blue tie and a dark blue windbreaker. His hair was near shoulder length and a bit greasy. He was probably an intern working for the court. He asked, "Is Jeremy Messier here?"

Jeremy didn't say a word. He raised his hand slightly at the young man.

"Sir, you're being served. Please take this envelope."

"We already have a copy of the lawsuit," Tom said. He held up the papers to show the young man.

He said, "I'm sorry sir, but that's not possible. I just received the papers from the judge at the Fairfax County courthouse. I have the only defendant's copy in this envelope. He held up an envelope, much thinner than the one Jeremy had accepted only moments before.

Jeremy took the second envelope. The young kid left the office as Jeremy ripped open the second package. He didn't care about being neat this time. He ripped the envelope straight down the middle, until he felt a pain in his side. He stared at the header. Plaintiff, Charles and Jody Williams, against defendants Messier Homes, Theo Messier, Jeremy Messier, and Aaron Messier. As he read the complaint, again his face was ashen.

He blurted out, "It says here that we put cameras and microphones in their house, too. Holy shit. What the fuck is going on?" He ran his hand through his bushy hair then slammed his fist on the desk. Again he felt the pain in his ribs. "I gotta get outta here. If you need me, I'll be at home."

Tom looked at him. Jeremy's face was contorted with tension, the lines on his brow tight together. Tom said, "You need to call Vince right away." Vince was the lawyer for the business. "He'll know what to do." Jeremy just stared at the lawsuit. He couldn't believe his eyes. Tom's suggestion didn't get past his ears and into his brain yet. Tom stood and handed Jeremy the first lawsuit and said, "Jeremy. Get your shit together, son. You can't let this go without taking some action to protect yourself and the business." He waited but Jeremy just stared at the papers. Finally Tom asked, "Do you want me to call Vince?"

He looked up at Tom. He looked beat, both physically and mentally. But he took a breath and said, "I'll call Vince. You call the crews together before they head out in the morning and tell them that they're not to make any comments to the press. I'm sure there'll be a team of investigators here to talk with everybody about both lawsuits. Hell, they're looking for a murderer and a pervert." He thought for a second.

Tom was about to say something but Jeremy cut him off. "We need to find out who planted the cameras. I have an idea, but I can't be sure."

"Who? Cause I have an idea, too."

"I can't say right now. I'll let you know when I find out for sure."

Tom had a feeling he knew who Jeremy had in mind. He didn't want to say, but he had the same suspicions himself. Aaron wasn't doing anything to quell those suspicions.

* * *

After Jeremy left the office, Tom decided to do some more investigative work. If Aaron was the one in charge of planting the cameras and microphones in the houses, he'd have to be working with someone else. Aaron didn't have the skills to pull this off alone. But who else would have the skills and balls to permanently mount the cameras? He'd have to look at the personnel files on his skilled tradesmen and see if anything jumped out. But in the mean time, he wanted to look through a few file cabinets and see if he could find anything that would point to Aaron or any accomplice.

He started at the file cabinets behind Aaron's desk. He opened the top drawer of the first cabinet and rifled through the papers. It was mostly purchase receipts for materials for houses that were in differing levels of completion. Tom knew that once a house was finished, the files would be removed from the active file cabinet and stored in a fireproof cabinet.

He continued to the next drawer. There was more of the same. He kept up the search through all the cabinets and found nothing. He reached the final cabinet and it was locked. He frowned. He tried it again. Nothing. He rubbed the rough stubble on his chin, thinking about his next move. If this was Aaron's cabinet, where would he keep the key? Tom sat at Aaron's desk and opened the center drawer. There was a set of four keys on a ring in the front tray. Tom returned to the file cabinet and tried each one. None of the keys worked so he returned them to the drawer. He opened each side drawer and rifled through each drawer. There was nothing of interest. He sat back in the chair, feeling frustrated. He looked around the room, trying to think like someone who had something to hide. *Where would I hide a key? Why would I lock the cabinet in the first place? If it was real important, I'd keep the key with me. But if I thought I was smarter than anyone else, would I be that careful?*

Tom stood and turned over the chair, looking at the seat bottom. There were dozens of old chewing gum wads stuck to the bottom of the chair. Tom shook his head. Aaron was like some junior high school kid, hiding gum from his teacher.

He leaned over to flip the chair upright. He looked at the underside of the desk when he did this. That's when he noticed the key attached to a magnet with double-sided tape. *Bingo.* He pulled the key from its hiding place and went straight to the file cabinet. The locked popped open.

* * *

Jeremy left the construction building heading for his condominium. He barely noticed the traffic on the two lane road. His mind was occupied with his mounting troubles. The lawsuits, the accusations of being a porn peddler, the psychopath trying to kill him, were all eating at his gut. But what was more troubling to him now was that he had no one to turn to. Aaron was useless when the pressure was on. He'd fold like a cheap suit. Tom didn't trust him. He said to talk with Vince and that was the right move. But beyond that, he didn't have the answers. None of the crew could help. They were all potential suspects in this camera scandal. Not to mention there was a dead body that was most likely the result of a murder. He had to check the files and see when the house had been built. It was just recently finished so that would put the pouring of the footer at about three to four months ago.

The blare of a horn made him jerk the wheel to the right. He'd been concentrating on his problems so hard that he'd crossed the center line and nearly sideswiped an oncoming car. Jeremy took a deep breath. Pain invaded his ribcage, but the painkillers were doing their job. He had to concentrate on his driving. He drove another mile to a gas station, filled up, and grabbed a six pack of beer from the convenience store. He turned and headed back towards the Messier Homes offices, but his destination was Aaron's house. No better way to get the real story than from the source.

* * *

Tom found what he was looking for. The drawings were in the bottom drawer of the locked filing cabinet, under a stack of electronics magazines. He pulled them out and spread them flat on Aaron's desk. The drawings weren't professional grade but they provided all the information that Tom needed.

The topographical drawings were of the Messier Homes construction offices, the adjacent lot, and the lots behind the two properties. The utilities were shown where they came off the street connections to the construction building as well as the outbuildings for Messier Homes. It also showed road frontage measurements and other land features, such as graded land heights relative to sea level. Finally, the base drawing showed all the utility connections to Aaron's house behind and down the hill from Messier's.

Tom's fingers followed the one set of dashed lines that weren't part of the original drawing. The parallel lines originated at the Messier Home's offices and went to the edge of the adjacent property. It ended in a square box on the lot. From the box, another set of dashed lines headed directly to Aarons house. They appeared to be tapped into the house at the westernmost corner. The legend on the drawings indicated that the path was for communications lines. It specified high bandwidth telecommunications lines, optionally, fiber-optic lines. *What the hell? Why would anyone need . . . ?*

Then the realization hit him. Aaron had high-tech communications lines running to his house from the offices. Aaron was never around to help run the business because he was running his own business. Aaron, the introvert, was also the pervert, running an illegal internet pornography business. He should have been the real target of Jake O'Connor's attacks. He was destroying Messier Homes. *He has to be stopped.*

Tom folded up the drawing. He picked up the phone to call Jeremy. He dialed but there was no answer and he hung up after six rings. Jeremy probably wasn't in any shape to help him anyway, so he took the drawings and headed out the door. He was going to confront Aaron with the evidence. Aaron was such a wimp, Tom figured he'd break down and wet his pants before he was finished with him.

Chapter 40

"We know the body is female, Caucasian, about five feet tall, with dark brown hair. She used artificial coloring but didn't need to. She had no gray hair. We think she was about twenty-five to thirty. The decomposition was pretty advanced but there was trauma to the right cheek bone and a bullet hole in the skull. Cause of death was the gun shot. She had been dismembered, apparently using the miter saw.

"Right. It was disassembled, under the footer of the foundation, right next to the body. The nameplate had been removed to prevent any kind of identification of the purchaser."

Sitting in his office just after lunch, Deputy Lyons was talking on his desk phone to forensic specialist, Dr. Ted Griffith. Dr. Griffith was very precise in the description of his findings. Even though he was set to retire in just a few months, he was very professional. He spoke like an instructor; as if he wanted to make sure Lyons understood not just his words, but what they meant. He explained the technical aspects of the body and the tool used to take it apart as if he were describing a mechanical process. It was all 'matter of fact.' No sense letting emotions get in the way of a murder, especially one that was obviously close and personal.

He continued, "We did find something out of place in between the woman's teeth. There was a piece of fingernail stuck between her lateral incisor and cuspid on the lower jaw. We think it might be the killer's. Whoever killed her got bitten. We know it wasn't her nail because they were manicured to perfection. The nail from her teeth had some skin roots on it. We're not sure we can get any DNA for testing from the sample, but we may be able to determine the severity of the bite. We're looking at that now. That's about all we have."

"Thanks Ted. Call my cell if you find anything else."

Dr. Ted Griffin hung up the phone in his lab. Lyons stepped out of his office to brief Johnny, Pat, Joe, and Hatch. He directed one of the other deputies to get a warrant for Messier Homes to do a search for blood, body fragments, and a purchase order or receipt for a miter saw. Pat recommended that they go to the home builders this afternoon to question employees of Messier Homes. They didn't have concrete evidence, but he felt that face-to-face interviews might narrow down the field of possible suspects.

Joe said, "I think we might be able to figure out who knows what by their answers and body language. If we do the interviews in teams we can watch for their reactions. It might tell us more than their answers."

Lyons agreed. It was worth a try. If they didn't move fast, whoever was responsible for the murder might flee, if they hadn't already? As they talked, a call came in on his office phone. It was Nelson Rockledge.

He asked, "So, Deputy Lyons, do you have a name for the body yet?"

"No sir, Mr. Rockledge."

"Deputy, what do you know? I need to calm my wife down. She's nearly in a panic."

In a calm, southern drawl, Deputy Lyons said, "Yes sir, I understand. I can only tell you a few things. First, the body is female. It was placed there before your home's footer was poured. We have a few other leads, but we can't talk publicly about them. Normally we wouldn't even tell a home owner this much, but you and your wife are not under suspicion."

"I understand. Thank you." He took a deep breath and continued, "I just wanted you to know that we've filed a lawsuit against Messier Homes. The suit should be delivered this afternoon. They may even have it by now. I don't know what that does to your investigation, but we couldn't wait. We can't live in our own home. We felt we had to do this."

Lyons mulled over what, if anything, the lawsuit would do. It was going to be in the news the next morning anyway. Lyons also knew that the Williams' lawsuit was going to hit Messier's at about the same time. Things were happening fast. When they questioned the crew this afternoon, he expected to get more pieces to the puzzle.

He turned to Johnny Poleirmo and asked, "How in the hell did you uncover this mess? It was right under our noses and you come up from Florida tellin' us we have a big problem in our back yard."

Johnny smiled, but it wasn't to gloat. He looked over at Pat and said to Lyons, "That man standing over there. He's the guy you should thank."

Johnny continued to explain how Pat came across the porn site and proceeded to track down its location through cyber space. He also mentioned that he and Hatch knew Charlie Williams, one of the victims. They'd been in the military together.

"Well you guys have got to teach us how to do them computer searches. That sounds pretty slick. Where'd he learn all that?"

Johnny's smile was broad this time. "That was my doing. I read about a cop in Vermilion, Ohio that was doing some sting operations from chat rooms. The cop learned how to do the chat room lingo from his daughter after she had a close call with a pedophile." Lyons frowned, one eyebrow raised. Johnny continued, "Anyway, he figured out how to get into these chat rooms and act like a fourteen year old girl. He learned the lingo. These creeps just started coming on to him. So he'd invite them over for a party. When they got there, they found out it was a surprise party, with a trip to jail and court. He still catches about three or four a month."

"Well it serves these bastards right. We've got to get better at shutting down this porn business. It's outta control. Hell they pipe it right into your home. All you have to do is do a search on a few sex words and there it is. How do you fight it?"

Johnny just shook his head. When he first started this task force just a few weeks ago, he was gung ho. He wanted to take on the perverts and clear them off the streets. Now that he knew the sheer size of the problem, he wondered how they'd ever make a dent in the business. It would take a multi-billion dollar, concerted effort from every law enforcement agency in the country. But who would take care of the rest of the criminals? The problem was astronomical in size. It wasn't isolated to any one part of the country, either. Anyone with a server and a few domain names could start peddling pictures and movies. There seemed to be no shortage of buyers either. Like they say, sex sells.

"I'll tell you what, deputy. After we're done here, Pat will show you what he knows and I can give you the number of the guy who really knows. Pat's pretty good, but the guy in Vermilion is a real pro."

"Alright. That's what I wanted to hear."

"And if your budget can afford a trip to Ohio and a new computer, you'll be in business busting these pervs in no time. If there were more of us busting down their doors, we might be able to make a dent in this thing."

The two shook hands, sealing the deal.

* * *

The team gathered in a briefing room. It was about thirty feet square, carpeted with very old industrial grade carpet. There were chairs lined up, six on a side, nine rows deep on either side of a center aisle, all facing a movie screen. A wood podium stood on the left side of the screen. A few six foot by two foot tables were along the walls on either side of the room. There was a small stack of handouts on one of the tables. Coffee cups, napkins, and crumbs from some pastry littered the tabletops.   Pat, Joe and the rest of the team took seats on the aisle near the front of the room.

The lights in the room were already darkened except for one set of four foot fluorescent bulbs near the back of the room. There were no windows. The paint in the room was supposed to be white, but the color was closer to beige, stained from previous years of tobacco smoke. Smoking had been banned the previous year. The room still bore the scars of years of smoke that had no place to escape. It made its final home on the walls, ceiling, and carpet.

Deputy Lyons moved to the front of the room and stood at the podium. He found the clicker for the overhead projector that hung from the ceiling. He tried clicking the power button several times. When the projector didn't respond he swore to himself and walked over to the projector, looking for the local power button. He found it and hit it twice. The projector came to life.

He made his way back to the podium where he tapped the keys on the computer keyboard that slid out on a tray. After two long minutes, the computer desktop was projected on screen. A few more clicks and a picture of the lot adjacent to the Messier property displayed on the screen.

Lyons cleared his throat. "I'm sure you guys recognize the property here." Everyone nodded. "Here's the area we found most interesting." Lyons used a laser pointer to highlight the left side of the property. "The thing we couldn't see well is in the next slide. What we do know is that there is something buried that requires ventilation. At least that's what we suspect."

He pointed the remote at the projector and clicked the forward button. The next picture popped on the screen. Lyons seemed surprised that the clicker worked and he gave a slight smile. "Anyway, this picture is an aerial photo of the property from two years ago. You can clearly see a very distinct line going from Messier's property, onto the trust property, then back to Aaron Messier's house. We suspect that there was a trench dug and an intersection vault installed where the trench makes an abrupt turn here." He pointed to the obvious change in greenery on the ground.

From the aerial photo you could clearly see the line from point 'A' to point 'B'. It wasn't illegal to dig a trench, and they had no real proof that it was associated with the internet porn business, but Lyons had an angle.

"So we know there's a trench with electrical and communications wiring under the ground there. We also know, thanks to our contacts at the county, that there was no permit issued for any kind of trench. And there was no electrical permit issued. So we have probable cause to search Aaron Messier's house and the Messier offices. We've got our foot in the door, anyway. What we do with it, that's the big question."

Lyons looked around the room. For a long moment, nobody spoke.

Then Pat said, "I've got an idea. What if . . ."

* * *

Aaron Messier was getting antsy. He wanted to get to the drive-through and make sure that his shipment was loaded and on its way to warmer climates. But Jeremy called and wanted to meet him at the house. He said he'd be over in half an hour. That meant he'd only have about two hours before he had to meet the FedEx guy. That would be cutting it close. He finished loading the programs for the evening on the web. There would be no live broadcasts for a few nights. The problems were mounting and it was time to cool it for a bit. His partner decided that they needed to back off for a few days and see what happened next. That was fine with Aaron. He'd be long gone by then.

Aaron was alone in the control room. He had a few minutes to think and go over his itinerary. *Leave tonight and make sure the packages are on their way. Head south and get closer to some warm weather. Catch the plane in Savannah to Grand Cayman. Screw Jeremy, I'm not waiting. I decide what I want to do and when I want to do it. Man, I'll finally be rid of Jeremy and all the rest of this bullshit. And I'll have more money than God.* He headed up the stairs to his bedroom. It would take him about fifteen minutes to finish packing and he'd be long gone before Jeremy arrived.

Roger and Gerry were parked down the road from Aaron's house. They were ready to wait him out as long as it took. Their hiding place wasn't well concealed, but it was the best they could do. Besides, it would be easy to spot Aaron's truck. This road had very little traffic.

Roger told Gerry, "You take the first watch. When Aaron heads out, you wake me and we'll follow him to the drive-through. We'll wait until he's inside, then we'll nail him. The prick."

Gerry just nodded. He looked all around the truck. There was nothing but trees with brightly colored leaves. It was mid afternoon and the temperature hovered around sixty degrees. The cloud cover was thick with just a few blue breaks where the sun filtered through. With the windows up, the temperature was rising in the truck to the point where it made Gerry drowsy. He yawned. Roger elbowed him and said in a stern voice, "Don't you fall asleep on me, now. You miss Aaron and I'll kick your ass."

"Don't sweat it, man. I'm fine." *If you're so worried, why don't you take the first watch?*

Roger turned and leaned his head against the passenger door. In minutes he was snoring. Gerry sat and watched. Nothing changed. His mind began to wander to the night that he and Roger assaulted Jillian Rockledge. He thought about Jillian's naked body and how she felt to his touch. After a few minutes, he was asleep, dreaming about his first and only rape victim.

Chapter 41

Tom Grayson rolled up the drawings he'd found in the file cabinet, tucked them under his arm and headed out the office door. He made his way down the steps and out to his truck, thinking along the way. He thought he had it figured out. The cool air hit him when he opened the office door to the parking lot. Most of the employees were just finishing up for the day. Only a handful of electricians were back from jobsites. They were out in the workshop, preparing for a service installation on Monday.

Tom looked around the lot and at the wooded area to the east of the offices. He figured that the search party was about the cable installation that was detailed on the drawings he now held. He didn't know if it was just the local sheriff's office or if a federal agency was involved in the search. Half the men were in plain clothes. They could have been FBI or some federal task force, he reasoned.

Then there was this Jake character, offering to buy a porn business. If they didn't have a porn business why would he be offering money, big money, to buy it? Nobody throws money around like that, unless they have good reason. He must know something.

He thought about the lawsuits showing up, suing the company for illegal cameras and a dead body. *This whole thing stinks. It has to be Aaron. Jeremy's not exactly a saint but he's always at work or at his condo. He doesn't seem to have time to plant cameras and transmitters in houses. He might be a playboy, but he's too busy to be involved with this, unless he's in partnership with Aaron.*

He still had doubts about Aaron. He was such an introvert that Tom didn't know what to think. Before all this, he didn't think Aaron was capable of much, except reading. But he did read about electronic gadgets. His desk drawer was loaded with magazines; *Modern Electronics, Micro Electronics Magazine, and Gadget Geek Magazine.* Tom always thought it was just because he was fascinated by electronics. He never figured that there was anything malicious or sinister about it. Now he knew better. This was much bigger than he'd imagined.

And what about the dead body? Was someone at Messiers guilty of murder? He wasn't sure it was even safe to be in the office alone. After all, he'd already been attacked once. At first, he thought that it might be Jeremy. Then he thought maybe Aaron was the attacker. Now he wasn't sure.

He took a deep breath of cool air and opened his truck door. He placed the drawings behind the driver's seat of the truck, got in and started the engine. He was off to confront Aaron.

* * *

Aaron smiled as he drove off towards Interstate 95. He was worried that he'd be seen leaving. He got to the end of the driveway and looked left down the road. He saw the front end of a beat up pickup truck among the trees. *Those two idiots. No wonder they're unemployable.* He wondered if they were going to follow him to the drive-through. He'd have to be careful. Heading out onto the road, he kept one eye on the road in front and the other in the rear view mirror. To his surprise, the truck didn't move. The sun was low in the sky and the fall leaves still filled the trees, producing a canopy over the road. But there was still enough light to see that the truck hadn't moved an inch. Finally Aaron rounded a bend in the road and the truck was completely out of view.

Aaron decided he had time to take a circuitous route to the drive-through. That way, if he was followed, he could easily spot his pursuers. And if they decided to go directly to the drive-through, they'd get there in front of Aaron. They'd see that Aaron wasn't there and go back to the house to find him.

Aaron kept his eyes out for Jeremy. The last thing he wanted now was to run into his older brother. He had time, but if Jeremy wanted to talk, it might take too long. The FedEx driver wouldn't wait forever, especially at an abandoned, locked drive-through store.

He smiled and looked at himself in the rear view mirror. He was almost done. He'd fooled them. All these years they'd called him the slow one. They made fun of him. They all deserved what was coming to them when they found their gifts. They'd preached to him about how to be good. *The hypocrites. Since the camera's set up, I'll even be able to see their faces when they figure it all out.*

Priceless!

* * *

"Diane, I think I'll be home tomorrow but it'll be late, probably around 10:00. We're going to do some interviews tonight then we'll finish up tomorrow morning. I figure we'll be on the road by about 9:00 in the morning."

Pat was talking with Diane, trying to keep her calm about the extent of his involvement in the pornography case. Since he was shot in the chest just a few months earlier, she had reason to worry. The Kevlar vest he wore was worth its weight in gold. She didn't want any more close calls. Pat wholeheartedly agreed with her. He wanted to keep clear of any potential danger. *They were questioning construction workers, what could go wrong?* He didn't say that to her. He didn't want to jinx himself or his brother, Joe.

Joe was on his cell phone to Lisa. She was also a bit worried. Joe was grazed on the arm by a passing bullet from a woman named Abbie Glover. He'd returned fire and shot her dead. He had no choice. She was charging a group of officers who were executing, what they had hoped to be, a peaceful arrest. Unfortunately, Bobby Garrett, one of the perpetrators, had other ideas. It ended badly.

"So, when are we visiting the house?" Joe was trying to steer the conversation away from the case to a more personal issue. He hoped that she would take the bait. She did, but only for a moment.

"If you get home early enough, we can stop over tomorrow." She paused. "When will you be home?"

"Pat plans for us to be on the road about 9:00 in the morning. But that would mean we won't get home before dark tomorrow night."

In a quiet, seductive voice she said, "We have other things to do tomorrow night anyway." She paused then said, "I miss you."

Joe could hear her sniffing tears back. It choked him up, but he took a deep breath and said, "I miss you, too. But we can celebrate tomorrow night."

"I know." With that, Lisa started to cry. He could hear the sobs through the phone even though she tried in vain to stifle the sound.

"Babe, what's wrong? Is everything okay?"

She sobbed louder, "Everything's fine."

"Then why are you crying?"

She laughed through her sobs then said, "I don't know. Maybe I just miss you." She blew her nose noisily into a tissue then said, "I'm sorry. I don't mean to worry you." Then, just like that, she stopped crying. She said in a calm voice, "Hurry home, Dear."

After exchanging love and kisses, they disconnected. Pat was staring at Joe.

"What?"

Pat said, "What was that about?"

Joe described Lisa's crying outburst and how she said she didn't know what the problem was.

Pat smiled and shook his head. "I'll bet dollars to doughnuts that she's pregnant."

Joe looked dumbstruck at Pat. He was speechless for several, long seconds. Finally he said, "No way!"

"Let me ask you something, Einstein. Is Lisa on the pill?"

"Yeah. I mean I'm pretty sure." Joe looked perplexed. "Yes. She is. I'm sure of it."

"You don't sound too sure. Maybe you should ask her." Pat was half smiling, half smirking. He hoped he was wrong. It wasn't because he thought that Joe and Lisa wouldn't make great parents. He knew that Lisa was taking college classes. She wanted to work in a profession for a while before they had children. This could sidetrack those plans, if Pat's suspicions were right.

He said, "Look, little brother, if she is, that's great. Lisa will make a great mom. And you, well, the kid will have one decent parent anyway." He smiled at his little joke, but Joe was still standing there with his jaw on his chest. He couldn't grasp that he might be on the road to fatherhood and there were no exits or rest areas.

* * *

The plan was for Sheriff Lyons, Johnny Poleirmo, Pat, Joe, and Hatch to meet a couple of Messier's electricians at the construction offices. They met in the electrical workshop where the team could get a first hand view of the work area and any storage that they had. The plan also included a search of the offices in the area. The trench on the adjacent property originated in one corner of the Messier offices. They wanted to get a look at the building and see if they could find any electrical cabinets or servers.

Brad was one of the young electricians. He seemed at ease talking with Pat and Johnny Poleirmo. He was even joking with them about how Messier's seemed like such a great, conservative company. Not much had changed since Theo left less than a month ago. Now all hell was breaking loose.

"This is like a Hollywood movie or something. Hell, a dead body, porn. What's next?" He smiled.

"You seem pretty happy for a guy who might lose his livelihood real soon."

"That's okay. My real passion is writing mystery novels. The way this is going, I'll have more ideas than I'll have time to write. I can't wait to hit the keyboard."

Pat and Johnny smiled in spite of the serious nature of the interview. They were looking at Brad with interest, but not as a suspect. It was obvious he was way too relaxed with the situation to be seriously considered for this crime. The interview was going well, but Brad had no useful information. They thanked him for his time and started to head out the door when they heard a vehicle roar into the parking lot. They looked out the window and saw Jeremy's truck stop in front of the offices. As he stepped out of his truck a dark green BMW pulled in behind him. A man jumped out of the car. A woman was in the passenger seat. She remained in the car. A golden retriever paced in the back seat from side to side, watching his master quickly walk up to Jeremy. Even from a distance of about thirty yards, Pat and Johnny could tell Jeremy was caught off guard. His face was etched with anxiety.

He spoke as the man approached, stones and dust kicked up as he walked. "Mr. Rockledge, I don't know what to say, sir. I . . ."

The man's voice was business-like, no anger or sign of malice. "Jeremy, I guess that's not what I wanted to hear. I wanted you to tell me who the hell buried a body under our house. Was it you?"

Jeremy was shocked. He considered that he might be suspected of planting the body, but he never thought anyone would come right out and ask the question.

"No sir. Absolutely not. I . . ."

Before he could get another word out, Nelson cut him off.

"Did one of your crew do this? Who is it?"

"Mr. Rockledge, you need to get off this property now. I'm not answering any more of your questions. You shouldn't even be here. You've filed a lawsuit against me and my company. This isn't right that you're here, accosting me like this. This is harassment."

Nelson Rockledge pointed his finger in Jeremy's face and shook it for good measure. "I'll leave alright. But I'll be back when I sue you into bankruptcy and I own this place."

Just as Pat and Johnny started walking towards the two men, Nelson got back in his car and left, heading out the way he came in. Jeremy was so incensed that he just stood there, red in the face. He was already pissed. He'd stopped by Aaron's house and he wasn't there. *I even told him that I was coming over to talk. Maybe the bastard's back by now.* He got in his truck and peeled out of the parking lot, heading towards Aaron's house.

* * *

Jody Williams was in her Mercedes on her way to Messier Homes offices when she saw Jeremy pull out of the parking lot. She decided to follow him. She watched the truck accelerate and head towards Interstate 95. After nearly a mile, but well short of the interstate, the truck slowed and turned left. Jody slowed to keep distance between her and the truck then turned left, following the pickup. She looked over at the passenger seat at the 9 mm pistol she bought at a gun show many years ago. She never thought she'd actually use it. She didn't think the gun was traceable. At least that's what she hoped.

She looked back up the road as the truck made its way down a beautiful winding road. The trees hung over the roadway in bright, fall colors. The wind was picking up a bit and dozens of leaves were falling onto the road. Jody thought how beautiful this road was with the colorful corridor, but how gloomy it would look in just a few short weeks.

She thought of her husband and how devastated he would be if she killed someone and went to prison. But she couldn't live with herself knowing that there might be some sex tape of her and Charlie, circulating around different porn sites. It was all too humiliating. The more she thought about it, the angrier she became, again. *They're not going to get away with this.*

* * *

As Pat and Johnny watched Jeremy speed off, Joe and Hatch came out of the main office. They were walking quickly towards them. Just then, a white Mercedes sped past following Jeremy's truck. Hatch and Pat saw the striking blond hair of the driver and both thought that it must be Jody Williams, their friend, Charlie's wife. Then Nelson and Jillian's BMW sped by, following the white Mercedes. The four looked at each other in stunned silence.

After a few seconds, Pat said, "Let's go. We've got to see where they're headed. If looks could kill, Jeremy's a dead man."

As they made their way to the car, Johnny chimed in, "Jeremy didn't look real pleased either. I'll bet he's headed for Aaron's."

They all closed their doors in quick succession. "Only one way to find out . . ."

The rental headed out onto the road behind the BMW which was behind the Mercedes, which was behind the truck. They were all headed for trouble.

Chapter 42

Tom Grayson grabbed the rolled up drawings from behind the driver's seat of his Ford truck and headed for Aaron's front door. His apprehension grew with each step. He felt that there was no other option but to confront Aaron. The plan was to convince him to turn himself in. He rang the doorbell and heard muffled chimes inside the house. There was no answer. He rang the doorbell a second time followed by several loud raps on the door. Still no answer. He looked back at the driveway and finally noticed that Aaron's truck was gone. He tapped the drawings on his forehead and started to leave. Then he thought, maybe he should do a little more investigative work. If he's running a porn business from this house, maybe I can find the server.

Tom rang the doorbell one more time expecting that no one would answer. To his surprise, the door opened. Tom's jaw dropped, then his stunned expression was replaced by a big smile. He extended his hand to the gentleman behind the door.

"Theo, how are you? It's good to see you."

Theo's smile wasn't nearly as warm. He said, "Tom. Come in."

Tom stepped past his old boss into the entry of Aaron's ranch style home. He looked around the house. It wasn't nearly as well kept as when Theo, Jeremy, and Aaron lived there many years ago. Even though Theo was busy building Messier Homes and raising two boys, the house was always clean and well maintained. He took a moment to gather his thoughts. He'd expected to talk with Aaron, but now that Theo was back from Paris, maybe it was time to let Theo in on what was going on.

"So, Theo, I know it's been less than two months, but how's retirement treating you?"

Theo hesitated before he spoke. The look on his face was difficult to read. His body was tense. There were dark circles under his eyes, more than Tom had ever seen in the past. Retirement didn't look like it agreed with him at all. He forced a smile as he extended a hand indicating that Tom should sit in one of the living room chairs.

"Well, Tom, let's just say that I should have done it long ago. Paris is fantastic. The little chateau we bought is perfect for the two of us. I think we'll be quite content."

"Is Natashia here with you?"

"No. She stayed over there. I plan to head back once I finish a little business with my sons." Theo was still standing as he spoke. He looked nervous.

Tom took a deep breath. This was going to be hard. But Theo needed to know.

"Theo, there've been some problems with the business that you should know about."

Theo's posture shifted and he frowned, but the expression on his face looked forced, plastic. "Problems? What sort of problems?"

"The sheriff found a body under the footer at the Rockledge home. It had to have been planted the day after the basement was dug. They haven't identified the body yet but it's a young woman."

Theo's eyes appeared to stare off into empty space as he recalled the dark, damp summer evening when he placed the trash bags under the footer. He was a much older man now and the task was more difficult than he imagined. The weight of a person, even one so petite, was difficult to carry down a ladder at night, under cover of complete darkness. Now that the body was found, it would only be a matter of time before they determined that the body was that of his former wife, Natashia. He was still amazed that no one questioned why she'd never called him from Paris after she had supposedly gone there to find their new chateau. Tom continued talking, but Theo wasn't listening. He was still shell shocked by what he'd just seen in the basement of Aaron's home, his former home.

"Then there's the lawsuit from Charlie Williams, and the miniature cameras found in their home. There were also cameras found in . . . Theo, are you listening to me?"

Theo's dazed look came back to Tom. He simply said, "Tom, why couldn't you just do your job and mind your own business?"

Tom looked at Theo as if he were speaking a different language. He didn't understand the question. "What did you say? I mean . . . I think I heard you, but what do you mean?"

Theo's voice was louder now, and he spoke in staccato punctuated words. "I said, why . . . couldn't . . . you . . ." his anger was rising and the volume of his voice along with it, "just . . . mind . . . your own fucking business?! It was working perfectly! Everything was going along smoothly until you stuck your nose into that attic! You couldn't even get the message when I shoved you down the stairs!"

"That was you? You damn near killed me. How could you? I've worked for you from the beginning. We've been friends for thirty years!"

Tom's thoughts were spinning out of control. First he thought Jeremy was the culprit, then Aaron. But no way did he even suspect Theo was involved. Even now, the idea that Theo was behind any of this was beyond his comprehension. He was always so proper, so refined. He catered to the wealthiest professionals in the home building market. How could it be possible that he was selling porn?

"Theo, what are you saying? Tell me you're just saying this to protect your boys. You can't really be mixed up in this?"

"Shut up, Tom! Just shut up. I want to show you something. Come with me."

"I'm sorry, Theo. I'm not going anywhere with you. In fact, I'm leaving. I have to sort this out."

"You're not going anywhere!"

"The hell I ain't! Watch me!"

Tom took three steps towards the door. Theo picked up a gun that had been on the kitchen counter where Tom couldn't see it. When he saw the barrel pointing directly at his head, he stopped. Fear immediately seized him and his knees got weak. He just froze and didn't move a muscle. His breathing became irregular, and he began to sweat.

"Let's go, Tom. I really need to show you something. Remember when Angela left? She gave me a hard time about the business. She always told me it would never work, that the business would fail. She nagged me constantly. I didn't spend enough time with her, or I never helped her. Or what about her dreams? She had a life, too. It went on and on, late into the night. I never got any sleep. I was making mistakes on the houses. I was just so damn tired all the time." He paused, looking at Tom to see if he was getting through to him. Then he continued, "When the boys were very young, she threatened to leave me and take the boys away. She was taking my sons from me because I was too busy trying to build a successful business. I was trying to make it so they didn't have to suffer through the life I had, where I wasn't sure if my mom would make enough money for us to eat any given night. I was trying to make sure my family never had to suffer like that."

He paused again, his face twisting into a distorted snarl. He asked rhetorically, "But did she appreciate that? No. You know what she did? She nagged even more. From the minute I got up in the morning and left for the day, and the minute I returned home from a construction site, she was on me. It continued all night. I finally couldn't take it anymore." Theo's face relaxed. His expression remained blank. No smile, no frown, no emotion at all.

Tom was trying to piece together what Theo had just told him. *The body at the Rockledge's? It couldn't be. That body was new.* He heard the report that the body had been dead for just a couple of months. Tom's puzzled look put a hint of a smile on Theo's face.

"Okay Tom, let's go." He waved the gun in the direction of the hallway towards the basement steps. Tom's legs weren't cooperating. He tried to move, but had no feeling in his legs. It's like they went to sleep while standing in the one position for so long. Finally he coaxed his left leg in front of him, then his right leg followed suit. He had no idea where Theo was taking him, but he feared that his boss had lost his mind. He knew that this wouldn't end well.

Theo said, "Down in the basement. I'll explain. It turns out Angela was right. I know how to build quality homes, but I never did learn how to make money at it. But we have a little while to talk."

Tom started down the steps. He felt Theo's hand on his back.

"Don't worry. I'm not going to knock you down any more steps."

They'd only made a few steps progress when they heard tires on gravel. Tom thought that maybe the cavalry had arrived. He looked back at Theo who was looking up at the basement door. He smiled and said, "Here comes my traitor of a son."

Tom had no idea what that meant and he wasn't sure which of his two sons he was talking about. A truck door slammed closed. Moments later the front door to the house swung open.

"Aaron, where the fuck are you?!

* * *

Gerry heard the sound of several vehicles approaching Aaron's house. He was watching as the truck rounded the corner into the driveway, spitting gravel as it did. It was obvious that Jeremy was in a hurry. Shortly after that, a white Mercedes turned into the drive followed by a dark green BMW. Then a plain looking black car. The last vehicle had at least four people in it.

Roger stirred just in time to see two of the four vehicles turn into the drive. He was still clearing the sleep from his head. He asked Gerry, "What in the Sam Hill is going on? Is Aaron still there?"

"I think so. I mean . . . I don't know for sure."

Roger frowned at his partner. "What do you mean you don't know for sure? Weren't you watching? Shit, it doesn't matter. We couldn't go up there now, anyway, with all the company he's got."

"And that first truck was Jeremy. He didn't look too happy from here. He was driving like a bat-outta-hell."

Roger thought for a second before he spoke. He yawned deeply and stretched. Gerry could smell his raunchy breath. Roger said, "Okay, let's just drive by real slow-like and maybe we can see if his truck's still there. If it ain't, we can head for the drive-through. That's got to be where he's headed."

Gerry agreed. When they drove slowly into the drive, the cars and trucks were empty but the dust was still in the air where they stopped.

"Gerry, my man, we don't want no part of that. Let's head to the drive-through. I think there might be a payday waitin' for us. I don't think we're going to ask Aaron nice, either. We deserve it."

Gerry nodded. He backed out of the drive and headed down the road towards the Interstate.

* * *

Jeremy looked around for Aaron. Then he saw that the basement door was opened. He started walking towards it when he saw his dad standing at the top step. He was holding a gun at his side. He looked past his dad and saw Tom Grayson further down the steps. He wondered about the gun and why Tom was there. With a puzzled look on his face, he looked around the house, trying to find Aaron. Then he turned back to his dad. His mind raced as he thought about all the problems that were coming to a head in the last few hours. Now his dad was here. Had he found out, beforehand, that his sons were destroying his business and he'd come back to straighten them out?

With an edge in his voice that made it clear that Theo's presence was not welcome, Jeremy said, "Dad, what are you doing here? I thought you were in Europe."

Theo didn't say anything for a moment. He took one step up and another towards Jeremy. "I had to come back and tie up a few loose ends."

"What loose ends, Dad? And why are you carrying a gun?"

"Come downstairs with Tom and me, and I'll show you."

Before they could move towards the stairs, more tires worked the gravel outside. A car door slammed. Jeremy went to the window and looked out. A beautiful blond woman was coming up to the door. Her face was beet-red. She wore jeans and a light-weight, tan coat. She carried a matching purse. She knocked on the door hard. Jeremy recognized Jody Williams, owner of the last house Theo finished before supposedly leaving the country. He looked at Theo who motioned for him to open the door.

Jeremy opened the door and backed into the living room, away from his father. Jody walked in and looked around the room at each of them. Tom made his way back to the hall and was trying to get past Theo into the kitchen. Theo held the gun behind his leg so Jody couldn't see it. Her face was still red. The men thought it might be some kind of makeup, but that only lasted until Jody yelled at them.

"Which one of you planted cameras and microphones in my house? Who was it?" She looked from one face to another. She could tell they all knew about it. Not one eye blinked. Not one jaw dropped. None of them made any pretense that they had no idea. "Then it was all of you. Is that how it is? You're all partners?"

Tom said, "No ma'am. I had no part of this. I was trying to find out who did it. I never found out for sure."

Jeremy looked at Jody then turned to his father. "I'm innocent in this, too. So, Dad, who is it?"

The smug look on Jeremy's face was like a knife in his back. He looked at his eldest son and said, "How can you sit there and act so holy. You tore us apart, you and that whore of a wife of mine."

Jeremy's jaw dropped. He knew what was coming.

"You and Natashia! You didn't think I'd find out? I knew she was cheating on me, but with my own son! I gave both of you everything that you could ever want! And this is the way you repay me?! By fucking my wife?! Your step-mother! You sick bastard!" Theo's face grew redder and more contorted by the second. Jeremy knew he still had the gun at his side. He also knew that his dad was losing control.

Jody didn't know what to say. She shouted at them, "I don't care who slept with who. I want to know who planted those cameras! And I want to know now!"

In one swift motion, Jody reached into her handbag and drew out her 9mm Glock. Jeremy and Tom turned their attention to Jody. Theo continued to glare at his son. Jody moved the gun from man to man. There was about ten feet between her and Jeremy. He was standing in the living room. Tom was now in the kitchen about fifteen feet away and behind Theo, who was nearest to Jody.

Jeremy's head turned towards the front window. More gravel was kicked up in the driveway. Jody didn't even turn her head. She didn't care who was coming. She wanted answers.

Chapter 43

Roger and Gerry road in silence until they reached the abandoned drive through. There was no one in sight and no evidence that anyone had been there recently. They drove slowly around the parking lot, past the garage door that used to allow cars to drive into the store. It was the same door that they'd pulled into when unloading the bags of cash into the walk-in cooler. The door was padlocked now and they didn't bring bolt cutters.

Roger swore. "That asshole. He screwed us over, big time."

"I'll bet he already took the cash." Gerry's voice trailed off like a little kid about to be punished. "What can we do now? Should we wait for him? Maybe he'll be back. Maybe the money's still in there."

There was silence in the truck again. The only sound was the engine idling, coughing occasionally, as if it was about to stall. Roger turned and looked out the passenger window. The sun was setting to the west behind the hill. He took a deep breath and turned back to his partner. "I'll tell you what we're gonna do. We're goin' back to the Kirkwood house and get the rest of that money. There had to be at least a million bucks left."

Gerry looked at Roger with fear in his eyes. "But the cops were there yesterday. Don't that mean they found out about the break-in? What if they're back from wherever they were? What if they catch us?"

"Don't you remember what Aaron said? They're gone for at least another few days. We'll be outta there long before they get back. That cop out there. That was just a coincidence.

Remember, there weren't any flashin' lights back by the house."

Gerry still looked like a scared junior high school kid. Roger went on, "Look, man, anything you do has some risk. We've done riskier things for a lot less money. Come on. Get a spine, would ya?"

Gerry seemed to be coming around. After another five minutes of pep talk from Roger, Gerry was finally ready. At least he appeared to be. Inside his brain was screaming that they should stay away.

The truck left the parking lot and headed for the Kirkwood residence. It was a forty-five minute drive through hilly, winding, two-lane roads. It would be dark by the time they arrived.

* * *

Aaron watched the parking lot through his binoculars. He saw Roger and Gerry head out on the road in the direction of the Kirkwood residence. He figured they'd be stupid enough to try and go back.

Ten minutes after Roger and Gerry left, a FedEx truck pulled into the parking lot. The driver looked around for a sign of life. He was about to pull away when Aaron pulled up next to his truck. He greeted the driver and opened the garage door. Then he opened the walk-in cooler where the boxes of cash were waiting. Within five minutes the boxes were loaded and the FedEx driver was on his way. Aaron smiled. He got in his truck and headed for the airport. A tropical paradise was waiting.

* * *

Jake and Shamus were riding around looking for Jeremy. They'd pulled into Messier Homes' parking lot. It was empty. Jake had been barking orders at Shamus all day. Shamus knew he was in a foul mood.

"Where is that lousy prick? I'll squash his fuckin' pin head like a grape. Head over to his punk-assed brother's house."

The limo left the parking lot, heading towards Aaron's house. They made the left turn and headed towards Aaron's house, following the same path as the earlier parade of vehicles.

As Jake's limo slowed to make the turn into Aaron's drive, they saw all the cars in the parking lot. Jake told Shamus to stop. The car was halfway up the long driveway. Jake looked around for a few seconds and said, "Let's get outta here. Too much company. We'll come back later." The limo backed out and left.

* * *

Nelson Rockledge yanked the door to the house open and walked in. He stood behind Jody. He noticed she had a gun pointed at the men in the room. Nelson held his own gun by his side. The sight of another person holding a gun on Jeremy, Theo and Tom unnerved him. He planned to be the only one with a gun in the room. Whoever she was, she was spoiling his plan. Then he figured that she must be another dissatisfied customer.

He said quietly to Jody, "So they screwed you, too?"

"Yeah," she responded, still holding the gun at the three men. "Actually, they watched us screw each other." She quickly looked down at his side and noticed the gun. "You too?"

"Yep. Me too. Did anyone fess up?"

"No. They're all cowards."

* * *

Jillian Rockledge remained in the car with her dog, Fenton, while Nelson went to the door. The windows to the BMW were rolled down to let in some cool air. She watched Nelson disappear in the house. As he did, Fenton began to whimper.

Jillian said, "Don't worry, boy, Daddy will be back in a minute."

She turned and looked at her precious pet, but Fenton's eyes weren't on the front door of the house. He was looking to the side yard. The whimper turned to a whine then a loud howl. Jillian said, "What wrong boy? Why so sad?"

Fenton moved into the front seat and before Jillian could react, he jumped out the driver's side window. He made a beeline for the side of the house and began to dig with his paws. Jillian looked on in horror. She jumped from the car and ran after her dog. She knelt beside him and tried to stop him from digging. It didn't faze the poor dog as he dug with all his might, howling the entire time.

As Jillian tried in vain to stop Fenton from digging, a plain looking car pulled into the drive. Four men quickly got out of the vehicle. Three of them headed for the house. They were all dressed in plain clothes; blue jeans, golf shirts, and light weight jackets. As Johnny, Pat, and Joe went to the front door, Hatch went to see Jillian. He noticed the dog digging at the side of the house. He was curious. Besides, they had plenty of help inside.

He slowly approached Jillian. "Ma'am, my name's Hatch. I'm here with the sheriff's department. Do you know what's going on inside?"

Jillian looked distraught about the dog. She didn't appear to be too concerned about what was happening inside the house. She kept trying to get her dog's attention, but Fenton continued digging. He had a pretty good hole started as he continued pawing the earth.

Hatch said, "He seems pretty intent. Do you know what he's looking for? I've never heard a dog whine like that while digging a hole. They're usually pretty happy to be doin' stuff like this."

Jillian looked at Hatch. Her face was twisted into deep sorrow for some untold reason. He could see the tears in her eyes as they spilled onto her cheeks. In a broken voice she said, "He thinks there's a body down there, at least I think that's why. We just found out the other day. He's a cadaver dog . . . or he was." Her eyes watered even more. "He's been retired for a bit. But he can sense a dead body. We know 'cause he found one at our house. That's how we found out."

"I'm very sorry, ma'am. Does he respond well to strangers? I'm pretty good with animals."

She shrugged her shoulders but didn't say a word. Her expression said, "Why not? It couldn't hurt."

Hatch moved closer to Fenton. He put a hand confidently on the dog's neck and rubbed. Fenton continued his digging. The hole was a little less than two feet deep now. Hatch continued to rub his neck and started a high-pitch, low volume whistle. Fenton at first didn't respond. But he slowly started to slow down his digging. His whining was less persistent, too. After nearly a full minute, he backed out of the hole and laid down. Hatch continued to rub his neck and whistle. Then he rubbed the top of his head, slowly maneuvering it towards him.

Jillian looked on in total amazement. The day Fenton found the first body, she and Nelson weren't able to get him to calm down. He was so upset. This total stranger walked up and put their tormented pet at ease. Hatch talked to Fenton briefly, saying, "That's a good boy. You stay nice and calm. You need to enjoy your retirement, not get all worked up. You did your job. Good boy."

Hatch looked at Jillian and said, "I didn't catch your name, ma'am."

"Oh, right. I'm Jillian Rockledge. My husband, Nelson is inside."

"Don't tell me. You own a Messier Home, and you're lookin' to get a rebate?"

Through her tears, Jillian smiled at Hatch. The way he spoke made her feel at ease. She stroked the back of her precious pet and said, "Yes, in a manner of speaking. Do you know what these bastards did?"

"Yes ma'am, I believe I do. Jillian, let's just stay here and keep our heads down, because this little pow-wow they have going on in there, could get rough." Just as Hatch finished, they heard a gunshot from inside the house.

* * *

Pat, Joe and Johnny got to the front door, the brothers on one side and Johnny on the other. They looked in the door. The situation looked tense. They were behind Jody and Nelson and could clearly see their guns. Pat was watching Jeremy and Theo. They were staring at each other, ignoring the rest, even though Jody and Nelson had guns pointed in their general direction. He noticed Tom looked scared. He was watching Jody and Nelson, but he would briefly look down at Theo's side. What is he looking at?

Nelson asked in a loud voice, laced with anger, "So which one of you bastards was it? Or were all of you in on it?" He and Jody were moving their guns from Theo to Tom to Jeremy and back again. It still had no affect on Jeremy and Theo.

Pat looked at Johnny and shrugged his shoulders. Johnny nodded, but he motioned to Pat and Joe, saying in almost a whisper, "Nice and slow. They know we're here, but we don't want to set off a fire fight."

Pat slowly opened the front door and allowed Johnny to move into the house behind Jody and Nelson. He turned his gaze to Tom who caught his eye. He nodded towards Theo indicating that he had a gun. It didn't seem to matter because Theo still stared at his son. If looks could kill, Jeremy would be six feet under.

Pat and Joe were inside now. They didn't like their position. They were all cramped into the entryway of the house behind Jody and Nelson. Pat and Joe moved into the living room and spread out. Jeremy moved towards the far wall, not wanting the brothers to move in behind him.

Johnny spoke in a calm voice, "Okay everyone. Let's calm things down here a bit. Jody, Nelson, how about you two lower those guns for me."

Jody was first to answer and she wasn't about to lower her gun. "There's no fucking way I'm putting my gun down until I get answers. Somebody in this room put cameras in my bedroom and I want to know who." She gritted her teeth. "And I want to know right now." She squeezed the trigger and fired a shot into the refrigerator next to Tom. Tom dropped to the floor, nearly wetting his pants. He was shaking like a leaf. Everyone jumped at the report.

Theo turned slowly towards Jody and smiled. "I always liked you, Jody. You show spunk, even with that dork of a husband." He looked at Jeremy again, his face turning ugly with an expression that emitted hatred. "It seems like there's always one partner in a marriage that has the balls to make things happen." He looked directly at Jody again. "Pardon my French. Even in business, you sometimes have to take risks. But it's time to settle things." He slowly raised his gun from behind his leg. He moved it so slowly that it appeared to be in slow motion.

Johnny said in a commanding voice, "Stop, Theo."

But Theo kept raising his gun. It was still angled towards the floor, but it appeared that he was going to shoot Jody. Then he quickly moved the gun and leveled it at Jeremy. Everyone hesitated. It was like time was frozen. He didn't pull the trigger for several seconds.

While he had the gun pointed at his eldest son, he said, "Jody, Nelson, I planted the cameras. I'm sorry if I caused problems for you. We weren't making money building houses, but we finally hit a gold mine on the internet. It was just business."

Jody's face turned a deep red, then nearly purple as her anger skyrocketed. "Just business? Just fucking business? You ruined our lives. You violated us just as if you'd personally raped us. You son-of-a-bitch!"

She tensed and fired a round. The bullet hit Theo on the left side of his chest. The impact threw him backwards. As he fell, he fired a shot at Jeremy. The bullet missed. Theo hit the ground, but he held onto the gun. He steadied himself and fired again before anyone could get a clear shot at him. The bullet hit Jeremy in the center of his chest. He went down like a sack of potatoes. Theo swung the gun towards Pat, but Pat was ready. He fired two rounds into Theo's chest. Theo's gun fell to the floor, followed by the loud clunk of his skull on the kitchen tile.

The room fell silent. Everyone's ears rang from the loud reports. The strong odor of cordite hung in the stagnant air of the house.

After a few minutes, Hatch and Jillian walked up to the door. Fenton, now calm and back to normal, stood between them.

* * *

Roger and Gerry pulled behind the Kirkwood house the same as they did a few nights earlier. They took their time, looking around to make sure nothing was out of place. It was like they never left. The motion lights came on, just as Aaron told them they would. Roger took out the magnet and placed it on the alarm controller. They unlocked the patio door and walked into the house like they owned the place. Roger turned to Gerry and smiled, his face conveying a look of *I told you so.* They didn't realize that the door should have already been unlocked.

They made their way to the master bedroom and to the vault that was still open. They went to work stuffing black trash bags full of cash. They had one bag each filled when they looked up into the faces of six armed men standing at the entrance to the vault. Roger's jaw dropped and his stomach immediately became nauseous. Gerry wet his pants. They both started to babble some nonsense that was inaudible. They thought they knew their fate, but they had no clue what they were about to endure.

Two men grabbed Gerry and stood him up straight. Without a word another of the men pounded his fist into his stomach so hard that all the wind was knocked out of his lungs. The men kept him on his feet not allowing him to collapse.

Realizing what he was about to endure, Roger stood up and tried to barrel his way past the men. They grabbed him and pushed him against the wall. One of the men laughed and said with a strong middle-eastern accent, "Where do you think you are going? We want to talk to you for a while. You see, you took something of ours and we want it back."

Roger knew what was going to happen after they talked. He wished he had something to bargain in exchange for his life. In a flash he thought, *Maybe I do.*

"You know, we couldn't have done this by ourselves. Will you let us go if we tell you who took all your money?"

Sheik Al Salil smiled. "You help us get our money back and of course we'll let you go."

Roger spilled his guts, giving Sheik Al Salil everything he knew about Aaron. He told them of his plan to steal the money and how there must be cameras in the house because Aaron knew exactly where the vault was and that there was lots of cash. He also knew the combination to the vault.

When Roger was finished talking, he looked at his captors and asked, "So can we go now?"

Salil looked at his associates and said, "Kill them, slowly and painfully."

Rogers jaw hit the floor. "But you said . . ."

Salil smiled broadly. "I lied. Allah will forgive me. We are going to retrieve His money so that we can continue our jihad against Satan's army. You are obviously part of that army so you must die." He nodded to the others. "Take them to the chamber, have some fun, then dispose of them in the landfill. And record it. We may be able to use it later."

Roger lost control of his bowels as he and Gerry were unceremoniously dragged through the house, out the back door, and to the garage. Adrenaline coursed through his body tightening his muscles, causing him to buck against the tight grip of the men holding his arms, all to no avail. Outside, they screamed as loud and long as their lungs would sustain. But the beautiful Messier home was so isolated that no one was close enough to hear. Once inside the garage, they were strapped to chairs and tortured for more than an hour before they were shot in the head with a 9mm. No one heard their cries of terror and pain, or the shots that killed them.

Chapter 44

Johnny Poleirmo called Deputy Lyons and gave him an update on what happened at the house. He left out a few details. He, Pat, Joe, and Hatch talked a few minutes among themselves and decided that they should say Jody shot in self defense. Pat pointed out that it was going to be tough to convince anyone that Jody didn't come to the house with murder on her mind. The others said they felt it was justifiable, regardless what others thought. They were willing to go to court for her, Jillian, and Nelson. All they did was come here to get their self respect and privacy back.

Hatch pulled Nelson and Jillian aside and spoke briefly to them. "Fenton sure is a beautiful dog. So, how'd you get a cadaver dog for a pet?"

They talked for more than ten minutes on the history of how they got Fenton and that he was fine until they moved into their new home. "You saw how he acted out there. That's exactly how he reacted at home. We'll never be able to live there, at least not as long as we have this poor dog." Jillian leaned into her husband's chest and put her arm around him. She continued, "Frankly, I'm not sure I can stay there now. We'll always feel like we're being spied on."

"I'd like to make you an offer. If you let me, I'll take Fenton with me for a few weeks and see if I can deprogram him. It's not very good odds, but I think I might be able to get his mind off the dead and get him back with the livin'. That way you can have some time in that nice place of yours and decide if you're gonna stay there. When you decide, call me and I'll deliver my man, Fenton, back to ya. Deal?"

The couple looked at each other and smiled. Nelson said, "You've got a deal. We can work out the details before we head out." They exchanged phone numbers and addresses. Jillian started to tell Hatch about Fenton's habits, type of food, toys, and times that he liked to go for a walk. Hatch listened patiently, smiling as Jillian rambled on.

Finally, with a broad smile he said, "Miss Jillian, I think I can handle it. You two need to go talk with my friends, Pat and Joe and get your story straight before the police get here." They looked at each other with a bit of alarm. They shook Hatch's hand and walked over to where Pat, Joe, and Johnny were talking with Jody Williams. They seemed to have everything in hand, just as Charlie Williams showed up. Several Sheriff's cars followed with their lights flashing and their sirens screaming.

The rest of the evening was nothing short of an adventure. Pat, Joe, Hatch and Johnny made their way into the basement. They found the hidden door that opened up into the control room. The smell of rotten food and dried sperm made breathing in the room difficult. The nine small monitors had pornography going non-stop. But on the large screen, a young man was sitting on a stool in front of a dark backdrop. He was giving a silenced monologue to the camera. As the monologue went on, the man would smile. Then his face would frown. He made a face like he was scolding a child, shaking his finger as if to say, stop doing that. Pat found the keyboard on a slide out shelf. He moved the mouse and found the icon for the audio. He unchecked the mute button and the young man's voice boomed into the room. The men covered their ears with their hands until Pat adjusted the volume.

". . . and Dad would yell at me again to get my homework done. Hell, I wasn't even in kindergarten." He paused. "Yeah, Dad was always preaching to me about being honest with everyone. Treat everyone with respect, especially your parents." He paused again, this time his facial expression became dark, a mood coming over his whole body. Then his face tensed and tears rolled down his cheeks. "That's what Dad said. But is that what Dad did? Well let me show you.

The scene on the monitor changed to darkness. A grainy appearance filled the screen. The team couldn't see anything on the camera. Then the picture seemed to come into focus. They could see what appeared to be mounds of dirt, the camera moving along, pointed at the ground in front of whoever was holding it. The camera came to the edge of a pit. Slowly, the lens peered over the edge of the pit at a man digging a small hole. The camera stayed nearly stationary, though it moved in a way that made the viewers feel a bit of vertigo. The camera zoomed in on a man in the pit. There was an extension ladder into the pit. It was dark, but he had a drop light that illuminated the area around him. The camera zoomed in tighter. As the picture zoomed in on the man digging, the movement of the camera was exaggerated. But Pat and Joe could clearly see the young face of Theo Messier, digging away. They could see the boards that were set up for the footer for the basement walls.

They continued to watch as Theo climbed the ladder, grabbed a dark trash bag from the back of an old van and climbed back down into the pit. He deposited the bag in the freshly dug hole. He went up the ladder a second and third time. Each trip he brought back another bag and dropped them into the hole along with the first. Then he covered them with a thin layer of concrete. Finally, he shoveled dirt on top of the makeshift grave.

The camera shifted back to the young man. "I guess I was a pretty good cameraman back then for the lousy equipment I had. But I did clean it up a bit over the years. Just for you, Dad. So when you told me to always be honest with people, all the time, I guess you really meant *When it's convenient.* I guess it wasn't real convenient for you to tell your sons that our mother didn't run away. She didn't leave us. You thought I believed it all these years." Aaron was starting to laugh now, but his laughter was through tears pouring down his cheeks. The pitch of his voice was rising, his voice getting hoarse with each angry word. "So, when the cops find you here with this recording, and they see what you did to your wife, my mom, they'll have all the evidence they need to fry your sorry, good for nothing, ass."

Pat noticed a small green light in the lower right corner of the monitor. He looked at the nine smaller monitors. They all had blinking red lights. He looked at Joe and asked, "What does the light mean?" He pointed to the blinking red lights then the green light on the main screen.

"I'm not sure. I thought you were the computer geek."

Pat shrugged and continued to watch Aaron Messier tell his story. Hatch said, "Hey fellas, I think I know where we can find the late Mrs. Messier." He told them about Fenton, the retired cadaver dog and how he was digging at the side of the house. Johnny said he'd call Deputy Lyons and let him know about the possibility of another body. He bet they'd have a backhoe here before morning.

Aaron continued his monologue. "Then there's my older brother, Jeremy. Big brothers are supposed to set the example, right?" Joe gave Pat a friendly elbow in the ribs. Pat returned the elbow.

Hatch smiled and said, "You two need to go to the principal's office until you graduate to eighth grade."

They smiled at the joke and continued to watch in fascination. "So what do you suppose my brother Jeremy does when our old man marries a Russian mail-order bride? He moves in on the action, of course."

The scene shifts to a bedroom, where two people, already naked and in a passionate embrace, fall into bed. They are immediately in a frenzy of love-making." The men stare in awe until Joe asks, "Can't you fast forward past this? Now we know why Theo was burning holes in Jeremy's head with his stare." The scene zoomed in on Jeremy's face, then Natashia's.

The monitor shifted to the next screen. It showed another pit, very much like the first, but this one was much larger. The picture was better quality than the last pit and it had a greenish color on the monitor. *Night vision.* The similarities to the first scene in a pit were striking. A man, whom they easily identified as Theo, though much older now, carried dark trash bags down into the pit and buried them, just as in the first scene. This episode obviously was much rougher on Theo as he labored to catch his breath with each trip up and down the ladder. At one point he looked startled. He looked up and almost stared right at the camera. But Aaron must have been hiding well because Theo went right back to work. The men now knew that Natashia wasn't in France enjoying her new chateau. She was at the morgue awaiting identification. That mystery was now solved.

The monitor was back to Aaron, sitting on his stool, his voice back to a normal tone. He wiped away tears with his right hand and continued. "Now you know why Messier Homes was such a success. Honesty, integrity, above all, family values." He took a deep breath. "Dad and Jeremy, by the time you see this, I'll be long-gone. I've already made arrangements for my financial future. Oh, and I've already mailed copies of this to the sheriff's office and the attorney general's office, along with a list of houses that have our special modification; the cameras and microphones. As you're watching this, so are our internet customers. They're seeing the real Theo and Jeremy Messier; my mentors."

"The money that we made from the website is gone. I managed to get that moved to a more secure location where I can access it if I run low on funds. That isn't likely, though."

Aaron's face took on a dreadfully, sad expression. His lips curled down, so pronounced that it almost looked like a caricature of his face. The tears started to pour again. He started to speak, but stopped to clear his throat. Then he started again, his words broken. He was choked up so badly that they had to listen hard to catch any of his words. "Dad . . . you . . . made me . . . what I am . . . today. I hope . . . you're . . . proud. Jeremy, you . . . can go . . . fuck yourself."

Music started and the camera faded to dark. Closing credits started to roll down the screen. Cast, Theo Messier,

Home Builder, Father, Murderer. Son #1- Jeremy Messier, Son, Brother, Home-wrecker, All Around Bastard. Son #2 – Brother, Son, Cameraman, Survivor.

A real professional job.

After a minute, the film began to play again from the beginning. The men looked at Pat, shrugged their shoulders as if to say, *What are you waiting for? Turn the damn thing off.*

* * *

Nelson and Jillian pulled into her parents' driveway. Before they got out of Nelson's car, his cell phone rang. It was his friend, Sammy Jones.

"Well, did you get 'em? I heard on the news that there was a shooting and two people got themselves killed."

"It was the right guys as far as I can tell, but it wasn't me. Some detectives from out of state."

"Too bad. But maybe it's best that you didn't actually pull the trigger. Who knows? You might have been charged with murder and your lovely wife would be a victim for the third time in just a few weeks. She can't afford to lose you right now."

Nelson looked at Jillian and smiled, though the smile had a touch of sadness. Jillian had been through a lot. He knew that going back to their house to live might not be possible. He knew one thing for certain; he loved Jillian with all his heart. He would do whatever he had to do to help his wife recover. The physical rape was bad, but you could build a more secure house to keep the bad guys out. What could you do to keep the boogey man away? He thought that by building a house, they would have the greatest, most secure home in the world. How could he have been so wrong?

Sammy said, "Nelson? You still there?"

"Yeah, Sammy. I was just thinking. We've got to make some decisions on what we're going to do next. At least these bastards are dead. The younger brother is out there somewhere, but he seemed harmless. I figured it was the older brother, but the cops say it was Theo. That's a tough one. He was always so professional."

"Nelson, my man, one thing I've learned in this business is you never really know people. You think you do, but people do very strange things behind closed doors. Trust me on this one."

Nelson just nodded to himself as he held his wife's hand and gave it a light squeeze. "Hey Sammy, I have to head inside. Thanks for running down the info for me. At least we got to see their dead bodies. That's some consolation."

"No problem. Take care of your wife. Good night, my man."

Nelson folded his cell and dropped it in his jacket pocket. He took a deep breath, looked at Jillian, who'd fallen asleep on the way home. He stretched his other hand and put it on her shoulder.

With a jolt, she sat upright in the car and screamed, "No, stop, get your hands off me." She was flailing her hands at Nelson. He grabbed her hands and subdued her, trying to calm her, while trying to wake her from her nightmare. She finally calmed down when she saw Nelson sitting next to her. She broke down in deep sobs as she leaned into his shoulder.

Through her sobs she cried, "When will it end? I can't take this much longer."

"We're going to make it through this, dear. I'm here with you, whatever it takes."

While he held Jillian tight, he silently said a brief prayer. "Dear God, help my wife through this ordeal. Let me be your instrument in her healing. Amen."

All he had to do now was chase the demons from his wife's mind and body. It would be his toughest job ever.

* * *

Early Sunday morning the backhoe finished digging at the foundation of Aaron Messier's house. Fenton, the retired cadaver dog, was two for two. The body, that they were pretty certain was Alicia Messier, was pulled from the hole. Dental records would be required for a positive ID since the body was no more than skeletal remains.

Jeremy and Theo Messier had been declared dead at the scene. Both were shot through the heart and died instantly.

When Tom Grayson was questioned, he told his story about finding the transmitter and attempting to find out who was responsible. He described how Jake O'Conner tried to muscle in on the operation. He told them that he believed Jeremy knew nothing about the porn end of the business. The story was so fantastic that the detectives taking his statement had a hard time believing that he knew nothing of the porn business. But after hours of questioning, his story remained consistent throughout. He was free to go. The rest of the crew at Messier's was cleared as well. But the business was shut down since none of the principals were left to run the business. Tom was sure that the company would fold and all his men would be out of work.

The sheriff's office thought about hunting down Jake O'Conner, but they decided that they had nothing to charge him with. The idea was dropped almost as quickly as it was suggested.

After the sheriff's computer experts were called to the scene, they determined that the porn business was run from the house on two servers, a primary and a backup. The elaborate system allowed the operators to monitor as many as ten programs at once. The lights on the screen indicated what monitors were broadcasting out on the net and which were just showing on the local monitor. They learned that Aaron had rigged his farewell video to Theo and Jeremy so that it ran continuously on the high priced website for all their customers to see. Aaron hadn't burned his bridges. He'd blown them up with an atomic bomb.

The customer list for Sensuous Exotic Couples Club was a who's who of the wealthy in America. The clubs price tag guaranteeing privacy was useless now that the operators of the business were dead. But the names of the rich and famous members of the club wouldn't be released. They would be spared any humiliation. But there were dozens of people who had cameras in their homes and someone had to tell them.

That was going to be a delicate operation, one that Pat, Joe, Hatch and Johnny were glad that they didn't have to help with. There was no doubt that lawsuits would be filed, but the only winners in this episode would be the lawyers. That was the second most obscene part of this entire saga.

The four investigators from Florida said their goodbyes to their Virginia counterparts and loaded into the rental car. It was after 12:00 noon and they wanted to get down the road to a restaurant for a decent meal. It had been a long night.

They sat at an Applebee's restaurant finishing their meals when the TVs broke from their normal sporting events for breaking news. A terrorist cell had been broken up in Baltimore, Maryland. The newscast was short on detail, but the FBI raided an apartment and found high explosives, bomb making equipment, and military grade small arms. The FBI had little to say about the suspected terrorists except that the cell had been under surveillance for a number of weeks.

As soon as they finished eating, Pat and Joe both got on their cell phones to Diane and Lisa. They let them know that they were on their way home.

Chapter 45

It was mid November on Grand Cayman. Hurricane season would officially be over in just a few weeks. The islanders were going about their daily lives, catering to the cruise ships that anchored in the West Bay off of Georgetown. The sun was setting. The view from the Caribbean Cove Condominiums was nothing short of spectacular. Every suite in the twelve-story building on the stretch of land called Seven Mile Beach had a balcony with an ocean view.

"That'll be all, William. My compliments to the chef."

"Thank you very much, Mr. Smith. You are most kind, sir." William left the room and closed the door behind him.

Aaron Messier, who now called himself John Smith, turned back towards the sunset and watched the water. It turned from blue with an orange streak from the sun, to a shimmering red. After several minutes it turned to a deep orange. He smiled as the half globe of the sun slowly inched below the water. The sparse clouds in the sky remained bright orange for another ten minutes before fading to a light pink, then disappearing altogether. Aaron concentrated on finishing his meal of lobster, crab, and scallops. He sipped his one hundred and fifty dollar per bottle Merlot, savoring the taste that lingered after he swallowed. He drew a deep breath of fresh, Caribbean Sea air, leaned back in his patio chair and relaxed.

Jillian Rockledge invaded his mind. He saw her exit the shower, her perfect body glistening with beads of water, her hair dripping until she wrapped it in a towel. She was in slow motion now, moving from the shower to the bathroom. Standing in front of the vanity, she faced the mirror, examining her face, leaning over slightly, showing Aaron the roundness of the fair skin on her perfect butt.   Even in his sleepy state, Aaron smiled.

His mind shifted to Jody Williams. She was on top of a man who was lying down on their bed, red silk sheets in a heap at the foot of the bed. This, too, was in slow motion as Jody moved methodically up and down against her mate. When she leaned her head back and tossed her hair to one side, Aaron saw himself laying there with Jody. He was smiling broadly as she continued her sensuous dance on top of him.

The scene changed slowly.   Now he was walking around the bedroom with a mini camera in his hands. He was filming the walls of the bedroom. He raised the camera to a mirror on the ceiling and caught the reflection of another beautiful woman.   She was smiling at him by way of the reflection in the mirror. He mounted the camera on a tripod that appeared from nowhere. He pointed the camera down to the bed where she lay naked. Aaron slowly moved around the camera to lie down next to her.   He placed a hand on her stomach and slowly caressed her soft, smooth skin. He moved his hand up, cupping one breast then lightly touching a nipple. He smiled again. She was saying something. He couldn't hear her.

He asked, "What is it?"

Her lips moved, but no words came out. He asked her again, "What?"

Again, her lips moved. He began to hear a repetitive sound in his ears. There was silence. Then there was the sound again. She disappeared and the sound grew louder. It was a pounding sound. He stirred for a moment then drifted off again. The knocking returned.

He sat up straight, shaking his head, rubbing the sleep from his eyes. It was dark outside. He looked at his watch and saw that it was nearly ten o'clock. Then he heard the pounding again.   It was coming from inside his condominium.   He rubbed the sleep from his eyes, rose, and headed into the living room to answer the door. He looked through the spy hole in his door. It was one of the servers.

"What is it?"

The voice on the other side of the door said, "Mr. Smith, you have an urgent message." Nothing more.

"Okay. One second." He rubbed his eyes again, reached for the door handle then remembered that the secondary locking device was not in place. He flipped the bar across the metal ball that stuck out from the door. No sense taking unnecessary chances. *Whatever the message, he can give it through the opening in the door.*

He opened the door a crack and looked out at the server who stood there looking back through the crack. Aaron said, "What have you got?"

The door flew open, knocking Aaron to the floor. The safety latch was jerked out of the wall with a loud bang. The wall shook and pieces of cheap metal and screws flew across the room. Three men quickly entered the room. Two of them grabbed Aaron by the arms. One of them grabbed his throat so tight that he couldn't breathe. They pinned him to the floor, face down, gagged him, and bound his arms behind his back. It happened so fast that he didn't have time to shout for help. The men held him tight in their grip. Aaron couldn't see anything but the carpet and the legs of his coffee table. The room remained quiet for nearly two full minutes. He wondered who these guys were. As more time passed, he grew more frightened. A man walked in front of him. His shoes were so close to his face that he could smell the leather.

The man said in broken English, "Aaron Messier, you've been a very foolish man. Do you remember your friends Roger and Gerry? Just nod if you do."

On hearing the names of the two men who did his dirty work, his adrenal glands started working overtime. Fear coursed through his body as the shoe man waited for his response. He didn't move. His head remained still, looking at the carpet and his captor's shoes.

Shoe man just waited. The longer he waited, the more fearful Aaron became. He finally asked again in a voice that sounded almost friendly, "Do you remember Roger and Gerry? It is a simple question and you need to be cooperative."

Again, Aaron remained still. Shoe man didn't wait this time. He said something in a language that Aaron didn't understand. Aaron could hear someone go to the entertainment center and open the doors. He turned on the set and loaded a video in the player. The men holding Aaron to the floor now yanked him up and forced him down on the couch facing the television. After a few minutes, the screen came to life.

Aaron's eyes grew to the size of quarters and his face drained of all color. He watched in horror as Roger and Gerry were stripped naked and doused with water. A pair of jumper cables were hooked to a large truck battery. Before either man was touched with the cables, they cried, pleaded, and begged for their lives.

Gerry was first. The cables were thrust against his chest and he screamed in pain. The cables remained in place for several seconds. When the cables were pulled away, square burn marks were on his chest. A wisp of smoke trailed upward from the burns. Next, one cable was held to the side of his head and the second cable thrust into his crotch. The screams were louder this time, his voice becoming hoarse from the strain. Again, the cables were removed. He slumped in his chair.

The camera swung around to Roger. His eyes were so wide they looked unnatural. The same pattern of torture was used on Roger with the same results. Aaron tried to look away, but a man held his head towards the television. When he tried to close his eyes, shoe man said, "Open your eyes. Be a man. You Americans are so . . . soft."

A knock came at the door. Aaron hoped that someone had heard the break in and was here to rescue him. But when one of the men answered the door and let another middle-eastern looking man in, his hopes were dashed.

The man carried a suitcase which he tossed on the coffee table. Aaron watched the man as he opened the case. When he pulled out a set of jumper cables, Aaron lost control of his bladder and wet his pants. The room started to spin and he passed out. When he came to, his shirt had been removed and he was soaking wet. There was a battery at his feet, the cables were connected and were being held by shoe man. The television was off.

Shoe man spoke. "My name is Sheik Al Salil. I am going to remove the gag from around your mouth. If you scream, we will kill you." One of the men showed Aaron the silenced 9mm. "I am not a patient man. I am going to ask you a question and you will answer or we will put the gag back on and we will torture you until you are dead. Do you understand?"

Aaron vigorously nodded his head.

Al Salil pulled the gag from Aaron's mouth. He drew in a deep breath.

Al Salil said, "If you answer correctly, you will be spared the pain and suffering that your friends endured. They should not have resisted." He paused for what seemed like ten minutes. In reality, it was only about ten seconds. "Where is our money?"

Aaron immediately decided that he didn't want to suffer the same fate as Roger and Jerry. "The money is in the Grand Cayman Bank. I'll give you the codes and you can transfer it wherever you want. Just, please let me go. I beg you."

Al Salil smiled and wrote down the codes that Aaron recited from memory. He nodded to one of his men. Aaron swung his head around, too late as one of the men plunged a syringe into his arm. The strong sedative took affect quickly. Aaron remained conscious but couldn't function under his own power. The men took him under his arms and carried him out of the condominium complex. No one questioned them about where they were taking this sorry looking soul. Al Salil already had a story that he was a friend and had too much to drink.

They loaded Aaron into a van and drove to a marina. He was escorted to a boat that already had its engines running. They left the dock and headed for the open sea.

* * *

The next day, Sheik Al Salil made the money transfer without a hitch. Aaron was locked in the cabin of the boat, still drugged. Al Salil stood on the bridge of the boat looking around in all directions. There was not another boat in sight. He looked down at his comrades and yelled over the sounds of the sea, "It is time."

Two of the men went below decks and pulled Aaron up to the aft deck. They tossed him on the deck. His head hit the teakwood. He stirred. One of the men grabbed a bucket, leaned over the port rail and scooped up several gallons of salty seawater. He dumped the bucket of water in Aaron's face, causing him to stir. He finally came to.

Al Salil nodded again to his men. They grabbed him, stripped off his clothes, and tied a rope around his ankles. They hooked the rope to an electric wench and raised him up, feet first, until his hands couldn't touch the teakwood deck.

Aaron looked around as his body slowly spun. He saw four men, upside down, holding knives. One man grabbed his leg and spun him faster. The others started to laugh. They continued to spin him faster and faster. He was getting nauseous. Suddenly, he felt sharp metal against his back. The deep cut immediately stung from the salt water. He screamed in pain. Then another cut opened his chest. More stinging invaded his senses. He screamed louder. The men around him laughed. He felt warm blood running along his torso to his shoulders and neck. Then it ran into his eyes. After what seemed like an eternity, the cutting stopped. Aaron was losing so much blood that he started to lose consciousness.

The wench started again. His body was raised high enough to clear the starboard rail. Then the I-beam holding the wench was swung out over the sea. Aaron's blood dripped and pooled in the sea beneath him. After a few minutes, the blood had the desired effect. A school of Tiger Sharks gathered, their hunger stirred by blood in their presence. Slowly, the wench motor turned, lowering Aaron towards the blue water now defiled with a pool of blood. With what little strength he had left, he shouted, "I gave you your money! Why are you doing this? You promised you'd let me go!"

"Ah, yes. But I lied. Allah will forgive one little lie, especially told to a member of Satan's army..

Sheik Al Salil watched as Aaron was lowered towards the ocean. He said, "Goodbye, infidel."

The sharks attacked him before he made it to the surface. The video camera ran to capture the example of what happens to those who oppose the jihad. It was a gruesome site to behold.

* * *

It was mid-November. Diane McKinney was getting ready for the barbeque at Joe and Lisa's new house in Winter Garden. Their friends were all planning to be there. She packed the cooler with the vegetable tray and assorted cheeses. She put the lid on and set the cooler next to the grocery bag of buns, chips, and crackers. She hollered back to Sean and Anna and told them that they'd better be getting ready to go to Uncle Joe and Aunt Lisa's.

She wondered what was keeping Pat. She walked back to the bedroom, but Pat wasn't there. She looked in his office. It was empty. Then she walked out onto the patio outside their bedroom. Pat was sitting in a lawn chair, staring at the open field behind their house.

"Uh-umm."

He didn't move. She watched him, trying to figure out what had him so preoccupied. He hadn't been himself in the weeks since he came back from Virginia. He hadn't talked much about this case. They only made love a few times since he returned. Even then, he seemed detached and distracted. She was worried about him.

After a long moment, she said in a voice that was steeped in concern, "Pat? Are you alright?"

He turned to see Diane looking at him with a puzzled look. He forced a smile and said, "Yeah, I'm fine."

But she wasn't fooled. "Listen, we're almost ready to leave, but before we do, I think we need to talk." She paused. "What happened up there?"

"What do you mean?"

She gave him a stern look that spoke volumes. Her eyes burned into him. He knew he had to tell her what was bugging him. There was no turning back. He returned her stare with one of his own. His eyes were empty. The usual life that made his face alive and energetic was gone. Diane worried for a moment that he'd had an affair while away. She dismissed the thought as quickly as it came.

"Alright. I said I'd never keep secrets from you and I guess this is one of those times." He took a deep breath and started to speak. Just then, Anna ran through the open patio door and said cheerfully in her three year old voice, "I'm weady to go!"

Sean followed her and said, "I tried to tell her that you were talking about grown up stuff, but she doesn't understand."

Pat smiled at Sean. He was trying to be so much more mature than his age would allow him to be. He was nearly seven now. It seemed to Pat that he was trying to grow up too fast. He was a lot like his uncle Joe in that regard. He said to Sean, "We can wait to talk grown up stuff, right Mom?"

She gave Pat a look that said, *You aren't getting away that easy.*

They loaded into the car and headed for Uncle Joe and Aunt Lisa's for the barbeque.

* * *

The barbeque was a hit. Lisa was giddy about her new house. Joe was pleased, but kept talking about all the work ahead. Twenty of their friends gathered to celebrate with the new home owners. Brian Purcer and Ginny Parks were there. Johnny Poleirmo and his wife, and Hatch joined in. Nancy Brown, who had worked with Joe when he'd been recalled to active duty, showed up, too. She and Hatch seemed to hit it off well. Nancy announced that she was resigning her commission with the Marine Corps at the end of the year. She'd been offered a civilian position in a new anti-terrorist task force and was excited about the new challenge.

When the barbeque was in full swing, Diane took Pat by the hand and whispered, "I want to show you something in the house."

His heart sank as the moment of truth was upon him. He followed her lead into the house to Joe's new office. She closed the door behind them, turned to Pat and playfully grabbed him by the lapels.

"Okay, McKinney, spill your guts."

Pat took a deep breath, let Diane's hands fall from his shirt and backed against Joe's desk.

"I don't know where to start. I . . . We . . ." His eyes started to tear up. He took another deep breath and his chin started to quiver. He started to speak again. "I killed a man. I shot him, and I killed him."

Diane felt weak. She could see the pain behind Pat's eyes. They weren't the eyes of a killer. She heard about the shooting at the house in Virginia and knew that Pat had been the one who shot Theo Messier. But it was obviously self defense. Why was he so distraught?

"Pat, I know. I heard about it. You didn't have a choice. You can't let it tear you apart like this."

Pat shook his head. He was thinking of a different shooting; the one that was giving him nightmares. Before, he would wake up in a cold sweat every three or four weeks. Now it was more like twice a week. He knew he couldn't go on like this. He had to tell someone. He now knew it couldn't be Diane. But if he didn't get help soon, he'd blurt it out in his sleep, and she would know he was a murderer.

He started again, shifting to a different topic that was bothering him, "This case, the child porn part of it . . . it's ripping me apart. I can't get the images out of my head. Those poor little kids. I can't believe how many sick bastards there are in the world."

Diane moved closer to Pat and put her arms around his neck. "I was afraid of this. I hoped it wouldn't happen, but you can't watch that kind of trash without it having some effect." She held him closer. She could almost feel his tension. She continued, "When you started this case, I read a few articles on it. Some of the cops who were on these cases . . . they went crazy."

"What do you mean?"

"Some got sucked into it and were arrested themselves for selling kiddie porn. Others went extreme in the opposite way, setting up vigilante groups to hunt down these sickos. If you decided to do that, I guess I couldn't blame you, but you'd be putting yourself on their level. Where would it end? You can't solve the world's problems, Pat."

"I know. I've got to take a break. I've got to get this stuff out of my mind, get deprogrammed. Then I think, 'What if I don't stop this crap? What if something happens to Anna?' I'd never forgive myself."

"Oh, God, Pat. Nothing's going to happen. We keep close tabs on her, and Sean. They'll be fine. I'm more worried about you. What's happening to you?

"I wish I knew, Babe. I wish I knew."

They embraced, Pat feeling the warmth of her body against his. His mind conjured up the image of a man through a rifle scope, the crosshairs centered on his forehead. He felt Diane's breathing, her breasts pressing against his chest. The image was steady, he was taking a slow, deep breath. Diane's breath was warm on his ear. He put pressure on the trigger. His embrace tightened. The image of Danny Vallero's brains exploding onto the drywall behind his head burst into Pat's mind. He jerked.

Diane jumped and looked at Pat, worry etched on her face. Her gaze penetrated his eyes, trying to see into his brain. She was hoping that he hadn't done anything that would destroy their family.

In a quiet, measured voice, she said, "Whatever it is that we need to do to bring you back, we'll do it. You're not alone. Let me help you." She embraced him again.

He held her tight. With tears in his eyes, he whispered, "Oh God, how I love you."

The End